Attended with Miracles

Attended with Miracles

Jack Dewhurst

The Pentland Press Limited
Edinburgh · Cambridge · Durham

© Jack Dewhurst 1993

First published in 1993 by
The Pentland Press Ltd.
1 Hutton Close
South Church
Bishop Auckland
Durham

All rights reserved.
Unauthorised duplication
contravenes existing laws.

ISBN 1 85821 013 5

Typeset by Elite Typesetting Techniques, Southampton.
Printed and bound by Antony Rowe Ltd., Chippenham.

For Hazel,
For Everything

"The Christian religion not only was at first attended with miracles, but even at this day cannot be believed by any reasonable person without one. Mere reason is insufficient to convince us of it's veracity; and whoever is moved by faith to assent to it, is consious of a continued miracle in his own person, which subverts all the principles of his understanding, and gives him a determination to believe what is most contrary to custom and experience."

David Hume (1711 – 1776)

Chapter 1

The palace of King Eadbald of Kent dozed in the unaccustomed warmth of early April in the Year of our Lord 625. With so many preparations to be made for the departure of the princess for her wedding in Northumbria there should have been signs of activity everywhere but few were to be seen. It had been a bitter winter. Until the end of February snow lay piled high and the drifts had collapsed huts, buried animals, brought down branches of trees and frozen fingers and toes. Biting winds had blown throughout March and Old Ketch, who had lived so long that nobody knew his true age, said that he could not recall a worse winter for forty years when on April 1st they had skated on Flatbridge Mere. Then all of a sudden the countryside had burst into life and it was spring, the mornings brisk, the days warm and the evenings getting longer and longer. The palace took its ease in the warm sunshine.

Inside however there is some desultory activity.

James, son of Eadfrith, is trying to decide how many of his worldly goods he can take with him on the long journey to Northumbria – wherever that may be – which he must presently make to accompany his mistress, Princess Ethelberga of Kent. James is twelve years old and a Christian. Almost everyone in Kent at that time is a Christian although, James has been led to believe, much of the rest of Britain is pagan. He is not quite sure what being a pagan means but it is a bad thing and no decent boy is supposed to think about it for fear of falling into mortal sin.

Mortal sin was something James did not like to think about, partly because he was not always sure which sins were mortal and which venial. Was taking the big red apples from the orchard of Archbishop Justus a mortal sin, James wondered, since the archbishop was never tired of telling them that these apples were so good that the apple in the garden of Eden was probably one of them. Stealing one of the small green ones may only be a venial sin, he supposed, since His Grace was not fond of them and was happy to give them away.

This had always made James wonder how things might have turned out if the apple tree in Eden had been one of that kind and Eve had had the same opinion of them as Archbishop Justus. The Devil, of course (James always thought of the Devil with a capital D) would have found a way round the difficulty, James supposed, perhaps by clouding Eve's judgement or tempting Adam instead – although *he* might have fancied a pear.

James stopped thinking about sin since he always became alarmed when he did so, and opened the door of the chamber so that he could hear his companions who were also getting ready for the journey. Four of the attendants to Princess Ethelberga, of whom James was the youngest, were going in the royal entourage. Godwin, a bumptious youth of eighteen with spots and red hair, was supposed to be in charge but lately he had been so preoccupied with the maidservants, and occupied with any he could get his hands on, that the other three youths had a free rein. Abnef, aged fifteen, might have taken advantage of this and bossed them about but he was an easygoing lad, big and gangling, as strong as most men and willing to work his fingers to the bone provided he got a lot to eat and eight hours sleep at night. James and Aldrith, who was a year older, and shared a chamber with James, were left much to their own devices. In addition to Archbishop Justus' orchard, this meant, in Aldrith's case, carving graceful little figures from the most unpromising bits of wood, and in James' case, drawing and painting, and, lately, sacred illumination which he might have known nothing about had it not been for a chance meeting with Father Birinus.

'Did you draw these, boy?' had been Father Birinus' first words.

James had been so absorbed in his task that he had not heard the old priest come into the room behind him. A flight of geese had stirred the boy's imagination when he had seen them coming in rapidly over the marshes and now he was trying to record their formation and their elegance and beauty on his tablet. But neither the first nor the second attempt had captured their grace to the boy's satisfaction and he had laid the wax aside and closed his eyes to visualise the moment when they came into view.

When he opened them an old priest, with long jowles and gnarled hands, was standing beside him and had taken up the tablet and was studying it intently.

'Well. Did you?'

'Yes, Father, I did, but,' admitted James truthfully, 'they won't go right.'

'Perhaps not,' this strange old man replied, 'but they nearly did. See,' he added, 'take up your stylus and change this leading goose so – to bring it below the line of the rest which you can broaden, ever so little, to make a wider V to give your picture depth. You must do it yourself. I fear my hands have long ago lost their ability.' Then, as James hesitated, 'Go on, do it.'

Before the boy had half completed the revision he knew it was right, and in a few strokes the geese were as he had seen them, bursting into his sight, urgent and powerful.

'Bring them and follow me,' the old priest had said. 'Let us find something more permanent than that wax, for this picture we must preserve.'

And so the strange partnership between James and Birinus, youth and age, had begun. Birinus had been among the priests who had followed Augustine to Britain once reports of his favourable reception by King Ethelbert had been received in Gaul. The priest had been a much younger man then although he was still too senior to have been part of such a hazardous expedition had he not insisted upon it. The word of God was to be preached by Augustine and his companions but it must also be seen to be present in a copy of the four Gospels worthy to be installed in the new Cathedral Church at Canterbury when that was constructed.

Birinus, in his earlier days had been an illuminator of exceptional talent. He had been a master of the formal capitular script known as uncial and he had been among the most ingenious in his construction of the decorative and initial pages of gospel manuscripts. He had insisted on being the one to accompany the majestic copy of the gospels which had been designed, written and illuminated by Pope Gregory's command when preparations were being made for Augustine's mission. If the gospels were to be spread in Britain there must be books such as this produced in that island and, although Birinus had lost some of his former dexterity, he was still an able and excellent teacher and he was hopeful that pupils of merit would be discovered in this new land. But he had almost given up hope that real talent would emerge. There had been craftsmen of a kind but no artists – until now. Several volumes had been produced under his guidance but the ideas had been his and the execution of what he had devised not wholly pleasing to the eye.

Now, in his seventieth year, he had found a boy with such talent as he could scarcely believe. There was so little time left and none must be wasted.

'Come, young man,' he had said. 'I must show you something that will delight your eye more than that of any who has yet seen it. Come.'

And beckoning James to follow him he led him into the sacristy of the archbishop's chapel and opened a cupboard where James saw a large assortment of sacred vessels and altar coverings.

'Bring that stool and place it so. No . . . nearer. What you must take from here is heavy and must not be damaged when you are lifting it down. Now take that book,' pointing as he spoke to the highest shelf.

James, with some difficulty and not without some apprehension, pulled the large volume towards him over the edge of the shelf so that he might grasp it more securely. It was so heavy he could, only with difficulty, lift it down to the table. The binding was crimson hide and glistening smooth, except where it was raised in the form of a large cross in the centre of the front cover. Each corner was protected with a silver triangular fitting on which a simple step design had been embossed. The whole majestic book was almost as long as James' arm and he could not completely span its thickness with one hand.

'Go on, boy, open it.'

James did so in a gingerly fashion. Line after line of regular script in a single column covered each of the two pages open before him. He turned the page and then another and on this one, beneath where the script ended about halfway down the right hand page, was a simple, coloured, criss-cross pattern which James gently touched with his finger, feeling the different texture of the paint and the nearby untouched vellum.

'Turn one more page.'

James glanced up at Father Birinus and then, obediently, did so. He caught his breath at what he saw.

On the left hand page was a decorated coloured border, divided into panels filled with two alternating designs. Within this border, at the corners, was a cross constructed of the same arrangement of panels but with the alternating patterns reversed and the colours different. In the centre of the page, which the four crosses did not reach, was the figure of a winged animal. On the right hand page of the pair, in the lower half, was the same regular writing as on the other pages but the upper left quadrant was given over to an immense and gorgeously decorated capital 'I', whilst the upper right portion contained smaller and less colourful, yet still illuminated, letters, which James could not understand. He stared and stared, captivated with the beauty of colour and design and was lost in admiration of it when Father Birinus brought him back to reality.

'What you are looking at is the beginning of the gospel according to St Mark,' the old priest explained. 'Here on the left there is always a large illuminated page, perhaps containing the evangelist's symbol like this one does, a winged lion, or perhaps filled with pure design. The right side is the beginning of the gospel itself. That enormous 'I' is the first letter of the word

'Initium' – the beginning, and then you see several smaller letters for the 'nitium' but still elaborately ornamented as you see; then there is a smaller line for the next few words followed by the usual script. The first pages of all four gospels are the same, see – 'and the priest carefully opened, first, the gospel of St Matthew, then Luke and finally John, all showing the same layout and appearance but with varied designs and colours.

James could have looked for hours but, after he had been totally absorbed for a while, Father Birinus touched his shoulder.

'Come boy. Enough for the present. You may come again soon.'

'Where did it come from? Who made it?' James could not resist the question.

'It came with me soon after the holy St Augustine first arrived here in five ninety seven. The Pope himself directed that it should be made in honour of the establishment of the Christian Church in this country. As to who made it . . .' Birinus shrugged. 'An Italian artist, of that I have no doubt. This fine uncial script and the single column is characteristic of the trained Italian illuminator. It is a fine book and it was a privilege to bring it here once we knew it was safe to do so.'

Birinus seemed to be considering something and remained silent for some time, merely closing the book and indicating to James that he should replace it. When the boy climbed down from his stool the old priest spoke again.

'You could do work like that – if you wanted to that is. You have the talent and I have the knowledge. Would you like me to teach you? It will be hard work and you must really want to do it or you will never succeed. But with your ability you could do work at least as good as this and probably better.'

There was no reply for a moment.

'Well, would you like to learn?'

'Yes please.'

His Grace of Canterbury, Archbishop Justus, was also preoccupied with thoughts of the princess's journey to Northumbria.

Justus had still not got used to the notion of being an archbishop nor was he quite at ease living at Canterbury. As Bishop of Rochester since 604 he had led a quiet life and had been in the habit of leaving all important decisions to his predecessor, Archbishop Mellitus who revelled in the big occasion.

Now that poor old Mellitus had gone to his maker the previous year –

may God have mercy on his soul – and already being proclaimed a saint, His Holiness, Pope Boniface V, had appointed Justus Archbishop of Canterbury before you could say chalice. It was the Kentish King Eadbald who had done it of course. No sooner had His Majesty been baptised by Justus than he was writing to Rome to say what a fine fellow Justus was; how he had everyone in the church spellbound during his sermons; how the children sat quietly listening to him in Sunday School instead of causing an uproar as they did when Father Romanus took them.

Pope Boniface had been very complemetary in his letter to Justus. He had written of his 'devotion and diligence in spreading the Gospel of Christ,' stressed how God had 'opened the hearts of the nations to receive the mystery of the Gospel through your teaching.' He had gone on to say that he learned 'from our son, King Eadbald, how your profound knowledge of God's holy word has guided him to a real conversion and acceptance of the true Faith.' And the pontiff had gone on to write the fateful words, 'Moved by your devotion, my brother, we are sending you, by the bearer of this letter, the pallium which we grant you the privilege of wearing.'

Justus absentmindedly fiddled with one of the crosses as he tried to make his big decision. Whom should he send to Northumbria with the princess as her spiritual adviser? Paulinus, who had been his secretary for so long, was the obvious choice, since if anyone could convert King Edwin to Christianity he could. Paulinus could sell woad to ancient Britons in Justus' view. But Northumbria was a long way away, much too far in fact for Justus to seek Paulinus when knotty problems came up. Justus would rather promote Paulinus to the See of Rochester, which was only a little over twenty miles away, to which messengers could be sent in a trice to command his presence in Canterbury if the Celtic Church started being difficult about Easter again or if complicated encyclicals arrived from the Holy Father, Boniface. It would be splendid to have Paulinus just down the road so to speak instead of a month's journey or more away in the north of Britain. But Justus knew perfectly well that he could keep Paulinus with him no longer. Romanus would have to become Bishop of Rochester for if he were sent off with the princess he would probably get lost on the way let alone succeed in converting King Edwin.

Sadly Justus rang for his servant and asked that Father Paulinus be brought to him at once. Best get it over with if it was an uncongenial task had always been his motto.

Paulinus had been in Britain for more than twenty years, coming as a young man in 604 with a party sent by Pope Gregory to bring much needed help to

Augustine. Mellitus had been the leader, Justus his right hand man with Paulinus and Rufinianus, as newly ordained priests, eager to convert the heathen.

They had come with a number of other clerics, including Father Birinus, and had brought with them all the adornments of sanctity which Augustine and his party lacked – church ornaments, vestments for the clergy, relics of the apostles and martyrs, sacred vessels, candlesticks, altar coverings, devotional books and as always a letter to Augustine from the Pope.

These letters had been a great comfort to Paulinus when, in the cold and damp of this northern island, he had sometime yearned for the warm Italian sunshine and the laughter of Roman children and perhaps a glass or two of the red wine of Tuscany. In his zeal to bring the Faith to the heathen he had not expected to feel the isolation from Rome so much. It had been he who had actually carried the letter on that occasion – the letter written by His Holiness in answer, Paulinus later learned, to the many questions which Augustine, in his uncertainty, had asked of him. Paulinus could still remember when St Augustine (which was of course the title they all gave him now) had assembled his clergy and instructed them by telling them the questions he had asked and reading the pontiff's answers. Everyone had been deeply moved by the simple wisdom of the Pope.

'Why does the method of saying Mass differ in the Holy Roman Church and in the churches of Gaul?'

'You are familiar with the customs of the Roman Church but you may come across others of greater merit. Select from each church whatever things are devout religious and right and when you have bound them, as it were, into a sheaf let the minds of the English grow accustomed to it.'

Paulinus never forgot that when he had been reluctantly brought into discussions on the tonsure or the date of Easter. He had been impressed too with the Pope's answers to the difficult questions of sex and childbearing.

'May an expectant woman be baptised?'

'Why should not an expectant woman be baptised? The fruitfulness of the flesh is no offence in the eyes of Almighty God.' It seemed so simple expressed in that way.

'How soon after childbirth may she enter church?'

That too had been answered equally simply.

'You are familiar with the old testament rule: for a male child thirty three days and for a female sixty six. But this too is understood as an allegory, for were a woman to enter church and give thanks in the very hour of her delivery she would do nothing wrong.'

'May a woman properly enter church at the time of menstruation? May she receive communion at these times?' Paulinus had wondered what the reply might be but had not been prepared for the answer.

'We know that the woman who suffered an issue of blood, humbly approaching behind our Lord, touched the hem of his robe and was at once cured of her sickness. If therefore this woman was right to touch our Lord's robe why may not one who suffers nature's courses be permitted to enter the church of God? Moreover a woman should not be forbidden to receive the mystery of communion at these times?'

Paulinus had ever since tried to make himself reason simply in this way, to see through the question and through the customs and ask if that was really what Almighty God wanted. But although he was generally able to do so, and was already noted for his wise solutions to difficult problems, he had not always succeeded and he sighed at his inadequacy and returned to his thoughts of the journey north. The archibishop had not yet sent for him but Paulinus had an extraordinary faculty for realising what was in the minds of others and often anticipating their instructions. So, confident that a message would come soon, he began, like James, to consider how much he could take with him. His thoughts were soon interrupted.

'Father Paulinus.'

The priest turned to see Brother Egbert shifting uneasily from one foot to the other. Egbert never seemed to be comfortable but was forever on the move, tugging at his habit, twisting his girdle, twidling unruly locks of hair on his shaggy head and rocking from side to side.

'Yes, Egbert, what is it?'

'His Grace requests your presence Father. He is in his chamber and asks if you will be good enough to attend upon him as soon as you are able.'

Egbert, for all his nervousness and agitation, always delivered every message with absolute precision. He had been Father Paulinus' personal servant for the last three years and the priest would be sorry to leave him behind when the princess's party travelled northward. Egbert would wish to go, Paulinus knew, but he was a local man whose father and mother, both growing old, would be distraught if their only son – the only one left alive out of their seven children – were to leave them. Paulinus would tell Egbert presently, and break the news as gently as he knew how, but now he must attend the archbishop and learn, he was confident, of the decision to send him with the princess.

His Grace, meanwhile, was awaiting Paulinus, sunk in his chair and chewing his lower lip as he always did when he was about to do something he disliked. He pointed to another chair as Paulinus entered the chamber, indicating without speaking that the priest should bring it to his side.

For a few moments His Grace still said nothing and then he looked up and smiled in a way Paulinus had seen so often in the past. It transformed his face immediately and filled the younger man, as it always did, with a wave of affection. Paulinus had come to know the old man well and to understand his moods and uncertainties and to realise how much Justus had relied on him. They had been together for a decade and parting would not be easy. As if the archbishop had read his thoughts this time, instead of the reverse, he spoke quietly.

'Paulinus, my son, I have known you too long not to understand your gift of divining what is in the minds of others. You will already know, as I see from your face, that you can no longer continue as my secretary but must go to a far more important task. It is you who must accompany our beloved princess as her spiritual adviser, preserve her faith and that of her attendants when they are among the heathen. More important than that however,' the archbishop continued, rising and gazing with such fixity at Paulinus that he almost discomfited the priest until his features relaxed again in a gentle smile, 'is your task of converting the king and bringing all the northern fastness of this island to our Lord.'

'I need hardly remind you,' he went on after a moment, 'that permission for the marriage of King Edwin to Princess Ethelberga was at first refused. My predecessor in this holy office Archbishop Mellitus, had judged that it was not seemly for a Christian maid to be married to a heathen husband. Our Christian faith and the holy sacraments could have been profaned by such a relationship with a king who was wholly ignorant of the true God.'

The archbishop paused for a moment as if uncertain whether to continue his account, as people often did with Paulinus who seemed to know already what he was being told. Then, deciding that everything must be said, he continued.

'You will recall too, I have no doubt,' that little smile again as if reminding himself that Paulinus would indeed have no doubt 'that King Edwin was grieved by this decision and sent messengers again with a firm assurance that no obstacle would be put in the way of the Christian faith, and that his queen and her attendants would have complete freedom to live and worship in accordance with their Christian belief and practice. But what was of even greater significance, and what undoubtedly swayed the venerable Mellitus in his decision to permit the betrothal, was that the king expressed himself willing to accept the religion of Christ if,' and Justus held up his finger as if to stress the significance of the point, 'on examination his advisers decided that it was more holy and acceptable to God than their own.'

The archbishop took up a parchment and glanced at it as if reminding himself what to say next; then after a moment he went on.

'It was on this understanding that the betrothal was allowed and it is on this understanding that I am sending you to King Edwin so that he, and after him his kingdom, may belong to the one true faith. Of all the priests I might have chosen for this task,' and a wistful expression came over the old man's face as he said the words, 'you are the one most likely to succeed although you are also the one I would in truth keep here with me. You have a wisdom that is not granted to many and certainly,' added the old man modestly, 'not to me. I have many times benefited from your wise advice and I can only hope that without it I will not fall into too many errors.' (Nor need to ask advice from Romanus very often, he added silently to himself.) 'I am not a wise man except in this one respect that I have learned from you and it is a wise man who learns from those who assist him. And that is the reason,' continued the archbishop almost choking over the words in his affection for the younger man, 'why I will miss you more than I can say.'

Archbishop Justus turned towards the window and stood for a moment as though he had finished. Then turning back to Paulinus he spoke again in a more businesslike tone.

'You have never sought preferment, Paulinus, that I know. You had no thoughts for yourself but only for others. Thus, gifted though you are I do not think you will know what I must tell you now. It is not fitting that a simple priest be sent off, in the company of a queen to the court of a king, with the task of converting the heathen in the north. It is fitting that *you* be sent,' the archbishop continued with a twinkle in his eye, 'but not as a priest. You must go as a bishop. One week from today, on the twenty first of April, Easter Day, you will be consecrated in this church and may the blessings of Almighty God go with you.'

Princess Ethelberga, second daughter of the late King Ethelbert of Kent by his first wife Bertha, was spitting mad. Sixteen gowns was a paltry number for a queen elect to take to her wedding in Northumbria. She had planned on taking at least twice as many but her stepmother, Salfrith had vetoed the notion of travelling with so many and for once her brother, King Eadbald, had sided with her.

Perhaps Eadbald was beginning to fancy Salfrith again thought

Ethelberga, only to blush with shame at the blasphemous thought. For Ethelberga, although fractionally conceited and arguably less beautiful than she imagined and just the teeniest bit jealous of anyone else in the limelight, to say nothing of her – some might say – waspish tongue on occasions, was at heart a good girl and a true Christian, and she said 'God forgive me' three times as she had been taught to do when wicked thoughts came into her head.

Ethelberga, never one to dwell on matters, gave a long sigh and told her maid to choose sixteen gowns – any sixteen – and began to think about King Edwin of Northumbria.

The princess seldom envied anyone, and certainly not poor people but at least, she thought, they had the opportunity of seeing their prospective husband or wife before the wedding day. Would Edwin be tall and handsome? strong and silent? or – she pulled a face – fat and boring, dull and stupid or even old and ugly (ugh)? Reports had it that he was a righteous man, whatever that might mean, and was generally considered comely: Ethelberga had only lately learned the word 'comely' and it rather pleased her especially, of course, when applied to herself. And the stories told about Edwin were without doubt romantic! Ethelberga mused over the various accounts which the wandering minstrels who visited her court had given her.

Forced to escape from Northumbria to escape capture by the usurper Ethelfrid, Edwin had spent several years trying to keep one jump ahead of his pursuers until they finally caught up with him at the court of King Redwald of the East Angles. According to one minstrel, who had seemed better informed than the rest, Ethelfrid put all sorts of pressure on Redwald to give Edwin up but, for reasons best known to himself, Redwald refused. At least he refused for a time but, eventually, he agreed to let in two assassins who would despatch Edwin before he could, literally, say knife. Then came the part that Ethelberga couldn't quite understand although she had to admit that it showed Edwin in a very favourable light and gave her all kinds of romantic notions when she thought about it.

Edwin was told about the plot, urged to get out as quickly as he could but, with plenty of warning and lots of opportunity he refused to go. Just like that! He said, evidently, that he had to honour Redwald's trust in him and it was not seemly to creep out like a fugitive. And would you believe it, Redwald had a change of heart, refused to let the killers in and before Ethelfrid knew what was happening Redwald invaded his territory and put Edwin back on the throne. Of course there must have been a lot going on that no one knew about, and you could never be quite sure what was true and what was minstrel's licence, but she had to acknowledge that she experienced a warm glow somewhere inside her when she heard the story.

He was a heathen of course and it was Ethelberga's solemn duty to do all in her power to convert him to Christianity. The Pope himself had written to tell her so in no uncertain terms.

Well she would try, Ethelberga promised herself, but how was she to go about it. Prayer? Certainly. Good example? Of course. Don't insist too soon on fish for Friday? By all means. Read passages from Holy Scripture in bed at night? Well perhaps. Better ask Father Paulinus whom Archbishop Justus had said would be coming with her in order to do some converting of his own. She raised her voice.

'Enid, ask James to come to me. I wish to send him on an errand.'

It was four hours before James found Bishop-elect Paulinus still at prayer in the archbishop's private chapel. For some minutes the kneeling figure seemed unaware of the presence of the waiting boy by his side until James, seldom able to keep still for long, fidgeted uneasily, dropped his cap and disturbed the priest's concentration.

'Who are you young man?' Paulinus asked kindly.

'James, Father. James please Father.'

'And who do you serve, young James, and what do you wish of me?' continued the priest.

'I serve our beloved Princess Ethelberga Father and come at her request that you may attend upon her,' replied the boy, adding, 'though I fear it was before vespers that she sent me and I have spent a long time searching for you Father.'

Paulinus noted the ease of delivery of the princess' message and was reminded of his servant Egbert who was to be told the news that he was to be left behind and someone else found to take his place. A thought came into his head as he studied the child's solemn face.

'How old are you, boy?'

'Twelve Father,' and then hesitantly, 'all but thirteen really.'

'All but thirteen,' repeated the priest, studying James so intently that he began to fidget again and wonder if he had done something wrong.

'What do you do for the princess James?'

'Whatever she should ask, Father, but mostly go on messages like this one, or ask for her horses to be brought, or carry her terrier puppy out to . . .' and James got quite embarrassed at the notion of mentioning canine defaecation to a priest in the archbishop's private chapel, so that, for the first time, he stumbled to a halt, adding after a pause, 'things like that Father.'

Paulinus was scarcely listening, all his attention focused on the boy before him. What an engaging child, he thought to himself. He had been long away from children in his clerical duties and it was refreshing to be with such an eager young man again.

'And what do you do when Her Highness does not have a task for you, James? What is your pleasure then?'

James was silent for a moment, uncertain how his passionate attachment to art would be received by this important man. He considered a white lie such as professing to follow some manly pursuit like hawking or archery, but something about the man before him made James think that only the truth would suffice.

'I draw, Father,' he replied, 'and sometimes when I can I paint. Animals and birds mostly,' he added, 'but anything really, sometimes from life but often I make pictures up in my head. I am decorating a prayer book with them, but of course,' he ended in case the priest might not have understood, 'to the glory of Almighty God.'

Father Paulinus, Bishop-elect of York, Chaplain to the Queen-elect of Northumbria, had understood only too well. Over a quarter of a century ago, whilst still in Rome, he had been just as this boy was now. It was as if the holy St Luke, that venerable patron of artists, had bewitched him and, for a time, he could think of nothing but the wonderful decorations on the scriptures which had been the proud possession of Santa Maria Maggiore where Paulinus had spent his boyhood. But just as he thought that nothing would attract him like a life dedicated to sacred embellishment, he found that something could – his love of God – which was so overpowering that Paulinus knew that he could only serve Him as a priest. All his energies went into his studies for holy orders. Art fell behind and then well-nigh disappeared when he came to this land where there was so little, whilst in his busy life as secretary to the bishop he had scarcely given it a thought. And now, standing before him, was a fair haired, chubby, Saxon boy with a solemn shining face and a passion for painting. Apart from the obvious physical differences between them – Paulinus was more than forty years of age, tall, dark, stooping with a thin hooked nose and undeniably Italian – this boy could be himself. Suddenly he did not want to lose this child, so different yet so much the same. Scarcely trusting himself to speak, lest he should be disappointed, and for once not knowing what the answer would be he asked his question.

'James, do you think that, if Her Royal Highness would allow it, you would like to come to me, to be my servant and to do for me the things you do for her? You see,' he added gently, 'art once meant as much to me as it does to you: then I lost it and perhaps, with you, I might find it again.'

There was silence for a long time, or so it seemed to the priest. He had closed his eyes thinking, 'he doesn't want to do it, you were foolish to ask.'

Then the boy's hand was in his own and, opening his eyes, he saw the broadest grin he could imagine and he realised that he too was grinning in the same gleeful fashion.

'Yes please, Father,' said James. 'I do hope she will agree.'

She agreed of course. Paulinus, at his most persuasive, was well-nigh irresistable. James although well liked by the princess was not such a favourite as Aldrith was. His little wooded carvings fascinated her while James' drawings had less appeal and, although she was always polite about them, he knew that their real message was lost on her.

So now, five weeks later, he was walking beside the bishop's horse and humming gently to himself. He glanced up at Paulinus at the precise moment when the bishop looked down at him and they smiled secretly together like conspirators.

Then they breasted the hill and James saw before him a broad green valley and there, in the far distance, the outline of a city.

York.

Chapter 2

Edwin, King of Northumbria and master of all England north of the Humber, had toothache!

What was the good of ruling such vast lands where, as everybody knew, peace reigned so securely that a woman could carry a newborn child across the country from sea to sea without fear of molestation; where a weary traveller could refresh himself from handsome brass bowls placed by Edwin himself at every spring along the highway; where sacrifices were made to the gods twice a day by the High Priest, Coifi; what was the good of all this if no one could suggest anything which would take away his pain. He had been given fermented extract of juniper berries which had stained the inside of his mouth purple but had left his pain as bad as ever. Then his so-called doctors had applied a revolting paste which tasted like a mixture of cow-dung and linseed oil. Edwin had tried to spit it out at once but it was a cloying, sticky glue which he hadn't got rid of for hours. Worse still, he had choked on his fingers while attempting to remove some from the back of his throat and, when someone slapped him on the back to try to relieve him, he had swallowed some. In despair Edwin had become more and more morose and had shut himself in his bedchamber and sulked.

It didn't take much to start Edwin brooding. By nature a solemn man, he now had to contend with toothache, a new bride he had never seen, his son, Osfrid, who was having trouble with his Anglo-Saxon irregular verbs, and also of course, his 'experience'. The King began to think of his new bride to take his mind off his tooth, which was aching worse than ever, and off his 'experience' which always nagged him.

How would his two sons take to a stepmother? Osfrid would be glad of the diversion but Egfrid, the younger boy, had been very close to his mother, Coenberg, and still seemed to miss her. Coenberg, daughter of Cearl, King of the Mercians, with whom Edwin had lived while in exile, had been a vision. Tall, slim and fair with a gorgeous figure, a lovely placid temperament, which perfectly compensated for Edwin's doubts and self-analysis, she had given him seven years of happiness even in exile. Edwin had never really believed that Cearl would agree to the marriage – after all a king in exile might have expectations but he had little in reality – but the two were so obviously deeply in love that the normally crusty old man had not only agreed but had given Edwin protection, a position in his household and his blessing.

Then suddenly an epidemic had devastated Mercia. Coenberg's fever had carried her off in just two days along with their baby daughter born only three months earlier, while Edwin and Osfrid had recovered. King Cearl himself had been a victim too which brought Edwin's sanctuary in Mercia to an end, obliging him to seek refuge with King Redwald of the East Angles and leading eventually to his 'experience'.

Perhaps, he mused, Egfrid would find a substitute for his mother in Ethelberga. By all accounts she was beautiful but what would she be *like*? Would she add to his problems by pestering him?

And then there was the Christian religion!

He had that very much on his conscience. He could remember his 'experience' precisely and the words the mysterious stranger had used.

'If a man can assure your good fortune,' he had said (and Edwin in regaining his throne had certainly continued to enjoy good fortune) 'can also give you better and wiser guidance for your life and salvation, will you promise to follow him faithfully?'

Edwin had said that he would but had not done so. Yet the stranger, and the promise the king had made, never went completely out of his mind. Christianity had somehow pursued him regardless of his attempts to forget about it. Now here it was again and it was all his own fault. He had no need to ask King Ethelbert of Kent for his daughter Ethelberga. Penda of Mercia had two beautiful daughters, staunch pagans like Edwin, so why was he going out of his way to marry a Christian and promising, moreover, to accept the religion himself if, after due consideration, he found in acceptable. Well, Christianity in the persons of Princess Ethelberga and her accompanying chaplain was on his doorstep and wouldn't go away now.

Curse his own foolishness. Curse Christianity. Curse his toothache!

In the great hall, which was used for anything from banquets to archery in wet weather, hasty preparations were being made for the reception of the queen-elect.

Everything should have been ready days ago when the news was first received that her party was approaching but the king had been so brooding and silent and so absorbed in his own affairs that no one could get him to say what was to be made ready. Usually, when Earpwald, son of Redwald, and now King of the East Angles, dropped in for a chat about Penda of Mercia, who may have been reported to be exercising his army, or about what Cadwalla, King of Gwynda was up to in the Welsh mountains, they prepared two thrones under the stags head in the south west corner; in the winter time they brought in a brazier since Earpwald suffered from chilblains. But this meeting of the bride and groom seemed to call for something more special.

Gundred, who liked to think of himself as Master of Ceremonies on these occasions, had wanted to suspend from the rafters two hearts transfixed by an arrow. Lilla, the Chancellor, who was also the king's friend, and to whom Edwin usually listened even in his more morose, withdrawn moods, had vetoed that notion. Instead the two thrones, hastily varnished (one was still tacky and Lilla hoped that Ethelberga wouldn't arrive too quickly) had been moved into the centre of the north wall beneath the three stuffed boars heads so that the sun, shining in through the large windows to the south, would illuminate the happy couple. Two miniature fir trees had been hastily potted up in brass containers and were placed to the right and left of the thrones whilst some large branches of honeysuckle, which was just coming into bloom, had been wound in and out of the decorative apertures in the back of the king's throne to emphasise masculine dominance but to retain the romantic effect. Clean rushes had been laid down the length of the hall for the entry of Ethelberga and her party and, in a final flash of inspiration appropriate to such a sentimental occasion, narrow bundles of rushes had been stained red and blue, woven into two capital Es and propped up against the back of each throne making it very difficult for the royal couple to lean back in comfort.

Sadly Edwin's toothache was worse and he was like a stag with sore antlers when he appeared.

'Lilla,' he croaked pathetically, 'what am I to do? How am I going to get through my wedding night if nobody will help me?'

'Your Majesty may take heart,' replied Lilla, ad libbing rapidly. 'News has come of a healer whose great great grandfather learned his art from the Christian, St Brigid of Kildare,' he went on helping the sorry figure of the king to his throne. 'They say that this illustrious ancestor was present when St Brigid performed the miracle of turning the water in her ablution chamber into beer for the refreshment of the bishop and his clergy. I am told,' added the Chancellor 'that it was a truly exceptional brew. This healer is even now hastening to Your Majesty's court,' (Lilla had in fact only heard of him that morning and his agents were desperately trying to find him) 'with what I have been told,' he concluded, more in hope than in expectation, 'will be an infallible remedy.'

Any reassurance his words might have given was destroyed by Edwin sinking back in his throne and getting the prickly end of one of the rushes in the small of his back. He shot up in exasperation, bellowing like a bull, clutching the wounded part with his left hand whilst supporting his aching jaw with his right. At that precise moment a messenger entered at the far end of the hall and ran panting down the line of rushes scattering them on each side. He slid to a halt in front of the king, bowed as low as his breathlessness would allow and gasped, 'May it please Your Majesty, Princess Ethelberga and her party are at this moment at the door.'

'Oh Tor. Oh Twi. Oh Odinn,' moaned the king and collapsed again onto the seat of his throne remembering, at the last moment, not to lean backward and thus finished bolt upright and staring in an alarmed fashion at his bride-to-be who was, even now, advancing towards him.

Ethelberga viewed this staring figure with alarm. Why was she having such a disturbing effect upon him? Was her clothing disarranged? Did she have a smut on her nose? Unused to affecting men in this strange fashion she turned to Bishop Paulinus by her side in some agitation.

She need not have been concerned. The bishop was well in control of the situation and was thinking what a heaven-sent opportunity (literally) the king's disability was. Paulinus had instantly grasped the significance of Edwin's swollen jaw and the gingerly fashion in which he was cupping his face in his hand. This was Paulinus' chance. Nothing, he knew, impressed heathens like a good miracle. Realising Ethelberga's worry Paulinus stepped forward and bowed in stately episcopal fashion to the king.

'Your Majesty,' he began in measured tones, 'I bring greetings from King Eadbald of Kent. It has been my privilege to escort your bride-to-be on this long journey to your illustrious court. She, I know, is overjoyed to be with you at last but she is deeply concerned, as I am, to see you in such pain and distress.'

Edwin looked up, somewhat mystified by this unusual, and he had to admit, perceptive opening by the bishop. After the briefest of pauses, as though Paulinus had not expected any comment from the king, he continued.

'We at the Christian court of Kent, members of the one true church of God, servants of our Lord Jesus Christ, understand full well that human frailty can only be sustained by God's grace and a true faith in His Holy Name. It will be part of my duties in Your Majesty's kingdom to promulgate the message of Jesus Christ, with the gracious permission of Your Majesty of course.' Edwin, who had taken his hand away from his face was listening intently and found that he was already nodding in acquiescence.

'. . . so that together we can enjoy that ineffable peace which no one, who is not of our faith, can understand, and ultimately come to our everlasting reward in heaven.'

Edwin was craning forward now following every word the bishop spoke.

'The power of Almighty God,' Paulinus went on, warming to his theme now that the crunch was approaching, 'is limitless. There is no human condition so abject that it cannot be relieved, no soul so tarnished that it cannot be made clean by the blood of the lamb, no disorder, no distress so great that Almighty God cannot, should he choose, instantly relieve it.'

'Her Royal Highness, Princess Ethelberga, and I . . .' the bishop turned half aside to include the princess in his words' . . . rejoice that the holy St Apollonia has already interceded on your behalf with our Blessed Lord and He has elected, so early in our aquaintance, to demonstrate his mercy by relieving Your Majesty of the distress you have suffered these last few days.'

'But I haven't . . .' began Edwin, about to expostulate at the presumption that this God could cure his toothache, only to find that his pain had vanished. There was silence for a moment, then the king could contain himself no longer.

'It's gone,' he shouted. 'Gone I tell you.' And leaping up from his throne he turned first to Lilla who, understanding the tenor of Paulinus' words first, was beaming back at the king. Edwin seized him by the shoulders, shook him, clasped him to his chest, thumped him on the back and almost did a little dance for joy. Gazing round in his relief the king's eye caught that of the diminutive Coifi the high priest behind Lilla and, putting his face to that of the high priest, he shouted in indignation.

'Ha, what about that Coifi? Gone d'you hear. Gone.'

Coifi, not understanding this any more than most of the others, was edging backwards behind a phalanx of lesser councellors who had come in as soon as the news of the bride's arrival percolated through the palace. But the king was too excited to upbraid the high priest further. Turning to Paulinus in his delight he spluttered,

'H..h..how did you do it? Tell me.'

Paulinus, now thoroughly master of the situation, was intent on bringing the king back to the main business in hand; there would be plenty of time for explanations later.

'Your Majesty,' he answered gravely, 'I rejoice in your so fortunate cure, and,' he added, turning aside and indicating, deferentially, the waiting Ethelberga who, if truth be told was only slightly less mystified than the other spectators to the scene, 'so does Her Royal Highness whom I have the great pleasure in presenting to Your Majesty.'

Protocol had been re-established. The happy pair gazed at each other for a moment – for slightly longer perhaps then would have been expected of normal polite behaviour, each suppressing an audible sigh of satisfaction at the sight of the other. Then Edwin bowed in a brusque but not unpleasing manner and Ethelberga sank into an elegant curtsey, in which she remained so long that Edwin, wondering if she was able to get up and simultaneously remembering his manners, stepped forward and helped her to her feet.

A moments gaze was all he needed. Brimming over with relief at his restoration to health and enthralled by the appearance of his bride, he drew her gently to his chest, encircled her with his arms and kissed her fondly.

Ethelberga was receiving congratulations from Lilla and the other members of the king's court. Osfrid and Egfrid, who had crept in at the back and had just managed to work their way to the front, were seen by Edwin and brought forward to meet Ethelberga. Even Paulinus, who had seen it all before and knew that there was nothing like a good miracle to break the ice, was smiling warmly at James who had been trying to listen to the consort of viols until he remembered his duties and edged his way back to his master.

Only Coifi, in an agony of doubt and distress, was silent and in a few moments crept away alone.

After that there was a lot of introducing to be done. The king brought his sons forward to meet the bishop, already a figure of fascination to Osfrid who had arrived just in time to witness the cure of his father's toothache. Egfrid, however, was strangely silent with the bishop but became more animated when Paulinus, seeing two boys of the same age, and ignoring their difference in rank, introduced him to James who was waiting a few steps behind.

The two boys said nothing at first but grinned uncertainly at each other and edged away from the main crowd. They were of the same age and height but very different in appearance, James' chubby face and fair complexion contrasting sharply with the thin somewhat sallow appearance of Egfrid. James, never quite still for long, fidgeted a little trying to think of something to say and was surprised to be asked a direct question.

'James. What kind of a name is James? I've never heard it before.'

Egfrid maintained a solemn expression as he made his direct remark, but it was not said in a scornful or abrupt fashion and James was not disturbed.

'Well, just an ordinary one, I suppose,' he replied, adding quickly, so as not to seem unhelpful, 'Christian of course.'

Egfrid digested this information for a moment before making his next comment.

'Christian? Does that mean what your priest was talking about to father – I mean when he took the pain away?'

'Yes it does,' James answered. 'Christians are followers of Jesus Christ who is our God and one of the Trinity although,' he added hastily, 'that's a bit complicated and you'd better get His Lordship the Bishop to explain it. All Christians,' the boy went on, feeling something more was called for by way of explanation, 'are called after a saint and I'm called after St James.'

'Who was he?' Egfrid was at his most direct again, scarcely altering the solemn expression on his face.

'Well, there were two of them, called the Greater and the Less.'

'And which are you called after?'

'The Less, I think.' James wasn't really sure but there was something about James the Less that appealed to him more than James the Greater.

'What did he do?' Egfrid, an avid searcher for information, was keen to learn all he could from his new acquaintance. James was getting into his stride too and remembering what Archbishop Justus had told him.

'He was one of the twelve apostles,' he began; then, seeing for the first time an expression of puzzlement on his friend's face, he added, 'they were followers of Jesus Christ our Lord, except that one of them betrayed Him and hanged himself and then there were only eleven. You see . . .' But he was interrupted by Egfrid.

'Is there a lot to tell?' he enquired. 'Because if there is I know a secret place where we could go and you could tell me all about it. Come on.'

James looked around, feeling that he ought to get Bishop Paulinus' permission first. But Paulinus was being led by the king to meet members of the Council and . . . well, after all, he was the king's son. If he said, 'come on,' you went.

'Right,' said James. 'Come on.'

The secret place was up a tree.

Close by the palace to the south stood a great oak with enormous spreading branches. Halfway up, where three boughs came off the trunk at almost the same point and ran horizontally, two pieces of wood, which had once been the sides of a cart, had been lashed together to make a platform roughly six feet square. Egfrid, who knew every convenient foothold of the climb up, reached the platform several minutes before James who was less agile and just a little perturbed by heights. Determined not to show anxiety, he pulled himself over the platform's edge and slid across until his back was against the main trunk where he felt more secure.

Egfrid was stretched out face downwards, his chin cupped by his two hands, watching James expectantly. Perhaps he sensed his new companion's unease for he did not at once resume his questions. Instead he spoke reassuringly.

'It's quite safe here you know, so don't worry. I've been up here hundreds of times. Osfrid used to come too but he doesn't like it as much as I do.'

James, feeling safer in his new surroundings with the broad trunk behind him, began to look round. The castle was only barely visible through the leaves and branches over to his right. A small gap in the leaves to his left revealed rolling countryside with blue hills in the far distance. Overhead the branches were thinner and a few fleecy clouds were seen against a brilliant blue sky. James decided not to look down.

Egfrid broke the silence.

'How long did it take you to travel up from Kent?'

'More than five weeks.'

'Are all of you Christians?'

'Yes, everyone.'

'How many . . . priests do you call them? . . . are there?'

'Three,' replied James. 'Bishop Paulinus, whom you met and who cured your father's toothache, is the chief priest,' (James smiled to himself as the phrase reminded him of the chief priests and the scribes and pharisees in the New Testament) 'and there are two who are newly ordained who will help him.'

'Does Bishop Paulinus often do marvellous things like he did for my father?' Egfrid enquired.

James studied the matter before replying. 'No,' he said eventually, 'not often. In fact,' he continued, 'Paulinus doesn't do it himself you know although it may look as if he does. Only Almighty God can work miracles but he always does them through one of his bishops or priests. In fact,' the boy admitted, 'I've never seen one before, although I've heard of many of course.'

'What sort of miracles have you heard of?'

So James gave Egfrid a summary of Christianity that he hoped Bishop Paulinus would have approved of.

Egfrid had rolled over onto his back and was squinting up at the top branches of the tree, trying to keep them in view as they waved about in the gentle breeze.

'It all sounds a lot more interesting than our old religion,' he admitted. 'All we ever do is to sacrifice to the gods all the time or else they will destroy us. Catch them sacrificing themselves for us. Some hopes.' He scrambled to his feet. 'Will you tell me some more later? Now I want to show you something. Come on.'

'Come on' seems to be his favourite words, thought James and was about to obey when he found that Egfrid was going up not down. James hesitated and was still only half upright on one knee when the prince, already ten feet higher up the tree, looked back and called again, 'Aren't you coming?'

'I don't think I can,' the other boy admitted. 'I'm not used to trees like you are.' And not wishing to appear afraid he added, 'It's not that I'm scared. I just don't know how to get up there.'

Egfrid seemed to understand. 'I'll come back and show you,' he said at once, and before James could blink, or so it seemed, he was beside him again on the platform. 'Now you go first. I'll be behind you to tell you where to put your feet and hands,' he instructed. 'Take that branch – no that one – right foot here; now left there and take that branch higher up.'

It was amazing how easy it was as long as James did what he was told. They seemed to have climbed a long way when Egfrid called to him, 'Now wait a moment for me,' and a few moments later the two boys were side by side on the same branch.

'Look.' Egfrid pointed to the trunk where there was a crude circle in the bark with 'E of N' scratched inside it.

James started to read. 'Egfrid,' he began and as he hesitated the prince completed it for him, 'of Northumbria.'

'I did that when I was seven,' he stated proudly, 'and up there –' up there seemed dizzy heights further on to James 'where you can just see is one I did on my ninth birthday.' Perhaps it was the look on his companion's face which made him add, 'We'll go there another time.'

James heaved a profound sigh of relief and closed his eyes for a moment.

When he opened them he realised that the prince had spoken and was holding something out to him. 'What,' he spluttered. 'What did you say?'

'I said here is my knife. Now you carve your initial beside mine,' and as James hesitated added, 'go on. Put it there,' pointing to a smooth part of the trunk just below and to the left of his name.

It took James a moment to wedge himself firmly. Then taking the knife he began to carve.

Minutes went by in complete silence except for the sound of the blade steadily chipping into the bark. Egfrid watched entranced as an elegant J emerged under the point of the knife. The J was slim although the main stem was relatively broad with gently curving margins. These diverged slightly at the top and merged into two spirals, one curving from the right, the other from the left. The lower end of the upright was cut away on the left side leaving a cavity into which the right margin was extended in, again, a graceful spiral fashion.

Then, just as Egfrid opened his mouth to speak, James began to frame the initial in a rectangle of four lines overlapping at each corner into the angles of which a curvilinear design was introduced, as if by magic.

If Egfrid was about to exclaim at this extraordinary artistry he was prevented from doing so by a roar from his companion. Moving backwards as he always did to view his completed work, and forgetting his precarious position in the tree, James lost his footing and would have plunged downwards through the branches had Egfrid not made a hasty grab, caught him by the collar of his jerkin, and hung on until the boy, legs flailing wildly, got one of them over a branch and held it tight.

It took several minutes to get him back to his original place on the bough. Both boys were panting with exertion and neither spoke for some time until James loosened his left hand gingerly from the tree, touched Egfrid lightly on the shoulder, and said, 'Thank you. I thought I was done for. Thank you for saving me.'

Egfrid wasn't really listening. He was tracing the gentle lines of the J with his index finger, circling the cirlicues and brushing away tiny fragments of wood. At last he spoke.

'It's marvellous,' he uttered. 'Wonderful, and you did it in a few minutes. However did you learn? Who taught you?'

James was suddenly diffident again in contrast to his assurance while carving the trunk. 'I suppose I could always draw,' he answered, 'but Father Birinus taught me the art of lettering and decoration. I just seem to know how to do it – like you know about climbing up trees,' adding after a moment, 'and down.'

'Well I think it's splendid,' the prince said admiringly, 'and I'm proud to have my initial next to yours. Could you do mine do you think? On parchment? Father has some.'

'Of course. But we'll have to get down first and Bishop Paulinus may be wanting me. Perhaps tomorrow.' And the two boys smiled happily at each other as Egfrid slid off his branch and tapped James on the right foot.

'Fine,' he said, 'Now we'll go down. Put that foot there. I'll go first and tell you where to make each step. Come on.'

Edwin and Paulinus faced each other in uneasy silence across the king's private audience chamber.

Edwin shuffled irritably, crossed his legs one way and then the other. Twice he caught Paulinus' eye and each time looked away immediately. He coughed and cleared his throat and, more than once, seemed about to speak before retreating into uncertain silence.

Meanwhile, Paulinus' easy confidence and urbane imperturbability ruffled the king still further. He felt so uncomfortable that he almost wished his toothache had not been cured so that he could hide behind its protective façade to avoid what he knew was coming.

He tried to meet Paulinus' eye but was unable to do so. He looked away but somehow was obliged to bring his gaze back to that of the priest who had begun speaking again.

'In my mind's eye, Your Majesty, I see an exiled king – as it might be you – living on suffrance at the court of another and in great danger of assassination. And I see this exiled king – as it might be you – sitting alone outside the palace of the king who had offered him sanctuary, wondering how he might regain his kingdom, as indeed Your Majesty has regained yours.'

Edwin seemed stuperose during this account and kept his eyes tightly shut to avoid Paulinus' intense gaze. The bishop went on more quietly.

'I see this exiled king – such as you, sire – meeting, on that occasion, a stranger who asked him three questions.

"What reward would you give," the stranger asked, "to the one who can deliver you from your troubles so that you can escape harm?"

"Any reward," the exiled king replied.

"And what if the same one promised that you would be king, crush your enemies and wield great power?"

'You answered,' Paulinus went on relentlessly 'that you would give ample proofs of your gratitude.'

In the brief silence which followed there was a low moan from the king.

'The third question.' Paulinus was now standing immediately in front of Edwin and speaking insistently, 'was; 'if this man, who can furnish such good fortune, can also give you better and wiser guidance for your life and salvation than any you have known, will you promise to obey him and follow his advice?'

'And the answer,' Paulinus was almost whispering yet his words were clearly audible in the silence, 'was that you would faithfully follow anyone who could do these things.'

Paulinus stopped speaking for so long that the king opened his eyes and found himself staring into those of the bishop. At that moment Paulinus stretched out his hand and placed it on the king's head saying 'And I think Your Majesty will recall that the stranger, who so mysteriously disappeared immediately afterwards, then put his hand on your head, as I do now, and said, 'When you receive this sign and recall our conversation do not delay the fulfillment of your promise.'

The bishop said no more but kept his hand on the king's head while Edwin closed his eyes again. In a moment his face contorted and tears began to flow freely and his sobbing became distressing.

Paulinus removed his hand and encircled the king's shoulders in a comforting gesture. When he spoke again it was with infinite gentleness.

'Our Lord Jesus Christ loves all men, Your Majesty, and must gather into His fold those who are not worthy of salvation. It is not easy for everyone He calls to follow Him, but He is omnipresent and no one can hide from Him. He sees you, King Edwin, as a convert to the one true faith, a loyal and steadfast Christian, and He would recruit you to His service as you well know. My task, sire, is to provide the means of your instruction and enrol you, and thereafter your kingdom, into the Church of God.'

Edwin rubbed his eyes with his sleeve to wipe away his tears which had run down both cheeks onto his chin and even dripped onto his robe.

'I've wanted to become a Christian so often,' he began, 'and then I would start to doubt and wonder if I had remembered correctly what the stranger said. You see,' he went on, after sniffing and rubbing his eyes again, 'I have always been the sort of man who can see both sides of an argument – a man who has difficulty making up his mind. I have tried to stop myself doing it but I can't. So when I had this strange experience I thought at first that it clearly meant that your God was wanting me to give up my religion for His. Then I began to ask myself was I right? Had that really been what the experience had signified? And anyhow,' he went on almost defiantly, 'I knew nothing about Christianity and' almost accusingly 'there was no one to teach me.'

'I will teach you, Your Majesty,' replied Paulinus, 'and if you will have faith in Almighty God it will be easy.'

'Faith! All right, you say it will be easy with faith, but I'm not that kind of man. I can't take things on trust. I have to see them and touch them or have them proved. So I know I won't really accept your Christ until you prove Him better than my gods.'

Paulinus did not immediately reply and the king looked up enquiringly and asked, 'Well. Can you?'

'I have faith in my God, Your Majesty, if you do not and I know that if He wishes to do so He can demonstrate His power. I also know that your gods are futile man-made images with no power whatsoever. So, sire, if that is what you wish, what would you have my Lord Jesus Christ do?'

'Make rain,' said Edwin rather surprisingly. 'Rain, that's what we need and if we are going to have a miracle we might as well have a useful one. You and your God versus Coifi and mine. Tomorrow. Here,' throwing a coin to Paulinus, 'you can toss this silver piece to see who tries first, you or Coifi. One must make rain within the hour and if he does, the other must stop it also within the hour. If the first one fails the other will have an hour to see if he can do it. Proof. That's what I need. Proof. Now we'll see if the stranger meant what he said.'

Coifi had been up all night working with frenetic energy. Tor, Twi and Odinn would show them. Rain? Easy. Just let him get a few things together and his gods would soon put that Christian, Jesus, in his place. Toothache. Ha! Anyone could cure toothache but making rain was something else.

One of his assistants, Cynbad, a hugh gangling dullard, had obtained from – only Tor knew where – a skeleton which was to be hung from the protruding branch of a tree. Garth, a diminutive but willing member of Coifi's team, had collected a black cat, which had been stuffed into a sack for safe handling, whilst a third minion, Readrid, provided a black calf and a black and white hen. Since black was the order of the day to simulate dark rain clouds, the faces of Coifi and his band, together with the white feathers of the hen had been stained with soot. At the appropriate moment Cynbad, holding a large jar of water, was to be stretched out on a bough above the skeleton over which Readrid was to hold a riddle purloined from the gardener. At a given signal a trio of hags in Coifi's employ, and a group of palace attendants, who had been pressed into service, were to shriek, "Rain, rain, send us rain" and the animals were to be sacrificed.

All was ready except that His Majesty, King Edwin, had not arrived. Coifi and his grisly gang waited. Cynbad, having at last managed to get onto his bough with the jar of water more or less full, was forbidden to come down and lay stretched out on the branch with the container balanced in front of him. Garth was having great difficulty controlling the cat, wild with fear and rage inside its small sack, and the hen kept up a ceaseless cackle and shed feathers right and left.

The sun climbed into the heavens. The sky was cloudless. It was going to be another beautiful day.

At length a stately procession emerged from the palace. Edwin had put on his best clothes to mark the occasion but was far less resplendent than Ethelberga, who had chosen her most elegant gown to show herself off to the populace. Paulinus however, in full episcopal regalia, stole the show.

Three chairs had been placed in full view of the tree and the river bank and the royal party seated themselves. The hour glass was turned and placed in front of the king. Edwin signalled Coifi into action.

The high priest, whose black face was becoming streaky in the hot sun, brandished his sacrificial knife, grasped the hen firmly and slit its throat with a flamboyant gesture. The subsequent sacrifices were less efficient and failed amid pantomime chaos as the chorus of 'rain, rain, send us rain' burst forth.

This was Cynbad's big moment. Tilting his jar he tipped water through Readrid's riddle onto the skeleton below. At first he splashed it only a little but, as the jar needed to tilt more and more, a continuous stream flowed down onto the sieve, which Readrid was shaking from side to side in a desperate attempt to simulate raindrops. Coifi swung the legs of the skeleton. Raedrid wiggled his riddle like a tambourine and Cynbad, in a final attempt to empty the container, lost his balance.

He crashed onto the riddle, grasped wildly at Readrid on the way down, clutched the dangling skeleton to his chest and felled Coifi beneath a mass of writhing legs and rattling bones.

The palace servants began to applaud the dramatic finale of the rain making ceremony. Readrid began slowly to descend. Garth made his escape and the hags shuffled forward to extricate their high priest and Cynbad from the mass of bones and fragments of jar at the foot of the tree.

The sand trickled steadily through the hour glass. The sun climbed still higher. It was a beautiful day.

At noon Edwin formally announced that Coifi's time was up, he had failed to make rain.

It would have been hard to imagine a more unnecessary statement. The populace, who had clearly decided that such an important occasion constituted a holiday, were basking in the sun and many had stripped off to bare torsos to soak up the warmth in their unaccustomed idleness. Ethelberga had departed to change into something cooler. Edwin had moved his chair beneath the shade of the skeleton's tree and was preparing to have forty winks. Even Paulinus had laid aside his mitre and was gently fanning himself with the ends of his long, loose sleeves. Coifi, suffering from concussion, had been taken away in a wheelbarrow.

James had been sent off to bring the only item the bishop seemed to want for his attempt to make rain. The boy returned with it presently and took it over to Paulinus who replaced his mitre, took up his crozier and instructed James to follow him, bringing his burden with him.

They approached the king who was dozing quietly. The bishop, indicating that James should put the object on the ground in front of Edwin, cleared his throat to get the royal attention and spoke in his usual confident manner.

'Your Majesty will indicate when you would like our Lord Jesus Christ to make rain,' he began. 'It is the custom of Almighty God to perform these deeds through the agency of some earthly creature. Since His saints are often chosen to be the instrument of His power, and since I am one of the least of His creatures, who would not presume to such an exalted position, Your Majesty will see that I shall call upon this statue, which my servant has brought from the chapel, to act in this way. It is of St Peter, the first Bishop of Rome, to whom our Blessed Lord entrusted the keys of the Kingdom of Heaven.'

St Peter's statue, to which the king turned his gaze, had been brought from Kent to grace the cathedral at York when this should be completed. It was three feet high, delicately carved in wood and stained a deep brown colour. The saint looked an imposing figure, his tiara on his head, a large bunch of keys in his hand and his massive locks falling in graceful waves to his shoulders.

Paulinus was speaking again.

'If Your Majesty is ready I suggest that we approach nearer to the river bank. See, the queen is returning. Perhaps, sire, you and she and the princes, along with your Chamberlain and the other members of the court, would like to assemble as close to the bank as possible to see everything that happens. The common people,' to whom Paulinus waved his hand beckoning as he did so, 'may, with your permission, gather behind on this higher ground, for I would wish to demonstrate to them too the infinite power of the one true God.'

Edwin took Ethelberga's arm and moved towards the water, eager to see this next attempt at a miracle but less happy to be on the windward side of the commoners, who were already pressing forward in a mass, craning their unwashed necks to see what was happening.

'We must abide firmly by the rules,' Paulinus insisted, 'and set the hour glass. Here,' he called to a servant, 'place it there on that mound so that all can see. My servant, and this statue of St Peter, are all I shall require,' he continued, and speaking to James said, 'bring the statue carefully James; I will require your help.'

James was excited to be a part of the miracle but anxious not to do anything wrong and he obeyed at once. He caught the eye of Egfrid who grinned at him and nodded his head in encouragement. The bishop turned to face the audience, every eye upon him.

'The one true God, through whom alone salvation can be achieved, does not require any of the paraphenalia your high priest collected, nor need He resort to the ridiculous antics you have witnessed. If the Lord God wished he could bring rain now, instantly.' One or two nervous souls looked apprehensively up at the sky, still blue and cloudless. 'But,' went on Paulinus, 'since Coifi chose to use water to try, vainly, to make rain, my God will do the same to show you all that only through the water of baptism can you be saved.' Then turning to James he commanded 'bring St Peter, James, and follow me into the river.'

He turned and began to march purposefully towards the water. James hastily gathered up St Peter and followed. Edwin sprang to his feet in alarm calling out, 'Stop. Don't wade in. The boy will be washed away and drown.'

Paulinus paused briefly in his progress, half turned and spoke with some asperity to the king.

'I think not, Your Majesty. Our Blessed Lord, who walked on the waters of the Sea of Galilee, will not let that happen.' And then, to James, he added more quietly, 'Follow me and do exactly what I do. Have no fear, God will watch over you,' and with that he stepped out boldly.

James was so intent on following the bishop's instructions precisely that he was several feet out into the water before he realised that he was *on* the river not *in* it. His Lordship in front was *on* it also, striding out towards the middle over the surface of the current. Then he paused and said to the boy, 'Place St Peter there facing the king.'

James, his mind boggling at what was happening, did as he was told and looked up at the crowd on the bank. There was consternation on all sides. The king was on his feet shouting although so many others were yelling too it was impossible to hear what he said. Many of the women had buried their heads in their hands in terror. Two of Ethelberga's ladies-in-waiting had fainted but lay where they had fallen since everyone had their eyes on the trio resting gently on the surface of the water as if standing on solid ground. The Christian members of the party were on their knees praying. One of the curates had started to sing a hymn.

In the midst of the panic and shouting and gesticulation James noticed a strange thing. Behind the crowd, and getting closer every minute, were thick, black clouds where a short time ago had been blue sky.

The bishop stretched out his hands before him and began to walk back to the bank and towards the king. James followed clutching the increasingly heavy St Peter. The bishop came to a halt before Edwin. Silence fell.

'Your Majesty will soon be gratified by the miracle of rain,' he remarked smiling broadly, 'so soon in fact that I fear many of us will not reach the shelter of our homes in time. If you look round, sire, you will see why.'

Edwin craned his neck round frantically and the rest of the crowd did the same. The black, menacing clouds were almost upon them. A clap of thunder rolled and the first few drops of rain began to sprinkle the surface of the river behind them. Ethelberga seized a shawl from one of her attendants, praised God three times that she had changed out of her best dress, and, casting her dignity to the winds, set off for the palace as fast as she could run. Edwin, stunned by the whole proceedings, sat motionless in the now steady downpour.

Only Paulinus, James and St Peter, retaining their immunity to water, returned to the palace dry-shod under the protection of an invisible umbrella.

Not for some time was it realised that the king was still sitting motionless on the bank in the pouring rain which hid the tears streaming down his cheeks.

In the temple Coifi was weeping with rage and frustration.

The gods – his gods – whom he had faithfully served for several years were humiliated and he with them. This Christian, Paulinus, must be right after all. His Jesus Christ must be God and all-powerful and Coifi's days as high priest were over. Unless that is . . . unless, he thought cunningly, he could transfer to the new religion and become a priest again – even in time a high priest. Coifi smiled to himself in a conspiratorial fashion. The old religion had let him down; now he would see what the new one could do.

But first there was the final act to perform which might secure his bona fide with the Christians. The idols and the altar must be destroyed, smashed, crushed out of all recognition. Coifi would willingly have done it himself, so deeply had his humiliation bitten into his soul, but his attempt – his vain attempt – to bring about their destruction had brought him further humiliation. He had been unable to lift the hammer which was needed to make any impression on them. In a rage he had brought in Cynbad who was standing beside him poised ready to strike.

'Destroy them,' shouted the ex high priest. 'Annihilate them. Beat them into dust.'

Cynbad brought down his hammer with a crash and the altar stone split in two. Down again and Tor and Twi fell into pieces right and left. Once more and Odinn, now minus his neanderthal head, swung violently on his rope. Cynbad beamed happily and continued his orgy of destruction.

Paganism was dead in Northumbria.

Chapter 3

There was silence in the bishop's room in the palace – the room which they now all called the scriptorium. The large table, beneath the window to catch all the light, was strewn with James' materials – parchment, styli, little jars of pigment, brushes and two sharply pointed instruments which he used for pricking through the pages for exact ruling.

James laid down his stylus and studied the page on which he had been working for so long. It was the initial page of the gospel of St Mark and he had been illuminating it for two months. At last it was completed.

'Initium Evangelii Jesu Christi, Filii Dei,' James read to himself out loud, examining each letter as he did so in case there should be a blemish previously overlooked. But there was none and he allowed himself a quiet smile of satisfaction at his accomplishment.

The capital 'I' of the word 'Initium' was elaborately embroidered at its upper and lower ends with a clever arrangement of two large and several, interwoven, small curved pelta designs. The body of the letter comprised six alternating panels, each occupying half the thickness of the stem, three displaying an intricate pattern of knot work and three writhing reptilian creatures folding in and out of each other in remarkable complexity.

Red green and blue had been the colours used to give greater beauty to the designs and the whole was contained in a slender buff frame.

James mused for a moment on the beasts curving in and out of each other up and down the stem of the 'I'. Beasts were all his figures could be called since they seldom had any true counterparts in nature. Some resembled dogs, sometimes placid, sometimes ferocious with teeth bared in a snarl. Some were cat-like. Once or twice he had included a stag or a wild boar which could just be identified for what they were. Snakes had often been used especially in difficult angles or curves of his designs, when they would be intertwined in a complex fashion. He was starting to include birds more often but here again, although graceful and pleasing to the eye, they were fanciful in concept. All were symbolic representations of the animal kingdom, James decided, just as his flowers and trees, novel in both form and colour, were imaginary representations of that part of nature.

The completion of such an elaborate design was a source of immense satisfaction, James thought. Some time before he had finished the great decorated page of his manuscript, which was next to the initial page, and now he turned to it and examined it in the same meticulous fashion. It was a splendour of colour and intricacy of design, just as the beginning of the gospel text was. James found himself gazing with pride at the elegant work he was preparing for God. Perfect he thought.

No sooner had this notion come into his mind then another followed it. He could hear his old teacher, Father Birinus, saying the cautionary words he had spoken so often to James. 'Man is imperfect, only God is perfect. If you think you have created a thing of infinite beauty for Him, and if your pride leads you to think you have achieved perfection, remember that pride is one of the seven deadly sins. Do not forget that what you have been doing for Him, for perhaps a year, Almighty God could create for Himself in an instant should He choose to do so. Never aim at absolute perfection: that is presumptuous and if you are so misguided to think that you have achieved it make sure that you have not.'

James, suitably humbled by this reminder of the pride in which he had been indulging, said a silent 'thank you' to Father Birinus and took up his brush. Where there was a descending pattern of knot work alternating in red and blue he selected one whorl from the lowest portion and with the application of a little yellow ochre changed it to a much paler shade than the rest. It was enough. You had to look carefully for the blemish but it was there. It was enough.

Retreating into humility and not wishing to yield to temptation again, James set aside the finished pages and began to consider the remainder of his work.

Two years ago Bishop Paulinus had given him the task of illuminating a copy of the four gospels which would grace the new stone cathedral in York. The first church which Paulinus had built had been for the baptism of King Edwin, and it had been small and made only of wood. The bishop had requested its rapid construction so that on Easter Day, in the year of our Lord 627, His Majesty, King Edwin of Bernicia and Deira, could be baptised within it with something approaching proper solemnity.

The king had revelled in his detailed instruction in the Christian faith. Everything had to be explained and discussed time and again with the bishop, or with one of the priests, or with James or with anyone who would listen. Once convinced of the truth of Christian teaching he had thrown himself wholeheartedly into absorbing as much of it as he could in order, he said, to be fully prepared on his baptismal day.

The king's baptism had transformed everything and James had never ceased to wonder at the change which had occurred in the lives of them all since the miracle of rain had washed away all the king's doubts. His baptism had been the signal for Paulinus to evangelise the entire region. James had accompanied him on many journeys through the wild, beautiful Northumbrian countryside, where the bishop had instructed and baptised the people almost continuously. On one occasion, James remembered, when they had been guests of the king and queen at their palace at Yeaveney in Glendale in the province of Bernicia, they had both taught the crowds who flocked to them and Paulinus had baptised people for thirty-six days without ceasing. In those days there were no baptistrys nor oratorys, which were only now being constructed, and the converts were baptised in the River Glen as Christ Himself had been in the Jordan.

Later, when it seemed that everyone in the region must have accepted Christianity, James and the bishop had come south, into the province of Deira close by the town of Catterick, and it had been the same story with hundreds being baptised in the River Swale. A small chapel, one of the earliest in the province, had been erected there and it had a special significance for James for it was there that the bishop had first broached the subject of the young man's future.

After a long day travelling from hamlet to hamlet they had made a brief visit to the chapel. Paulinus had been silent for some time making James think that he had something on his mind. The servant was happy to leave the master undisturbed since their relationship was a close one and they could be entirely at ease with each other without speaking. Finally the bishop had turned to James and placed a hand on his shoulder.

'My boy,' he had begun, 'you have been a great help to me since coming as my assistant, and,' he added, 'my friend. You have developed an ability to teach our faith to these simple people for which Almighty God will one day reward you. But we must look further ahead than tomorrow. This province will soon be wholly Christian and then there will be a need for more clergy and more churches, and the word of God will be widely proclaimed. I have many times wondered how best you could serve Almighty God. You would make an excellent priest. Our Blessed Lord needs young men of your quality and fervour. So I must ask you; have you considered the priesthood?'

It had been a long time before James had answered, he remembered, and then reluctantly and with sadness.

'I have considered it, my Lord, perhaps as many times as you have wondered about it,' he admitted. 'I love God and want to serve Him but,' he continued truthfully, 'I do not feel that the priesthood is the way for me.

You have told me, my Lord, that when there are more churches in the north, and especially when the new cathedral at York begins its construction, there will be a need for the decoration of His house so that all His subjects can see due reverence paid to Him. I have some skill in illumination my Lord, as you know and I wondered if I might take part in that decoration. Since my instruction by Father Birinus I have practised everything he taught me and even,' he had added tentatively, 'developed ideas of my own which seem promising. I could show Your Lordship some examples of my work.'

And Paulinus had sent him to bring them and had studied them all, from the simple illumination of letters with which James had begun, to the more intricate designs which had evolved, as well as the transition from the application of a little colouring at a few special places to the riot of gorgeous colour which was now beginning to characterise his work.

The bishop had gazed at it for some time before speaking. When he did so it was slowly and with great deliberation.

'I had expected your decision on the priesthood James, for I had felt that although you would make a fine priest, you did not really want to be one. But, busy with my own affairs as I have been, I had not realised the extraordinary extent to which your artistry had blossomed. Father Birinus could never have been guilty of the sin of pride but he would have had a feeling of deep satisfaction, had he been able to see these examples of your work. You have a rare talent, my boy, greater by far then ever I had. Your skill is something which must be used for God, whether you perform it as priest or layman. Not only should you develop your talent further – if such a thing is possible, so advanced have you become – but you must teach others who will come after you, so that the Gospel of our Lord can be fittingly displayed throughout the whole of the land.'

The bishop had then paused before fulfilling James' wish to a greater extent than he could have dreamed of. Paulinus turned the page towards his servant and pointed to it.

'This, James, this is what I want you to do for our Lord and for me. When we made our journey here five years ago I was able to bring with me only one old gospel text and, it must be admitted, one of only mediocre quality. But it was, nonetheless, a fair copy of the four gospels, as revised by the blessed St Jerome in the fourth century, at the command of His Holiness Pope Damasus. It has with it, although even more roughly prepared than the texts themselves, a series of canon tables devised by Eusebius, Bishop of Caesarea, to allow similar passages in the account of the four evangelists to be identified and compared easily. Despite its modest artistry,' Paulinus admitted, 'it is nonetheless a complete account.

'Listen carefully to me James,' he had then said slowly and insistently as if emphasising the importance of the task he was assigning to the young man. 'I wish you to prepare a worthy edition of these four gospels with their canon tables, decorated and illuminated in the glorious fashion of which you have shown me you are capable. I relieve you at once of your duties here with me. Go to York and see Father Melchior. He will give the gospels into your keeping in accordance with my instructions in a letter you will carry with you. He must send someone else here to help me – not' Paulinus smiled 'to take your place, James, no one could do that, but to provide what assistance I require. Meanwhile you are to move yourself and your materials into the room next to mine. Obtain, by my authority, whatever else you require. Do not be hasty though. This is a noble task I am giving you so plan it carefully and execute it faithfully with all the skill you so clearly possess. And in due time when my work here is done I will come to see your progress.'

And that, James remembered, had been that.

Two years had since gone by. He had spent months planning and experimenting, accepting and discarding ideas, creating designs and choosing colour schemes, until he was satisfied about what had to be done and how. He had worked incessantly, buried in his task, revelling in it day after day. Almost a year had been needed for the Gospel of St Matthew. James had early hit upon the idea of giving the first letter of each new chapter some additional elaboration and this had proved to be a development that pleased him and added further beauty as the gospel pages unfolded. Bishop Paulinus had been specially complementary about it all.

Now a beginning had been made on St Mark's account. The great decorated page and the initial page were complete and would no doubt be carefully examined by the bishop who was returning to York soon. But now the light was beginning to fade and James was surprised to find how late he had been working. No more could be done that evening. He would walk to the refectory by the walled garden where the queen and her attendants often enjoyed a summers evening. Sometimes the ladies were still outdoors even as late as this. Perhaps, James fondly hoped, she would be there.

Edith had been merely one of the attendants to the queen when he had first seen her. He had accompanied the bishop to the queen's quarters when Ethelberga had expressed a wish to learn what progress James was making with his illumination of the gospels. It had been a considerable surprise to her to discover that his artistic abilities were held in such high regard by Paulinus, since she had been no more than politely interested in the little sketches James had done as a boy. Now, here he was with the responsibility of producing a manuscript of such importance. Edwin had seen the Gospel of St Matthew several times and had told her about it in glowing terms. Everything Christian impressed him these days, of course, but perhaps, the queen had thought, she had better see for herself. Paulinus had been commanded to bring James and some of his work to show her.

James chose to take the decorated page and the initial page and the first two chapters which would, he thought, be sufficient for her to see what was being done. He had set them out on a large table which stood beneath the window in the queen's reception chamber. Ethelberga had been surprisingly complementary, he thought, since he knew that his early efforts had not impressed her so much as Aldrith's carved figures had done. But now she was glowing with praise and James became embarrassed and tried to look away to avoid her direct gaze. That was when he caught sight of Edith.

He had not known her name then. Indeed, it had taken him some time to learn it. Like all young men, attracted for the first time by a pretty face, he had not wanted to ask one of the other palace attendants outright for fear of being made fun of, and a good deal of oblique questioning had been necessary before she was identified as Edith.

He had seen her in the company of the queen and her other ladies many times although, of course, he had not spoken to her, nor would he have known what to say had the chance arisen. It was worship from afar for the moment and likely to remain so it seemed to James. Yet he continued to take those routes through the palace and its grounds which seemed most likely to lead to a sight of her.

On that first occasion, whilst Ethelberga, who was a little shortsighted although seldom prepared to admit it, peered closely at his designs, he had stolen glances at the girl, trying not entirely successfully, to be unobtrusive as he did so. She had seemed unaware of his interest and had continued with some task or other along with the other ladies. He had allowed his attention to wander from the queen and her examination of his manuscript and, with a start, he realised that she was addressing him.

'Beautiful, James,' she had said. 'How long have you worked on this so far?'

'Almost a year and a half, Your Majesty.'

'And how long do you think it will be before it is complete?'

James had hesitated and it had been Paulinus who had answered.

'Perhaps three more years, perhaps more, Your Majesty,' he had replied. 'James knows that it is the quality of the finished work that is important not how soon it may be accomplished. He may have as long as he wishes.'

That had been six months ago and James had seen Edith many times since then. She was among the smallest of the queen's ladies. Dainty was the word that always came to his mind. Soft, fair hair, gathered neatly beneath a tiny, lace cap, regular features and a ravishing figure. She must surely have a lovely smile, James thought, but so far he had not been able to catch sight of her laughing. Always she had a composed, rather demure, expression which sent little shivers down his spine in a way that the bold stares of some of the other palace girls did not. What would she be like when (if) he was able to meet her?

He began dreaming away happily, thinking of the many sketches he had made of her since he had seen her first. Perhaps he might include one among one of his designs, carefully hidden away of course so that only careful examination would reveal it. Where might be best?

The horseman had been seen by the lookout when he first breasted the hill to the south. He was travelling slowly and, as he grew near, it was clear that both he and his mount were showing signs of fatigue. The rider was slumped forward in the saddle and the horse was blowing stertorously and weaving from side to side in its exhaustion.

When he reached the gate he had to be helped from the saddle and supported for a moment or he would have fallen. Those who helped him would have laid him down on the ground to recover but he signalled impatiently and gasped hoarsely, 'take me to the King. From Mercia . . . they are coming.'

Edwin was in the Queen's chamber fondly watching his son being bathed. He was gurgling happily, kicking his tiny feet in the water and waving his chubby arms in delight. Ethelberga caught his eye and smiled and squeezed his hand in a spontaneous gesture of affection. Both had been deeply saddened by the deaths of their first born son, Ethelhun, and their daughter, Ethelryd, who had been born a year later, leaving them with only their eldest child Enfleda, born a year after their marriage.

When another pregnancy did not follow immediately Ethelberga had become desperate with anxiety which only the King's tenderness and solicitude had calmed. They had prayed constantly, often side by side, in their private chapel and their faith in God had been rewarded when this beautiful little boy whom they had christened Wuscrae, had been born a year ago. Edwin squeezed his wife's hand in return and put his arm gently round her for a moment. Almighty God had been wonderfully good to them.

A noise outside the door disturbed him and he dragged his eyes away from his son to see what was happening. Lilla, clearly in great agitation, was framed in the doorway waiting to be bidden to enter. Edwin beckoned to his friend and rose to meet him. Lilla spoke softly but urgently, anxious not to disturb the queen who had turned back to her infant.

'Your Majesty, there is grave news. May I beg you to come at once. A messenger has arrived with alarming information.'

Edwin followed his Chancellor, pausing only to say a reassuring word to Ethelberga as he did so. Lilla led him hastily to the audience chamber where the King saw Osfrid, kneeling beside a mud-stained figure who was sunk into a chair, eyes closed as if asleep. The man in the chair opened his eyes, roused himself at the approach of the King and with difficulty rose to his feet. Again he swayed and would have fallen had Osfrid not steadied him.

'This man has ridden all night from the south west, Your Majesty,' reported Lilla. 'What he has to tell is tragic news. Tell His Majesty what you told me,' he commanded.

The man, still unsteady despite Osfrid's help, looked at the King for a moment, as if to bring him into the focus of his glazed eyes, and gasped, 'An army Your Majesty. Soldiers . . . hundreds of them . . . and marching here.' His voice trailed off as fatigue overcame him. It was Osfrid who took up the story.

'Cadwalla, Your Majesty, and Penda must have formed an alliance and raised an army and are marching north and east from Mercia and Gwynda. I got the whole story from this man while you were being summoned. He was returning from visiting his father's home where the old man had died some time ago. Near Leek he saw several horsemen moving slowly and stealthily as if anxious not to be discovered. Knowing the countryside he hid until they had passed him by, and he was about to resume his journey when he realised that they were scouts of a large force which was heavily armed and coming this way. He has some experience of military matters and believes that he saw the standards of Cadwalla of Gwynda on one flank and of Penda, the dog of Mercia on the other. He watched for as long as he dared before he had to make his escape or they would have been upon him. He was able to detour to the south and east to avoid the advance party and then rode here as fast as he could. He was not able to watch them for long but he believes that there might be more than six hundred men in the two armies. He is at the limit of his endurance, Your Majesty; we will learn no more from him for the moment. He is incoherant already.'

Edwin closed his eyes and took a deep breath when Osfrid finished speaking. There was silence whilst each of them digested this alarming information. At last the King spoke, almost in a whisper.

'Penda and Cadwalla. The barbarian and the apostate. What an unholy alliance. However did they come together in this way without us finding out? We are in terrible danger. How far away do you think they might be, my boy?'

'Perhaps as little as four days march, father,' Osfrid replied. 'They must be moving fast to have come so far without being discovered.' And when his father seemed to hesitate he added, 'we must raise what force we can but we are ill-prepared. The garrison here, in York, is less than one hundred men, with seventy more or so at Hatfield. If we scour the countryside we might find another fifty or hundred but they will be ill-equipped and without fire in their bellies. We cannot face Penda and Cadwalla as we are, father. Our only course is to retreat north, get what reinforcements we can on the way and meet them when we are not so heavily outnumbered.' He looked at his father expectantly, waiting for agreement. He did not receive it.

'No.'

Edwin had drawn himself up and was standing almost to attention, looking out over the heads of those assembled in the chamber as though seeing his two arch enemies approaching. He had the look of determination and aggression which he had shown in his warlike days before becoming a Christian.

'No,' he repeated. 'No. We will meet them. Almighty God is on our side and, with His help, what good will their greater numbers be?'

'But father,' Osfrid stammered, 'even Christ's armies have been defeated as you know. Over six hundred against less than a third of that number is madness. We cannot stand and fight. If we retreat now we can avoid a battle for weeks and gather many more men in that time. They, on the other hand, will get no reinforcements and may lose men if we make them follow us further and further north.'

'What Prince Osfrid says is sound advice, Your Majesty,' put in Lilla. 'We know the power of our God but He does not always choose to intervene. How can we know His will? It is surely safer to act as the prince suggests. That way we will get stronger and they perhaps weaker and the battleground, in the end, can be of our choosing. Do you not think, Your Majesty . . .'

But Edwin was no longer listening. He had fallen to his knees and with eyes closed and hands joined, was praying silently, his lips moving as he said the words of the prayer to himself. After a moment the others did the same, Osfrid kneeling last and shaking his head in disbelief.

Some time later Edwin got to his feet and the court followed him. At once he became incisive in his instructions.

'Osfrid, go with Lilla and take a small party from this garrison. Gather what troops you can. Scour the countryside but do it quickly; we must move off south as soon as we have sufficient men together. You have two days and then we must be off. Send scouts out at once. We must know all we can about the enemy – their numbers, how fast they are moving, their arms, their supplies, everything. Have the force at Hatfield alerted and instruct them to prepare what defences they can for that is where we must meet the invaders. The Queen must be prepared to leave at a moment's notice, if Almighty God does not choose to support our cause. I am aware,' he added, turning to Lilla and placing a hand on his friend's shoulder as he said the words, 'that we cannot know His holy will, and that it might not be in His divine plan to grant us victory, but what He has already given to me and my family and to Northumbria must be defended and we must not be of little faith. Were we to retreat north into Bernicia the whole of Deira would be devastated by this army. I cannot leave my people to die in this fashion. We fight and we win or lose.'

'But we must be realistic,' he went on after a pause. 'Her Majesty will have to make her escape if we are defeated. Send Bishop Paulinus to me at once please. He must assemble the few church treasures we have collected for they too must go if we lose the day. They cannot be allowed to fall into the hands of the heathen, Penda, nor, the apostate Cadwalla. Now go quickly, all of you, to your tasks. I will await the bishop.'

As he stopped speaking he waived them all away and sank into the chair which had been vacated by the exhausted messenger. Not for some moments did the King realise that someone was still standing by his elbow. Looking up he saw it was Egfrid.

'May I go too father,' the boy asked. 'To the war I mean. I am twenty years old and strong and,' he added almost defiantly, 'I believe in God as you do.'

The king looked at his son with the same affection he had shown for his baby boy only a short time ago. He rose and placed his arm round the young man's shoulders and drew him to his breast for a moment. Then he stood and looked critically at him.

'We are of the same height, Egfrid,' he said, 'and, if you are perhaps a little too thin for fighting, I am a little too stout. At your age I had fought in several battles and even been wounded . . . here,' he slapped his thigh as he said the word. 'Yes, my son, you may go but I think your friend James may not. God's word must be fittingly written by his artistry. He is to leave with the bishop, for Kent if need be. He will want to be with you, I know, but that cannot be helped. The bishop will tell him – where is he by the way? He should be here for there is much to be done. Go and find him, my boy, and ask him to make haste. But he is not to come here,' he corrected himself. 'Have him come to your mother's quarters. I must go at once and prepare her for what might happen. Find him Egfrid. Find the bishop and send him there.'

James had at least travelled with his friend as the tiny force marched out of York. He had argued his case fluently. Every man able to fight – and permitted to he added bitterly – would have to stay in the field until the end. If the king's forces were overcome by the invading armies someone must bring the news back to York.

So he rode with Egfrid, each aware that this might be the last time they would be together. There was so much to say and yet so little. Their few attempts at conversation had been stilted and unreal and they soon lapsed into silence. They moved closer to each other, knees almost touching as they rode along. Then Hatfield was ahead and immediately everything was activity. Egfrid disappeared into the thick of the preparations and James was left to his own devices to lend a hand where he could.

The reality of their position at Hatfield was alarming. Hasty defences had been constructed on higher ground to the south of the town. Sharpened staves had been hammered into the ground and angled in the direction from which it was expected the attack would come. A few trenches had been dug in front of crude stone walls which, in that region, criss-crossed the face of the hillside. Weapons, such as they were, had been distributed. The regular troops were massed in the centre of the defence line but they numbered, in the end, fewer than two hundred men; a motley group of peasants armed with clubs and wooden staves comprised half as many more; a few had brought rusty spears or old and broken farm implements as their only means of offence. Some had also collected rocks which they had piled into little cairns at their feet. These pathetic irregulars were stretched out towards the flanks of the line but their numbers were pitifully few and none seemed to have much stomach for fighting.

Even Edwin, who had at first been full of determination and encouragement, seemed to lose heart as he surveyed his men and let his eyes come to gaze upon the massed forces taking up their positions with practised skill on the moor ahead of them. Cadwalla, short but thick set and powerful, could be made out, swaggering through his lines with a massive sword and shield. Penda, who was a much taller, blond figure, Edwin could not yet make out and even after a careful search was nowhere to be seen. Even his standard could not be identified and Edwin wondered for a short time if their messenger might have been mistaken about the alliance between the two kings. He even allowed himself a moment of optimism at the notion before remembering that whether Penda was there or not was of little moment. The numbers facing them were formidable whether there was one king or two. Edwin drew his sword, moved across to Osfrid, Egfrid and Lilla to say a few words of encouragement, then pushed through towards the front of his line. He gazed out across the slender strip of moorland separating them from their implacable enemy. Get ready. They were coming!

The full horror of it all was starkly visible to James. He was hidden near the summit of the hill behind two large, grey boulders, which leaned obliquely against each other, giving him shelter from the sight of the enemy but allowing him to see the battlefield clearly through the gap between them.

In the tense moments before the battle he registered the entire scene with his artist's eye. There was a vast expanse of moorland in front and on either side. Even during the desperate waiting for the attack he instinctively recorded the blaze of colours laid out before him like one of his own designs. The foreground was purple with heather of a myriad shades as the wind ruffled its surface. On the lower ground, between the two armies, patches of yellow at first broke up the purple carpet which was then replaced by a border of bright green grassland edging a narrow stream. On the far bank the heather was more broken, and of a violet shade, and was soon obscured by the seemingly infinite number of Cadwalla's soldiers. Against this mass of colour Edwin's forces looked nondescript and bedraggled, whilst the bright colours of many of Cadwalla's officers, and the reflection of their spears, underlined their superiority.

James had no time to notice more. Cadwalla's men were moving forward at a steady insistent walk, line after line pressing inexorably onwards. Crossing the stream they increased their pace and, at a shouted command, each man lowered his spear, thrust it forward in front of him and broke into a run.

Edwin uttered a roar of command to his forces and leapt behind the protective stakes which gave him some shelter against the line of advancing spearmen. Many of his men followed his example and, from their relative protection, they eluded their enemies' early onslaught, and the advancing forces were held. Attackers and defenders were soon locked in a grim struggle during which the the advantage of the higher ground, and the shelter of the line of staves, allowed Edwin's men to inflict many casualties on the van of the enemy troops.

On the right flank however the spearmen had met little resistance. Edwin's peasantry, facing superior numbers and more powerful arms, were savagely mauled and many broke and ran in panic. What little opposition had been put up crumbled rapidly. They were soon overrun and Cadwalla's men began to surge across to turn and fall upon the centre of Edwin's men from their flank.

Even then James had hoped, for a short time, that the assault might be held. Edwin was magnificent, his sword thrusts striking man after man who came at him. James could see Egfrid by the king's side, his back to a rough stone wall, fighting grimly. As James watched one huge ruffian cleared the staves in a single bound to reach Egfrid, only to be impaled on the boy's sword. Seconds later he had kicked the legs from under another and stabbed him deep in the neck with a dagger in his left hand.

It was then that James saw Osfrid, and then that the whole pattern of the battle changed. Osfrid had run to help the peasants on the left who, fighting in more broken country, had put up a measure of resistance and were holding their ground. James heard Osfrid shouting encouragement and saw him force his way forward to take the fight to the enemy. In an instant they seemed to melt away in front of him and, at that same moment, James understood why.

Penda of Mercia, with his own army, *was* there after all. The waves of attackers who had earlier launched themselves against Edwin's men, had been merely a part of the numbers opposing them. No sooner had Osfrid reached the enemy on the flank than they turned aside to right and left and, through the gap they created, poured Penda's troops who, until then, had been lying low behind the trees and bushes on the raised ground James had noticed earlier. Osfrid was directly in their path. He had time only to run one through before ten were upon him crushing him to the ground, hacking and stabbing relentlessly.

James, in his hiding place, from which Edwin had forbidden him to emerge, could only watch impotently. He closed his eyes for a moment to shut out the carnage below and muttered a hasty prayer for Osfrid's soul. When he opened them again he saw that Edwin, disregarding the overwhelming numbers of these new attackers, had swung round to face them. In a frenzy of desperation he struck three or four who set upon him and was about to run another through when, in one horrifying moment, James saw that Cadwalla himself had climbed to the top of the stone wall by which, only a second before, Edwin had been protected, to launch himself at the king and plunge a dagger deep into his back. Edwin pitched forward onto his face with Cadwalla astride him, stabbing again and again. In minutes, it seemed, all resistance was at an end. The pitiful remnants of the Northumbrian army threw down its arms and begged for mercy.

They received none.

The massacre that followed was swift, bloody and complete. No one, so far as James could tell, escaped. Though he should have left long ago he was unable to tear himself away despite the awful horror of the holocaust enacted on the hillside below. The annihalation was systematic. Each quarter of the field was covered by an officer and a group of men. Anyone who might still be alive, and many who were already plainly dead, were hacked to pieces in an orgy of butchery.

How long he watched James could not tell. He was numb with horror and beside himself with grief but he was to witness two more atrocities which would remain in his memory ever afterwards.

At Cadwalla's command one of his soldiers raised a great sword and, with a single blow, severed Edwin's head from his body. The head was impaled upon a lance and waved high in the air, to the accompaniment of ironic cheers and laughter and shaking of fists. Then shouting broke out to the right, where James saw that a skirmish was taking place. A soldier had lifted his sword, as if to strike, when an officer stepped in and threw him roughly to the ground. A figure, who had evidently been lying at the foot of the wall, covered by a pile of dead defenders, was dragged to its feet. Filthy and bleeding though the figure was, James recognised Egfrid and almost revealed his hiding place by starting to his feet and uttering an exclamation.

It took him some moments to appreciate what had happened. A soldier must have found a defender left alive and was about to finish him off when the officer, realising who the youth might be, perhaps from the remnants of the fine garments he was wearing, parried the blow, pulled Egfrid to his feet and dragged him before Cadwalla and Penda.

James was sickened by the sight. Death was bad enough but what might face Egfrid now at the hands of this barbaric pair? His last sight of that field of dishonour was a broken Egfrid, supported by two guards, with Cadwalla gripping him by the hair, forcing back his head, spitting in his face and roaring with laughter. Thrust deep into the ground at Cadwalla's feet was the lance on which was impaled the battered head of Edwin, King of Northumbria. Then James saw why Egfrid's head was being forced back in that manner. He was being made to look upwards at the grisly battle trophy, the head of his father.

James had left the scene soon afterwards, creeping quietly over the hill to where his horse was tethered out of sight. He had walked the animal a long way, afraid that the sound of hooves might be heard by the invaders. But there was no pursuit. The victorious army had quickly become a drunken, ill-disciplined rabble, quarrelling among themselves, certain that the whole of Northumbria lay at their mercy.

It had needed six hours of hard riding to reach York. Many hamlets through which he passed were deserted as if the news of the debacle had already been heard by the women and children and old people who had scattered to whatever protection they could find. York, too, had evidently been alerted to the news and, as James slid to a halt in the palace yard, hasty preparations for departure were obviously being made. A wagon was drawn up by the entrance and was being loaded. Horses were being harnessed and spare ones gathered to be roped to the rear of the wagon at the time of departure.

James found Bishop Paulinus in the chapel where he was collecting a small pile of church treasures. The bishop, seeing that the young man was distraught, took him over to a bench, ordered him to sit down and sat beside him.

'Were any saved, James?'

'My Lord, I wish there had been none,' he replied, 'but I fear that Egfrid fell into the hands of Penda and Cadwalla, and Almighty God alone knows what they might have done with him.'

'Tell me of the king and quickly,' insisted Paulinus, 'for I must give Her Majesty the news without delay.'

James recounted the awful events, watching the bishop turn ashen at his story of the mutilation of Edwin and the torment of Egfrid.

'May God have mercy on them,' Paulinus prayed when the account was over. 'Now we must be away from here within the hour. I will go to the queen. Gather together your manuscript and whatever you were copying but nothing else mind; nothing. I will take the few treasures which you see here; there will be no room for more.'

On the altar nearby James could see a large, gold cross and a gold chalice set with precious stones which they had brought with them from Kent eight years ago. One or two lesser items had been wrapped in cloths and were standing beside them ready to be taken. It was a pitifully small collection but they must travel light and, James remembered, quickly.

'I will bring the gospels, my Lord,' he replied, 'and will await the readiness of Her Majesty and the ladies. How many will be in the party?'

'Only a few can go,' the bishop answered. 'The queen, six of her ladies, Father Melchior and Bassus, the King's Marshall, who, you will remember, was too ill to ride with the army. He will give us some protection. Father Linus had elected to stay and sustain, if he can, the faith of the remaining Christians. But I fear for his life,' Paulinus added, 'for I do not think those barbarians will spare him. May God grant that they spare some.' Paulins paused for a moment and looked at James with concern before speaking again. 'And you, James. Are you recovered enough from your ride to leave so soon? We should not wait. As it is we mean to strike north-east towards the coast aiming for Whitby where, by God's grace, we will find a ship to take us to Kent. To attempt the journey by land would be foolhardy.'

'I am alright, my Lord,' answered James. 'My manuscript can be ready in a moment. I will get what rest I can and be with you when it is time to go.'

In the event more than two hours went by before the queen's party set out. Ethelberga had elected to ride on horseback whilst Enfleda, Wuscrae, their nurses and the other women crowded into the one wagon which was fit to make the journey. All the serviceable transport had been sent with the army, and last minute attempts to repair an ancient cart had failed.

They left in silence, moving at as steady a pace as the horses would allow. They too, with the exception of the queen's palfrey and the horses ridden by the four men, were those which the soldiers had left behind as too old to be useful. Some, Paulinus feared, might never reach Whitby.

Despite the need for haste they were four days on the road. The queen, who had dissolved into torrents of tears at the news of Edwin's death, had rallied in an astonishing fashion. She rode uncomplainingly for hours at a time. When Bassus, who had assumed command of the group, suggested a rest she would often shake her head and continue in so determined a fashion that no one dared complain.

James soon recovered his energy and, having the best horse, took on the role of scout, roaming ahead looking for the easiest road, picking out good places to rest or spend the night, and keeping a sharp eye open for any danger. Several times he went back to look for any sign of pursuit but there was none. The invaders had probably decided that the need for haste had vanished, with the king and one of his sons dead, the other captured and his army annihilated. Which was just as well thought James since their little group was unable to travel fast. The four who were mounted could have made better time but the wagon, laden as it was with the women and children and provisions, could move only slowly and its occupants had a most difficult time huddled in such a crowded conveyance which rocked and creaked alarmingly.

There was one blessed moment for James on their second morning after leaving the palace. He had been far ahead considering the route and thinking that the time had come for him to return again and inform Bassus about a suitable stopping place. He had been unaware of his immediate surroundings in his contemplation of the wonderful countryside stretching far away into the distance. Then someone called to him.

'Master James.'

He was startled out of his meditations and turned in surprise. His surprise was redoubled seconds later.

Edith, mounted on a large ungainly mare, was coming up close behind him. He was taken so much off his guard that, for a moment, he was speechless, staring stupidly at this most unlikely apparition beside him. She was more beautiful than he had ever seen her. The warm sunlight caught her hair which shone and waved in the light breeze. The exertion of riding to catch up with him had brought a healthy glow to her cheeks and her eyes were shining merrily, as though she were revelling in her liberation from the confines of the wagon. James was entranced and allowed the silence to continue for so long that he became flustered and blushed, unable to think of anything to say. It was Edith who spoke again.

'I see I startled you sir,' she said in a low, husky voice which James found instantly enchanting. 'My apologies. I had not thought to alarm you.' She smiled as she said the words and the smile was everything James thought it would be. 'My Lord Bishop would speak with you, Master James, and, since you were so far ahead and no one else was available to bring you the message, and,' she added with a touch of pride in her voice, 'since I was the only one of the queen's ladies who dared mount this beast, he asked me to ride forward to request you to return. There has been a serious development I fear,' she concluded.

James was still staring enraptured, serious development or not, during the delivery of this message, and only when Edith raised her eyebrow in silent enquiry did he answer.

'My apologies, Lady Edith,' he began, 'I will come at once.'

He gathered the reins and swung his horse round in an instant. 'Let us return,' he urged and set off back towards the wagon before realising that Edith's mount could not keep up with him. At once he was all apology again and stopped for her to catch up. For a while they rode on companionably side by side.

'My Lady,' he said after a moment, glancing covertly at her out of the corner of his eye, 'how did you know my name?'

Edith did not answer immediately and was at pains to guide her mount with great care over a patch of rough ground. Then, half turning in the saddle to look at him following a little way behind her, she answered him softly.

'I could say quite easily that my Lord Bishop told me your name, sir, when he sent me after you – as indeed he did. But if I am truthful I must admit that I have known it for a long time – ever since you brought your wonderfully illustrated pages for Her Majesty to see.'

'My pages? Did you see them then,' said James in a puzzled fashion. 'I thought only the queen herself had looked at them. You were engaged in some task over the other side of the room.'

'You forget, sir, that at one point in your visit Her Majesty took you through to her chamber next door to see the curious lines of a tree outside her window, which she thought attractive and wondered if you might include it in one of your designs.'

James did remember. It had been a most graceful tree of arching branches which appealed to him immediately so that it was not entirely to satisfy the queen that he had transposed it into a capital T for one of his later chapter headings. He spurred his horse to ride beside her. She waited until he came abreast before continuing.

'We all crowded round to look. We couldn't resist it.' And after a second she said quietly with genuine admiration, 'They were beautiful; delightful.' She looked at him shyly for a moment and admitted, 'It was then that I enquired your name.'

There seemed to be no suitable reply to this and James sat silently wondering at the seeming impossibility of this splendid girl wanting to know his name. They rode on in silence for a time, Edith's horse too ancient to increase its speed. James continued to ponder and was surprised a second time when she spoke again.

'Master James?'

'My Lady?'

'And how did you know *my* name? Or did you enquire the names of all Her Majesty's ladies?' she asked teasingly.

James chose to be serious despite her lighthearted question.

'No, my Lady,' he said quietly. 'Why would I want to know the names of the others. I asked only about you.'

It was Edith's turn to blush.

Grim news awaited them when they rejoined the party. The bishop drew James aside to explain their predicament.

The Lady Eldrena, who had been Ethelberga's nurse as a child, and who had come with her from Kent to look after the queen's own family, had been ill for hours without telling anyone. Before they had left their overnight camp she had been seized with pain which, at first, had been in the middle of her stomach; she admitted later that she had been sick but had managed to conceal the fact from the others. Knowing how pressed they were for time she had said nothing, even when her pain became worse and moved down towards her right groin. Now she was gravely ill and they could clearly go no further that day. A resting place must be found, and quickly, so that she could be given some relief from the jolting and lurching of the wagon.

'There is a small defile ahead, my Lord,' the young man said hastily, 'I did have it in mind to stop there but then thought that, whilst there was still some daylight, it would be best to push ahead.'

'She is in such great pain, Master James,' Edith said, 'so great that she lies motionless for the slightest movement is agony for her. They tried to give her a little broth but, at once, it all came back and her distress during the retching was pitiful to see. Now she breathes so shallowly that it is barely possible to see any movement of her chest. Her lips are blue and her eyes sunken. Oh, James, I fear she will die. She has the look of a corpse already.'

'I have thought it ever since Bassus and the bishop and I lifted her from the wagon, Edith,' he answered. 'I know little of sickness but her pain was terrible. We should be on our way too, if we are to keep ahead of those barbarians behind us, and save the queen and her children. If they overtake us we are lost but we dare not move with her so ill.'

In his anxiety he took Edith's hand and held it in both his own for comfort. Presently he released it and smiled and, leaning forward, took a lock of her hair, which had fallen over her cheek in her agitation, and gently replaced it.

'We seem to have become Edith and James,' he remarked as he did so. 'That pleases me. May it remain so?'

'Oh, James, of course,' she responded instantly and took his hand and squeezed it affectionately in so natural a manner that they laughed aloud in their new-found companionship.

For a while they sat together without speaking, each happy to be with the other, until James became aware of movement over by the sick woman and saw the bishop cross to her and kneel by her side.

'Edith, he is to adminster extreme unction I fear. Let us join them. We must all be together to pray for her soul.'

A small chest, which contained the church treasures which Paulinus had collected together, had been placed so that the old lady could see it. A linen cloth had been laid upon it with two candles and a vase of holy water. A second linen cloth had been placed gently on the breast of the dying woman. The bishop held the Holy Eucharist between the candles and murmured the opening words of the Viaticum.

Edith, kneeling just ahead and to James' right was huddled down with her head close to the ground and the movement of her shoulders told him that she, like several of the other women, was weeping.

The Kyrie Eleison and Pater Noster followed and James found himself making the responses to the bishop's words.

At dawn Bishop Paulinus said a hasty Requiem Mass and Eldrena was buried.

They made a forlorn little group gathered in a half circle round the portable altar which Paulinus always took with him on his travels. Ethelberga was stony faced throughout the Mass but several of her ladies were openly weeping and others were moist-eyed and barely able to keep themselves under control. Everyone was able to receive Holy Communion since no consecrated hosts had been left at York for fear of desecration by the barbarians.

As the bishop spoke the words of committal, ending with the familiar prayer, '*Requiescat in pace*,' all the women were crying and James found the corners of his eyes pricking and could not prevent one or two tears from rolling down his cheeks. He was almost glad of the activity of replacing the earth over the body, wrapped now in an old linen cloth, on the breast of which the queen had insisted on fastening a tiny, gold crucifix which she had always worn.

At the head of the grave they planted a crude, wooden cross which Father Melchior had made, at the base of which they rested a white stone which James had found and with the point of a dagger written

The Lady Eldrena
A Christian
May God have mercy on her soul.

He had no inclination to attempt its decoration in any way and it lay, wedged against the foot of the cross, perhaps the crudest work he had ever performed.

Bassus and Father Melchior with the help of Edith and one or two of the younger ladies completed the loading. No one had any appetite for food and, by mutual consent, they climbed aboard and set off again to the north-east, hoping to make up some of their lost time.

How important that lost time might have been was soon brought home to them.

They had been on the road some four hours and the sun was high when they saw ahead a hamlet where they hoped that fresh water, and perhaps even a little fresh food, might be obtained. But reaching it they discovered it deserted, or so they thought until James, looking for a place to answer a call of nature, stumbled across an old man lying upon a crude pallet and near to death. James had brought the bishop at once and the man had been overjoyed to see a priest and to be able to receive the last sacrament. Having been well nigh comatose when found by James he revived sufficiently to say a few words after he had been given Extreme Unction.

'Where have they all gone? Why have they left you,' enquired James, wishing instantly that he had not asked the second question; it was all too obvious that the man was unable to go anywhere and would soon be in the next world. It took a moment for him to reply.

'Army coming. Barbarians,' he managed to say. 'All gone . . . coast. Will have sailed by now.'

'Sailed!'

Paulinus, behind James with his back to him, had nonetheless heard the old man's words and realised their import.

'Sailed! If they have made for the coast James, and fled by sea there may be no ship left for us. Perhaps all will be gone. This is serious news indeed. We cannot reach Whitby until tomorrow afternoon at the earliest and that might be too late. The news has travelled far faster than we have I fear. What can we do? We must get Her Majesty away at all costs.'

James digested this alarming information for a moment noting, as he did so, that the old villager had lapsed into unconsciousness again. There was only one course open to them, he realised, and even that may be too late. When he spoke his voice was full of urgency.

'My Lord, there is one thing I can do. I must ride ahead now to Whitby. If there is a craft left I will keep it there in the harbour until you arrive – by force if necessary. The only other possibility would be for you and the queen to ride ahead, perhaps with Bassus or me, but that would leave these ladies stranded and certain victims of Cadwalla and Penda when they reach here. On this horse I can be at Whitby before nightfall and, if there is a ship, rest assured I will detain it until you come.'

Paulinus considered for a moment before giving his consent.

'Very well, James. You are right. You must go alone to find us a vessel if you can. We will follow with all haste. Yes, that is what you must do. Get a few things together at once and be on your way. We will stop a short time and then press on as fast as possible hoping to be with you in good time tomorrow. Go, my boy. God be with you.'

It took only a few minutes for James to fill his water bottle, take a few morsels of food for the journey, throw a cloak across the saddle, and he was off. He had no time to explain his errand to anyone much as he would have hoped to find Edith to tell her why he was leaving so abruptly. But Bishop Paulinus would have to tell them trying, at the same time, not to upset them too much.

James set off at a good pace and the village quickly dropped behind him. He was alone in a deserted countryside with only one thought in his mind – reaching Whitby whilst a ship was still there.

Below him as he gazed down into the little port lay a deserted harbour. James could see no sign of a ship, either tied up by the harbour wall or anchored in the bay. He was too late. Too late! It was all he could think about. The queen, Bishop Paulinus and the whole party were marooned with Penda and Cadwalla pursuing relentlessly and, he had little doubt, laying waste to the countryside and slaughtering God's children as they advanced.

He must go down, he decided. Perhaps, just perhaps, there was a craft of some sort still remaining. He turned his horse and made his way carefully down the steep path which led to the town and the harbour beyond it.

He saw and heard no one – and, as it turned out, no one saw or heard him. He had traversed the length of the main harbour and was about to retrace his steps in utter dejection when he heard a sound and stopped dead. A fat man, red-faced and swarthy was staggering under the weight of a table, from a door in a line of cottages beyond the harbour.

One glance at the scene was enough for James to take in what was happening. Avarice might just have saved the day. This fellow – the last in Whitby James had no doubt – had stayed behind to steal what he could of his neighbours belongings, abandoned in their flight.

James shrank back to study the position for a moment. This man, to all appearances at least was a thief, and a ruffian too. He would not be likely to let James stand in the way of his escape with those rifled goods and certainly would not willingly offload them to make room for the queen's party. James looked like having to use force after all; but . . . but he would be obliged to give the man one chance to agree first. Better be ready for tricks though he decided. This was a slippery customer by the look of things. He must hurry, too, since there wasn't much light left. James adjusted the knife in his belt and moved out into the open.

The effect of his appearance would have been comical had the affair not been so serious. The man stopped dead in his tracks, gasping under the weight of a table. His mouth opened and closed but no sound emerged. His wife, who had been looking at him when James appeared on the scene, was obviously puzzled by her husband's reaction, then, following the direction of his gaze, she turned slowly and stared silently at the intruder. The man stirred himself, lowered his burden to the ground and quickly became a crawling, obsequious beggar.

'Beg your pardon, sir,' he whined. 'Just loading our few, poor possessions, sir, before leaving. Not much more to bring out, my Lord,' James had been promoted it seemed 'but all we have you see, all we have. Poor folk we be, poor folk.' He almost licked James boots with his unctious fawning before beginning again. 'Can we direct you anywhere, my Lord? All gone here, I'm afraid. I'd move on, sir, if I was you. We're just off to catch this tide if we can. Just get this aboard. Catch the tide.'

James stood for a monent, surveying the pair before he spoke.

'I'm afraid you will miss this tide, my friend, and likely tomorrow morning's too; very much afraid but there it is. What is your name and your good wife's,' James asked, giving the bedraggled specimen a gentle smile.

The response he received was more brusque than before and the man looked shifty and no longer compliant.

'Miss it. What d'yer mean, miss it. Why should we miss it? We're going if you're not. Come on Meg, help me with this last table,' and turning away from James he shook his wife furiously and pointed to the table in front of him.

'I wouldn't bother with that, Meg, if I were you,' James replied in a quiet but determined tone, although his stomach felt hollow at the thought of violence about which he knew next to nothing. Neither of them must suspect that, however, and the more fierce he could look the better. 'You, sir,' he continued, 'should know that Her Majesty, Queen Ethelberga of Northumbria, wants your boat to help her to escape her enemies.'

There was no immediate reply to this as husband and wife looked at each other as though thunderstruck. Then Meg, recovering first croaked, 'What's he mean Jeb?'

'I mean,' retorted James, in the most authoritative voice he could muster, 'that Her Majesty, with her ladies-in-waiting and Bishop Paulinus are but a short distance behind me, fleeing from invaders – as I am sure you are,' he added. 'And she must be transported to Kent and your's is the only boat left so it will have to be your's. So,' he ended still keeping the gaping pair in his direct gaze, 'may I ask you politely to unload this stuff so that she and her party can be your passengers. You may fear no loss. She will pay you well for the hire of the boat and for your services.'

'Pay, will she,' was Jeb's first response, followed by, 'Queen of Northumbria, you say? Where is she then? Go and get 'er and we'll see how much she can pay.' Jeb was at his most mendacious whilst saying the words until he suddenly remembered what else James had said.

'Kent? What d'yer mean Kent? This leaky thing will never make Kent. Won't try. Not with me aboard I can tell you.'

'There is no other craft that I can see. Produce another instead if you can and we will go in that. Kent it must be and in this by the look of things. So start unloading. I'll give you a hand.' And with that James turned and strode towards the vessel.

'Leave it,' roared Jeb, and launched himself at the young man with a sudden leap. James was nearly taken off his guard and probably would have been had it not been for Jeb's hoarse cry.

Reacting instinctively James lowered his head and butted the advancing Jeb in the stomach forcing him backwards onto the ground his arms flailing wildly. In a few seconds breathing space the young man drew his dagger and, falling on Jeb's held it quivering before his throat.

It would have been difficult to know who was the more frightened, but James had the upper hand now and wasn't going to lose it. He rose steadily to his feet never taking his eyes off his attacker.

'Turn over face down,' he ordered. 'Now you, Meg, get something to tie his hands and feet – and you . . .' to Jeb, 'don't make one false move or it may by your last.' James was sure that that was the thing to say but doubted if he could ever bring himself to do it. Please God let Jeb not resist.

Resistance seemed beyond Jeb as he lay prone on the ground before the young man who was trying to look as threatening as possible even though Jeb, face to the ground, could see nothing. Meg's return with thongs to tie him was a welcome relief.

Tying her husband hand and foot was evidently an activity Meg indulged in with relish. The knots were pulled so tight that James had to order her to loosen them a little for fear the man would not be able to steer next day. With some reluctance she did so and then, lumbered to her feet, and glowered angrily at her prostrate husband.

'I've been wanting to do something like that for years,' she chortled, beaming happily. 'He led me a dance, he did. Well not this time; not this time,' and turning to James she added, reassuringly, 'take no notice of what he says about the boat, sir. She doesn't look much but she's seaworthy and she'll get us there. She'll get us there, don't fret.'

The next morning it was she who volunteered to go to the cliff top to keep watch for the queen's party whilst James, not wishing to waste any time, unloaded from the boat everything but food – quite a lot of which he found stowed away. Unloaded, the shortcomings of the barque were all too obvious. She was a fishing boat which had seen service over many years, throughout which James doubted if she had ever been cleaned on even a single occasion. Scales of fish, caught long ago, were engrained in the planking. Dirty water sloshed mournfully from side to side as she rode the gentle swell of the harbour. Bailing, James considered, looked like being a continual task. The one feature which gave him any encouragement was a flimsy hut-like construction near the stern, giving some protection to the steersmen and allowing, James hoped, two or three women to get some shelter from the elements.

One thing was plain however. The whole of the queen's party, plus Jeb and Meg, could not be accommodated on board. James ran over their numbers in his mind. It couldn't be done he thought. Nine certainly, perhaps ten might just squeeze aboard. Three left – who? Himself for one of course. Jeb had to go since no one else could manage the vessel and his wife couldn't be left behind. The other women could not be left behind either which left Paulinus, Bassus and Melchior. The bishop had to accompany the party, that was clear; Bassus too since there was no telling what tricks Jeb might get up to unless someone watched his every move. Melchior and James left behind; that would have to be it. Pray God the others would get aboard.

It was a vain hope, James saw at once, when he realised that room had to be found for extra provisions they would need for the journey, and the few church treasures they were carrying. Space had to be left for bailing too if they were not to sink. The distress of the group had been instantly apparent when they saw the vessel and some, James was sure, were reluctant to go aboard despite the frightening alternative of being left behind.

It seemed an insoluble problem and James, tired of wrestling with it in his mind, had seated himself on a bollard on the jetty, exhausted by his fight with Jeb, his exertions in unloading the boat and a night virtually without sleep. He had closed his eyes and was dozing a little when he heard the bishop address him and felt a hand upon his shoulder.

'James, I must speak with you for a moment.'

'Of course, my Lord,' he hurriedly replied, 'forgive me. I dozed off when I ought to have been . . .' and his voice tailed off as he realised that Paulinus was not alone. Standing a few paces behind him was Edith who smiled and nodded her head to him as if in encouragement.

'This lady would speak with you, James,' said the bishop, 'and you will, I trust, feel able to agree to the suggestion she is going to make.'

James did not know what to say and looked from one to the other in some surprise. It was Edith who broke the silence.

'Master James,' she began, perhaps feeling some formality was called for in the bishop's presence, 'the Lord Bishop has told me that you and Father Melchior are not to accompany the rest in this . . .' she hesitated, glancing at the boat, evidently wondering how to refer to it '. . . this craft. Indeed, could not accompany us as I can see. But even so,' she continued in a more determined fashion, 'the remainder cannot all be taken or all will sink. I too wish to stay behind. You will not know this but my home is not far from here, near a village called Catterick, in fact, and I cannot flee to Kent without knowing if my family are safe or if they have fled their homes too; if they are alive or . . . ' she hesitated '. . . dead. So if you will have me stay with you and of course,' as an afterthought, 'Father Melchior, with your help I might reach my family before the barbarians do and perhaps see them again before . . .' she hesitated again and showed the first sign of real distress '. . . perhaps we all die.' Her last words were so softly spoken that James could scarcely hear them.

'Before you answer James,' put in the bishop, 'let me assure you that if Mistress Edith were to come with you, we could just manage to take the rest aboard. Aldeth has slung a hammock for the infant across the shelter in the stern so that three can lie beneath it and he will occupy no space needed for anyone else. We can just manage it, I'm sure of it. Cramped and uncomfortable though it will surely be.' Then drawing James aside for a moment the bishop continued in a low voice, 'There is, of course, another reason too. You have some regard for this lady, I can plainly see, and, unless I am very much mistaken, she for you. Oh yes, James, that surprises you I see,' noting the astonished expression on the young man's face, 'but I would wager on it – were bishops betting men of course,' he added with a grin. 'I know she wishes to do it James. Can you say yes?'

'But the danger, my Lord. The country will be ravaged by those savages. How can I protect her?'

'By God's help, should He so wish,' replied the bishop 'and what is the alternative? We are taking a risk as it is with such a small craft. It is for the best, I do assure you. Father Melchior has already agreed and we hope you will too.'

James hesitated only a second longer and when he turned to look at Edith he knew that he could not leave her behind. It was all he could do to restrain himself from taking her in his arms there and then. He caught Paulinus' eye and laughed and saw Edith laughing too. Well, he thought, if she wants formality, formality it shall be.

'My Lady Edith,' he said with a little bow, 'it will be my pleasure and I'm sure Father Melchior's to escort you;' and unable to maintain the formal tone any longer added, 'oh, my pleasure it will certainly be.'

Bishop Paulinus, feeling that enough had been said on that matter for the present spoke again.

'I must say one thing more that may be painful for you. Your manuscript – your wonderful manuscript – should come with us. It is the word of God in all its beauty and cannot fall into heathen hands. When you will see it again I do not know – maybe never if that is Almighty God's plan. Pray to him that I may return with it myself so that one day you can finish it. And now,' he added, in a more businesslike tone, 'it is time to go. All are aboard, I see, and it remains only for us to say our farewells. We have so much to thank you for. Without this vessel, crude though it is, we were doomed. Come, say goodbye to the queen and I will give you my blessing.'

So all three knelt to Queen Ethelberga who, distraught and frightened though they knew she must be, was gracious and full of thanks to them for their faithful service to her and to her children. Then they knelt to Bishop Paulinus who pronounced his blessing, clasped James to his chest choking back the tears and they were gone.

The forlorn trio stood watching from the shore for a long time and, when the boat was all but out of sight, they ran up to the top of the cliff to keep them in view just a little longer.

Then they were alone in a deserted country at the mercy of barbarians.

Chapter 4

It had taken them longer than expected to reach Catterick. They set off westward out of Whitby but somehow drifted off their route and travelled for more than two days before Edith was able to get her bearings and to realise that they were to the north and west of their destination. It was a mistake that probably saved their lives.

Father Melchior was a poor horseman and with his slowness and their roundabout route it was noon on the third day before Edith was able to tell them that they were close to her home. They had entered a thickly wooded area some hours earlier and, as they emerged into more open country, she reined in her horse and pointed ahead.

'Look. Do you see that small copse on the high ground ahead? When we reach there we will be able to see Catterick which is only a short distance further on. We should catch sight of it when we breast that hill. Hurry please Father. I must know if they are safe.'

'I will not slow you down any more,' replied the priest. 'I can never keep up with you but, now that I can see where we are going, I will follow at my own speed. Go along with James. I won't get lost.'

Taking him at his word they rode on towards Catterick, Edith racing ahead in her eagerness to find her family. It was all James could do to catch up with her and steady her pace with a hand on her bridle.

'Edith, wait. We must be careful. We don't know what we are going to find when we get there. If the invaders are in the town we must be sure they don't catch sight of us. We might be able to escape by running for it but Father Melchior never would. I hear no noise but we must take no chances nevertheless. We'll ride on to your copse, up there on the right, leave our horses and move forward on foot to find out what is happening. If all is quiet it will take only a short time to go back for the horses and ride down into the town.'

Edith realised the sense in what he said and reluctantly agreed. They tethered their mounts under the trees and moved forwards quietly, covering the last part, as they approached the brow of the hill, crouched low to the ground to be sure to keep out of sight. James had to restrain Edith again and spoke to her quietly but urgently.

'Stay here and keep down whatever you do. I will creep up to the edge and, if it is safe, signal you to come. Please! It is important. There may be soldiers there,' and giving her no chance to argue he pushed her down to the ground and crept ahead on all fours.

Edith watched impatiently, ready for his signal. She saw him stop short of the summit and raise his head slowly. Then he rose on one knee and stood up and turned to look at her with alarm written all over his face.

'What is it?', she cried out, but now seemed rooted to the spot, afraid to go forward to see whatever it was that had so appalled him. James looked back again at the sight over the hill and then back to Edith and, as she started to move towards him, bracing herself for whatever might be there, he ran back to meet her. She tried to push past but he pinioned her arms and held her firmly.

'Not yet, Edith,' he urged, pulling her down with him onto one knee. 'Wait just a moment before you look. My dear, I'm so sorry.'

'James, tell me quickly. What has happened?'

'All burned. The whole town I think. There isn't a building standing, nothing but charred remains. The entire place is razed to the ground.'

Edith looked incredulous for a moment and then her face puckered and she burst into floods of tears. James held her close, making soothing noises and stroking her hair. Presently she became calmer.

'Did you see any people?' she asked. 'Is anyone alive?'

'I saw no one but I looked for only a moment. Still,' he continued, 'I don't see how there could be, not in the town although some may have escaped.'

He released Edith gently while she dried her tears. In a moment he asked softly, 'Would you like to wait here for Father Melchior while I go down to see how bad it is? Would that not be best?'

But she would not agree and together they rode slowly down into the charred remains of the town of Catterick. As they approached it they passed the blackened remains of the chapel where – so long ago it seemed – Bishop Paulinus had asked James to illuminate the gospels and sent him off to York to begin his task.

A little further on, in the town itself, they found the first bodies, some scarcely recognisable as human remains, so fierce had the holocaust been. There were a great number of corpses, many of them children. The stench of burned flesh was nauseating, and the mutilated bodies, severed limbs and hacked torsos were gruesome and repellent. Mercifully, for Edith, none was recognisable. After a short time they could bear it no longer and, by mutual consent, they turned their horses back up the hill to await the priest.

It was only later, when they had recovered from the first shock, that James realised their good fortune. He had been silent for some time, sunk in his own thoughts. Father Melchior, who had insisted on going into the town to pray for the dead, had returned exhausted and was sleeping. Edith was crouched alone, stunned by the events, unable to comprehend what was happening. James came over to her, knelt by her side and took her hand.

'My dear,' he began, 'I grieve for you more than I can say and I know it will be a long time before you get over the horror of this day. But now we must decide what to do. Are you able to discuss it? It won't help if we fail to protect ourselves. Edith, look at me; can you talk?' and she met his eye, forced a little smile, nodded her head and said at once, 'Yes. I will be alright. Let us talk.'

James wakened Father Melchior, and, huddled in a tight group beside their horses, as if for mutual comfort, they made what plans they could. James gave them his assessment of the position which he had been considering for some time.

'The town was burned only recently,' he explained. 'Some of the embers were warm and a little smoke was rising so it may have been only yesterday that the atrocity occurred. That means they cannot be far away and it also means that we have been very lucky not to run into them already. We have been to the north and east of here for the last two days and seen nothing, which probably indicates that they have gone west or east although they may have gone north after we passed by. My guess is that, sooner or later, in their search for the queen, they will go east, aiming for the coast, thinking that she will try to get away by sea. I think our safest plan is to continue north-west, to try to get as far from here as we can and hope to find safety with the southern Picts, who are Christian I understand, although converted by the Celtic Church. Still, we are all of one faith and if we are fortunate, and Almighty God wills it, we may find shelter with them.'

He paused for a moment to give either of his companions a chance to speak but both remained silent.

'I remember from the journeys I made with Bishop Paulinus, that he told me of several monasteries and priories in these northern regions which we might try to find. One, I think, was at a place called Melrose but I cannot recall how far away it might be nor in which direction. Then there is another called Whithorn or Whitehouse – 'Candida Casa' he used to call it – which had been founded long ago by the great St Ninian. I think it was to the north-west of here on the coast, in a region known as Galloway, but if it is three days journey or twenty-three I don't know.' Then, smiling gently at his two companions, he added, 'Unless either of you has a better plan I suggest we aim for Whithorn.'

Gradually the mood of black depression, which had marked their retreat from Catterick, had lightened. Edith and James often found themselves together ahead of Father Melchior, who plodded on steadily behind them. At first they had tried to stay with him but this seemed to make their progress funereal and they had evolved a system of riding ahead, keeping him just in sight, and having everything ready at their stopping places and overnight camps when he finally caught up with them. They passed through several villages where they replenished their supplies and got fresh water. There was little news of the enemy but no one knew where they might be and James was unwilling to relax their precautions for a moment.

Not until they had travelled for a week after leaving Catterick did they feel they had put any risk of pursuit behind them. At first the weather had been kind, then rain for two days had slowed their progress and had been followed by a keen north-west wind, blowing straight into their faces and making them huddle inside their cloaks for warmth and ride in silence, since only a shouted remark could be heard above the wind.

That night they had been fortunate. Instead of having to sleep in the open, under whatever protection they could find or fabricate from trees and bracken, they found an empty shepherd's hut, crude and dirty but weatherproof and dry within.

The priest had eaten hardly anything and had maintained his silence during the meal, finally withdrawing a little distance away and kneeling down to pray. It was a long time before he returned to the silent pair who had not wished to disturb him by talking. He stood beside them for a time smiling benignly, in strange contrast to his sombre mood of a short time earlier.

'My friends,' he addressed them, holding both his hands out towards them, 'my good friends; I have something to say which I would like you to listen to carefully and, if you please, don't interrupt.' He smiled as he said the words since James seemed about to speak. 'Hear me out. It has taken me a long time to decide what to do – almost the whole of the time since we left Catterick – perhaps even since we left Whitby. Now I know where my duty lies.'

'But Father,' began James, before Father Melchior's hand restrained him. 'Sorry,' he muttered and lapsed into silence awaiting the priest's words.

'Both of you are right to seek the Christians of the north, just as I am wrong to do so. In my mind I suppose I always knew I must be wrong to accompany you, but it has taken until now for me to see it clearly and to know that I can come with you no further. I do not know how many Christians are still alive in Northumbria but, if there is only one, how will it help him if the only priest alive runs away? I will go back tomorrow and give what help I can to any of the Christian faith I might find. If they are to die they may at least have a priest with them. If I am to die what does that matter so long as I have not abandoned the faithful.

'There is another reason why I must return,' he continued, speaking with a confidence they had never seen in him before. 'There are some who may try to save themselves from the barbarians by lapsing into idolatry, hoping that their lives will be spared. I have seen some evidence of this already in one or two places we passed through. That I must prevent, or hellfire stares them in the face for denying the God they once accepted. I am not a brave man,' he admitted, 'and that is perhaps why it has taken me so long to realise my error in trying to flee this country with you. But I know what I must do now, and tomorrow, when you continue on your journey northwest, I will return the way we have come. I pray to Almighty God that you will find the Christian community you are looking for to keep your own faith strong in the face of all temptation. You will find,' he smiled, 'that the Celtic Church calculates the date of Easter differently – incorrectly too I fear – and their monks wear a strange tonsure unlike our own, but – ' and an impish grin passed over his face 'I do not think our Blessed Lord will hold it against you if you celebrate His glorious resurrection a week too early. That you celebrate this greatest of Christian feasts at all is the important thing.'

After that they had made no attempt to dissuade him from his resolve and they had spent their happiest time since the queen and her party left them. He had spoken with delight about James' texts which he had seen grow from their first words until they had to be abandoned when they made their escape.

It was while he was praising what he called James' 'incomparable artistry' that he returned to the idea of aiming for the 'Candida Casa' of St Ninian.

'A holy establishment like that is dependant on the abbot,' he said, 'and may, from time to time, fall short of the holy observances which St Ninian decreed. If you find what you seek there, well and good. You may resume your work as a scribe and they will be lucky, indeed, to have you. But, if you do not find that all is well, remember that further afield – almost on the edge of the world, so I have been informed – is the holy Celtic community called Iona or Hii, in their language. I have heard that they have a great tradition of embellishing sacred texts which began in Ireland and came to that far away place with the Abbot Columba, of whom Bishop Paulinus used to speak with reverence. So,' he ended rising to his feet, 'if you cannot find what you are looking for in one place perhaps, with God's grace, you will find it in another. And now goodnight. Tomorrow we go our separate ways. Sleep well. I will pray a while longer. Pray for me and I will pray for you.'

The time following Father Melchior's departure was an idyllic one for Edith and James. The weather immediately improved and the cold wind they had had to endure for the previous few days was replaced by a perfect spell of warm, autumn sunshine. They travelled steadily north-west, riding contentedly side by side. Their anxieties over any possible pursuit were behind them and they chatted easily together, getting to know each other, learning about their lives before they had met, totally absorbed in each other's company.

Edith was eager to learn about all the drawings James had made as a young man. She listened with rapt attention to his description of the gospel book Father Birinus had brought from Gaul, and how the old priest had trained James in this form of illumination. He mentioned his plans to use her picture in some hidden place in his work. At first she pretended to be alarmed by the notion but, when James teased her about it, she seemed secretly pleased and even joked with him about that part of the gospel in which she would most like to be.

On the third day they reached a river running south-west and they realised that they would have to turn north-east for a time to find a crossing place. James had learned, from questions he had asked of villagers on their route, that Whithorn was to the north and west of this firth, as they described the river, perhaps four or five more days journey.

They were both delighted by the many birds they saw as they followed the river bank and James described the different characteristics which needed to be brought out in any drawing of them, and outlined some of these by little sketches which he made with a pointed stick in the mud of the river bank. They spent two long afternoons in leisurely dalliance without any thought of completing their journey, idling through the peaceful autumn days without a thought in the world for anyone else.

So absorbed were they in each other that one evening, when something recalled the memory of Catterick to Edith's mind, she became conscience-stricken and troubled that she had not thought about the possible fate of her family for several days. It was then when she became upset, and wept a little at the memory of Catterick, that James sought to calm her by taking her in his arms, and before either of them realised what was happening, he was kissing away her tears and holding her tightly to him. In a second she raised her face to his and kissed him gently on the lips, burying her head in his chest afterwards and clutching him as if her life depended on it.

James turned her face up to his and began to kiss her again, this time more passionately. She responded, readily at first, then seemed to get upset and moved her head away but did not free herself from his arms. He sensed her uncertainity and did not press her for a moment, cradling her head gently. Then she looked up at him once more and said softly. 'I love you,' and, as he bent his head to kiss her again, she placed a finger on his lips to restrain him saying, 'Wait just a moment, darling, I have something to tell you.'

He smiled and nodded, happy to indulge her in any way she wished. In a few moments she drew him over to a fallen tree trunk, motioned him to sit down and then, crouching at his feet, rested her chin upon his knees. He stroked her hair gently waiting for her to compose herself.

'My darling one,' she began, speaking hesitantly at first, 'I love you more than I can say – I have loved you I suppose since the first time I saw you. I wanted to be with you every minute of the day if I could and, when you had gone to Whitby to find a boat, and I could not be with you, I was so miserable. It was then that I knew that I could not go to Kent and risk never seeing you again. I knew that I must somehow find a way to stay with you. It was a godsend that the tiny boat could not take us all and I was determined to make the bishop allow me to stay.

Edith released him, laughing and crying at the same time. She seized his hand and held it to her cheek and began kissing it repeatedly. Then, unable to resist, she wound her arms around him once more and snuggled up close, reluctant to let go for a second.

In a little while her excitement calmed and she lay contentedly in his arms, her breathing and his the only movements. James, with great tenderness, kissed her hair and said softly, 'Edith, I love you and no one but you and always will. From now on we live our lives together, that is all I want. When we find a priest – please God may it be soon – we will be married. I want you so much, my darling. You are the only thing I can think about. Don't say anything,' as she moved as if to speak, 'just let me go on talking for a moment. I can't believe this is happening to us,' giving her an extra hug and receiving one in return. 'Why would someone like you love me? That's what I can't understand and I'm not going to try. It's enough for me that you do.'

And then he began telling her about his feelings the first time he saw her in the queen's audience chamber, and how he used to plan his routes through the palace in the hope of catching sight of her, and the problems he had trying to find out her name without anyone knowing. She was so still he thought she might be asleep and stopped speaking.

'Go on I love it.'

'Edith, you hussey,' he laughed, but went on all the same, telling her of the many drawings he had made of her – so many that he feared he might fall behind in his work, and had to ration the number he drew each day. 'I had to make sure,' he said, 'that I left one to do just before dusk. The only thing I was sorry about was that I had no picture of you smiling. Whenever I saw you with the other ladies you were so solemn,' a little squirm of delight and a hug from her at the idea, 'that I thought you must be a very serious little mouse. Do you know, I had to wait until you came up to me on that old horse, on our journey to Whitby, before I saw you smile. But,' he added, 'it was worth waiting for.'

She had lain happily in his arms for a long time afterwards until it was quite dark, their bodies close, kissing softly and longingly and passionately and, once, so abandondly that Edith became quite embarrassed and turned her face into his chest to hide her blushes. It was she, nonetheless, who broke the silence.

'Jamie,' she said, haltingly at first, 'I know nothing about . . .' and she paused briefly before saying the words '. . . physical love. A woman isn't supposed to, I accept, although I realised from others around the palace that many did. Perhaps I shut it out of my mind deliberately because, you see . . .' and again there was hesitation '. . . I think I was afraid of what it,' and she repeated 'it' with emphasis, 'it would be like. I couldn't imagine it at all until I met . . . until I began to love . . . you . . . and want you.' Her last words were almost inaudible but after a moment she continued with more certainty.

'Don't laugh at me Jamie when I say this. I know, just from loving you before I had touched you, and now from the feeling of having you in my arms with our bodies close together, that I want to be yours – physically yours – in a way that I hadn't thought possible until now. I had never imagined that I could talk about it like this – you don't think I'm abandoned, do you,' she put in quickly, looking up into his eyes for reassurance. He did not answer but shook his head several times and presently she began to speak again.

'What I am trying to say, dearest Jamie, is that, although I *have* had a fear of physical love, I have none with you. I want the time to come quickly when we can be together. May we find a priest soon – very soon. I hope I do not have to wait, longing for you as I do,' and she shook her head and frowned before rushing on again. 'Dear one, I'm not saying this properly and I haven't yet told you what I really want to say. What I mean is this. I can wait for a priest if it is not too long, but things are different for men and if you cannot wait,' and she lowered her eyes as she finished, 'I will be yours now, if that is what you want.'

She stayed with downcast eyes for some time after she had stopped speaking. Then she felt James' hand beneath her chin and he raised her face up to his but still did not immediately reply. Instead he shook his head as before and smiled so broadly that she too relaxed her expression and began smiling also.

'Thank you, my little mouse,' he said at length. 'I can wait – a little while at least – until we are man and wife. I would love to do this,' and he gently stroked her breast as he spoke, and Edith closed her eyes again and gave a little cry of pleasure, 'and more,' he added, his fingers sliding over the neck of her gown between her breasts for a moment before he withdrew them. Hugging her to him as he did so he felt the shiver of excitement that passed through her body. 'But I can resist, I hope,' he went on and laughed at her and she at him now that the delicate moment in their relationship had passed.

For a few seconds they looked silently into each others eyes and at the very same moment said,

'I love you,' which sent them both into peals of laughter. Edith was the one to speak first.

'Oh, Jamie, I love you so. You are an adorable man and I don't know what I have done to deserve you. I know our love will be wonderful when it happens. Oh please let there be a priest at Whithorn.'

At Whithorn there was no priest, only a monk, *not* in holy orders.

Edith and James had encountered problems on the last stage of their journey. A deep inlet from the sea, to the east of the peninsula where Whithorn lay, forced them to detour northwards for a considerable distance around this long stretch of water, and to return due south to the tip of the promontory before reaching the Candida Casa. Their hopes of finding a refuge with a thriving Christian community were immediately dashed. For a while they found no one, and were wandering disconsolately in the gathering dusk, when two men came towards them from the cliffs to the south, where they had evidently been on the beach.

Edith saw them first and waved. The two men stopped, as if wary of strangers, and then began moving forward again very slowly and cautiously. They visibly relaxed when they saw that one of the newcomers was a woman, and the smaller of the two, a bent, gnarled, aged figure, greeted them pleasantly.

'Mistress, sir,' he addressed them, 'are you alone?' peering anxiously behind them trying to pick out anyone else who might be there.

James realised his concern and answered reassuringly.

'Yes, quite alone. Have no fear. I'm sorry we startled you. My companion is the Lady Edith and my name is James. We . . .' He stopped as he glanced at Edith, who was shivering and trying to find shelter behind her horse from the rain and wind blowing stiffly off the sea. 'We have a lot to tell you, sirs, and will gladly do so but my . . . this lady is chilled to the marrow. May we beg the hospitality of a shelter where we can come in out of this wind and recover from our long journey?'

The little man answered at once.

'Aye, that ye can. Come along, missy and sir, this way,' and he set off at a surprising pace, Edith and James following, leading their horses, with the second man bringing up the rear. They were led past a white stone church, clearly the Candida Casa, to a collection of buildings behind it, which James saw at once must be – or have been – a priory.

They were taken through a low door, along a dark passage, into a large room containing several long, crude tables with benches beside them. Some were in a poor state of repair and one or two had legs missing which seemed to have been broken up for firewood. Most, however, were intact, and at the end of one were some dishes and the remnants of food, where, it seemed, the two men had earlier enjoyed a meal.

The little man marched past this last table to a large hearth where a fire was dimly glowing, and began to rake it into life and put on more wood, the leg of one of the tables being clearly evident among the pieces he used.

'Let the missy have that stool beside the fire,' he began. 'She can warm herself and talk to Fursa here, if she can,' and he gave a high pitched cackle of enormous amusement before speaking to James again.

'Come with me. I'll show you where you can stable your horses and unload them and feed and water them. You're welcome. Welcome.' And he set off again at a half run the way they had come in with James following, after getting a reassuring nod from Edith.

She moved closer to the fire and warmed her hands. After a moment or two she took off her cloak and spread it before the fire to dry. In a while she breathed a sigh of contentment and turned towards her companion.

He was taller than his friend and very fat. He wore a dark brown monk's habit which was voluminous, with a girdle, which had once been white, but was now a nondescript grey colour, stretched across the vast expanse of his stomach. His tonsure was quite unlike any she had seen before, the hair having been shaved from the front of his head but that at the back left long, covering his neck and overlapping his cowl. He had still not spoken since they first met, and Edith was beginning to wonder if he was dumb, which might explain the little man's strange remark about talking to him 'if she can.'

'It is very kind of you, Father,' she began, watching his face closely to see if her words evoked any response, 'to take us in like this. Thank you,' giving him a beaming smile to express her gratitude.

Its effect upon him was electric. He grinned from ear to ear and burst out laughing, advanced towards her, patted her hand – which Edith, just a little alarmed, had to try not to snatch away – and said, in a deep booming voice,

'?????'

Whatever he said was incomprehensible to Edith who looked blank in amazement at being addressed in a totally foreign language. He repeated whatever he had said, or so it seemed, leaving her as baffled as ever. Then, after an interval, when Edith was beginning to think this linguistic deadlock might never be resolved he said,

'Fursa,' and pounded himself on the chest, clearly indicating his name. He repeated it, 'Fursa,' and pointing to her, and raising his eyebrows in interrogation, said his first intelligible words so far.

'You, who?'

Edith, now laughing with relief that something had been said that she could understand, replied, 'Edith,' and for good measure, pointing towards the way James had gone, said, 'James.'

'Edith,' pointing to her, Fursa rumbled, and went on as if trying to imprint the names on his memory, 'Edith, James, Edith, James,' ending with a smile of satisfaction, 'James,' pointing to the door, 'Edith,' pointing to her.

There was silence for a while after that which Edith was wondering how to break when Fursa did so.

'Not Father,' he said, clutching his habit and holding it out towards her, 'Brother – lay brother.' Then getting into his stride, as if he had not spoken this language for a long time, he proceeded. 'Brother from Hii,' pointing several times at what was clearly intended to be a long way off. 'Sailed here. Find if anyone left. Only Calen.' And seeing Edith frown he gave a lifelike imitation of the little old man going about at his half running pace.

'Calen,' replied Edith. 'Yes, Calen. I understand.'
'All other gone,' continued Fursa. 'Picts drive away. All gone.'
  Edith digested this disconcerting news while Fursa got up to replenish the fire. No one here but Calen! So there was little chance of staying here. She began to get very disheartened and must have looked glum for Fursa came across to her, patted her sharply on the shoulder and said, 'Laugh, not cry,' and grinned at her so mischieviously that she could not resist laughing in return.
  This was how James and Calen found them soon afterwards when they returned from the stables. Edith told James in a rush what she had understood from Fursa, and James nodded adding, 'Calen told me something of this while we were out. He says he will tell us everything in a short time but first he must make us a meal. It is to be a celebration, he says in our honour.'
  And celebration it was. Calen had made a large fish stew earlier in the day and now he began heating it in a huge iron pot on the hearth whilst he set out platters and new bread, which he made each day in the priory ovens. There was ale to drink and a basket of little cakes, which were clearly another of his specialities, and which melted in their mouths after the rough fare they had been having for so long. The pot of fish stew was enormous but there was very little of it left at the end of the meal. This was partly the result of James and Edith's hunger, and the novelty of such succulent seafood, but mainly because Fursa showed them all why he was so fat. His capacity for food was prodigious and he mopped up every bit of juice on his plate with large chunks of Calen's new bread and quaffed great draughts of ale.
  An enormous belch from Fursa, which set them all laughing, gave the signal for the meal to end and the talking to begin. Calen refilled their tankards first and motioned them over to the fire, where James and Edith sat close together on one side, Calen in the middle and Fursa, who began to doze almost at once, on the other.
  James felt that it was polite to tell their story first and gave a long account of their adventures and their search for a Christian sanctuary. Calen listened attentively and, when James came to the end of his story, rose from his chair and came across to take them both by the hands, squeezing them in a friendly fashion, before beginning his own account.
  'I've been watching you both,' he began, 'and I must say, first, that it's an honour to have two young people such as you here with us. I'm glad you're here. There's only one thing I'm sorry about – that we have no priest whom I expect you hoped for to marry you. Oh yes, I know,' seeing the surprised looks which they gave each other, 'I told you I was watching you carefully

and you can't keep young love hidden from an old man like me. You could have been married here once – not so long ago too – but not now. Please God, before long, this will be a Christian priory again as it has been for so long. But it's had it's ups and downs and just now it's downs. Listen.

'It began, they say,' he explained, 'with St Ninian, of course. He must have been a fine man, big and strong, people used to say he was although,' he admitted with a grin, 'I suppose we don't really know what he looked like. He came from the Welsh mountains well south of here, and went to Rome as a young man, became a priest and then a bishop. The Pope – Celestine they say he was called – made him one so that he could come back to these parts and convert all the people to Christianity. And so he did too. Not immediately though. The story is that he visited the town of Tours, which is in Gaul I'm told, where they had a great saint called Martin. Ninian determined to be like Martin so he brought back with him from Tours builders and these stones – the white stones – to erect this church, which is why it is still standing in spite of the fighting.'

Calen gazed at the fire for a moment and seemed to be remembering better times long ago. James looked at Edith and moved closer to her to take her hand. Calen caught their eyes and smiled and, seemingly reassured, continued.

'In those days – I don't know how long ago – the whole of this region was Christian, for miles and miles in every direction. It went on for a long time too after Ninian died, because there was another priest further north called Mungo who kept on where Ninian left off. But then,' went on Calen looking very fierce whilst telling this part of the story, 'the king of one of the Pictish tribes – Aldred, or some such he was called – a man who had been a Christian, apostacised.' Calen almost spat out the word in his indignation. 'He began destroying everything that our beloved Ninian had built up, well nearly everything. He raided here last year and the brethren fled, all but one that is,' grinning at them as he said it, 'but they couldn't destroy the stone church and for some reason they didn't burn down the priory. They were looking for precious things, I suppose,' he whispered sadly, 'as if we would have any here. Poverty. That's what St Ninian preached and what he practiced too and that's why they went away I suppose – nothing to steal. I'm the only one who stayed,' he added proudly, 'and they couldn't find me because I hid in St Ninian's cave, which they didn't know about and never discovered. Perhaps the brethren will come back one day, please God. It happened once before when a warring tribe came down. But the devil knows his own and Almighty God will defeat him and, –' he hesitated so long that James thought he had stopped 'they will come back. I know they will. And if they don't,' he added wistfully, 'I will get help from Iona.'

James and Edith started at the word and Calen, seeing their surprise, said, 'That's where he comes from, you know,' nodding at Fursa whom they now saw was awake but sitting absolutely still trying to follow what was being said. 'They sent him here to find out what the state of things was, and if the Christians needed help, because he's the best sailor they have. He's the lay brother who looks after all their boats you see. If the brethren don't come back Iona will help me. Fursa came last time there was a raid but they all came back before help was needed.'

Calen fell silent for a long time before saying in a quiet voice, 'You are welcome here but there is nothing for two young people – and no priest – ' he smiled again, 'so I suggest you go with him to Iona, tomorrow, when he leaves.'

'Oh, do you think he would take us?' Edith cried. 'James, that is the place that Father Melchior told us about. Do you think he would?'

'Yes. He take.'

Brother Fursa, who had replied, was watching them very carefully, but seemed hardly to have moved since he fell asleep.

'Yes. I take you. Understand some he says,' nodding towards Calen, 'You come. Welcome.'

The young pair were so excited they could hardly contain themselves. This curious conversation went back and forth in their own saxon tongue and, what they now learned was gaelic, the language of Ireland across the sea from where the Christian monks had come to Iona.

Finally, when they were all so sleepy they could talk no more, it was Calen who first fell to his knees and they all prayed to God in thanks for His goodness in bringing James and Edith to safety, and to ask His blessing on their journey the following day. Then, nearly asleep on their feet from weariness, they were given a monk's cell each and were dead to the world in an instant.

They did not sail the next day nor on the three following ones.

The wind, which had risen during James and Edith's journey down the peninsula to Whithorn, blew strongly for the next two days. Giant waves beating against the rocks on the shore sent showers of spray high in the air. The boiling maelstrom of churning water, which made it impossible for Fursa to put out in his boat, filled the young couple with alarm since neither had any knowledge of the sea. They were appalled at the prospect of the journey they were about to undertake in such conditions.

Fursa was full of cheerful confidence, however, and took them down to see his boat which was more substantial, and in far better repair, than Jeb's.

Although relieved by this they still found it impossible to believe that one person could sail her single handed, especially with two passengers, but the monk laughed at their anxieties and told them of his voyages up and down the northern coasts as well as to Ireland itself which he had visited, he said, more than ten times. James regretted that he and Edith knew so little that they would be no help to him, which sent Fursa into more peals of laughter and a fit of coughing, which seemed likely to choke him, until relieved by James pounding him several times on the back.

'You help,' spluttered Fursa. 'Yes, you help. I give you this – ' one rope, 'or this – ' another. 'Say hold, you hold. Say pull, you pull. I teach you steer – easy, see,' and he demonstrated the use of the tiller to them and amazed them by insisting that they would both be able to take it and would be quite good seamen when they reached Hii.

Their four days with Fursa and Calen at Whithorn were a delight. Edith, eager to help Calen in any way possible, went with him into the gigantic priory kitchen and he showed her the huge cauldrons, the massive utensils and the immense hearth where everything for thirty or more monks had been prepared. She was allowed to help in the preparation of several of their meals, using the smaller hearth and oven in the refectory, although Calen was so adept at cooking that she realised he only let her help out of politeness. He had been the priory cook for many years, he told her, but he had never taken vows nor been a member of the community in the religious sense; but he was so good a cook that no one ever suggested he should be replaced.

Since her help was clearly not required she offered, instead, to mend his clothes, as well as their own, which he was only too willing to accept . He produced a motley collection of tunics, cloaks, ragged trousers and leggings, decrepit sandals and a variety of other garments which defied description. Edith, although used to work of a very different kind in Queen Ethelberga's household, was an accomplished needlewoman and with the application of much ingenuity she produced a wardrobe of strange but sound garments for the little man which so pleased him that he capered about with delight in his excitement.

Edith would bring her mending into the warmth of the refectory and, whilst he cooked, she would sew. They talked for hours and she found this strange little man a source of immense interest. She asked him all kinds of questions about the Celtic Church and its differences from that of Rome about which he seemed quite unconcerned.

'Differences there are,' he admitted, 'but none is important. Oh, they work out the date of Easter differently and wear a different tonsure, like Fursa's as you will have noticed, but we both worship Almighty God, and follow the teaching of Jesus Christ, and that's what matters. I tell you missy – ' Edith had failed to persuade him to call her by her first name 'I've seen the Roman Church and its customs, because St Ninian brought them here, and I've seen the Celtic Church and *its* system, since the monks of Iona travelled far and wide spreading Christianity after St Ninian died. So things have been a bit of a mixture, you might say, and I've seen both sides.'

After a while, when he had added herbs and spices to his cauldron suspended over the hearth, tasted it several times and expressed satisfaction with a wink at Edith, she said, 'Go on Calen. Tell me more please. I want to know everything.'

'Everything? Well that's a tall order isn't it,' the little man replied, shaking his head from side to side then nodding so that she wasn't sure if he was agreeing or disagreeing. After a moment he continued with his tale.

'The Celtic Church is organised differently, for one thing, you see. In our Church the bishop's in charge, although answerable to the archbishop, if there is one, I suppose. His Lordship the Bishop's the head man, like St Ninian was, with the whole of the diocese under his care. But the Celts do it a different way, so Fursa says and so I've seen in the north. With them the monastery's the centre of everything and the abbot's the boss – even over the bishop. The abbot may not even be a priest but the bishop can only carry on his duties, like ordaining priests for example, when the abbot tells him to.'

Calen stopped, watching the puzzled expression on Edith's face, and then resumed the story.

'Oh, I know it sounds strange but they tell me that in Ireland, where the Celtic Church is the only one, there aren't any towns like York where you used to live, just a monastery as the centre of a particular area. I don't understand it all although Fursa and I have discussed it many times,' he admitted grinning at Edith. 'But I do know this, they follows the teaching of Jesus Christ and so do we, and if Fursa lets his hair grow on the back of his head and the monks here shave it off, what's the difference? It's the Christian faith which is all I care about.'

There was silence for quite a long time after Calen stopped speaking. Edith was deeply impressed by his sincerity and comforted by the notion that the faith of Iona would be the faith she understood. She was considering this when Calen interrupted her thoughts.

'I've heard some marvellous things about the Irish monks who come from Iona, I can tell you, but I'm no sure how many of them are true,' another mischievous grin at Edith. 'They have the gift of the gab and no mistake which they get, so they tell me, from kissing some stone or other in one of their castles.' He carried a large pan over to the sink to drain as he went on talking. 'Take St Mungo, for instance. They tell so many stories about him you don't know what to believe. They say his mother was thrown over a cliff when she was carrying him but came to no harm. Then she was set adrift at sea in a little boat and when Mungo was born he was so holy, from the moment of his birth, that he refused his mother's milk on Sundays and feast days. And another yarn they tell,' Calen continued, warming to his theme so enthusiastically that Edith began to wonder if he had kissed the mysterious Irish stone too, 'is that one of the kings up north found out that his queen had given his gold ring to her lover. In a rage the king threw it into the sea and told her that she had three days to get it back again or he would chop her head off. 'Don't worry,' says Mungo and sends one of his monks out in a boat to catch a fish. When he brings the fish back to Mungo there is the ring in its mouth.'

Calen shook his head in bewilderment, saying as he did so, 'It's a puzzle, and no mistake. But,' he added after a pause, 'there is one thing the Celtic Church can do better than we were ever able to do here – or so Fursa tells me,' he added in a tone of voice which expressed some doubt about the monk's veracity. 'They are very good artists to hear him tell it. Columba, who was the first to come to Iona, used to illuminate psalters and gospels which *he* says,' jerking his head towards the sea to indicate Fursa, 'are the most beautiful things you could ever see. One of them – the best, Fursa says – is known as Columba's Cathach.'

He looked round from the pot he had been tending on the hearth to find Edith staring at him, her work put aside, intent on what he was saying.

'Go on, please. Go on,' she pleaded. 'Did you do the same things here?'

'We tried,' answered Calen, in disparaging tones. 'At least two or three of the monks did but they were never successful. When he,' indicating Fursa again with a jerk of his head, 'saw them he shook his head and couldn't find a good word to say about them.'

'Where is it – the scriptorium? Can I see it?' asked Edith quickly, rising to her feet in her excitement.

'Aye, I suppose you can,' replied Calen, surprised at the interest the young woman was showing. 'Just let let me set this aside and I'll take you.'

The moment Edith saw the scriptorium with its styli and parchments and pigments, neglected and ill-used though these were, she knew she had to find

James and bring him there at once.

He too had been lending a hand wherever he could. Calen's stack of wood was running low, and the remaining refectory table legs were at obvious risk, so James took one of the horses as a pack animal and set about gathering as much wood as possible, from the surrounds of the priory, and steadily reducing it to manageable size. Slowly the pile of logs grew beside the door to the refectory, then a second one beside it. James found a small outbuilding, whilst poking about out of curiosity, and was filling it with wet wood, gathered from the beach, when Edith found him.

'Jamie. Oh Jamie, come and see. You'll never believe it.' Edith was ecstatic but refused to tell him more until he agreed to follow her.

His reaction to the scriptorium was as enthusiastic as hers. Some of the pigments were dried and useless but he found several in good condition as were many of the styli, and there were quantities of parchment which the monks had obtained before their indifferent efforts had led to discouragement.

Edith watched him in silence at first whilst he examined everything he could find. He opened cupboards and peered into corners and searched through piles of long-neglected materials, heaped haphazardly together. He seemed to be so absorbed in what he was doing that she thought he might have forgotten she was there until he called her over to a chest he had opened in one corner.

'Oh dear. Oh dear. They were no great artists here I'm afraid,' he said woefully, lifting from the chest several examples of the monk's attempts at sacred illumination.

She came to stand at his shoulder, peering down at the garish colouring and inept design on the vellum sheets he had discovered. James shook his head sadly and she put both her arms round his waist and hugged him tight.

'Fursa was right,' she remarked presently, and went on to tell James what Calen had said about the skill of the Iona monks and the poor opinion Fursa had had about the work at Whithorn.

James made no reply but returned to his examination of the chest in case there might be something of better quality to be found. He was kneeling on the floor, sitting back on his heels, when Edith spoke again.

'Now you know what Father Birinus felt like for so long, Jamie, until you came along. How depressed the poor man must have been seeing work of this kind and always hoping for something better. Well, you came along – that was something better,' and she hugged him again, kneeling beside him on the floor, consoling him at the memory of Father Birinus her words had evoked.

'Jamie,' she said suddenly, 'I have such a good idea. Couldn't you do something – I don't know what, but something – for Calen and Fursa, to say thank you for all their kindness. Couldn't you Jamie?'

'I might perhaps. I might. It couldn't be very much, there isn't time. But I could do something.'

He thought for a moment then took up an old fragment of parchment, already marred by earlier attempts, saying, 'What about something like this.'

Something like this quickly took shape as Edith watched him sketching out his rough plan.

He began with a large flowing capital 'C'. 'Hm,' he murmured after a moment. It won't do like that. We need some interior decoration. Perhaps . . .' he mused again for a moment 'a monogram of 'CA' to start with. There, that's better. How's that for a start?'

'Oh, Jamie, splendid,' exclaimed Edith, clapping her hands with glee before she realised that he had started to draw again. 'What are you doing to it?'

'I thought it would be better with one of my dogs – and a bit of extra decoration too,' he answered, sliding the finished effort across for her to examine. 'Well?'

'Oh yes, Jamie, splendid. Then you will finish the name, I suppose?'

'Yes. Now I have the idea I can complete the name and maybe, if I have time, put a little picture of Calen in too. But that can wait. Now for Fursa.'

James pondered for quite a time before he began to draw again.

'We need a large 'F' first . . . that's a bit lopsided, don't you think. We had better have some more decoration on the left, like so. That might do for a start.

'Mm, of course. Does he get any dogs?'

Again James didn't answer at once but considered the question carefully.

'What about . . . giving him two in his last letter for a change . . . the 'A'. And I've got another idea too. You know how he pronounces his name with the accent on the last 'a'; we'll give him two 'As' one inside the other . . . like this.'

Again Edith clapped her hands, so delighted was she with the sketches.

James sat back and grinned at her. 'Well, mouse? Will something like those do? I could manage that. We won't be able to leave tomorrow so I should have time. But remember, not a word. Now please help me to find everything I need.'

Far away to the south Father Melchior lay helpless before Cadwalla.

The priest was spreadeagled on the ground, each limb lashed to a peg driven into the earth, making scarcely any movement possible. A livid bruise disfigured his cheek, a trickle of blood ran down his arm from a stab wound in his shoulder, and his left ankle, twisted in a grotesque fashion, had been broken by a vicious blow from Cadwalla's club as the priest lay at his mercy. Mercy was not a word in Cadwalla's vocabulary.

A woman, Reda, had taken the priest through the perimeter of Cadwalla's camp, returning with interest the barrage of bawdy comments from the rabble as they threaded their way through. She had sought out the captain of the chieftain's personal guard and, somehow – and Father Melchior had preferred not to know how – they had been led through the cordon until they were standing immediately outside Cadwalla's hut. Only then did Reda show any sign of nervousness which the priest, his gaze fixed intently on the hut door, scarcely noticed.

She put her ear to his lips and whispered, 'He'll come out of there sooner or later. You'll know him at once. He's deformed and hates everybody because of it.' Then, glancing round quickly she went on, 'You're a fool but a brave one.' Father Melchoir felt her lips pressed gently against his cheek but, when he turned to look at her, she was gone.

He eased his crucifix from his ragged roll, keeping it out of sight in the folds of his tattered garments, then edged to one side trying to be as inconspicuous as possible, hoping not to be challenged until the chief himself emerged.

After a time a shadow moved in the doorway of the hut. Father Melchoir was aware of a stirring among those around him and a huge figure lumbered out into the daylight.

He was not tall but in bulk he was massive. His shoulders, thick and strong like a bull's, were twisted, the right higher than the left. His left arm, flexed across his chest, was thin and shortened whilst the right one was correspondingly huge, as thick as any man's thigh, the hands large and hairy and in continuous motion, the fingers clenching and unclenching in menacing fashion. Cadwalla's head was enormous and he had a steely, glittering eye and an expression of such malevolence that Father Melchior, despite the strength of his resolve, felt a momentary stab of fear. The mouth was set obliquely, drawn up at one corner, a thin line of saliva trickling from the other. His eyes flicked rapidly from side to side missing nothing.

They focused instantly on Father Melchior.

'What the devil! Who the hell are you?'

'A priest, Lord Cadwalla,' answered Father Melchior, holding up his crucifix to this shambling creature, 'and a priest who is pleased to learn the you acknowledge the existence of satan and hellfire, both of which await apostates. By this holy crucifix I abjure you to cease the wicked killing of innocent Christians and to allow the Word of God to be preached again. It is my sacred duty to urge you to repent of the error of your ways and . . .'

The priest got no further.

'Kill him.' Cadwalla was purple with rage as he bellowed the order.

Two soldiers leapt forward immediately, one catching Melchior a glancing blow with his spear as the priest turned to avoid him, the other felling him to the ground with a swinging blow from a club. The first was drawing back his spear for a final thrust when Cadwalla bellowed again, 'No. Stop. Seize him. Bring him here.'

Melchior, bleeding from the wound in his shoulder and dazed from the blow to his head was dragged to his feet.

'How did you get to me – into here?' demanded Cadwalla, gesturing to the enclosure round his hut. Then, seeing that the man was incapable of speech, he screamed in fury.

'Captain of the guard. Here. Now. NOW.' The last word was in such a piercing shriek that it penetrated even Father Melchior's dazed senses.

The captain, fear oozing from every pore, cringed before the tyrant.

'You let him in – a priest,' shouted the deluded creature. 'A priest! I loath them. I detest them. I demand to be kept away from them and you . . . you . . .' spitting with rage, 'let one in.'

The captain had sunk to his knees on the ground before this gibbering maniac. He looked to right and left for help, moistened his dry lips, swallowed and finally croaked, 'I didn't know, my Lord. He looked a beggar. She never mentioned a priest.'

'She? A woman brought him? Who is she?'

'A whore, Lord Cadwalla. A whore I've been w . . . with. Reda is her name but she never mentioned a priest.'

'Find her. Find her. Now,' barked Cadwalla. 'You and you; all of you – scour the camp for her. I want her brought here. Leave this one to me.'

Soldiers scattered in all directions, frantically trying to get out of the chieftain's way, knowing that in his rages he was capable of thrashing wildly about with his sword at anyone in the vicinity. The captain, pathetically whimpering unintelligible sounds, crawled on all fours towards Cadwalla to beg for mercy. He was bent low to the ground by Cadwalla's feet, almost touching them with his lips, when the massive right hand drew the sword from its scabbard.

'You will not die, you cur,' he gloated, 'but you will move no more in my service.' And taking the sword in both hands he lowered the point ever so delicately to the back of the captain's neck and then, suddenly, with tremendous force and a terrifying scream, drove in deeply into his victim's spine between two vertebrae.

The prostrate man collapsed sideways, his spinal cord severed, all muscular power drained from his limbs. Cadwalla shambled to the side and kicked him three or four times as he lay helpless on the ground. Then he turned to a page hovering beside the hut door.

'Get the physician. Get him now. This blackguard will not move again but he is to be kept alive, do you hear. Those are my orders – kept alive and paralysed.'

Father Melchior had collapsed onto the ground when his two supporters had been despatched with the others in search of Reda. His head was still swimming and his shoulder bleeding but, with infinite slowness, he crawled towards the motionless figure of the captain, holding out his crucifix and praying for the stricken soldier.

'Lord Jesus Christ, have pity on this man who was Your creation. Ease his suffering and grant him the grace of acceptance of Your word before his last breath. Let a knowledge of Your goodness enter his soul and, after paying for his sins, may he enter eternal bliss. And this creature, Cadwalla, whose cruelty and bestiality so offend Your goodness and love, may, even he, be brought into the fold of the one true Shepherd. May he be forgiven Lord. Like those whom You pardoned on the cross, he knows not what he does.'

Father Melchior turned his eyes up to Cadwalla as the prayer ended. There was an expression of terror on the tyrant's face. His sword had fallen to the ground and his hands were pressed tightly to his ears trying to shut out the sound of the priest's words. His head, turned to one side so that his deformed hand could reach his left ear, was shaking from side to side and the creature who, a moment before, had committed such a blatant act of ferocity, was whimpering.

'No. Stop him. No. No. Peg him down. Gag him. Make him stop.'

So Father Melchior had been pegged to the ground in front of Cadwalla's hut and a filthy rag was stuffed into his mouth so that he could scarcely breathe. He drifted in and out of consciousness, aware of the pain in his head, shoulder and ankle where Cadwalla, in a last brutal act before fleeing to his tent, had bludgeoned him. At times, for short periods, his mind was clear and he realised that Cadwalla was terrified of Christ, trying to hide from God, aware of his apostacy and desperately trying to blot it out of his mind. Perhaps, thought the priest, I might somehow manage to get through to him – and then unconsciousness overwhelmed him again. At one point he was dimly aware of a commotion and of screaming and of something thrown down over one of his legs. He was able to raise his head enough to make out the mutilated body of Reda but, no sooner had he begun to pray for her, then his senses left him again.

When he became aware of his surroundings once more Cadwalla was standing over him, his face twisted with fury and hatred, his former arrogance returned. Father Melchior strove to keep his mind on the task of convincing this animal of the goodness of God.

'Cut him free and bring him here.'

The priest felt his bonds severed and he was dragged upright, hanging helplessly on the two soldiers, unable to put his broken ankle to the ground.

'You have troubled me enough, you scum,' mouthed Cadwalla, who was now lounging in a chair before his hut, drinking from a huge goblet. 'We are all considering how we can best dispose of you once and for all, but it must be something slow and agonising to amuse us all.' He laughed and looked round at his men.

'You,' he roared to the soldier holding Father Melchior's left arm 'how shall we do it?'

The man licked his lips but made no reply. Cadwalla snarled and turned to another and then another.

'You then? Or you? Any of you?'

It was Melchior who replied. The priest had suddenly found resources he did not know he possessed. The man in front of him was the sworn enemy of the Lord Jesus Christ and Melchior was his priest. With God's help he could face anything of which Cadwalla was capable.

'Perhaps, my Lord Cadwalla, I might be allowed to make some suggestions. You see, Almighty God's servants have been suffering for Him in many ways for over six hundred years. If He allows it, they may even die for Him, but He does not make it easy for the murderers my Lord.'

Cadwalla had fallen silent again at the mention of Almighty God and was showing signs of his former anxiety.

'You may recall, from your own Christian teaching, my Lord – ' Cadwalla blanched at the word and chewed his lip ' – that the holy martyrs, Cosmos and Damien, were tied to crosses and stoned but the stones rebounded and killed those who threw them; they were thrown into the sea but were caught by angels and returned to land; they were thrown into the fire but the flames turned aside and refused to burn them. Perhaps my Lord remembers St Sebastian, pierced full of arrows but still refusing to die. Or St Catherine, lashed to a spiked wheel which collapsed and killed her torturers. Or St Margaret, eaten by a dragon which burst assunder. Or St Panthaleon who survived burning, the wheel, the sword, liquid lead, wild beasts and drowning. So you see, Cadwalla, the servants of God have endured every kind of execution for Him and there are more, many more. St Lawrence was roasted on a grid iron but was so sustained by Almighty God that the saint suggested they turn him round that he might be more evenly done. And don't forget the holy apostles, my Lord – there are several new ways there for you to try; St Bartholomew, flayed alive; St James the Less, beaten with clubs; Simon the Zealot, sawn in half – all supported and sustained by God to withstand brutality far exceeding anything you are capable of.

'Do you not see, you pathetic, muling creature, you can kill me – kill any of God's servants in one of a thousand ways but you will never escape Almighty God Himself. You know this Cadwalla. I see it in your eyes. You have tried to get away from Him – are trying every minute of the time – but you know you can never escape him, never never, nev . . .'

Cadwalla had clenched his fists and thrown them up in the air in a gesture of outrage. His face was contorted with fury. Flecks of foam appeared at the corners of his mouth. His withered left arm began to twitch, his head jerked sideways and his back arched. Blood oozed from his mouth as his clamped teeth bit into his protruding tongue. A spreading stain of urine marked the front of his breeches and the stench of faeces arose as his incontinence was complete. In a last desperate move before the convulsion, rocked his entire body he managed to point a shaking finger at the priest and, through clenched teeth, ground out the one word.

'Kill.'

It was the soldier behind Father Melchior who reacted first. The spear entered his back below the ribs, slicing through his liver and severing the main artery of his body. He was dead before the remaining spear thrusts began to rain down on him.

On the ground, beside the martyred priest, the massive bulk of Cadwalla jerked and heaved and writhed in his fit of epilepsy, watched dispassionately by his silent soldiers.

James and Edith had decided to give their gifts to Calen and Fursa after the evening meal on their last night in the priory.

James, suddenly eager to get to work once more, had begun at once to convert his rough sketch of Calen's name into it's final form. A double sheet of vellum, deeper than the length of a man's arm, had been divided into two so that the friends should each have an equally imposing gift. He had worked at remarkable speed and had accomplished a great deal by the time dusk had obliged him to stop. Even then, by a flickering rush light he had made adjustments to both names. Below Calen's name was a neat white church inside a circular border of pots and pans, knives and spoons. Peering round the last stroke of the 'N' was the inquisitive face of the little cook. Across the upper horizontal of Fursa's name were clouds, through a break in which could be seen pursed lips blowing a fair wind down to the monk's boat which was scudding merrily along, a portly Fursa at the tiller and two passengers who would, in the final version, be Edith and James. Propped up against the last upstroke of the final 'A' was Fursa himself, fast asleep, hands clasped over his ample stomach.

James had been at work at first light on the following day and was able to complete both before dusk.

Fursa, although anxious to be away before the winter gales set in, had said that they would have to stay one more day since a considerable sea was still running. While he made last minute checks to his boat, James and Edith enjoyed a splendid last day exploring widely under Calen's guidance. He showed them the grave of St Ninian just behind the stone church. Then, with the two young people on their own horses and Calen mounted on one of the pack animals, he took them to all his favourite places around the peninsula. He pointed out a tiny island to the east which he said was called Whithorn Island where there was a church built on the spot where, some said, St Ninian had first landed. Calen chattered away about the places he remembered as a boy, the things he had done and the life in the priory where he had spent the last ten years. Fearing that he would be lonely when they had gone, Edith asked him if he minded being alone again.

'Lord bless you, missy. I shan't mind really. I've been alone a lot in my life. I had a wife once but, sadly, not for long. She died, poor creature, after we had been wed only two years. We were happy too – so happy that I suppose that was the reason I never took vows; I always hoped I would meet someone else and want to marry again. But I didn't,' and he gave a great sigh and for a moment looked quite sad.

But only for a moment. Soon he grinned at Edith and started talking again.

'I won't be alone for long, missy, now that you are leaving these horses with me. I'll set off when you have gone and find some of the brethren. I have a good idea where they might be and I think I can persuade a few to return. So, you see, we might have the place going again in no time. I should have done it before but I'm too old to get very far on my own two feet. Now, with your horses, it will be different. And now, young sir,' turning in the saddle to address James who was riding behind them, 'I have something to show you both. Come with me.'

Without another word he led them to the cliff edge and dismounted, indicating that they should do the same. Then, tethering the horses, he set off down the cliff face, using a tortuous track that they would never have found without him and which, although steep, had many easy steps and hand holds and places to rest to get one's breath, so that Edith negotiated it without difficulty. When they were standing on the seashore Calen spoke again.

'We cross that pebble beach that stretches out to the west. Will you be alright, missy?'

'Yes, fine, Calen. Is it far?'

'No, not far,' he replied. 'Just there where the cliffs are. That's where we are going.'

They traversed the loose pebbles of the beach quite easily and were almost at the cliff face when Calen stopped and asked, 'Can you see that black cave mouth? Just a little way up from the shore? That's St Ninian's cave where he used to come to pray alone and where I hid from the Picts. It's a holy place and I want you to remember it after you've gone with Fursa.'

A few minutes later they were standing at the entrance to the cave peering into it's blackness. In the rock, to the right, by the cave mouth, a crude cross had been carved, and just within the cave itself, leaning up against the wall, Edith could make out a second simple cross made out of two pieces of driftwood lashed together. Calen, seeing the direction of her gaze said, 'You'll see a lot of those inside. Many pilgrims used to come here – but not for some time – to ask for St Ninian's help, and they would make a cross like that or scratch one on one of those stones or perhaps on the cave wall. Let's go inside.'

The cave itself was enormous and stretched back into the gloom an unknown distance. Calen, answering their unspoken question, said, 'Back there there are nooks and crannies and caverns and hidey holes – those Picts would never have found me even if they had discovered the cave.'

The two young people held hands, gazing up around the grandeur of the cave. In a little while they all knelt to pray to the saint for their safety on the journey the following day and for Calen to find the brethren and bring them back to the priory. Then Calen said it was time to go but, first, they must leave something, however small, in memory of their visit. Edith arranged a cross of loose stones whilst James, finding a stone with a sharp edge, gouged out a second cross from the softer rock at the back of the cave.

Calen nodded his approval. 'Well done. Now we go, or no food tonight.'

It was another evening meal to remember. There was fish, of course, and succulent roast goose which Calen had obtained from heaven knew where. There were cakes of different kinds and new bread and ale. Fursa consumed such gargantuan quantities that they feared he might burst but the only explosion was the sound of his ultimate belch, for which the others now waited, signalling the end of the meal.

James motioned for Edith to keep them busy in conversation and went to the scriptorium for the parchments. He returned presently holding them out of sight and nodded to Edith to begin as they had agreed she would. She smiled her approval and, taking a spoon, rapped gently on the table.

'Calen, Fursa,' she began. 'We have to thank you for so much I hardly know where to begin. You have taken us in, given us food – and what food – and shelter and kindness and,' she hesitated, 'friendship. We want to give you something in return, something James has done with a skill of which I hope Fursa will approve; something which we hope will remind you of us.'

She stood aside to let James come forward to the table and place each man's parchment before him.

Fursa was the first to respond with a mighty roar of approval and a stream of incomprehensible words in gaelic. After a moment he changed to his own brand of Saxon.

'Good,' he shouted, clapping James on the back so hard that the young man staggered forward. 'This good – good as Iona – maybe better.'

Calen too was entranced and for a long time they poured over their illuminated pages, glancing quickly at each other's and then back to their own, scrutinising every detail. There were constant remarks like, 'Look at this,' 'that's marvellous,' and 'did you ever see anything like it.'

Calen went into fits of laughter at the picture of the sleeping Fursa to which the monk retorted by pointing to the wicked expression on Calen's face and saying, 'He look like that all the time; naughty.'

How long they would have gone on James could only guess but it was he who reminded them of their departure at dawn. Calen even wept a few tears and was uncharacteristically incoherent in his thanks. Fursa hugged them both to his ample stomach and said, 'That good. Thank you. Fursa thank you,' and then, mysteriously, 'wait till he see this. Come on,' he continued, 'see here,' tapping the parchment, 'I sleep. Now we all sleep.'

They left soon after dawn. Calen cut a pathetic figure on the shore as they watched him getting smaller and smaller. Edith and James were reminded of themselves at Whitby when they were just able to make out the little old man scrambling up the cliffs to watch them as long as possible.

Then he was gone and James was brought back to reality by Fursa with a gruff command.

'Right. Now you steer.'

Chapter 5

Almost two weeks after leaving Whithorn Fursa's boat came smoothly alongside a simple wooden jetty on the eastern side of the island of Iona.

With two passengers aboard, who had never before been to sea, the monk had chosen the gentlest route. He had attempted no long crossings which would have kept them at sea overnight and had not risked being caught in stormy weather which, as winter was approaching, became increasingly likely. For the most part they had hugged the coastline, moving slowly northwards, seldom out of the sight of land and always putting into a sheltered anchorage before nightfall. Only twice had it been necessary to leave the protection of the coast, once when they crossed, what Fursa told them was, a wide bay soon after rounding the headland south of Whithorn, and the second time when they had left the west coast of the mainland to pass, by way of a large rocky island which Fursa called Arran, to a long peninsula of land which he said was known as Kintyre.

They had kept well inshore after that, creeping slowly up the eastern coast for the longest continuous section of their journey, and had then waited impatiently until a near gale from the west, bringing squall after squall of rain, had been followed by a gentle easterly, which had blown them quickly across the narrowest part of the sound to the island of Mull, off the south west tip of which, Fursa told them, lay Iona. They had seemed almost to have arrived at their destination when again they were frustrated by further contrary winds, and Fursa had to use all his skill to beat steadily round the south of Mull over the final narrow strait to Iona.

Their arrival was greeted by a brief spell of evening sunshine, bathing the monastery and its motley collection of buildings, in a glow of welcome for the weary travellers. As they ran gently in towards a shallow bay Fursa pointed out the large wooden chapel within two rings of single cells where the monks lived. The abbot's house was hidden from view by the chapel itself whilst, further away from the ring of cells to the south, lay a little huddle of dwellings of varying size which Fursa called the 'hospitium'.

Here, he said, lived a number of lay folk who came to the monastery from time to time, as they were doing, some of whom spent just a few weeks and some several years doing a variety of tasks within the life of the community. One of these, Fursa told them, was called Oswald who had been some kind of nobleman in Northumbria before he had arrived about three years ago and stayed ever since. There were several women, wives of men who worked around the island tending cattle, sheep, goats and a few pigs, and helping generally with the monastery, so Edith would be assured of some companionship.

The two young people had finally come ashore with a feeling of relief. They had endured the discomforts of the journey stoically but had found little pleasure in it. Edith had adapted more quickly to the choppy motion of Fursa's little boat and had been able to help the monk whilst James was fit only to lie listlessly, half over the side, for the first two or three days of their journey. Gradually, as they moved slowly towards their destination, he revived and began to take an interest in the workings of the boat under Fursa's patient instruction. Several times the elegance of the sea birds, which wheeled and soared around them, captured his attention and the scudding clouds and the filling sails gave him ideas for future designs.

For the most part however it was an uncomfortable voyage, cold with brisk winds and squally rain. Conversation was difficult in the roar and screech of the wind and each night, when they came ashore, they were too tired to do more than eat a frugal meal and fall asleep, wrapped in their clothes, under whatever shelter they could find. Fursa had caught a number of fish to supplement the stores they had brought from Whithorn, most of which he had eaten himself, neither of the others having much appetite at the end of each tiring day.

Their arrival on Iona was like a blessing. James helped Edith ashore and both fell to their knees to give thanks for their safe arrival in the Christian community they had searched for for so long.

He took Edith's arm and together they surveyed their surroundings with interest. A path led northwest from their tiny harbour, up a gentle slope towards a stone building in the distance. A stream, emerging from behind this building, flowed towards them for a while before veering eastwards to reach the sea a little way north of where they were standing. North of that again, the monastery buildings now, in the early evening, lay in the shadow of a hill to the west which was the highest point they could discern on the island.

As they were cautiously inspecting their new home two figures emerged around the corner of the track ahead of them and made their way down to the boat. Both were lean, rugged men, dressed in a fashion similar to Fursa's, but looking altogether fitter and stronger than he. Fursa introduced them by names which Edith and James did not catch, nor did the men, who evidently spoke no saxon, understand theirs. Fursa, who seemed as delighted to be back as his two fellow travellers, greeted the monks in his usual jovial fashion and loaded them up with an assortment of goods which he had brought from Whithorn. Handing James and Edith their few possessions he said, 'You go with them. I stay. Put boat to bed,' and laughing uproariously at his joke he patted them on the shoulders and pointed to the distant monastery buildings.

The quartet moved off in silence back along the path, Edith and James feeling uneasy again, being unable to converse with the monks. They passed close by the stone building which they now saw was a kiln with other buildings behind – a mill and two larger barns for storing grain. By the look of the fertile plain which extended, James could now see, well to the north of the monastery ahead and well south of where they had come ashore, grain seemed likely to be plentiful. Their path turned right by the kiln, over the stream and continued directly northwards towards an earthwork rampart ahead.

Passing through this they approached the first of three large wooden buildings which were linked together and which they recognised as the guest houses which Fursa had pointed out from the sea. One monk motioned them to follow him to the door whilst his companion, muttering something incomprehensible, but smiling in a way they took to mean farewell, continued on his way towards the monastery.

At the door to meet them was a short stout woman who, to their relief addressed them in Saxon.

'You are welcome, in God's name,' she began. 'You will be tired, I'm sure. Come in, come in. I'll show you where you can sleep. We have a dormitory for men and another for women. You can bring your things along with you. My! You haven't brought much,' when she saw their small bundles. 'We'll have to get you some more things if you're going to stay with us very long. I'm called Fara, by the way, and my husband is Maban. We are guest master and mistress and we will make you comfortable I can tell you – very comfortable, like home. If you want anything just ask. Maban or I will be glad to help you. That's why we're here. We both speak saxon and gaelic. I'm Saxon originally and my husband is a Scot. We lived in Ireland and I didn't like it; we lived in Northumbria and he didn't like it so we ended up halfway between the two. This suits us both. There's nothing we enjoy so much as looking after folk. There you are.'

The seemingly endless flow of words – music to the ears of James and Edith so long used to broken saxon and incomprehensible gaelic – came to an abrupt end as Fara paused before the door of a dormitory for women.

'Come on, dear,' she began again, taking Edith comfortably by the elbow, 'we'll get you settled first and then I'll go to find Maban to look after your . . .' she paused for a moment, looked quizically at James, grinned and said, 'friend. Friend? Well that will do for the present.'

Turning to James she pointed to a bench against the wall a little further along the passage and said, 'Rest your weary feet, dear. You look all in.'

James *was* nearly all in and was nearly asleep when he came to with a start to find a short, plump man, Maban he presumed, standing before him. The little man was so like Fara they could have been twins rather than husband and wife. James remembered hearing it said that husbands and wives often came to look alike but he had never thought to see them as near identical as Fara and Maban.

There was a difference though. He was as silent as she was loquacious but he was no less capable nor hospitable. Taking charge of the young man he led him along to another part of the building to a men's dormitory, showed him his pallet, carried his little bundle of clothes, took him out to a pump in the yard and pointed out everything James would need with scarcely a word spoken. Then, when he had seen to all James' comforts, he spoke his longest sentence yet.

'Food now, or else you'll be asleep before you can eat it.'

Edith was already waiting in a refectory further into the building. Fara was busy setting out a meal and James was surprised to find how hungry he was. It was simple fare but delicious. There was bread, which Fara said was made from barley, eggs poached to perfection, and a little meat – or was it fish. James couldn't decide. It looked like one and tasted like the other and was quite unlike anything he had tasted before. Edith and he became quite convulsed with laughter, trying to decide what it might be until Fara returned from an errand and told them that it was seal, many of which Fursa had shown them on their voyage. As a special treat they were given goats milk to drink although Fara said they would usually have water unless it was a special feast day. Ale – much to Fursa's disgust – was not allowed on the island.

It was a wonderful welcome after so many weeks of danger, uncertainty and discomfort. In the few hours they had spent on Iona they had felt at home at last, as though the threat of barbarism had receded completely to be replaced by the Christian protection of the island and it's monastery. Edith took James' hand and squeezed it happily and, when she thought Fara was occupied with something else, rested her head gently on his shoulder.

They were contentedly enjoying their new-found peace when Fursa arrived to make sure they were being properly looked after – or perhaps, they thought, to beg a slab of seal meat on a huge slice of bread from Fara. The monk was soon seated beside them telling them that he had seen the abbot, Segenus, to inform him of their arrival. The abbot wanted to hear all their news, Fursa said, but not until they were rested and properly fed (Fursa winked at Fara) and had enjoyed a good night's sleep. They would probably have to meet someone else tomorrow too, he suggested, someone he had already talked about.

James and Edith looked at each other in a puzzled fashion, unable to think, in their tiredness, whom it might be. They both looked enquiringly at Fursa?

'Oswald,' he said, 'Prince Oswald.'

Prince Oswald, nephew of the late King Edwin of Northumbria, knelt at prayer in the chapel of the monastery of Iona. Three years on the island had given Oswald a contentment he had never previously experienced. The turbulence of his young life had been exciting, but in what Oswald now saw was a barbaric existence. He had exulted in the victory of his father, King Ethelfrid of Bernicia, over King Edwin of Deira, who had then fled into exile leaving the whole province in the victor's hands. Oswald had been too young to fight in that campaign and, although he had later fought bravely in his father's army, when Edwin regained the kingdom, Oswald had been obliged to flee the field with his elder brother, Eanfrid, leaving their father dead and his forces routed. Oswald had wandered the wild northern wastes of the country brawling, fighting, drinking and wenching but always nursing bitter resentment against Edwin and plotting revenge.

Then the remarkable news reached him of King Edwin's conversion to Christianity, Oswald, unable to understand it, had seen it as a sign of weakness and had redoubled his efforts to raise an army and march against Northumbria. But the Pictish chieftains had seen little in it for them and viewed each other with too much suspicion to commit substantial forces so far south and Oswald had gone westward in the hope of finding more support.

He had found none. Instead he met a monk from Iona, Falla by name, who had been preaching his pernicious Christian doctrine in the region. Oswald, in his cups, had been abusive and had reviled Falla and mocked his Christianity. The monk's calm acceptance of the personal insults had further enraged him until, provoked beyond endurance, he had leapt forward, flailing with his fists, bent on inflicting injury. The outcome, had Oswald not been befuddled by drink, might have been different but, as things were, he was astonished to find his blows easily parried, his wrists seized and himself pitched head over heels into the corner. The monk, sitting none too gently on Oswald's back, had twisted his right arm up behind his shoulder and had begun to preach to him.

'Our Lord Jesus Christ,' the monk's words only dimly penetrated Oswald's mind 'taught us to turn the other cheek when someone strikes us, which shows you what a poor Christian I am. Had you been attacking me alone I might have done so, as I tolerated your insults, but when you reviled our Blessed Lord I could not stand aside and do nothing, especially when I realised you knew nothing about the faith you were attacking. So now that I am sitting comfortably, and you are in no position to object, let me instruct you.'

For the next half hour Falla expounded the basis of Christianity, explained the love of God for all His creatures, described how Christ died for our sins and rose again on the third day. Oswald, despite himself, found he was listening. Something he could not define caused a quickening of interest in his fuddled brain. When he should have been seething with indignation at his rough handling by this man of God he found himself listening to the monk's gentle voice and trying to follow his argument. When released from the monk's grip, and freed from the weight on his back, he remained prostrate on the floor, puzzling over his odd reaction to the doctrine which had hitherto been anathema to him. More surprising still, on the following day, he had actually gone to the lengths of seeking out Falla again and asking him to repeat his instruction. Oswald listened carefully on that occasion and on the next and the one after that as, each day, Falla taught him the word of God.

Oswald was baptised only four weeks later and when Falla returned to Iona, after completing his task of evangelising the region, Oswald went as well.

He had been assiduous in his Christian observance from the moment of his arrival. The Holy Office, which the community monks attended, seldom found him absent. He contemplated making his own vows but the abbot,

Segenus, had been curiously reluctant to encourage him. Though disappointed he had accepted the abbot's ruling yet he continued to conform to the abbey routine.

He had remained in prayer for a long time after Terce and it was in the chapel that the abbot's servant found him with the request that he attend upon the abbot as soon as possible.

'My Lord Abbot.'

'Prince Oswald.'

Formality had always characterised the initial exchanges between these two as though the proper rank of each needed to be acknowledged before they could relax in friendly discussion. Someone of Oswald's importance might easily have been a disruptive element in the life of the community. Not only was he a constant reminder of the outside world, from which the clergy and monks had voluntarily withdrawn in the service of God, but his rank as prince in the House of Bernicia, albeit an exiled one, was a sign of the temporal influence and power which was directly opposed to their frugal and austere way of life. Yet, so far from being an upsetting factor in their lives, Oswald's devotion and humility, his failure ever to stand on his dignity and his willing acceptance of the religious life of Iona, had served as an example of resignation to misfortune and submission to the will of God.

The abbot, especially, had appreciated the prince's admirable qualities but had discouraged him from making religious vows, feeling that the contribution he might make in the outside world to the spread of Christianity would be far greater than any he might make within their own community. That opportunity might now have arrived.

'Two young people, escaping from Northumbria, arrived last night, Oswald, and, from what I have been told, in a very brief meeting with Fursa the boatman, they have news of considerable importance to us all but especially to you. I will let them tell their story presently but you should know that Edwin is dead and paganism rampant again in his former kingdom. You must question them in detail. They speak only saxon so, although I would willingly be with you when you see them, I would understand little of the discussion. They are waiting in the next room. May I have them brought in here? I will leave you alone and you can tell me everything later.'

Oswald indicated his agreement and closed the door softly behind the departing abbot. This sudden reminder of the Kingdoms of Northumbria, thoughts of which had once occupied his every waking moment, had unsettled him. He realised that he had scarcely given it any consideration for months, and now here it was again, obtruding violently into his life – his peaceful contented life.

Edwin dead! Well, he had given *him* little thought either. As his father's enemy he had no cause to love Edwin but now, so far from relishing his death, Oswald found it impossible to feel anything but sadness. He murmured a 'de profundis' for the soul of the dead king who had accepted Christianity as Oswald had and, by all accounts, almost all of Northumbria as well. His thoughts were interrupted as a young man and woman entered the room.

Edith and James bowed politely to the prince and stood waiting uncertainly for him to break the silence. He addressed them in saxon.

'I am Oswald of Bernicia, nephew of King Edwin, about whose death I have just been told. You, I understand are refugees from Northumbria although I fear I know little else about you. Perhaps you will tell me your story?'

The two looked enquiringly at each other and with a nod Edith indicated that James should begin.

'My names is James, Prince Oswald, and I formerly served in the household of Bishop Paulinus of York at the palace of King Edwin. This is the Lady Edith, once lady-in-waiting to the queen until she and the bishop and a small party were obliged to flee Northumbria and escape by sea – and to safety we can only hope – to Kent. Northumbria was invaded by the unholy alliance of Penda of Mercia and Cadwalla, King of the Britons of North Wales. They overcame King Edwin's army at Hatfield, killing him and his elder son, Osfrid, and capturing his younger son, Egfrid. The barbarians decimated the region, Your Highness, and we were fortunate to escape with our lives.'

James stopped, wondering how much the prince would want to know. 'Do you want me to go on, Your Highness?'

'Go on please. I want to know everything. Here – the Lady Edith may take this chair – I fear there are few comforts here. You and I can sit before her on the ground and I will listen carefully. Tell me everything; everything.'

James' tale took a long time in the telling. Several times he went wrong, confusing the sequence of events in his mind; each time Edith gently touched his arm to interrupt the flow of his account with a correction. At last all was told and James fell silent, waiting for the prince to speak.

'So,' mused Oswald aloud, 'Edwin dead, Osfrid dead and Egfrid captured – and, if I know anything about Cadwalla and Penda, also dead by now. Edwin's children by Ethelberga were a daughter and a son you say,' glancing enquiringly at the pair? In response to James' nod he continued. 'Do you have any news of my brothers, Eanfrid and Oswy.'

'None, Your Highness. We know nothing of either.'

'Nor of Edwin's cousin, Osric?'

James shook his head.

'What was the state of Northumbria before the attack James? Much was Christian I believe. Is this true?'

'Quite true, Prince. Several years ago I travelled far and wide in Bernicia and Deira with His Lordship, Bishop Paulinus. We would both instruct and he would baptise and many, very many, became Christian. Once King Edwin renounced his worship of heathen gods and the idols were destroyed, word of these events spread rapidly and the people were eager to follow the king's example.' James hesitated for a minute before adding, 'Perhaps too eager.'

'Too eager? To become a Christian? Surely no one can be that?' Oswald's tone was quite sharp in his retort.

'Your Highness, I accept that our religion is something all should be encouraged and taught to accept. What I meant was simply that we found out, from our companion, Father Melchior, of whom I have spoken, that when the barbarians overcame the Christians many of our converts showed signs of lapsing into idolatry again hoping to save their skins. I should not criticise our efforts to spread the gospel, perhaps, but it seems possible that, in our enthusiasm to win souls for Almighty God, we may – ' James looked unhappy and looked anxiously at the prince who was watching him intently ' – I repeat, we *may* sometimes baptise too many too soon.'

There was silence for some time while Oswald digested these comments. After several minutes he spoke again.

'Perhaps you are right, perhaps not, Master James. It is a question of deep theological significance. We must not forget the inward grace of which the sacrament is merely the outward sign. Let us leave that for such as Abbot Segenus and his colleagues.' Then rising abruptly and walking up and down the little room as he was speaking he changed the subject.

'This Father Melchior, your companion, whom you mentioned, tell me more of him.'

James, perhaps disturbed by Oswald's rebuke to his criticism of mass conversions, looked towards Edith who took up the story.

'He was – still is, I fondly hope – a very brave priest, Your Highness, who refused to come with us to the safety of this island but returned, instead, to Northumbria to do what little he could do to sustain the Christians there. He had no illusions about the dangers he was facing. He had seen the charnel house of Catterick and he knew he was taking his life in his hands.

May God grant him protection in what he tried to do or eternal bliss in heaven if he has met his death.'

'Amen,' muttered James crossing himself.

It was Prince Oswald's turn to look disturbed and Edith felt that something she had said had troubled him although she could not think what it might be. He paced up and down in an agitated fashion for a while oblivious of the young couple. Edith smiled at James and took his hand and left her chair to sit beside him on the floor. He nodded to show that he was alright and both watched Oswald who seemed to have forgotten they were there. Eventually, when James was beginning to think he should ask if the prince wished to be left alone, Oswald smiled and spoke again.

'You have been very helpful to me, both of you. I hope we will have many more talks together while you are here.'

He smiled once more and looked deliberately at their two hands clasped tightly together and his smile became a broad grin. He extended both hands towards them to help them up and asked, 'you are married perhaps? I had not realised.'

It was James, now mollified by the change in the prince's manner, who replied.

'I wish we were, Your Highness. We would like to marry but, as we told you, there was only Brother Fursa at Whithorn and no priest to perform the ceremony. I wonder, Prince Oswald . . . may I . . . would you perhaps ask the Lord Abbot if he would allow us to marry? Do you think you could, Your Highness . . . please?'

'With great pleasure, great pleasure,' the prince responded without hesitation. 'I will put your request to him at once. He will be here presently to find out what I have learned from you. He has only a very few words of saxon and would not have understood what you have told me. Leave me now if you please and take my good wishes for your future happiness with you. The lay brother is waiting outside to escort you back to your quarters. Later, I expect, the abbot will wish to see you himself – perhaps with me present to interpret. I must go to the chapel now to ask our Lord for help in what I must do.'

The expected summons to the abbot's presence did not come for three days. They were days filled with fascination for the young pair. On the first Maban had introduced them to an older monk called Plenus who had been the guest master before him but was now relieved of these responsibilities and was allowed to pray and recite the psalter and meditate as much as he wished, without other duties to distract him. This solemn man had taken them on a conducted tour of the monastery. They saw the surprisingly small wattle hut, close by the guest houses, where Prince Oswald had lived for three years. Plenus pointed out the double line of monks cells built round a central courtyard for silent meditation. They were constructed in a semi-circular fashion, abutting onto the side of the chapel which ensured the monk's complete privacy since no one but they was permitted to enter the area. The cells were small beehive-like structures with doors that stood open to let in light for most of the day but could be closed at anytime to give complete solitude for prayer and meditation. It was, Plenus explained, one of the rules of their blessed founder, St Columba – or Columcille, as they sometimes called him – that every monk should have his own, 'fast place with a door to enclose him.'

There were more than one hundred and twenty monks in the monastery at that time. Sometimes there were more and he could not remember the number falling below a hundred. Plenus talked to them freely, perhaps because of the silence he was usually called upon to observe since, he said, another of Columba's rules was that they should not talk unless some business demanded it. He was permitted to speak to them, as he was doing at that moment, since it was the abbot's policy that visitors must be made familiar with the principal features of the monastery soon after arrival, so that they would then observe the customs of the community without inadvertently distracting the monks at prayer or meditation.

The members of the order – the monks clerical and lay, excluding people like themselves, Prince Oswald and a few families allowed to live there – were called the brethren. When they took their solemn monastic vows in the chapel they were tonsured, like he and Fursa were, from ear to ear. The whole of the front of the head was shaved bare, letting the hair grow only at the back. James was about to ask why they had chosen a tonsure so different from our Lord's crown of thorns, which the monks of the Roman Church adopted, but it seemed to him that Plenus, although happy to instruct them in a most informative fashion, did not welcome questions. James put his query aside and listened to what the old monk was saying.

'There are three groups of us,' he said, ticking them off on his fingers as he spoke. 'The first are the seniors, like me, who have been here for some years – older men who attend the religious services and pray for everybody – we all need it, you realise,' he interpolated with a rare flash of humour. 'Then there are the working brethren, as I used to be, including the lay brothers, who are younger and stronger and do the manual work,' Plenus seemed to underline the word as he said it giving it a special physical significance. 'There is much to do outside the monastery itself with the agriculture, or the livestock, or the mill, or the kiln, as well as within it like the "pincera" who is in charge of the refectory, or the "pistor" who organised the bakery. He's a Saxon, as I am,' he added smiling, 'and Fara would love to chat to him, as you can imagine since you have heard her talking already, but it isn't allowed as I have told you.'

'The most junior grades are the 'alumni' or the pupils, youths under instruction who haven't yet taken vows but will nearly all do so sooner or later.'

'What is your rule? Is that the word?' asked Edith who may not yet have appreciated Plenus' dislike of questions.

He paused before replying then smiled, as if prepared to humour so pretty a young lady. When he answered it was in his most polite fashion.

'The blessed Columcille,' he began, 'whom we Saxons know as Columba,' a little patronising smile at Edith, 'did not lay down a rigid rule. We keep all the canonical hours, of course – Lauds, Terce, Prime, Sext, None, Vespers, Compline and Matins – but not all keep all, if you understand me.' Plenus had clearly decided he needed to be specially explicit when talking to women so, in a moment, he elaborated, 'The senior monks keep all these if they can – so all go to most and most go to all.' He chuckled for a moment at his turn of phrase before continuing. 'Anyone may go, if they wish, even you,' nodding to Edith and James as if bestowing a great favour. 'We sing, we pray, we chant, we pray; I used to go whenever I could but my first duty, when I was younger, was to my visitors.' He inclined his head fractionally in their direction. 'Now, Fara and Maban do the work instead and there are others doing special tasks as, someday perhaps, will you. We are a community,' he went on, 'not just the brethren, although we are perhaps the chief part with the abbot at our head, but all of us who live here, as now,' he added gracefully, 'do you. Come, let us continue our tour. Soon it will be noon and time for Sext which I must attend.'

Plenus took them to the chapel, a large wooden building which they entered by a door on the opposite side from the monk's cells, and conducted them at once to a balcony at the rear of the building which, he insisted, was where they must go whenever they came to pray, the nave being reserved for the monks alone. The chapel was of considerable size, clearly capable of accommodating the two hundred or so souls on the island at that time with room to spare. Some monks, perhaps ten or twelve had already assembled awaiting Sext, and were kneeling singly at various parts of the church so as not to disturb each other. When James and Edith had prayed for a short time Plenus took them back down the stair and out again into the grey winter's day.

'We have no time left to visit everything,' he told them, 'but if you come over here a little way, I can show you what else there is so that you will know the extent of it all.'

They walked for a few moments before Plenus stopped and pointed to a two storey wooden building near by where they were standing. He resumed his account.

'That is the abbot's house, where he has a room to sleep and a room to pray and meditate; there is also a room kept specially for sacred illumination.' James and Edith glanced at each other as he spoke but did not interrupt. 'Such embellishments of holy writ have been a tradition here since the time of our founder, St Columba, who was himself – or so I am told by Brother Eligius – skilled in the art. Brother Eligius is "scriba", or as it is called in gaelic, "scribhnidh", who transcribes and preserves sacred texts and ancient records.' Plenus scratched his head and hesitated for a moment as if about to say something else about the 'scriba' but evidently changed his mind, simply adding, 'You will meet him presently perhaps.'

The young pair caught each other's eye again with a little smile as if to say, 'I don't doubt we will.' Plenus was speaking again.

'Over there – ' he was indicating a long building to the north of the monk's cells ' – is the refectory where you may sometimes go, although you will mostly take your meals in the refectory in the guest house. Perhaps you should be grateful for that,' he added, giving his fleeting smile again, 'since your rations may be a little more plentiful than ours. It is another of our blessed founder's precepts that we should never take food until we are hungry, and any food, over and above what is required to sustain us, should be given to those in need – which is deemed to be you.'

Edith and James felt they should make some comment on this but being unable to think of one wisely kept silent.

'Our refectory is a homely place, nevertheless,' Plenus admitted, 'although we take our food in silence with a reading from holy scripture to sustain us spiritually. We have a special stone too where our bread and other food are blessed before being shared out. It is a huge flat boulder lying on it's side and we – at least my Celtic brethren – call it "moelblath" or "the stone of division". No one knows for certain where it came from but where else than from heaven, a gift from God.'

Plenus broke off and spun round on his heels to point towards a tiny hut, evidently constructed of planks, lying against a long rampart which formed the western boundary of the monastic enclosure.

'There,' he said reverently, 'is the cell of our sainted founder Columcille. Visit it when you can but always with respect because it is a holy place.'

He paused as if to add emphasis to the solemnity of his words then smiled at them again but in a warmer fashion than ever before. 'You may go anywhere you wish about the island,' he told them, 'except for those parts reserved for the monks alone which I have indicated to you, and which include the abbot's house. I must go,' he concluded. 'You have been most attentive and,' as if relenting in a final magnanimous gesture, 'I have done all the talking. Do you have any last question?'

James shook his head and looked at Edith who spoke without hesitation.

'You have been very gracious, Brother Plenus, and I have found everything you have said absorbing. B . . . But do you . . . perhaps . . . have a moment to tell us a little about your rule?'

Plenus looked surprised but not displeased at the question and answered after a moment's thought.

'There is much to tell and it would take too long to go into detail but I will say this. There are, in our founders rule, precepts for the religious life such as an insistance on the love of God with all our hearts and souls; to love our neighbour as ourselves like our Blessed Lord taught us to do; to abide by God's testament at all times; to pray . . .' Plenus stopped and seemed to have forgotten they were there, then went on as if answering by rote, 'To pray until tears come; to labour until tears come; to genuflect to God until sweat comes; to forgive everyone from our hearts; to pray constantly for those in trouble and . . .' with eyes tightly closed, 'to prepare our minds for martyrdom.'

There was silence for a while and when they both thought he had finished he began again more softly.

'To practice penances before all things; to eat only when hungry; to sleep only when exhausted; to speak only when necessary and to occupy ourselves in prayer, reading and work.'

He stopped suddenly, touched each on the shoulder and said, 'We are pleased you are here with us. You are welcome. It is time for Sext; farewell.'

The young couple watched his tall figure enter the chapel and, after a moment's discussion, decided to follow him. They ascended the staircase to the balcony, moving as quietly as possible so as not to disturb a man already kneeling there, hunched up with bowed head. They chose a place with a clear view of the nave where close on fifty monks were already assembled but no longer scattered throughout the chapel as they had been before, but kneeling together in front of the altar now that the office had begun. Their voices, singing and reciting in perfect unison, carried majestically up to the balcony moving the pair deeply. Their desperate flight from Penda and Cadwalla, the horrors of Catterick, their long voyage to Iona – all were forgotten in this Christian sanctuary on the edge of the world. Edith found she was hugging herself in sheer delight at her good fortune in finding this haven of tranquility with James beside her. He, with closed eyes and moving lips, was affected by the same emotions, letting the pealing voices of the monks wash over him in waves of contentment.

The office had been over for some time when they finally returned to reality. As they began to move from their places the figure, who had shared the balcony with them, stood up also and they recognised Prince Oswald. He smiled and motioned with his hand, indicating that they should precede him down the stairway. Outside, in the grey of the afternoon, they turned to await the prince.

'Good day to you both,' he said. 'I was intending to come to see you after Sext and here you are. I would like to talk to you, if I may. There is a room at the guest house we might use. My own hut, although more than large enough for one, will scarcely accommodate three. Do you have time to talk?'

'Of course, Your Highness, it will be our pleasure,' responded James smiling, whilst Edith nodded emphatically and added, 'Yes indeed, a pleasure.'

It was cool now so they wrapped themselves in their cloaks and set off briskly to their new home, so briskly in fact that Edith had to trot to keep up with them. Oswald, who was in the lead, turning to address a remark to them, saw Edith's haste and was full of apologies for his thoughtlessness and slowed down to fall in beside her for the remainder of the walk.

Some time later, seated round a little table in a room adjoining the guest house refectory, Oswald began the conversation.

'The Lord Abbot is indisposed, I fear far from well, in fact – and will not be able to meet you for some days. You will be a little lost by yourselves and I would like to spend some time with you tomorrow if you agree. There is much to see on the island and, if the Lady Edith would find it congenial, I would be delighted to be your guide. The local weather expert – Fursa, whom you know – assures me that we will get no rain for a day or two so it will be a good opportunity for you to find your bearings and learn your way around your new home.' He looked enquiringly at Edith who glanced towards James to get his reaction. He nodded at once and Edith was quick to accept the prince's offer.

'We would love to come, Your Highness. When I lived at York, and before that at my home in Catterick, I was outdoors, walking or riding, a great deal and I found the confinement of Fursa's boat something of a trial. Nothing would please me more than to spend the whole day exploring,' and with a gracious smile she added, 'especially with you, Your Highness, if we will not be a nuisance. Are you sure you can spare us so much of your time?'

'Gladly,' the prince answered, 'but with one condition. Here, in the community, I am not a prince or Your Highness. I am Oswald only, which you must call me and I will call you Edith and James. It will be time enough for "Your Highness" and "Prince" if we return to Northumbria which perhaps I should. You can help me too as we talk and get to know each other. I will not question you now but tomorrow, in return for my guided tour,' Oswald smiled at the phrase 'you must let me share my problems with you.'

Edith and James might have been alarmed at the prospect of hearing all the prince's troubles had he not been beaming at them as he spoke. He raised an eyebrow at them in enquiry?

'Of course . . . er . . . Oswald,' James answered first.

'It will be our pleasure your . . . Oswald,' replied Edith.

And so it proved to be.

On the following day they set off to the north west of the monastery when they had breakfasted after Holy Mass. Oswald took them, via Columba's cell, through an entrance in the west rampart and up the steep hill they had noticed on their arrival. Oswald called it Dunii and said it was more than three hundred feet above sea level. It was a stiff climb into a strong wind and Edith and James were glad of their extra garments which Fara had insisted they took with them while she washed and mended their own, which had suffered badly from their travels. Edith protested that she could do them herself but Fara would not listen. 'Tomorrow,' she had said, 'Tomorrow is time enough. Today you are still guests. Tomorrow you are residents. Go and enjoy yourselves.'

Once they had completed their climb they were treated to a spectacular view of the island. It lay on a line which ran from north east to south west and was a little over three and a half miles long and almost one and a half broad. The monastery was below them to the south east, in the northern part of the plain which sloped gently downwards to the sea and was bisected by the stream which they had crossed on the way to the monastery on their arrival.

This stream arose from a small lake at the foot of the southern slope of Dunii, which had once been marshy ground, Oswald said, until it had been excavated and dammed to create a sufficient flow of water to turn the mill wheel. Oswald pointed out the mill beside a kiln for drying the grain, and barns for storing it. Grassy hillocks were dotted about the vista below them and on one of these, in the centre of a flat plain which ran almost the whole way from east to west across the middle of the island, was a circle of stones.

James, who was the first to notice them, drew Edith's attention to them, asking Oswald at the same time, 'What are those?'

'Druid stones for pagan rites,' was the answer. 'The druids were here before Columba – indeed they tried to prevent his arrival by deceit. Two men came to his boat, as he came ashore, saying they were bishops. But the saint saw the devil in them both and, holding up his crucifix, he drove them and the devil out and they fled, leaving him in possession of all this.'

'All this' did indeed look more impressive the more they studied it.

To the north of where they were standing the land ran gently downwards from the foot of the hill to the shore. As they looked east a magnificent stretch of white sand could be seen, sweeping round the north east corner and continuing south almost to the monastery enclosure. The west of the island was rocky and wild, as was the south beyond the east-west plain. Oswald pointed out twin pinnacles which he called "uchdachan" or breasts – looking rather embarrased and avoiding Edith's eye as he said it. Then, farther to the west, they were just able to make out a cairn which Oswald simply called Columba's place, and which marked, he said, the spot where Columba had stood to make sure he could no longer see Ireland.

Seeing them both somewhat puzzled by this he laughed and added, 'I shall have to tell you more about the founder, I can see. Let us find a comfortable spot and I will tell you the story.'

They found a sheltered place looking south into the watery, winter sun and James and Edith settled down side by side facing Oswald and eager to hear his tale.

'Columba is a saint,' he began, 'but was not always so. When he was a younger man in Ireland he was fired by tremendous zeal. He founded monastery after monastery, the first in Derry in the year five forty-six on land given to him by his own tribe, Clan Niall. Perhaps his success went to his head, as it did to many, and made him ambitious for even more wordly power and influence. Although highly regarded throughout the length and breadth of the island, for his holiness and wonderful eloquence, he was, it must be admitted, a man of fiery temper and even, at times, vindictive. Above all he was proud – proud of being a prince of the royal blood of Ireland. St Cormac called him "a king's son of reddened valour" – and his pride was indeed a deadly sin for him.'

Oswald paused briefly to collect his thoughts before resuming his account.

'Columba was, by repute at least, a transcriber of holy books of considerable skill. The beauty of the illustrated sacred text held a fascination for him which eventually brought matters to a head. On one occasion, when living in the house of his teacher, Finbar of Moville, Columba stole a codex of the gospels and copied it without permission. When this sly deed was discovered, the king, Diarmait MacCerball, was asked to rule on whether Columba should be allowed to keep the copy or not. The king made a famous judgement that the book should be returned since, in his words, "To every cow belongs her calf".'

The decision enraged Columba who, filled with bitterness, stirred up his clansmen of Niall to rebel against King Diarmait. Columba's tribesmen attacked the king's forces at a place called Cooldrevny and defeated them with greater slaughter. That it was at Columb'a instigation cannot be doubted, and it caused such resentment throughout Ireland that, on the advice of his confessor, St Molaise, he elected to make his reparation to God in a foreign land and chose to follow those Scots before him who had already evangelised part of south west Alban.

'Taking twelve disciples with him he sailed away from his native country, determined not to settle until he was no longer able to see it. How many places he visited we do not know – there was one for certain, called, Oronsay, where he climbed the highest hill but Ireland was still in sight. Eventually, on Pentacost Sunday, which was the thirteenth of May in the year five sixty-three, the saint's boat negotiated a difficult passage through the rocks on the southern tip of this island – there,' emphasised Oswald, pointing with his outstretched hand to the cairn, adding, 'at the foot of the cliff below that point. I am no sailor,' he admitted, 'but I do not think an expert, even Fursa, would wish to take his boat into the mouth of the tiny creek where the sainted Columba landed. We call the spot the "bay of the coracle" or in gaelic "Port-na-Churaich".

'It is a beautiful spot to visit, but not in winter,' laughed Oswald, pretending to shiver in an imaginary wind. 'In spring, when the weather improves, you must go there. It is spectacular – sheer cliffs falling to a beach of pebbles of marvellous colours; red feldspar, light green quartz and dark green serpentine, mottled and spotted like a snake's skin.'

Oswald stopped and began to look uncertain and troubled, as he had done when they had first told him of the barbarian's victory in Northumbria. Then he rose and turned half round to face south east with a strange expression on his face.

'Columba climbed to that spot where you can see that cairn,' Oswald was pointing due south towards the cairn but still gazing intently south east. 'It was from that spot that he realised that he could no longer see Ireland and had found a new home.'

Edith and James had no wish to break the silence which followed, each aware that, suddenly, Oswald's tale had become deadly serious but in a way they could not understand. The prince turned back to them again and came nearer to crouch down in front of them, taking their hands in his own as he did so.

'Columba was advised by St Molaise what he should do,' he said softly. 'Tell *me* what *I* must do. Columba went to war and caused bloody slaughter for which he was rightly condemned. Will I be condemned if I make war on Penda and Cadwalla and bring death and destruction to my own country? Will I?'

James remained silent as if too surprised by the prince's question to answer but Edith replied at once.

'I think I had just begun to realise your dilemma, Your Highness – I'm sorry, Oswald, but in this matter you are Your Highness. It came to me just now as I watched you looking out towards Northumbria, and I remembered your concern when we first met and I told you about Father Melchior. There is an easy answer to your question. No! No one will ever censure you if you wage war on that fiendish pair. Columba, from what you say, made his war out of bitterness and a desire for revenge. It would have been wrong for anyone to fight for those reasons but, especially, a man of God. But if you were to gather an army and attack Cadwalla and Penda bitterness and revenge would not be your motives nor a desire to seize the throne for temporal power. I know that you feel compelled to do it to bring your country back to Christ and to restore the peace of God which all enjoyed during the Christian reign of King Edwin. That would be something you would do for Almighty God, Your Highness, not, as Columba did, for base wordly reasons.'

James, who had been listening as intently as Oswald, looked admiringly at Edith. Oswald watched her too for some minutes and she steadily returned his gaze. Then he took her hand and slowly raised it to his lips. He smiled, including James also as he did so, and said simply, 'Thank you. Thank you for your wisdom and your honesty and courage. You have shown me what I must do so clearly that I wonder why I could not see it before. I think perhaps,' he continued, now in obvious delight that his doubts had been dispelled, 'that I did not want to see it. I was too content here, serving God in peace and tranquility. I didn't want to do what in my heart of hearts I knew I should. You were quite right, Edith – how perceptive of you to realise it – it was your story of Father Melchior turning his back on safety and returning into danger that upset me. Well – ' and he stood up decisively and offered a hand to each to help them to their feet ' – now I know what I must do, thanks to you. Let us continue our tour. I will show you what I can while the day lasts.'

Now all in high spirits they went first to the central plain and climbed the hillock with the ring of stones on it's summit. Oswald, as if fired by religious zeal, knelt to thank Almighty God and to ask that he too should overcome the heathen as effectively as Columba had the druids. Then they returned round the western and northern slopes of Dunii to the white beach in the northeast. They were like children, happily playing barefoot in the sand, coming as close as they could to the sea washing in towards them and jumping away with shrieks of laughter.

It was almost dark when they returned to the monastery. Vespers had just begun and without hesitation they made their way to the chapel to join the holy office. The hymn had been sung and the first of the two psalms was being recited with some solemnity when they entered. The versicles and the responses which followed were impressive but the magnificat was glorious and moved the trio deeply after their emotion and enjoyment of the day. When the final prayers were over Oswald leaned towards them and whispered, 'Go if you wish. I will stay a while longer. Now that I know what I have to do I must pray for the strength to do it. You have helped me more than you will ever know. Tomorrow I will visit the abbot to ask when he will see you. Goodnight and enjoy the rest you deserve.'

Their reception by everyone they had met on Iona had been so cordial that it came as a surprise to James that his acceptance by the scriba was less than willing.

Brother Eligius was an old man who had become intolerant of incursions by others into what he considered to be *his* scriptorium. The tradition of sacred embellishment, which had come with Columba to Iona, was something of which the scriba was intensely proud and the notion that others might possess similar ability was dismissed out of hand. What Fursa had told them all of the crude attempts at decoration made by the monks of Whithorn had confirmed his belief that no art worthy of the name existed on the mainland. A Saxon could not possibly be expected to be capable of anything other than the most amateurish efforts at illumination. Indeed it had taken a direct order from Abbot Segenus to induce Eligius to see James in the scriptorium at all. Not surprisingly the young man's reception was cool.

'I am told you aspire to be an artist,' were the old man's first words.

James had been left standing before the scriba who continued to devote the whole of his attention to the manuscript he was studying without even a glance at his prospective recruit. Grateful for the warning that Fursa had given him James answered quietly.

'It has been my hope since I was a boy that one day I might call myself that; but there is a lot to learn and I am sure much room for improvement.'

'I expect there is,' sniffed Eligius, 'we will see how much presently.' He raised his eyes to the figure standing patiently before him and continued in abrupt fashion.

'You have, I suppose, received *some* training?'

'Less than I would have wished,' responded James disarmingly. 'My initial training was from the holy Father Birinus, who came to Britain some years after Augustine and his party landed in Kent and evangelised the region. Father Birinus had been a skilful artist when younger and was able to instruct me for almost two years before he died – God rest his soul. Since then I have tried to put into practice what I learned from him and to develop ideas of my own of which I hope,' James added modestly, 'he would have approved.'

Since Eligius had returned to his manuscript, and no comment was forthcoming upon what had been said, James thought he ought to continue.

'I hope that I might learn much from you, Brother Eligius, with your great knowledge of the tradition which your blessed founder brought with him. It is clear to me,' James went on, 'even as I stand here before you that there is much from which I may benefit.'

Eligius looked up abruptly as though suspecting flattery but found his companion looking so intently at the manuscript on the table that, intrigued despite himself by the young man's obvious interest, the monk became more affable.

'You will never have seen the like of this, I know. You had better come round this side and look at it properly. This is the Cathach of St Columba – the psalter he himself copied before leaving his native land for this island. Did you ever gaze upon such artistry?'

James was, indeed, fascinated by the psalter, not because of its design and colouring so much as for the script in which it was written which was entirely foreign to him. The lettering was neatly executed with a fine nib and, although some variation in the width detracted a little from it's regularity, it was altogether a creditable work. It was bold and striking if a little garish in concept, which did not surprise James when he recalled Oswald's account of the kind of man Columba had been. However this was plainly not the moment for the expression of anything other than praise. With as much fervour as he could muster he exclaimed, 'Marvellous, such artistry, wonderful,' and unable to bring himself to dissemble longer lapsed into silence.

There was a chuckle of satisfaction from the scriba whose expression had become almost benign at the apparent effect the Cathach had had on this presumputous Saxon.

'I thought that would startle you. Do you think you, or anyone else, could ever produce a work like that?'

James unable to think of a suitable reply to this shook his head solemnly from side to side.

'May I enquire about the script, Brother Eligius,' he asked after a moment. 'I have seen nothing like it before. It is quite different from the uncial lettering I am familiar with. Can you tell me about it?'

Plainly mollified by the impact the manuscript had had Eligius began to expound.

'It is called Irish Majuscule and has been used in that country for over two hundred years. It is comparable for those Gospels which are to be used on ceremonial occasions. There is a simpler form of it employed only for everyday work known as miniscule – which I could show you,' the monk added, now clearly accepting the notion that James *might* enter the scriptorium. 'You will have to master it if you are to be any use to me, and,' returning to his early brusque manner, 'the good Lord alone knows how long that will take. Whatever you learned of Roman ways you had better forget. If you are to work here you must do things our way.'

There was a pause during which Eligius seemed to be trying to decide whether to accept James or not, subjecting him to critical scrutiny the while. Eventually, when James was beginning to become distinctly uncomfortable, the scriba, somewhat grudgingly grunted and said, 'It's too late today to make a start. Be here tomorrow early and, if you have any of your own work to show me, bring it with you.'

That had been that, James, dismissed, had departed uncertainly wondering whether to ask Fursa if he might borrow the parchment prepared on the last days at Whithorn, or if this would be regarded by the critical Eligius as too frivolous a subject.

Fursa left him in no doubt.

'Should you take it to show him? Certainly you must take it and I'm coming with you. I wouldn't miss it for worlds. I want to see the expression on his face when he sees it as I told you before.' And James remembered the fat man's words at Whithorn, which he had not understood at the time 'Wait till he sees it.'

However much Fursa was looking forward to the encounter James was not since he had no wish to be the instrument of discomfitting the old man whom, in a curious fashion and despite his cantankerous nature, James had quite liked.

In the event Eligius, true artist that he was, had taken the demonstration of his new pupil's skill surprisingly well. He had bent over the painting for some moments with a frown, glaring up just once at Fursa as though realising how much the grinning boatman was enjoying it. Finally he straightened up and, ingnoring Fursa completely, took James by the hand.

'It is not God's work,' he said solemnly, 'but it is fine work.' And he could not resist adding, 'would that your subject had been worthy of it. You are already a fine artist – better I admit than I had thought possible. I can teach you nothing about art but, if you are to work here – and I accept you willingly – you must learn majuscule. *That* I can teach you.'

Then giving James a little smile which was immediately followed by a frown, he turned to Fursa.

'As for you, this is more than you deserve – far more. Take it and be gone. We have work to do.'

James was accepted.

Two days after Christmas the chapel was filled with the entire community for the marriage of Edith and James.

Oswald had been as good as his word and, soon after the abbot's complete recovery, the young couple had been sent for, not only so that Segenus could hear the news of the devastation in Northumbria at first hand, but so that he could give his consent to their wedding. Oswald again acted as their interpreter.

The abbot had been kind and gracious.

'The marriage of two young people,' he said, pausing patiently for Oswald to translate each phrase, 'has always been a cause for celebration in the Church. There is, as yet, no fixed liturgy for the marriage service but the Holy Sacrifice of the Mass should, if possible, be an integral part of it. At one time,' Segenus continued, clearly warming to his theme, 'even the presence of a priest was not essential since, in the early Church, priests were few and couples wishing to marry many. But, wherever possible, not only was it desirable that a priest should officiate but the permission of a priest or bishop was to be sought beforehand – as you are doing now,' smiled Segenus approvingly.

'St Polycarp one of the glorious martyrs of the early Church, wrote in such terms to St Ignatius saying, "It is fitting that the groom and bride enter matrimony with the advice of the bishop so that their marriage will be according to God and not according to concupiscence". Tertullian tells us, "Marriage is made by the Church, confirmed by the offering of the Holy Sacrifice, sealed by the bishop, proclaimed by the angels and ratified by our Father in heaven." So you see it is truly "holy" wedlock into which you are entering and I must satisfy myself that there is no impediment which would render the contract invalid.'

'Are you in any kind of blood relationship, the one with the other?' He looked enquiringly at both.

It was James who answered.

'No, my Lord Abbot. I was born in Kent and the Lady Edith in Northumbria and there can be no possibility of a close kinship between us.'

'Do you both consent to the union?'

'Yes willingly.'

'With all my heart.'

'Has either of you entered a previous contract of marriage?'

James shook his head and Edith said, 'No, my Lord Abbot.'

The abbot nodded approvingly, as Oswald translated the denial, then smiled and said, 'The consent of your parents should be obtained, if possible,' then, seeing the expression of dismay on both their faces, he continued quickly, 'but it is clearly impracticable since we do not know where they are nor, sadly, if they are still alive. So there remains only the matter of the banns – the publication of your intention to marry so that an opportunity can be given for any impediment, of which you may be unaware, to be brought to our notice. Even the banns, in special cases, can be dispensed with but we need not do so in your case. We can comply with the condition without there being any delay. It will be advent in a few days time and your marriage could not be solemnised then. The congregation will be told of your intention to marry when Holy Mass is said on the next three Sundays and your wedding can be – shall we say – a day or two after Christmas, our Lord's birthday.'

Preparations required to be made, Edith, with her experience as a needlewoman, undertook the unusual task of making not only her own bridal clothes but James' as well. Fara was in the seventh heaven and brought materials of all kinds for Edith to use. James feeling, like other bridegrooms, rather in the way, took himself off to the scriptorium where he and the repentant Eligius had established a relationship based on their mutual love for, and skill at, sacred illumination.

The bishop had specially asked to see them and had been warm in his congratulation and good wishes for their happiness. Neither Edith nor James had yet become accustomed to the notion of a bishop who was subsidiary to the abbot. A bishop was necessary for certain ecclesiastical duties, such as the ordination of a priest, but in all other respects the abbot ruled. Bishop Gobban, well known as a severe man, had a forbidding countenance, which they found alarming when they were shown into his presence, but he became more affable after Oswald had spoken to him for a few minutes and seemed genuine in his expression of goodwill.

The weeks of advent were filled with many delightful experiences for them both. Once the news became known they were stopped constantly by the people they met in the course of the day, with congratulations, hopes for their future happiness and offers of help. The entire community seemed to have taken them to it's heart and the notion of a marriage service, a rarity on the island, was clearly meeting with general approval.

Then the little presents started to arrive. No one had much to give but many wanted to give something. There was a little embroidered mat, for a small table in the room they had been given, from Briga, the wife of a herdsman, whose company Edith enjoyed; a delicate carved figure of a seal from one of the men who tended the sheep and was renowned for this skill; some sea shells gathered on the shore by one of the fishermen; an elegant fan of seabird feathers from Shilde, the teenage daughter of a tiny wizened pigman who donated a handsome leather belt for James to wear at the wedding, saying that he himself had become so thin now that it no longer held anything up; a cloak for each of them from the tailor, Brother Erasmus; a wedding cake decorated with two tiny figures from Brother Mark, the baker and many more simple offerings.

The abbot had been extremely kind and had said, through Oswald, that apart from a few of the brethren who had special skills, like Brother Erasmus, the rest had no way of contributing a personal gift; Segenus hoped that James and Edith would accept a collective gift of their wedding feast in the monk's refectory which, on this occasion, they would make as lavish as their rule allowed and the resources of the island could provide.

Three days before the ceremony Fursa brought a touching gift. It was a small piece of driftwood of elegant shape which he had dried and polished with great care. It's texture was now glistening smooth and the wood was shot through with patterns of light and dark which reflected the flickering candlelight with great beauty.

On the same day they received another surprise. Brother Eligius came to the guest house bringing six double sheets of parchment, several styli and a number of pots of pigment. The once forbidding 'scriba' offered his gift with simple grace, stressing that, although the resources of the scriptorium would always be at James' disposal for any work he might do for the community, these materials were for his own personal use. As James, delighted with the gift and the old man's kindness, offered his thanks Eligius turned with genuine sadness to Edith and said, 'I cannot, I fear, offer you any gift, my Lady; I can only hope you will share in whatever pleasure your husband-to-be will get from these.'

Edith was charmed and so far forgot herself as to give the monk a little kiss on the cheek whereupon he blushed deeply, then laughed, took both their hands in his and was gone.

Finally, on the last day before the wedding they had a visit from Oswald who had been unaccountably absent the previous day. They now realised why. Looking tired but cheerful he offered them a small wooden box saying, 'I have nothing left to give you since everything from my former life has been disposed of. So will you accept these as a tiny offering which I hope will please you.'

Inside was quartz, feldspar and serpentine gathered from Columba's landing place and gleaming in wonderful colours as Edith shook them out into the candlelight. She was almost speechless with delight.

'Oh, Oswald. Oh. You went all the way in this weather for these. They're beautiful. How can we thank you,' and she had tears in her eyes as she kissed his cheek whilst James, also entranced by their beauty, shook Oswald's hand and clasped his shoulder as the prince beamed in happiness at the reception of his present.

Now they were kneeling together at the foot of the altar in front of the entire community. The bishop, himself, had celebrated the High Mass and made it a sacrifice of awesome solemnity. He had a deep resounding voice and when he sang the opening words of the 'Gloria in Excelsis Deo' and the 'Credo in Unum Deum', to be followed by the brethren chanting the familiar words with practised skill Edith was so deeply moved that she leant towards James for the reassurance of their arms touching briefly together.

The Holy Mass contained a solemn litany of Irish saints sung in gaelic but, that apart, Latin was used throughout until the marriage service itself was reached. Oswald, as James' best man, had coached them both in the few words of gaelic they needed to know.

'Will you, James, take this woman Edith, to be your wife, to keep her, from this time forward, whatever may befall you and love her, in accordance with God's decree for the rest of your life?'

'I will.'

'And will you, Edith, take James as your husband and love him and minister to him and, in God's good time, bear his children and keep yourself only for him for the rest of your life?'

'I will.'

'Does anyone here know of any impediment to this union?'

The bishop had scarcely paused before continuing.

'I declare that you are man and wife, and may the blessing of Almighty God and of the holy St Columba go with you.'

Their wedding feast had been an occasion such as the monastery had not seen before. The wedding cake was enormous and was placed in the middle of the flat boulder stone, and there was much laughter when it proved to be too far away to reach across the expanse of rock when the time came to cut it. A monk had solemnly climbed onto the stone and moved the cake nearer to them. They used Oswald's sword to cut it – the only princely item which remained from his previous life – and everybody cheered. James and Edith, at the centre of the long refectory table at the top of the room marvelled at the splendid occasion which had been arranged for them and, time and again, squeezed each other's hands beneath the table as if still unable to believe their good fortune. By very special permission ale was allowed on that occasion and, when the health of the bride and groom was drunk, with the entire community standing and holding out their goblets before them, Edith could not keep back a few tears of happiness and James had some trouble doing so.

Then he had risen to express his thanks for them both. Everyone had cheered again with unmonastic abandon, when he said the only words in the speech he attempted in gaelic "my wife and I."

The rest, as always, Oswald had translated as James tried to stammer their gratitude.

'You are no strangers to hardship and penance here,' he had said, 'so you will understand what, 'my wife and I' endured in our escape from barbarians and what a haven of holiness and peace and happiness we have found in your community, of which we now feel a part.' He had stopped for a moment and shaken his head in a bewildered fashion before ending, 'I'm sorry, I am too full to find words except, "thank you".'

Edith slept in his arms after their lovemaking that night. It had been blissful – far beyond the expectations of either. James held her gently listening to her regular breathing until hours later, he realised that they had fallen asleep in each other's arms. The first glimpses of light were streaking the sky. It was the beginning of their first day of married life together.

Chapter 6

The rays of the late afternoon sun slanted into the scriptorium illuminating the text James was studying – or not studying for his attention had wandered. It had been a long, cold, stormy winter and it was already mid April before the few glimpses of the sun they had seen had any warmth in them. With this first sign of spring flooding in onto him at last he had abandoned his work and was basking in the unaccustomed warmth.

James remembered the Kent of his boyhood when days were long and hot and dry – had it ever rained he wondered? It seemed not now, so long after. Northumbria had been colder and bleaker but with a stark moorland beauty the soft south east had not known. Here, in the isolation of this island – and island off an island off another island, James remembered from their voyage with Fursa – there was both a savagery and a tranquillity he had not experienced before. The storms of the winter had been beyond his belief on some days. Sheets of rain had been driven by powerful winds from the west. They had shut their doors and barred their windows and stuffed crevices and huddled inside layers of clothing before huge fires which Maban and Fara always seemed to keep ablaze. James had thought spring would never come but here, at last, was the sun enticing him away from his study of this fascinating Irish calligraphy and encouraging idle thoughts in it's soft golden light.

He smiled to himself as he remembered that, despite the harsh winter, it had been an idyllic time for himself and Edith. Though only a few months married, it seemed he could hardly remember a time she was not there. So happy were they together that they could lose themselves in each other's company and be oblivious of their surroundings. For the first time, since he had been introduced to religious artistry by Father Birinus, he had been obliged to force himself to apply his mind to it and, at first, it had only been Edith's urging that had kept him at his work.

The prince had left them more than a month ago now and, as yet, no reports of his success had been received. Edith and James had missed him at first. He had been so much in their company and the three had formed such a friendly group together that they had felt his departure keenly. But their initial loneliness disappeared as their familiarity with the gaelic language allowed them to become more active members of the community; Edith was now speaking fluently and James was improving steadily.

Two small rooms had been given to them in a wing of the guest house affording them privacy when they wished it yet permitting them to live with the lay community and establish companionable relationships with several people. Edith enjoyed the company of Briga, whose husband tended the sheep and goats, and of Shilde, whose father was the pigman.

As James had returned to his manuscripts, Edith had begun an artistic endeavour of her own. Intrigued by the beauty of the vestments, which had been brought from Ireland after the community was established, she asked the abbot's permission to repair several which she had noticed were now old and tattered, with their embroidery frayed and stained. He had willingly agreed and, when the more important repairs had been done, she had begun to make new vestments, one of which, with James' help in designing the decoration, was almost ready.

Now that he was proficient in the Irish majuscule form of writing it intrigued him more and more. It was unlike the formal uncial script he had known when he came to Iona and, after his initial surprise at seeing a new way of forming letters, he was finding it increasingly to his liking. It had a more rounded flowing form to it, especially when written with a broad nib, a modification which Eligius had introduced. James had adopted these broad even letters from the beginning and was using them for the gospel of St Matthew which he was just finishing.

His designs were based closely on the original copy he had made at York but were more intricate and elaborate with a greater number of animals and birds weaving their delicate criss-cross patterns, leaving scarcely any part of the decorated portion free from his artistry.

Eligius had shown him some examples of another script called Irish miniscule which was simpler and less formal and used only for those books which would not be read on ceremonial occasions. James had practised it a little to achieve familiarity but had no occasion to use it since his St Matthew gospel was intended for formal use in the monastery chapel where only the best was good enough.

Now it was time to get on. St Matthew would soon be ready and he could move on to St Mark.

Oswald had always known that it would not be easy to raise a large army.

The Kingdom of Dalriada, which had been settled by the Scots from the northern parts of Ireland, had the same strong Christian tradition. Oswald had been hopeful that the king, Domnal Brech, could be persuaded to commit substantial forces to march against Cadwalla but His Majesty would not provide more than one hundred and fifty men whom Oswald was obliged to accept with a good grace and try his luck with the Picts.

The Picts had always been an uncertain quantity. Those in the far north occupied the full extent of the island from sea to sea. It was wild inhospitable country, where small groups of inhabitants lived in relative isolation in deep valleys, separated from each other by towering crags and harsh, bare hillsides. The southern Picts – sometimes united with those from the north under one king, but often boasting an independent ruler – occupied land as far south as the Firth of Forth which also formed the upper boundary of Northumbria. To the east they possessed a long seaboard and to the west they abutted onto the border of Dalriada. Columba himself had evangelised most of the region after converting the king, Brude, and although some of the later rulers had been less devout, Oswald was hopeful that his enterprise against the heathen would appeal to the present king, Garnaid. Again it had been a hard row to hoe and Oswald had come out of it with a promise of only one hundred men and as many volunteers as he could find. These had been few and he still had a total of less than three hundred in all when he went south to try his luck with Ednoch Brede, King of the Nidwari Picts of Galloway.

The unsettled state of Galloway which had led to the flight of the monks from Whithorn, when Edith and James passed through, had become stabilised under the new king. Whithorn had been re-established as a religious centre, although not yet approaching it's former glory. Ednoch had encouraged the monks to preach widely throughout the area and many of the population had returned to the Faith. Oswald was again hopeful of a sympathetic hearing, especially as the immediate territory to the east, Strathclyde, was settled by Britons who might choose to throw in their lot with Cadwalla and Penda, so threatening Galloway's new-found stability. Nonetheless the Nidwari Picts were few and Oswald considered he would be lucky to come away with one hundred and fifty. He got one hundred.

Now, as he rode with them north east, to join the main body of his force on the south bank of the Forth, he pondered the inferiority of his numbers. He could only hope to march into Bernicia and launch a surprise attack with rather less than four hundred men. And how many had they? Eight hundred? One thousand perhaps, more even? Oswald needed a brilliant plan, or a lot of luck, or Almighty God coming in on his side – or all three.

At least the preparations were complete. Midsummer was passed and within a month battle would be joined. Oswald decided that he needed supernatural help as never before. Well, if prayer could do it he did not intend to be found wanting. It would be a long ride and there would be plenty of time to ask the Lord's help.

'James, for the love of God, come at once.'

James, hard at work on the initial page of St Mark's gospel, was oblivious, as always, of his surroundings but the words finally penetrated his consciousness. Maban, purple in the face from running all the way from the guest house, was calling him again.

'James, it is Edith. You must come.'

Dropping his stylus, James seized Maban by the coat, shouting 'What is it? What has happened? Tell me.'

'Go,' gasped Maban, scarcely able to get his breath, let alone speak. 'Can't explain. Go.'

His urgency was not lost on the young man who was out of the door of the scriptorium and down the steps, running with all his might for the guest house. What could be wrong? She wasn't . . . she couldn't be . . . dead. Please God, let her not be dead. Don't let her die.

Shilde was there at the door as he panted to a halt.

'Where is she? Is she in our rooms? Tell me quickly.'

'James, thank God you are here. Fara and Briga are with her. Come at once. Fara says it is . . . must be . . . a miscarriage.'

'Miscarriage!' James could scarcely comprehend it as he paused before the bedroom door, fearful, at first, of what he might find inside. Shilde pushed it open, pushed him through without ceremony and followed him in.

It had been almost two weeks before James could bring himself to believe that Edith would not die. After a month, she could sit out in the warm sun and after two months she almost looked her old self.

But her physical illness had been so serious that the sadness of losing her baby had not impinged fully on her consciousness. She had wanted to get better for James but, as she grew physically stronger, she became emotionally more tense and prone to silence. James would find her sitting absolutely still, staring straight in front of her, the work she was engaged in forgotten. Much of her former spirit had left her and seldom, and only briefly, was her old spark apparent. He would return from the scriptorium at the end of the day to find her morose, depressed and silent. Thoughts of her lost child seemed to be always on her mind and, time and again, she would ask James to tell her about the baby, lying lifeless in his two hands, as Brother Linus the infirmariah baptised him, although she hardly ever reacted when he told her the story.

At last, James, at his wits end to know what to do, went back to Linus for help. The monk again listened patiently but, this time, could offer no assistance.

'I have little experience of these things,' he admitted sadly. 'The mind is a strange thing. It can rise above pain and it can cause pain when there should be none. But I do not know how to cure it's problems.'

He was silent for so long that James had given up hope that he would be any help, and was about to open the infirmary door to leave, when Linus spoke again.

'There is one here who might help – if he will. There was an occasion, some years ago, when one of the monks was badly affected in the mind – I need not tell you how – and this brother helped him. He would never tell us what he did but he might agree to try again. We would need the abbot's permission of course, but I think he will agree. Come with me.'

Segenus had listened to Brother Linus's account of Edith's state and, without hesitation, had agreed.

'We have all been given some skills – a few like you James of exceptional quality – and we must use them to the greater glory of God and not, as the poor man in the parable buried his five talents in the ground. You have my permission to ask Brother Aidan if he will try to help. I will not order him to do so. That must be his choice.'

Brother Aidan was reluctant to help – that much was clear to them both when James made his request. The monk was a small, thin, pale man, of perhaps thirty years of age, and with a fragility which made it almost impossible to believe that he was capable, by Brother Linus account, of extraordinary fasts and prolonged vigils without sleep in the chapel. His face had a distant expression as though he were looking beyond them into a totally different world. When James asked him to help he sat absolutely still for a long time and the young man was about to repeat his request before Linus motioned him to silence. Eventually Aidan turned slowly and addressed James.

'I recall with great pleasure your wedding at Christmas in which we all took part.' His voice was surprisingly deep and mellow for such a slight frame. 'The joys, and sorrows,' he smiled fleetingly, 'of matrimony are something we, within the brethren, have given up for God but that does not mean we do not regard the married state highly. It was a privilege to be present at your marriage feast and to see your wonderful happiness together. I was distressed to hear of your wife's miscarriage of your son and am deeply sorry to learn that she is so affected by the loss.'

Aidan paused for a moment, rose to his feet, adjusted his girdle around his thin frame and concluded, 'I will try to help. The mind is a strange thing. It is true that I have helped one or two in the past although I have not always known how. I will try. Take me to her.'

Linus had left them together and James had escorted Aidan to his room. Edith rose at their entrance and Aidan motioned her to be seated and smiled at her kindly. Seating himself opposite her he indicated that James should remain in the background, then began to speak in his beautifully mellow voice which seemed immediately to have a calming effect on her.

'I have been told about your sad loss, my child. What you have been through is disturbing to us all in the community who have come to regard you and your husband so highly. I know that you have not been able to put the memory of these terrible events out of your mind – even with God's help, for which I am sure you and James have asked. But God sometimes gives his help in unusual ways, and through strange agencies, and it is possible, my child, that He may choose to help you through me.'

Edith was staring intently at Aidan as he was speaking, seemingly unable to take her eyes off his face.

'You are watching me closely,' he continued, his voice even deeper than ever and so soothing that James was aware of a total calm pervading the room. 'That is what I wish you to do, Edith – to watch me carefully when we talk about it all.

'Do you recall that our Blessed Lord wept with compassion over Jerusalem? That the Blessed Virgin Mary wept for her dead son when she held Him in her arms after He was taken down from the cross? That St Peter wept at the appalling realisation that he had denied Christ three times? That St Mary Magdalen washed our Lord's feet with her tears? That the widow of Naim wept for her only son who had died and Jairus for his dead daughter?'

James, watching closely saw that Edith's eyes were half closed, her expression relaxed, her breathing so soft that the movement of her gown was scarcely perceptible. Aidan, he noticed, had raised a finger and was holding it straight up between Edith's eyes and his own. The monk continued to speak quietly to Edith.

'Tears cleanse the mind, my child. They wash away pain. They let grief flow more freely. Weep for your son, Edith. Weep for your memory of him. Your grief has been within you and must emerge. You have a torrent – a raging torrent – inside you that must force it's way out. Edith! Edith, let it break out. Let it come. Don't hold it back. That's right. Tears should flow . . . flow . . . flow.'

James watched fascinated, as Edith's face changed visibly while Aidan was speaking. The eyes puckered, the lids became moist, the trickle of tears fell and a torrent replaced the trickle, cascading down her face whilst she sat motionless, still facing directly towards the little monk.

'There are many more tears to come, Edith,' Aidan was saying, 'three months of tears which have been kept locked up inside. Sorrow cannot be confined like that without the mind suffering. That is good,' as more and more tears fell, 'you will be better now; so much better. I will leave you but James will stay. You can sleep for just a short time – that is right, sleep a little. Edith, for the first time, had taken her eyes off the monk and lowering her head to her arms she was fast asleep.

Aidan rose and spoke softly to James. 'Stay with her for as long as you can. She will not sleep long. Then talk to her about anything. Keep her spirits up if you can. You will find it easier than before. We have made a good beginning. I will come again in the morning.'

The next session followed a similar pattern with Edith watching Aidan intently and he talking in his sonorous voice until her tears began again. Each time Aidan left her sleeping but after the fourth occasion his instructions to James were different.

'Take her out, James. It is a beautiful day. Go anywhere, but if it can be somewhere with pleasant memories for her so much the better. You will find I think that she will enjoy it. I will come again tomorrow do not fear.'

Edith had slept for only a little while and afterwards they had gone out and climbed Dunii but, this time, in the heat of the summer. They were gasping for breath at the top and laughing together as they had not done since Edith's miscarriage. James could not believe the change and so was doubly alarmed when, after some time, she said to him:

'Tell it to me James. Tell me again . . . about . . . how you held him.'

He had told her, of course, with trepidation, at first, until he realised that this time it was different. She had begun to weep almost as soon as he had started speaking. He had stopped in alarm but she motioned him to continue. She had cried steadily throughout his account and, when it came to an end, she crouched beside him, lowered her head to his lap and wound her arms round his knees, as she had done by the Solway on their journey to Whithorn. Then she simply said, 'Thank you. I love you. Please love me again. Please. Like we used to do.'

So they had made love, passionately, blissfully, alone on the mountainside, for the first time since their son had been lost.

Aidan had come the next day and the one after that but the pattern of the earlier meetings had not been repeated. He had remained silent, except for the occasional probing question and Edith had been made to talk about everything relating to her illness.

What could she remember? When had she first realised she was going to lose the child? What had her reaction been? Could she remember James coming? Could she recall who else had been there? Had she known anyone else who had miscarried? Had they been affected by it as she had been? What were her first thoughts on regaining consciousness? How soon would she like another child?

She recalled a surprising amount it seemed. She remembered her panic when the bleeding began and being brought almost to her knees by the first pain as she went to find Fara. She sensed Fara's anxiety as she called frantically for Shilde to fetch Briga. She remembered being helped back to her room and the blood running down her legs and the pains – would they never stop? She remembered the room spinning and Fara's face coming and going and one enormous pain and then the blood; she supposed it was the blood – wetness, at all events, all over her feet and legs and the bed. Then she remembered nothing more until she had opened her eyes and found she was lying on her side with Jamie's face only a few inches away from hers. She had been unable to understand why, during the day, he was not at the scriptorium. Then it had all come back to her and, panic-stricken, she had felt for the swelling in the lower part of her stomach which she could no longer feel.

Edith paused in her recollection at that point before adding, 'I knew then that it had happened but I dare not ask as if not knowing would bring it back.'

Once into her stride she had been unable to stop and the monk had made no attempt to stop her. But whenever she hesitated for a few moments he was there with the next question. Edith answered every one readily and often at extraordinary length, showing no reluctance to discuss any subject Aidan introduced until he asked:

'How soon would you like another child?'

She hesitated and, for the first time, seemed unhappy. Then she smiled at Aidan and answered in a careful voice, 'I thought I was ready for that question and I said to myself that I would answer it at once. But if I had done that the answer would have been only partly true. Until yesterday I think I would have answered, "never", that I could not bear to go through that experience again, not even for you,' turning to James and smiling as she said it. 'But now I have no hesitation in saying, "at once" if that is what James would like. Immediately.'

Aidan's last question was the other she did not answer promptly.

'Has it affected your feeling for your husband?'

Although she did not reply at once she showed no uneasiness. She had been looking straight at Aidan as question after question came her way. Now she turned to face James. She was no longer addressing the monk but speaking directly to her husband.

'I hadn't expected that question, I must admit,' giving a little smile 'and again I almost answered at once, "no of course not".' James beamed as she said it and made to move towards her until she put out a restraining hand. 'But if I had said 'no' it would not have been true for it has affected my feelings for you – they are deeper and stronger than ever before, although I loved you so much, my dear, it does not seem possible they could be. But they are. Oh, yes, they are,' and turning to Aidan, she answered him this time.

'Yes, it has affected my feelings for my husband. I love him with all my heart and soul and all I wish to do is to make him happy.'

Then she had burst instantly into tears and James had left his chair and taken her in his arms. She sobbed as if her heart would break while he kissed her face and stroked her hair and murmured softly into her ear whilst she clung to him as if her life depended on it. Gradually her sobbing came to an end and she rested calmly against him. It was some time before he released her.

Only then did they realise that Brother Aidan had left them. He did not return.

'Prince Oswald. Prince Oswald.'

Oswald opened his eyes as his lieutenant shook him gently by the shoulders. It was barely light, the camp silent but for the commencing dawn chorus of songbirds.

'It is Wicktil, the scout, Your Highness. He has just returned and tells me that he has important news. May I bring him to you?'

Oswald swung his legs to the floor and stood up beside Alban, rubbing the sleep from his eyes. He stretched and moved to the tent door peering out into the early morning. He had been late to bed, unable to stop turning over and over in his mind the problem of Cadwalla's numerical superiority. Perhaps Wicktil's news would give him some help. He turned back to Alban.

'Give me a moment, Alban, and then bring him. I will get a cloak; it is still cool.'

When Wicktil came before him Oswald saw that he was an insignificant man of medium height, middle build, sandy hair and, in general, of such a nondescript appearance as scarcely to possess any memorable feature. He remained silent in the background until Oswald motioned him forward and offered him refreshment from a pitcher beside him. The scout, after hesitating for a moment, accepted the goblet of wine which disappeared immediately and was replaced empty on the table before Oswald had begun to speak. Perhaps spies had to take what was going as fast as possible, he thought, as he watched Wicktil wipe his mouth with his sleeve and await the prince's command.

'Alban says you have something important to tell us. Be seated here and tell your story in your own time.'

Wicktil, who was tired and drawn when observed closely, glanced at the lieutenant who nodded in encouragement. Then the spy began, haltingly at first, until he had overcome his nervousness in the prince's presence.

'I went south nearly a month ago, Your Highness. I travelled a long way but, from bits I picked up here and there, I thought it would be worthwhile. And so it proved,' he added, pausing for effect and looking from one to the other of his listeners to judge their reaction.

'Penda has returned to Mercia, Prince Oswald – about three weeks ago – almost a month in fact. It seems that he and Cadwalla had more than enough of each other's company for some time now. Penda, I think – although I can't be sure – had been keen to invade the Briton's of Strathclyde but Cadwalla refused. They argued about it for a long time before Penda stormed out and withdrew his troops to a separate camp some miles away. Two days afterwards he returned but it was the same story. Hammer and tongs they say it was, with both going at it for all they were worth, until – and this is what interested me so much, Prince – they say Penda screamed cowardice at Cadwalla. But when everyone thought they would fight Cadwalla backed down and Penda flung himself out in disgust and has been marching south ever since. I followed for more than a week. He's gone alright. If you were to attack now he's too far away to come back in time, even if he wanted to.'

Oswald had risen to his feet at the news and was gripping Alban by the shoulder.

'Penda gone! Listen to that Alban. Gone. We will never get a better chance than this. Wicktil, you have indeed done well and your time away has been well spent. You may leave us and get some sleep. You will be well rewarded.'

Wicktil rose and turned towards the tent entrance before pausing and looking back at the prince. Oswald, with his back turned, was thumping his fist into his palm in his excitement. Spinning round on his heel to speak to Alban he stopped in surprise, seeing Wicktill still there.

'What is it? Is there something more?'

The scout scratched his head in a puzzled fashion for a moment before replying.

'Yes, I think so, Prince Oswald, but I'm not sure and I certainly don't understand it. I . . . can . . . tell you sir. It might be important.'

Oswald motioned Wicktil back to his chair and resumed his own.

'When I heard Penda had gone I almost came back at once but I'd heard such strange things about Cadwalla that I thought it might be . . . could be . . . important.' He scratched his head again in evident doubt about the reception his news might get. 'Well, Prince, there was this business of him not facing Penda for a start. That would never have happened a short time ago. Then I heard he'd been sitting alone in his tent for hours on end, screaming abuse at anyone who tried to disturb him. Then he asked for a priest.'

Wicktil stopped to see the effect his words had had.

'A priest! Cadwalla?'

There had been a profound effect on Oswald, alright. He was again on his feet, staring at Wicktil in disbelief. The prince turned to Alban who shook his head and shrugged as if to say he didn't understand it either.

'A priest.' This time Oswald whispered the words as if talking to himself, and repeated, 'a priest.' He resumed his seat and spoke directly to the scout again.

'You were right to tell us this – right to go back to find it out. Tell me what else you discovered – everything.'

Wicktil, happier now that his hunch had been so well received, continued more confidently.

'They couldn't find one – a priest, I mean. Well of course not, they'd all escaped or been slaughtered.' Wicktil looked quickly at his two listeners before going on, 'slaughtered. Yes they were. How many I don't know but it seems there was one special one . He hadn't been captured but had walked right into the middle of Cadwalla's camp,' Wicktil shook his head in evident disbelief 'held up his crucifix and began to preach. Cadwalla was in a purple rage, they say, screamed blue murder and the priest was cut down in a flash. But afterwards, that evening, Cadwalla kept coming back to where it had happened to stare at the spot and once he even knelt down. Since then, everybody says, he's been a different person – shrieking in the night, spending hours alone in the dark, as I said, sending for girls and . . .' Wicktil glanced at Prince Oswald for a second before going on, 'not being able . . . to do anything, if you understand me . . . or so the girls always said. It was around that time that he began to ask for a priest and he's been doing so ever since.'

There was dead silence after Wicktil finished his account. Then Oswald smiled slowly to himself, stood up and came over to the scout who rose to meet him. Oswald clasped him warmly by the arms and said, 'Marvellous news. Marvellous. You have done exceptionally well and your information is of the greatest value to me. *Now* you may go. You will be doubly rewarded.'

He watched Wicktil, now showing every sign of satisfaction, leave the tent before turning eagerly to his lieutenant.

'Great news Alban. Great news.'

'What does it mean, Your Highness?'

Oswald did not immediately respond but remained looking far into the distance as if seeing a different scene altogether from that in the tent.

'It means, Alban, that the murder of this priest – a brave man whoever he was and I think I can guess – is preying on Cadwalla's mind. No murder can be shrugged off even, I believe, by such a creature as Cadwalla. But the murder of a priest, and by a professed Christian too, is something to answer for. Cadwalla must be looking straight into the fires of hell as he sits alone in his tent. He has no *need* of light. The flames must dazzle him – and singe him too, I think. Alban, we must turn this to our advantage. I must think. Leave me now but send me food. I must think this out.'

Seventy miles to the south, in another tent, Father Melchior stared relentlessly at the terrified Cadwalla. The figure never moved unless Cadwalla, goaded beyond endurance by the accusation in it's eyes, tried to launch himself forward, fingers outstretched to grip the spectre's throat. But he would clutch only thin air and find the priest, still silent and accusing, in the corner of the tent behind him. Once, in a fury of desperation, the chieftain had seized a sword and swung frantically at every part of the tent in which the figure appeared and reappeared. The fabric had been slashed in a dozen places until Cadwalla, letting the sword fall from his hand, had cowered, gibbering with fear, in the centre of the tent, eyes fiercely closed, not daring to glance in any direction and risk meeting those ghostly eyes.

Hours later he had still not moved but was crouching, incontinent and stinking when his attendants found him.

Oswald was brisk and decisive when he next sent for his lieutenant at noon.

'Alban, I want to know everything about the disposition of Cadwalla's forces. Send Wicktil again and any others you can rely on. Say we will be coming south close behind them so, as soon as they have learned what they can, they must come back to meet us. I need to choose my position carefully. I must know where Cadwalla, himself, is. That is crucial and whoever learns that must come back at once with the information.

'Next, Alban, I want ten monks habits. Get them made at once. Never mind if they are not perfect – just so long as they will pass muster at a distance. And I will need ten men to wear them who will agree to have their heads shaved – all the hair cut off the front and left long at the back, like the Celtic monks. Each man must carry a cross like our Lord's – but I want flaming crosses, Alban – with the ends of the crosspiece and the upright bound and tarred. They need not be too big for each 'monk' will have to carry his cross high.

'Then, Alban, I want a really big cross – huge. I don't care how many it takes to carry it but it must be gigantic. I need it up on a hillside in full view of Cadwalla so that he must see it. And then,' went on the prince, smiling at his lieutenant's bewilderment, 'I need everybody round the cross singing the praises of Almighty God so loud that Cadwalla cannot fail to hear them. I want sound poured down upon him that he cannot escape from.'

Oswald stopped and seemed to be considering something further before issuing his last instruction. When he did so it was in a quieter more serious tone so that Alban had to lean forward to catch what was said.

'Don't forget though, Alban, we must have fervent prayer as well, from everyone in the army who is Christian. Everyone must join in the singing round the cross – whether Christian or not. That is just to torment Cadwalla further, and our Lord will understand. But He is entitled to our proper devotion too and in that we cannot compel those who are not of the Faith to take part. The word must go round though, Alban, that all Christians must pray to Almighty God that our enterprise will succeed. Fervent prayer, Alban, fervent prayer, that is what we need.'

It was still dark on the Island of Iona yet the chapel was almost full. Only those who could not drag themselves there by reason of age or infirmity were absent. The abbot's instructions had been explicit and his messengers insistent – everyone who could possible manage to do so was to come.

Edith and James had been asleep when Fara's volley of knocking had aroused them. By the time they reached the chapel the monks were all assembled and more than half the balcony was occupied. All was quiet, every head bowed in prayer. A monk posted at the foot of the stairs had whispered to them as they entered, 'Kneel down quietly and pray, the abbot will speak soon.'

Segenus was kneeling alone and absolutely still on the altar. Presently, when the balcony was so full that a little group of people were only just able to crowd in at the top of the stairs, a monk came from the rear of the chapel, up the sanctuary steps and spoke quietly to the abbot. Segenus nodded but remained kneeling for a little longer to complete his prayer. Then he rose to his feet and turned to address the waiting assembly.

'Fellow Christians,' began Segenus, speaking in a clear ringing voice, 'members of the Community of Iona. One whose company we formerly enjoyed on this island is in need of our prayers. Our erstwhile brother Oswald is in dire peril and is calling on Almighty God for help. We too must ask God to help him. This has been made known to me during the night which has just passed,' went on Segenus, glancing at the earliest streaks of dawn appearing in the eastern sky, 'although I need not tell you how. Many miles to the east of us the forces gathered by Prince Oswald face those of the heathen which greatly outnumber his own. No! Not the heathen. Worse than the heathen – an apostate Christian. The Lord Oswald cannot win without Almighty God's help and we must pray for that help while they fight. We are his supporters, just as Aaron and Hur supported the arms of Moses and the Lord helped Joshua to vanquish the Amalekites.

'So, from this moment on, there will be a stream of fervent prayer rising to Almighty God from this chapel for the victory of Oswald in Northumbria. There are many here who can celebrate the Holy Sacrifice of the Mass, so many Masses will be said today. At the appropriate times the holy offices will be sung and we shall have hymns to praise God and litanies of the saints and private prayer. There must be prayer – public and private – rising to God all day long, and all night long if necessary, until victory is Oswald's. Let none leave here except for the purposes of nature or to minister to the few who are ill and cannot be here. Their prayers too will join with ours until victory is accomplished.'

And so the day passed as Segenus had directed and, despite the long vigil, fervour grew until, in the gathering darkness, the abbot turned to the congregation, and held up his hands.

'It is over, my friends, the end we all prayed for has been achieved.'

And then when the final prayers were sung and the blessing bestowed on all, the abbot made a last pronouncement.

'Now that victory is won I have something else to tell you. The victor, whom we knew as a humble member of our community, and we now know as King Oswald of Bernicia and Deira, made one more request of me before leaving our island. "Should Almighty God allow me to defeat our enemies", he said, "and permit me to rule over the whole of Northumbria, it is my dearest wish that the kingdom shall become Christian again. Send me a holy father to preach to my people and bring Christianity to my country. The choice I leave to you. I need a man of God who will convert a nation."

Segenus stopped speaking and beckoned Bishop Gobban forward to stand beside him before continuing.

'The priest who bears this special responsibility must have special powers. He must be able not only to baptise converts, which any here in holy orders could accomplish, but, since Northumbria will require priests of it's own, he must be able to ordain which only a bishop has the authority to do. I wish to send His Lordship Bishop Gobban on this mission carrying with him, as he does, full episcopal powers by which, we trust, the Kingdom of Northumbria will, once again, be brought to God. It is a hard task that I am asking you to undertake,' turning and addressing Gobban directly, 'and it my hope that you will accept it. We will seek a new bishop here, either from the Scots in Ireland or from our own number. If you accept this challenge – and I see you do' Gobban was smiling and nodding his head 'may all the blessings of Almighty God go with you.'

Oswald, King, by conquest, of Bernicia and Deira, drained the last of his goblet of wine and lay back in his chair exhausted in body but elated in spirit. Alban, his lieutenant, stood before him, patiently waiting to give his report.

'Sit down, Alban. You deserve some rest after this day's work. Have you completed the count? How many did we lose?'

'Around eighty, Your Majesty,' Alban replied, stifling a yawn not very successfully and bringing a smile to the faces of both men. 'Eighty dead, perhaps ten more who I think will die and about the same number wounded. More than a third of our force dead or injured in all. It was a near thing. Had we been opposed by them all we could never have done it.'

Both men fell silent recalling incidents in the battle, scarcely able, even now, to believe in their victory. Seeing the exhaustion in his lieutenant's eyes, Oswald stood up and brought over a large platter from the rear of the tent and placed it between them on the table.

'Here is meat and bread and wine, Alban. Eat and drink while you tell it all to me. What did you find out from the prisoners?'

Gratefully slicing a leg off the roast fowl in front of him and filling his cup with wine, Alban took a huge mouthful before answering.

'It was just as you said, Your Majesty. The captured officers told me that Cadwalla had given no orders for weeks. He refused to send out scouts and so had no notion we were so few in number. He wouldn't consider a battle plan and yelled abuse at any commander who tried to make him do so. He kept on saying, "You can't beat God with any plan," and, "God is on their side," and lots more in that vein.'

Alban hacked off both chicken breasts and the other leg while Oswald leaned across and refilled his cup. Both ate in silence until Alban was able to resume his report.

'What mattered most was that two of Cadwalla's princes, from some unpronounceable Welsh valleys, hadn't moved up their troops to join him, two hundred men or more they must have had between them. They had finally realised that, when our assault came, any battle with Cadwalla in command was likely to be a shambles. They thought we had a large army since no reliable information had been obtained and the false reports Wicktil and the others had circulated had misled them. Apart from which, Your Majesty,' Alban surmised, 'I expect they would never think we would attack with a force as small as we had. Well,' Alban shifted into a more comfortable position in his chair, 'one of the commanders got cold feet and set off back to the Welsh mountains, and as soon as the other realised that he, alone, was supporting a panic-stricken defeatist, he went too. In the end we were opposing only Cadwalla's army which was perhaps twice as big as ours.'

Alban took up the carcass of the bird and began to gnaw what was left. Oswald again refilled his goblet.

'I was lucky on our right flank sire. It seems that the commander of the opposing force was killed by an arrow as soon as our archers began firing. There was no effective second in command, since no one had planned for that eventuality, and we went through them and scattered them easily. Your flank got much the worst of it, I fear.'

Oswald had a far away look in his eyes, and when he began to speak, it was as if he was reliving the assault on Cadwalla's troops.

'At first, it was eerie, Alban. Our flaming crosses got nearer and nearer to

Cadwalla's lines and yet there was no move to oppose us. Every now and then we would see a man – sometimes thee or four men – turn and run for it before we reached them. Apostate Christians, we later learned these were, like Cadwalla himself, and infected by him, with a terror of Almighty God's revenge. The rest were waiting for a signal which never came and, when our monks flung their flaming crosses into their lines and fell to the ground for the archers behind them to shoot, the effect was devestating. They were disorganised and dispirited. Many fought hard, I'll give them that – fought for their lives in fact but without cohesion. As it was they outnumbered us and we were losing ground when you attacked from the rear after overrunning their left flank. I have a great deal to thank you for Alban. Your bravery today was something to remember. Without your support we would have lost many more men and perhaps lost the day. You and all our men were magnificent.'

'They had every reason to be, Your Majesty. *We* were fighting for what we believed in and were wonderfully led; *they* were fighting haphazardly without leadership since you had destroyed that before the fighting began.'

Oswald smiled and reached across the table to place his hand on Alban's sleeve in a gesture of gratitude.

'Not I . . . at least not I alone, Alban. I too have made enquiries among Cadwalla's captured retainers and they all tell the same story. It was that unknown priest – whether Father Melchior or not – who began Cadwalla's downfall. All I did was to fan the flames of his terror of Almighty God's revenge.'

Again there was a moment of silence, each almost too tired to speak. Alban had pushed aside the few remnants of food that were still uneaten and closed his eyes. He opened them with a start and struggled slowly to his feet. He looked with affection at the king before asking,

'And Cadwalla, sire. How did he die? I only know that he perished.'

'By his own hand, Alban. By his own hand. When the first troops reached his tent he was found kneeling on the ground holding a crucifix in his left hand – Almighty God alone knows where it came from. His right hand was still on the hilt of a dagger driven deeply into his belly. He must have died in agony but the agony he will be suffering now will be far worse. His soul must be deep in hell.'

Chapter 7

The refectory was filled with every able-bodied member of the brethren. As they arrived in their ones and twos few broke the silence to ask why they were there, but many an eyebrow was raised in interrogation and many a head shaken in ignorance. Less than a year after the last general assembly they were here again. More decisions! It was all very disturbing to the calm tenour of their service to God.

When everyone had arrived Brother Denis, who was counting them and marshalling them into place, nodded his head and left by the rear door of the refectory to return, moments later, with the abbot and a familiar figure whose appearance was so unexpected that few of the monks were able to suppress some exclamation of surprise. Behind the abbot stood Bishop Gobban.

Segenus came forward to the edge of the raised platform at the end of the hall and held up his hands for silence before addressing them in a serious tone.

'My brothers in Jesus Christ, we are come together again to consider a most surprising and, I have to say disturbing, development. What has happened affects us all and the reputation of this community. We must decide by the vote of the majority of you here, what must be done. That we may make this decision wisely let us first ask for God's help. We will kneel in silent prayer, tell Almighty God we are sorry for our sins and ask for His grace to help us to vote correctly.'

The abbot himself knelt immediately and the communtiy followed. For four or five minutes there was silence, every head bowed in prayer. The abbot's voice recalled them to their task.

'You may sit comfortably and listen carefully to what I and, in a few moments, Bishop Gobban, will have to say.' Segenus paused, closed his eyes briefly as if uttering a further prayer for help and began to speak again.

'You will all recall, I feel certain, that on the evening of the day on which King Oswald of Northumbria won his great victory over the despicable

Cadwalla, when we had given thanks to Almighty God for hearing our prayers and vanquishing the barbarians, I told you of a special request that the king had made before he left us. You will not have forgotten it, I think. It was to send a priest to convert the Kingdom of Northumbria to Christianity. Bishop Gobban was selected by me for this task and he left to undertake it soon afterwards. What I said to you then was this.' The abbot had a remarkable ability to recall his own words which he now repeated verbatim.

'I wish to send His Lordship, Bishop Gobban, on this special mission, carrying with him full episcopal powers by which, we trust, the Kingdoms of Bernicia and Deira will be brought to God.'

The abbot paused again, sweeping his eyes over the silent brethren. When he spoke again it was as if a deep sadness had overcome him.

'The outcome for which we all hoped and prayed, has not come about. The mission has failed,' Segenus turned suddenly and held up a restraining hand as he heard Gobban behind him hurriedly rising to his feet. 'Yes failed, Gobban. The fact must be faced. There may be reasons for failure but it remains failure nonetheless. Now, my Lord Bishop, you may speak. Tell us why the mission did not succeed for we must decide what is to be done – whether we can help King Oswald by sending another missionary or not.' He sat down and indicated by his outstretched hand that Gobban should come forward to speak.

Gobban took two strides to the front of the platform and stood upright and defiant before the watching monks. Every eye was upon him and he, in turn, stared stonily across the huge refectory.

'To send another monk to Northumbria would be futile – futile I tell you!' raising his voice to a shout and waving his arms. He looked round at the abbot and back at the brethren before launching himself into a torrent of defiance.

'The Northumbrians are a barbarous and obstinate race who rejected God's word and refused to listen to His representative. I was sent, as their bishop, to bring them Christ's teaching, to make them aware of sin, to call on them to repent and do penance. Did I not do these things? Was I not at pains to impress on each and every one to whom I preached – and they became fewer not more numerous as I continued my mission – that they must abandon their sinful ways and pray that Almighty God would forgive them their past sins if they confessed and were truly sorry. How many accepted the teaching I offered them? How many showed any fear of the fires of hell? How many were cowed by the thought of God's vengeance? A handful. Everywhere I met mute obstinacy. When I told them eternal truths and they could be persuaded to listen did they accept them? No. I was always questioned. Why this? Why that? The word of God does not call for questioning but acceptance. Reject this teaching at your peril, I told them. The fires of hell are for such as you. Fall on your knees and ask pardon of Almighty God.'

Gobban seemed almost to have forgotten the monks assembled before him and to be repeating his arguments over and over again to the absent people of Northumbria who had rejected him. His tirade went on for a long time and there was some shuffling of feet and fidgeting as he roared out his denunciation. Suddenly he stopped as if, once more, he had become aware of his surroundings. They thought he had finished until he finally burst out, 'Stubborn; obstinate; headstrong. To send further monks to them would be futile.'

The murmur, after Bishop Gobban's invective ceased, was longer than ever and the abbot made no move to stop it for several moments. When he did, holding up his hand, the silence was instantaneous. As if in deliberate contrast to Gobban's loud proclamation he spoke quietly but still remained audible across the silent room.

'Now you have been told Bishop Gobban's reasons for the mission's failure. He has told you that he was rejected by a barbarous, obstinate, stiff-necked people. May we hope for any better reception if we send someone else? Shall we tell our friend, King Oswald, that we cannot help him?' Then he raised his voice and went on more insistently, 'This is a vital matter which we, collectively, must decide. Let me hear from you.'

No one moved for several moments. Everyone, it seemed, was reluctant to be the first to his feet. Then, from over to the left of the refectory, Brother Falla stood up.

'I am disturbed – deeply disturbed – by what the bishop has said,' he began, turning half round so that all could hear him. 'I have not marshalled my thoughts fully yet but I must say one thing which does not seem to agree with what we have just been told. In my journeys, preaching God's word, I have met Scots, Picts, Britons and Saxons from Bernicia. I cannot – simply cannot – believe that one of these groups, the Saxons, is more resistant to God's word than the others, or that the Saxon is by nature a stiff-necked, stubborn man, an opinionated person who will not listen to reason if,' and Brother Falla turned back directly towards the bishop 'reason is what they were offered. We have Saxons here, even among the brethren. You know them as well as I do. Brother Mark here,' catching the baker's eye and gesturing towards him, Brother Erasmus, our tailor, Fara, our guest mistress and Edith and James, among our most recent arrivals who have made so many friends in the community. Are these, I ask you all – and you Bishop Gobban – obstinate, difficult people? I have listened to the Lord Bishop, Brother Abbot, but what he says about Saxons is not what I have found among that community.'

As Falla resumed his seat Gobban began to rise from his, but the abbot forestalled him.

'You have had your chance for the moment, bishop, and may, if you so wish, speak again later. But it is the monks' turn now. Who will speak next?'

Brother Aidan stood up so quietly that the abbot was not immediately aware of him. Then, with a tiny smile to himself, he pointed to Aidan, saying, 'Yes, Brother. We would all like to hear from you.'

Aidan began speaking in his beautiful melodius voice as soon as the abbot took his seat again.

'My Lord Bishop, I too find it difficult to believe that the Saxons of Northumbria who, not so long ago we are told, were converted to Christianity along with their then ruler King Edwin, by a bishop of the Roman Church, could remain so stubbornly insensitive to a bishop of the Celtic Church. I must tell you something many here will not know. The young man, James, to whom Brother Falla has already referred, was in the service of that Roman Bishop – Paulinus was his name – and travelled widely with him throughout Northumbria. James would tell you were he here, as he has already told the Lord Abbot,' Segenus nodded his head vigorously, 'that the Christian teaching of Paulinus, and even of James himself for that matter, was accepted with eagerness by the Northumbrians. There was no rejection, no obstinacy, no refusal to believe, no defiance of the will of God. Instead there was acceptance, willing acceptance.'

Aidan spread out his hands towards his listeners as if to include every one of them in what he was saying.

'The people who accepted the word of God from one bishop are the same people who rejected it from another. The word of God is the same. The people are the same. Only the bishops are different. Is it not likely then that it was the manner in which the Faith was preached that made the difference between acceptance and rejection.'

Aidan turned round slightly so that he was addressing the bishop more directly.

'We have heard you say, my Lord Bishop, that you were sent to make them aware of sin, to call on them to repent and do penance, and later you spoke of God's vengeance. Would it not have been much wiser to have talked to them of God's goodness and of how any sins, not just theirs, offend against that goodness? Would not anyone, made aware of the goodness of God and of His love for His people, not *want* to give up sin and be deeply sorry for having offended Him?

'Brother,' Aidan continued, stressing his words more forcefully that hitherto, 'it seems to me that your ignorant hearers found your words too severe. Should you not have followed the Apostle's practice of beginning with the milk of simpler teaching and, by degrees, nourishing them further with the word of God until they achieved greater understanding and were able to accept Christ's loftier principles. I cannot agree with the bishop, my Lord Abbot, that it would be futile to send another man to Northumbria. I believe it vital to send one. The people of that land have rejected God's word, that is plain enough, even though I have suggested that the manner in which it was offered to them may have been the reason for this. But we cannot stand by and leave matters as they are. We must try again to bring them to God. Do we preach only to those we know will listen? Oh, no, we do not. We carry God's word to everyone and, if it is not received the first time, we carry it again – and again and again, until it is.'

There was an audible hum in the refectory after Aidan's words but once more the abbot did not call for silence immediately. When he did so it was to ask if anyone else wished to speak. After a moment, when a faint murmur continued and heads were seen to turn in all directions, a plump, red-faced monk, in the body of the hall, got to his feet. The abbot indicated with his hand that the monk had the floor and said quietly, 'Brother Baithus.'

Brother Baithus rocked from one foot to the other in pendulum fashion for a moment then steadied himself by a hand on the shoulder of the monk next to him and addressed the gathering in resounding tones.

'It will not be necessary for me to speak for long, my Lord Abbot. First I wish to say that I can only agree with everything Brother Aidan has said. I go, as do others here – Brother Falla, Brother Dinanus and Brother Cromanus for example – to preach God's word far and wide. I know that I either reach the listeners with my words or find them deaf to them. In the event that they refuse to listen it is always I who have been at fault having chosen my words ill or having given them too harsh a message. I am sure Brother Aidan is right, that is what Bishop Gobban did.

'Brother Aidan's second point is equally valid. We take God's word to all as often as is necessary for them to receive it. Not to do so is a lamentable failure of our duty.'

Baithus stopped and smiled, swivelling round so as to beam at the entire assembly of monks.

'Brother Aidan's third point, my friends,' he continued, still grinning happily, 'was made more cogently than any, although I do not believe it was his intention to make it. If we agree that we should send a priest who will take the Lord's message, gently and lovingly, to the people of Northumbria we must also agree that we have been listening to the priest who must do this. Who better, my Lord Abbot, than Brother Aidan?'

Baithus sat down to cries of 'here here' and 'Aidan' and 'that's right' and similar expressions of approval, and for some minutes the abbot, who had walked to the front of the platform, could not restore silence. When he finally did so he addressed them all in serious tones.

'You have led me to believe that, by common consent, you choose Brother Aidan to be our next missionary to Northumbria but I must ask you formally to confirm this. Do you agree that he is the man?'

'Aye,' from every part of the room.

'Is there any dissenting voice?'

Silence. The abbot glanced briefly at Bishop Gobban who shook his head to deny dissent.

'Then, Brother Aidan, I must ask you if you will accept this task for which, I may say, you have shown yourself admirably fitted? Will you go?'

Aidan was still sitting in his place, his eyes closed, his lips moving in prayer. The abbot, seeing him so occupied, waited patiently until the monk opened his eyes and rose slowly to his feet.

'Yes, my Lord Abbot, I will accept the task. I would ask only one thing. That the brethren pray for me that, with Almighty God's grace, I may accomplish it.' He sat down again while the abbot remained standing as before in front of them all.

'There is one more thing to be done,' he remarked. 'The same conditions which prevailed, when our brother, Gobban, went on the first mission, prevail now. The missionary must have the dignity, authority and powers of a bishop. One week from today Bishop Giles, who succeeded Bishop Gobban here, assisted by Bishop Gobban himself, will consecrate Brother Aidan as bishop.

In the scriptorium two figures poured over the completed Gospel of St Luke. James had been standing behind Brother Eligius to let him scrutinise the finished work without interruption, but the scriba had called the young man forward so often, to share his pleasure at an elegant design or at the ingenuity with which a difficult corner of a letter had been decorated, that they now sat, heads together, examining the text minutely, the one searching for any flaw there might be – except the deliberate one – the other expressing frank admiration at everything he saw.

'I do not believe it could have been done better, James,' praised the scriba. 'I really do not. It will be a tremendous addition to the community's treasures when the fourth Gospel is completed. That is something I look foward to seeing. This one – Luke – I truly believe surpasses Mark which, in turn, is even better than Matthew. Will you be able to keep it up?'

Both were smiling together and returning to a further examination of the manuscript when a voice addressed them from the door of the room.

'Brother Eligius. Master James.'

It was Brother Albert, the abbot's servant, looking anxious as he always did when trying to deliver his master's messages accurately.

'Yes, Albert, what is it?' replied Eligius, only giving the monk half his attention as his eyes strayed back to the open book before him.

'My message is for Master James – from the abbot,' explained Albert somewhat unnecessarily. 'The abbot wants . . . wishes . . . asks, that is, if he may wait upon Master James here, in the scriptorium after Sext, and could the Lady Edith possibly come also so that His Lordship may see them together?'

Eligius looked enquiringly at James who, though puzzled, nevertheless replied without hesitation.

'Of course. I will go for my wife at once to be sure of finding her and bringing her back here.'

In the event however they were not back in time, since Edith had been out on some errand and it took James a little time to find her. When they reached the scriptorium, both a little out of breath, the abbot was waiting them but not alone. Brother Aidan was with him.

Segenus was gracious when he saw their laboured breathing and realised that they had been hurrying.

'You are out of breath. I'm sorry. I should have given you a longer time but we,' gesturing to Brother Aidan 'were anxious to see you as soon as possible. Take those chairs and rest a moment until you recover while we continue our examination of this . . . magnificent work.'

The abbot smiled kindly and Aidan nodded and both returned to their perusal of the manuscript. Presently the abbot turned and spoke again.

'It is wonderful. You have a great gift James. However, that is not what we wished to see you about – at least not directly. Brother Aidan has put a request to me but, before I consider it, I want him to put it to you first.'

The young couple glanced at each other but said nothing, waiting for Aidan to speak.

'Perhaps you know,' he said at length, 'that the brethren, with the Lord Abbot's consent, chose me to preach the word of God in Northumbria at the request of King Oswald. I shall leave for that country in one or two weeks time after I have been, however unworthily, consecrated bishop. When I arrive there it will be necessary to establish a church – several churches in fact, but one in particular which will be the episcopal centre of the kingdom. In the course of time that church must acquire whatever ornaments it can so that the worshippers may see the Lord's house decorated with many examples of man's artistry. Among such examples it is my wish that a copy of the word of God, as written down for all mankind in the Gospels, should be embellished for ceremonial use. Only the best we can offer is good enough for Almighty God and I know of no man capable of greater beauty in the illumination of sacred scripture, James, than you.'

James glanced at Edith and at the abbot and Eligius in turn, then dropped his eyes in embarrassment.

'You may perhaps realise now what I am going to ask,' Aidan went on. 'I am going to ask if you will both come to Northumbria with me to help me to make the bishop's church as near worthy of our Lord as man can devise. You both know the country well. You both speak Saxon and Gaelic. You would be of inestimable value to me. Do you think you could agree?'

The reaction of the couple was instantaneous. Each looked at the other, smiled happily and put their arms around each other, swinging round from side to side in their emotion. James whispered, 'Oh Edith, what an opportunity,' and she replied, 'I never dreamed we would have such a chance.'

Then, at the same instant, a thought came to them both and they turned guiltily towards the abbot. Edith lowered her eyes and James, keeping his arm round her shoulders, spoke to the abbot as if it had been he who had asked the question.

'My Lord Abbot, please forgive our churlishness. We were so overjoyed at the idea of returning to Northumbria – home for Edith and it seems like home to me too – that we must have seemed too eager to leave here as if we had been unhappy. Nothing could be further from the truth. We have been immensely happy and contented. But . . . this is not our home and the prospect of returning there overcame our gratitude to you for taking us in and allowing us to become part of your community. We have been blissfully happy, my Lord, but . . . given the opportunity . . . we would like to take it.'

Both young people turned to face Aidan.

'My Lord Bishop, if the Abbot will permit, we will gladly accompany you.'

After that it was smiles from everyone. Segenus clearly bore no grudge and he admitted that he would have been surprised if they had elected to stay. It was while Aidan and the abbot were discussing animatedly with Edith and James when they might leave and what preparations they would need to make that Eligius, whom they had almost forgotten, spoke.

'I have a suggestion to make, my Lord Abbot. I do not know how you will receive it but I must make it. This young man has given me endless pleasure with his artistic skills, as I'm sure you all realise. The elegance of the work you have been examining speaks for itself and, had it been finished here, would have been an enormous acquisition for our library of sacred books. But St John's Gospel is still to be transcribed and James will not, now, have time to do it. Were I to attempt it the contrast would be painfully obvious to all who saw it.'

Eligius stopped for a moment and walked over to put his hand on the decorated page at the beginning of St Luke.

'My Lord Abbot, may I submit that there is now only one thing to do – to allow the artist to take his work with him when he accompanies Bishop Aidan. The sooner the last Gospel is finished, the sooner will the bishop have a fitting object of reverence in his church.'

James looked from abbot to bishop, overcome by the scriba's generous gesture. Aidan closed his eyes to say a prayer while the abbot, walking over to stand directly in front of Eligius, touched him gently on the sleeve before replying.

'I wished to make the same suggestion, Brother Eligius, but could not bring myself to do so knowing, as I did, how highly you prized this young man's work and how much you wanted to have it here in our community. You will be remembered for your generosity. I know how much it cost you.'

Aidan and James,too, were full of thanks to the old monk who shook his head as if to say, 'no matter.' Then he took James by the hand and said softly.

'The book belongs to it's author. The work is yours. Take it with my blessing.'

Not for a few moments, when they were all feeling a little embarrassed by their emotions, did Edith, too, approach Eligius. She had tears in her eyes as she spoke to him.

'We will remember you, Brother . . . always.'

And for the second time in a few months she kissed him on the cheek.

Edith had been more moved than ever she expected when Fursa's boat pushed off from the little jetty. James, sensing the depths of her feeling, said nothing but placed his arm around her shoulders and held her protectively to him.

Only a few had come to see them off – Fara and Maban, of course, and Shilde and Briga but the members of the religious community had continued with their daily routine. What did arrivals and departures matter anyway? God's work had to be done and they were not to be diverted from it. So, in restrained fashion, most had said their farewells the previous evening, and a few that morning early, and the brethren had gone about their business.

Edith looked towards the retreating shoreline without seeing it, her entire mind absorbed in reminiscence. When they had arrived she was a . . . maid was one word often used for it . . . sexually unaroused or, if aroused a little, certainly unfulfilled. Her thoughts went back to the wonderful time of their wedding and the blissful lovemaking which followed it. You couldn't say she was unfulfilled now! Was everyone so lucky, she wondered – Fara and Maban for instance. Making love with the one whose love you returned was the most natural thing in the world but . . . somehow . . . you could never imagine anyone else doing it. Why not? Why did it seem strange for, Calen say, to make love to his wife, as she was quite sure he had done to the enormous pleasure of them both.

Their own lovemaking had got better she was certain but it had been so ecstatic the first time that it was hard to see how any improvement was possible. Perhaps it was what you were used to that made the difference. At first you had no standard for comparison so good might seem marvellous. But then, as you came to know how beautiful it could be and, she supposed, got better at doing it, the evoked response was better too. One might . . .

Gracious, she thought, as a sudden movement by Fursa brought her out of her pensive state, what a subject to be thinking about as you were leaving Iona which had meant so much to you. She forced herself to look back at the dwindling buildings with Dunii behind them but, in no time, she was seeing them no longer and was back with her thoughts again.

One reason Iona meant so much to her was precisely because this was where she was married and slept for the first time with her husband. You didn't do that many times in your life she hoped, so, naturally, it meant a lot to you. And becoming pregnant too that was another part of it but, although she was happy to dwell on the wonder of her conception, she refused to let the despair of her miscarriage enter her mind.

Edith looked around for a diversion. The shore was still visible but barely, the high ground beyond just a blueish haze. It had almost gone now and she had missed it. Not really missed it she thought at once; it was all there in her head, the good and the bad – mostly good although the bad had been shattering in it's intensity.

She turned her head in search of further diversion and her eye was arrested by Aidan. Now she could think of her recovery and not of her illness. This saintly man had done that for her and she would do anything for him in return. Would she ever have the chance she wondered?

In an instant her thoughts had gone from the past to the future. Northumbria again! But not quite the Northumbria they had known. Her life had been entirely in Deira and she had never been out of it until their journey to Iona. Now they were going to Bernicia which she did not know at all although Jamie had spent a lot of time there with Bishop Paulinus before she had met him. Would they be with Aidan there or might his episcopal see be miles away? She hoped he would be near her, not because she any longer felt the need of his help but because she might, one day, be able to do something for him.

Edith sighed and felt James' arm tighten around her shoulder. She looked up and smiled at him, her reverie over. He bent his head down to hers and whispered in her ear.

'You were miles away. What were you thinking about?'

Edith glanced round quickly to see if anyone was watching and gave him a tiny kiss.

'You. Us. Our lives together on that wonderful island – and my life with you wherever we are going. I don't mind where we go as long as you are there.'

Chapter 8

In the noon day heat of August, in the Year of our Lord 642, the inhabitants of the royal palace of Bamburgh, although seeming to go about their normal affairs, were desperately trying to conceal their deep anxiety. Oswald, King of Bernicia and Deira, had marched out with his army a month ago, bent on a once-and-for-all confrontation with Penda, King of Mercia. They had heard nothing since the news, a week ago, that Penda's forces had been sighted and battle would soon be joined.

Crown Prince Oswy, from his chamber in the palace, watched the ceaseless surge of the waves onto the rocks far below him. His ancestor, King Ida, had chosen well when he had selected this site for his palace. On top of a massive rock, one hundred and fifty feet above the sea, it could be approached only from the south east. It was well-nigh impregnable, as Ida had intended that it should be, and they might all, still, be grateful for it's stout defences, thought Oswy, if the king's attack on Penda failed.

It had always been Penda, it seemed to Oswy, for as long as he could remember. Penda ravaging large tracts of Deira and Bernicia; Penda defeating his uncle Edwin; Penda burning, looting, raping, pillaging and terrorising their lands. Even when his brother, Oswald, had finally won back his kingdom it had been only Cadwalla he had defeated. Penda had returned to Mercia from where he had been a thorn in Oswald's flesh ever since.

His marriage had been very much on his mind of late. What would Enfleda be like he wondered? She and her mother, Ethelberga, had escaped from Deira and returned to Kent in dramatic fashion, he knew, after her father, King Edwin, had been killed by Penda. Enfleda would be . . . how old? If she was born about 626 she must be, what? . . . Sixteen or seventeen by now. She was a Roman Christian too, which filled him with some apprehension, since the Roman Church was almost an unknown quantity to Oswy who had no idea what to expect. The notion of being a married man was beginning to appeal though. Let's hope Brother Uffa, who had sailed to

Kent to escort her back north, would have a smooth voyage and a safe arrival.

Meanwhile he could only wait, not even knowing if he were king or not.

In the scriptorium three young alumni carefully pricked and ruled the vellum on which they would transcribe the fourteenth psalm which James had set them as their allotted task. One of them, Paul, had been under instruction for only two months yet, already, he showed more promise than the others who had been with him almost a year. Paul might just be capable of great things, James mused, as he watched their painstaking measurement and careful ruling. Parchment, even of inferior quality such as they were using, could not be wasted and a sharp eye kept on them now might pick out a careless error before any great harm was done. Paul didn't make careless errors but Albin and Jude could still do foolish things if he took his eyes off them for long. He would make fair copyists out of these two but he hoped for far better things from his newest recruit. James had turned out several creditable copyists since Aidan had asked the king to allow the young man to establish a school of sacred illumination a few years ago.

What a lot had happened in the last eight years since Bishop Aidan and Edith and he had come here at Oswald's request. Not exactly *here*, of course, in Aidan's case, although he visited the royal palace not infrequently, especially in the early days when he was spreading the word of God among Oswald's people. The king had offered to let Aidan establish his episcopal see wherever he wished. True to form, as a monk with the whole Celtic monastic tradition behind him, he had chosen not Bamburgh but Lindisfarne, seven miles away. Twice each day this tiny outcrop of land became an island when the rising tide cut it off completely from the mainland. At other times, when the tide was out, it was possible to pick one's way carefully across stepping stones in the sand to reach Lindisfarne safely.

There Aidan established not only his episcopal see but a monastic community like that on Iona. It was an ideal site for such an enterprise, giving the monks an isolation from wordly affairs which they so much prized yet allowing the bishop ready access to the mainland for his missionary journeys and for visits to the king. It had taken Aidan time of course to gather dedicated servants of God around him but, with humility and manifest holiness such as he exuded, recruits had come in a steady stream and most had stayed.

James broke off his train of thoughts just in time to stop Brother Jude straying wildly in marking off his left hand margin. A glance showed that Brother Albin, tongue in cheek, was plodding on slowly but accurately. Brother Paul was well ahead of both.

James went back to recalling his first year before the bishop had become fluent in Saxon and the young man had frequently translated for him. Sometimes Oswald, himself, had done it, if James was not available, because his clerical duties occupied him elsewhere. Both men had found it a wonderful experience to translate Aidan's words. James had once asked him, 'How do you know, my Lord, that you are getting through to them when you cannot understand the words I translate?'

'I watch them closely,' the bishop had said. 'I just watch their faces. It is easy to tell if they understand or not.' And he added, 'It is a surprising thing that, even when King Oswald, himself, translates for me, they seem unconcerned at his royal presence and conscious only of the words of our Lord.'

There had been many converts. Very many. James remembered clearly how, on Iona, he had once questioned the wisdom of mass conversions with Prince Oswald, as he had been then. The prince had seemed to disapprove of what he said at that time but perhaps James' words had had a bigger impact on Oswald's mind then he had realised at the time. At all events, when Bishop Aidan was about to teach his subjects, the king always spoke first in this vein – 'I am your king and a devoted Christian but you must accept the word of God only if you believe it, not because I have done so. To become Christian because I am one is to become Christian for the wrong reasons. You each have a free will of your own and it is up to you to accept the bishop's teaching or not as you wish. You remain my people and I will rule you without fear or favour whether you are Christian or not.'

Oswald had insisted that James, when he translated, should tell them the same thing in the king's name so that there would be no easy conversions of those who did not truly believe.

The three young copyists were now deeply into their tasks and James could easily have taken up one of his own but the king's departure had filled his mind with thoughts of impending disaster. James found that the idea of the imminent battle disturbed his concentration and prevented him from doing his best work. He returned, instead, to remembering the halcyon days of Oswald's early reign.

It had been an idyllic time, especially when he had travelled with Aidan all over the two kingdoms so that the bishop could reach as many people as possible. Oswald, with pressing affairs of state to occupy him, had seldom been able to accompany the bishop and James had mostly gone instead. Vivid memories of Aidan's sanctity – there was no other word for it James had long ago decided – had stayed with him ever since.

Wherever they went Aidan had always insisted that they should walk unless the distances were too great. They invariably stopped to talk to anyone they met and, if these were poor people, Aidan had money or gifts to offer them which he himself had been given by some rich person he had visited. Such influential hosts were often disappointed at Aidan's refusal to eat heartily of the rich fare provided. The bishop always ate sparingly, however succulent the food he was given, whilst on Wednesdays and Fridays he would eat nothing until after None except during the fifty days following Easter. The example Aidan had given to all was wonderfully stimulating and converts were made in numbers which rivalled those made by Paulinus during Edwin's reign.

Then James' thoughts came back as they always did to the 'miracles'.

He had turned these over in his mind many times but, although he had tried to find a rational explanation for them, he had never been able to do so. There was one intriguing fact about these episodes. They only occurred when James and Aidan were alone with the one person the miracle benefited. There had, for example, been the fire in the haystack which was being fanned by the wind and the flames were beginning to get hold of the poor man's house. The man had called for help and had been upset when Aidan had assured him that there was no danger and had knelt down to pray. Whilst he was praying, and the man was pleading with James to do something more practical, they had both realised that there *was* no danger since the wind had suddenly changed and the fire, which was blown back across the part of the haystack already burned, was easily beaten out. When they had done this it seemed to James and the man that scarcely any of the hay had been destroyed.

That had been the first miracle but there had been many others. A child had fallen onto a pointed stake which had pierced his groin and blood was pumping out fiercely. The bishop had placed his hand upon the wound and knelt in prayer on the ground by the child's side. After a few moments the bleeding had stopped and there was no sign – not even the smallest mark – to show where the wound had been. On another occasion a cow, which had fallen into a pit and had obviously broken it's leg, lay bellowing in pain whilst it's owner, standing helplessly above, had been unable to help. Aidan had prayed first then, asking for a cloth, had climbed down into the pit and bandaged the leg of the, now, placid animal which stood up on its four legs and was later pulled out to safety without any sign of the injury.

Aidan had always insisted that nothing was said to anyone about these wonderful happenings but somehow the word would be spread abroad and little groups of people would be waiting expectantly for him at the next hamlet. But there had never been any miracle for them. James had once asked the bishop why he never worked a miracle for a large crowd as the Lord Jesus had done in the Gospel. Aidan had not answered at first and when he did so it was to ask another question.

'I believe you will find that you know the answer yourself, James, if you think about it for a moment?'

James, after some thought, had said hesitantly, '*You* don't work them my Lord. God does that I realise. If He wished to do so He could enlighten the darkness of all these people by His omnipotence without the need of anyone to teach them. But, I suppose,' James looked inquiringly at Aidan, 'that is not His way. They have to exercise their free will to accept Him or reject Him without the miraculous signs that I have seen. They have to have faith and to believe. Miracle after miracle would, I suppose, make it too easy for them.'

Aidan had smiled and nodded his head.

'Well done, James,' he replied. 'Remember what our Lord said to Thomas the twin when He appeared to the apostles after the resurrection – 'Because you have seen Thomas, you have believed. Blessed are they who have not seen and have believed."

James thoughts were interrupted by a commotion in the courtyard below his window. A horseman had clattered in through the gate and people were running from all sides eager for news. Could he be from Oswald, James wondered? Please God, if he were, let him bring good news. He tried to shut out of his mind the thoughts of the king's attack on Penda and returned to his pupils. It was idle to speculate. They would just have to wait for news.

Edith, in her own room, was preoccupied with her private thoughts.

Could she be mistaken? It seemed too much to hope for after all this time. More than nine years since the miscarriage and no sign of another pregnancy until now. Then, out of the blue, she had begun to experience the nausea and her breasts had been so tender that, when James last made love to her, she had almost cried out and had been obliged to disguise her pain in simulated passion.

If she had been regular with her 'little visitor', as Fara used to call her cycles, she would have had something more definite to go on but, ever since she had lost her child, she had seen perhaps only about two or three times a year and then the loss had been almost nothing. The last time had been in May and here it was mid August, but that had happened so often before that it didn't signify anything. Then the nausea had started and once she had been sick although, fortunately, James had not been there. Could it be imagination that her skirt was beginning to feel more tight?

She would love to ask someone, but whom? Fara would have known but she was not here to advise. She dare not raise James' hopes until she was sure – really sure.

She sighed and moved over to the window as if seeking inspiration outside. There was a horseman dismounting below her. He looked weary, as though he had ridden a long way. Could it be news at last of Oswald's battle?

Enfleda, Princess of Deira by descent from her father, the late King Edwin, Princess of Kent, as grandaughter of the late King Ethelbert, was contemplating the same problem which had faced her mother seventeen years earlier – what to take with her on the long journey to Northumbria.

It seemed that drastic reductions were going to be necessary. The party was to go by ship – 'now they tell me' she sighed, thinking of what might have to be sacrificed. Ships were far from commodious – cramped would not be too strong a word – and the wardrobe she had selected would take up far too much room. Something must go.

In truth Enfleda cared very little what she took. She was an easygoing girl and the dresses originally chosen had been picked by her mother anyway so her mother could have the job of deciding what must be abandoned. The 'old girl' had regarded herself as an authority on sea travel ever since she had survived the harrowing journey from Whitby after King Edwin had been killed. Of course Enfleda had been in the boat as well but she had only the haziest memory of the voyage which couldn't compare with Ethelberga's oft-repeated comments on their experience.

What had the trip really been like, Enfleda wondered, and would this one be the same? To hear her mother tell it they were in mortal danger every moment of the time. The pounding of the waves, the roaring of the winds, the pitching of the boat, she had heard Ethelberga reciting so often, 'Oh you cannot imagine it if you haven't experienced it for yourselves.' None of her audiences ever had experienced it, of course, so her mother was on safe ground except, of course, on that one occasion when a captain, who had just returned from taking her aunt safely over to Gaul to enter a convent at

Faremoutier, had been in the audience. Ethelberga had been very subdued and had refused to be drawn on the subject of sea travel. But later, when the good man had left them, she had taken up the theme of storms at sea, which they had all heard many times before, but was now embroidered with constant phrases such as, 'the captain and I know,' and 'we mariners who have been through it all.'

'Enfleda.'

'ENFLEDA.'

The bride-to-be was interrupted in her thoughts by her mother who, under the pretence of asking her daughter's opinion, was deciding what was to be taken aboard. Enfleda, compliant as always, knowing that resistance to her mother's ideas was seldom profitable, aquiesced with a nod. Ethelberga, who had expected nothing less, had passed on to the next matter and was ticking off the numbers of the party on her fingers.

'You, my dear, can have only two ladies-in-waiting, I fear – you will just have to hope that there will be some presentable girls at the other end. Try to get an older woman too, if you can as lady-of-the-bedchamber. If you are lucky and get a good one, and there are some quite intelligent women up there' (mother was an authority on the whole of England north of the Humber, Enfleda giggled to herself) 'she will keep the others in order don't you fear.'

Ethelberga paused, momentarily diverted from the counting.

'Let me see, where was I? Of course, that's three. Then there will be your personal chaplain – that's four; one other priest, I suppose – five; one or two servants for them, say seven so far. Who else do we have? That's all, I think.'

'The priest from the north and his party will have to return with us won't they mother?'

Enfleda knew that her mother had overlooked them since she seldom gave consideration to anyone beyond her immediate family circle.

'Of course child. Of course. How many are there; four perhaps? If there are more they will just have to go by land by themselves.'

There was silence for a moment while Ethelberga fussed over the clothes once more, removing one garment and replacing it with another.

'Mother.'

'Yes, child. What is it? I'm busy you know. If I don't do this no one will. Why can't you decide something for yourself sometimes?'

Enfleda ignored the injustice of this for a moment until her mother turned to her again.

'I think I have decided something.'

'Decided something? What may I ask?' Ethelberga seemed quite unaware of her own volte face as she said it.

'The present, mother. I've decided what I would like to take as my present to my . . . husband.' Enfleda blushed and stumbled over the word.

Ethelberga seemed momentarily at a loss but soon regained her composure.

'Present! But it's all decided. There is that silver cup set with rubies that your grandfather gave you when you came here after our ESCAPE,' the word acquired capital letters as pronounced by Ethelberga. 'A most suitable present I should have thought.'

'But it's so small,' Enfleda imparted just the opposite emphasis to her word 'since it was given to a seven year old girl. My . . . husband, Oswy, might like a longer drink than he would get out of that after . . .' Enfleda hesitated, not quite sure what physical activity Oswy might have been indulging in before attempting to quench his thirst in that miniscule goblet. 'You did say, mother, that I could choose what I liked. Yes you did,' seeing Ethelberga about to challenge the statement, 'didn't you?'

'Yes dear, I did.' Ethelberga was nothing if not fair. She was seldom called on to confirm a promise but never failed to do so if challenged. Then smiling, as if humouring her daughter she asked, 'What is it you want to give?'

Enfleda gave an inward sigh of relief knowing that she had succeeded, and, very carefully, answered, 'I would like to take . . . to take back, that is . . . to my husband-to-be the unfinished Gospels which we brought with us from Northumbria nearly ten years ago. Mother, please,' seeing Ethelberga opening her mouth as if to protest, 'let me finish.'

Enfleda, put out of her stride for a moment, paused, holding up her hand to maintain her mother's silence. Then slowly she continued.

'I have always found them beautiful – so have you because you have told me so many times. They weren't finished because of the war, I realise, but . . . it is almost *because* they weren't that I think they are appropriate. They came with us from the north and they were written in the north even if, I think you said, the writer was from Kent. They are, or ought to be, part of Christianity in the north and I think they should go back there, especially,' Enfleda rushed ahead, 'since the Church there now is Celtic and ours is Roman. I don't understand – don't perhaps trust – Celtic Christianity but I will have to live with it and I think if those Gospels went back with me they would not only be a gift – all right a ceremonial gift,' seeing her mother frown, 'if you like, but what other kind of gift can you give a man you have never seen.'

Enfleda wiped her eyes and bowed her head for a moment before collecting herself and continuing defiantly, 'It would not only be a gift, as I say, but would also be a bit of the Roman Church that I know in a Celtic stronghold which I don't know and . . .' she faltered again, 'something to remember Kent by.'

For once Ethelberga said nothing but took her daughter in her arms and held her gently for a moment. Then she released her and looked intently at her for some time before speaking again.

'Very well, Enfleda, so be it. I won't say it isn't a good idea. Indeed,' Ethelberga was a generous loser on the few occasions on which she lost, 'on reflection I think it an excellent choice. Your father was very proud of those Gospels. They were going to be the showpiece of the new cathedral at York until we had to leave. Yes, it is a good choice but we shall have to get them from Bishop Paulinus in Rochester. He will give them up if I ask him. You will have to go for them yourself though. I'm too busy. Far too busy.'

Bishop Paulinus was half asleep in his chair in his Palace at Rochester. He dozed quite a lot now, he realised, far more than ever before. He attended all his services, of course – well almost all – but did not get among his flock that way he had once done when first he came to the see.

Thoughts of Northumbria began passing through Paulinus' mind as they often did when he dozed. Edwin . . . his toothache (Paulinus mentally smiled although he had never done so openly at the time) . . . the king's conversion . . . the baptisms . . . James . . . the Gospels . . . and then the terrible invasion and the king's death. Ought God's bishop to have remained behind, he asked himself for the hundredth time? Would he have been long ago dead if he had? What happened to those who did stay? James . . . the girl, what was her name . . . it was no use he had forgotten. Father Me . . .me . . . who? No use forgotten again. Then that appalling sea journey. Paulinus always shut that right out of his mind when the reminiscences tried to bring it back again. What a blessed relief the land had been and how fortunate that this bishopric of Rochester was vacant at that precise time. To have succeeded his old master Justus in the see of Rochester was something which pleased Paulinus very much.

He smiled again at the memory of the archbishop. He himself might have been an archbishop too, Paulinus remembered. At the very moment when he was in that awful boat fleeing to Kent, he had later heard that the Pope's messenger was bringing him the pallium but, because of the war, could get no farther north than Nottingham by which time Edwin was dead and Paulinus had escaped. So he never received it. Never really wanted to, like Justus, he . . .

He came to with a start to realise that his servant was shaking his arm. He opened his eyes but it took him a moment to adjust to the light now pouring in through the window of his room. He pushed himself upright in the chair and blinked.

'What is it?'

'My Lord, you have a visitor. It is the Princess Enfleda who has come, she says, with a message from her mother, Queen Ethelberga. May I show her into your presence?'

Brother Egbert had lost none of his accuracy in the delivery of a message, thought Paulinus. What an extraordinary thing it had been that, on his return to Kent, who should appear but Brother Egbert, asking to be his servant once more.

Paulinus shook himself and rose to his feet. It would never do to receive the princess looking bemused and sleepy.

'Very well, Egbert. Please tell the young princess that I will be happy to receive her.'

The bishop straightened his robe and pushed down an unruly tuft of his thinning hair with the flat of his hand as he waited. Egbert soon returned, showing Enfleda gracefully into the room.

'My Lord Bishop.'

'Your Royal Highness. Pray accept this chair and tell me what brings you so far to visit an old man.'

'Bishop Paulinus, you're not old and you're not going to be all formal with me, are you? Please don't be? Can't we just be as we usually are? Please?'

Paulinus smiled. 'We have been friends for a long time, haven't we? After all, when you have shared a small boat with a lady for so long it creates a bond, does it not?'

They both laughed, their informality restored. These two had indeed had a happy relationship which defied their difference in years ever since their return in Jeb's ancient boat. Paulinus looked quizzically at the young princess.

'And what favour have you come to ask me?'

'Oh, my Lord, I ought to have known that you would anticipate what I have come for before I told you. You are right, of course, I have come to ask a favour.'

'Well then, ask away. I will grant it if I can. Have I ever not done so?' and they laughed again like children. Then presently the princess became solemn.

'It is in your power to grant it my Lord, although I fear it will be a sad loss to you if you do.'

'Then it will be my loss,' Paulinus replied. 'Tell me about it please.'

Enfleda spent some time explaining about the Gospels and the precise reason why she wished to take them back to Northumbria as a present for her husband-to-be. She was at great pains to make the bishop understand the significance of this gift, which was, at the same time, Northumbrian and Kentish, and as such would mean so much to her. Paulinus listened attentively and said not one word until her recital was over.

'My child,' he then said kindly, 'I think it is a wonderful thought. Nothing could be more appropriate than the return of the Gospels to the north. Indeed we would never have removed them if they could have been safely left behind. But it was all savagery, then, as you have heard so often from your mother,' the bishop added, grinning conspiratorially at the princess, 'and they would beyond doubt have been defiled, which we could never allow to happen. They were God's word, and God's word most beautifully worked by man.'

Both were silent for a moment until Paulinus, rising to his feet, took a large key from the depths of his robe and moved to the back of the chamber.

'I will take them out for you now and we will look at them once more together before you return them. I only hope,' he said with some asperity, 'that the Celtic Church appreciates what it is getting.'

He opened a cupboard in the corner of his room and, lifting out a single large volume, carried it over to a table placed beside his chair near the window. The book was bound in blue hide, each corner protected by a triangular cap of silver, and etched with a pattern of interlace based upon that used in the decorations of some of the pages. A large cross had been raised in the hide in the centre of the front cover in a manner similar to the St Augustine Gospels which Father Birinus had shown James to fire his enthusiasm so long ago. The binding of the volume, which Bishop Paulinus had commissioned soon after his return to Kent, had been closely based on that of the same Augustinian text and had been taken by the bishop to Rochester as his most prized possession.

The old bishop and the young princess poured over the beauty of the St Matthew Gospel and the beginning of St Mark which had come to such an abrupt end in the early autumn of the year 633. Nine years ago, mused

Paulinus, as he looked for the last time at James' masterpiece which had remained for all that time incomplete. Once or twice the suggestion had been made that another artist should complete it but the bishop had always steadfastly refused. No one – certainly no one in Kent – could have done it justice. It was better unfinished.

He was so caught up in his thoughts that he did not realise for a moment that Enfleda was speaking to him.

'Do you think he is dead? The young man who did this?'

'I don't know but I fear so. Few survived, or so I've been told. The carnage, they say was frightful – so appalling that I have been informed that many whom I baptised renounced the faith – may our Blessed Lord forgive them – in the hope that Penda and Cadwalla would spare their lives. But *he* would never have done that. He would have died first, I know he would.'

Paulinus stood for a moment, gazing into space as if seeing the Northumbria of those days. Then, as if anxious to let the Gospels go before their loss affected him too much, he became suddenly businesslike.

'Come along, my dear. Time is up. Here is your gift. What husband-to-be ever had one more beautiful? Take it now, it is yours. Where is your servant to carry it for you? Keep it safe always and when you look at it, think of me . . . and pray for my soul.'

The messenger with his tragic news was brought first into the presence of the stunned Oswy.

'The king is dead. Long live the king.'

Oswy did not react at once as the formal words were spoken. Then he shook his head as if in disbelief and barked:

'Dead? Are you certain? Is it beyond doubt?'

'Yes, Your Majesty,' the messenge replied. 'It is quite certain. Penda left us in no doubt of that. He displayed the body, Your Majesty, for all of us to see – mutilated and dishonoured. It was mangled beyond belief.'

Oswy looked at the attendants beside him before closing his eyes and muttering a prayer for his dead brother. Presently he opened them again and gestured for the messenger to come forward and take a stool beside him.

'Bring him food and drink,' Oswy ordered and added to the man, 'I want to know the whole story. You may refresh yourself while you tell it.'

The messenger, Dalla, gratefully accepted a goblet of ale and took three large gulps before beginning his account.

'As you know, Your Majesty, we went south east with a considerable army. The king's,' he hesitated, 'the late king's plan was to attack before Penda had collected all his forces which we believed he was gathering on our border. King Oswald intended to surprise him by attacking before Penda was ready but we were not in time and he *was* ready, Your Majesty. Our two armies came together at a place known locally as Maserfield. Our numbers probably equalled theirs but they were better positioned and well dug in at a spot we were hoping to occupy ourselves.'

Dalla drained the last of his ale and dragged the leg from a fowl placed before him; he took two enormous bites before continuing.

'The fighting was very fierce. For a time we held them but then we lost ground. That was when King Oswald, rallying a group around him, attacked ferociously. Their impetus took them through Penda's front line and, for a moment, it looked as thought we might split their ranks. But they had reserves in depth who held our attack. Worse still,' Dalla shook his head at the memory of it, 'the king's thrust had penetrated too deeply and the front ranks of Penda's men closed behind them cutting off their retreat. We counter-attacked fiercely but it was no use. We got close but . . . not close enough. The king . . .' Dalla seemed to be seeing the battle and the plight of the surrounded king' . . . once he knew we couldn't reach him . . . oh, my Lord God, receive him into heaven . . . he called to us all, 'God have mercy on your souls, God have mercy on you.' Dalla wiped both eyes with the back of his hand and waited until he had regained his composure. Then he looked up again at Oswy. 'That was what he said, Your Majesty. He thought of us, not of himself – just of us. He was a great man . . . a saint.'

There was shuffling of feet and turning of heads for a time after Dalla stopped speaking. Oswy pointed to the messenger's empty goblet which was refilled. The grateful man took it up and buried his face in it, glad of the distraction. Then he took another leg off the platter and gnawed off a mouthful or two before speaking again.

'Worse was to come though. Both sides broke off the engagement soon afterwards since each had been severely mauled. But Penda hadn't finished with us. In full view of us all he had King Oswald's body stripped, then he took a sword and hacked off first the head and then both arms at the elbows. He took the lifeless torso, full of so many wounds, Your Majesty, and with the help of two of his men hurled it off an escarpment onto the rocks below. And while we watched . . . we had to watch, what else could we do . . . he put a spear through the head and one through each arm and stuck them in the ground in full view of our men but guarded by his strongest force so that to try to get them back would have been folly. I think perhaps,' suggested Dalla somewhat hesitantly, 'he wanted us to try to recover them – to tempt us to attack his strongest position. But we had suffered too severely in the earlier fighting and many more of our men would certainly have been lost.'

Dalla leant over and swept into his palm the last bits of food before him, every eye still upon him.

'The survivors are returning, Your Majesty. Many were killed or severely wounded – half the force or more. But,' he ended, rising to his feet and stretching to relieve his cramped limbs, 'there is one good thing. Penda too, we feel, lost a lot of men. He retreated south as soon as he could and I'm sure he sustained more losses than we thought at first. If he comes back, Your Majesty, it won't be yet awhile.'

James heard the news from Brother Paul.

The three pupils had finished their tasks for the day and had departed, leaving their master to inspect what they had done. As usual Brother Paul's work was the best and much nearer completion. Albin and Jude had plodded on slowly, nonetheless, and the transcripts showed few errors and none serious. Perhaps, James thought, by the end of the year they could be allowed to return to the monastery at Lindisfarne to join the other copyists whom James had trained and who, under the watchful eye of Brother Sextus, were preparing quite presentable copies for use in Bishop Aidan's increasing number of churches. Sextus had come from Iona a year after Aidan's episcopal see had become established, already having received some training in Ireland. Brother Eligius, sensing James' need for someone like Sextus, who could be left to do ordinary work on his own or to supervise other copyists, had generously released him to join the monks at Lindisfarne.

Brother Paul looked like being his best pupil yet, thought James. His script was neat, his preparation exact and his nib kept admirably trimmed and even in width. He should . . . James thoughts were interrupted by someone speaking to him from the door.

'Master James.'

James turned and smiled when he saw it was Brother Paul but his smile faded at once when he noticed the sadness on the young man's face.

'Paul, whatever is it? Is it the messenger? The news is bad, I feel. How bad Paul?'

'Terrible sir,' Paul replied quickly. 'It could hardly be worse. One of the pages who was there when the messenger came to Lord Oswy told me. The king is dead and his body abused – mutilated and defiled. I am so sorry,

Master James, I know how close you were to him. More than . . .'

He broke off as he saw James sink to his knees with tears in his eyes, for the dead king.

Edith learned the news from James.

He came to find her immediately after hearing it himself, knowing how upset she would be. Her anxiety over her own condition, of which he was still unaware, seemed to magnify her grief for the king.

'He was never like a king to us, Jamie,' she kept on repeating 'never. He was our friend. Oh Jamie do you remember how much we missed him when he left Iona, and now he's dead. Poor Oswald. Poor, poor Oswald. Such a good man.'

She clung desperately to her husband who held her tight and kissed her hair and gradually calmed her. They were a long time without speaking until James raised her face, dried her tears and said simply.

'Come on mouse. We must go to the chapel to pray for his soul.'

No one needed to tell Aidan who already knew what had happened.

The bishop had been kneeling quietly at prayer in his monastery chapel when the knowledge of the outcome of the battle came to him with startling clarity. The whole scene flashed vividly into his mind as it was actually happening. The agony of the wounded, the screams of the dying, the naked fear of the besieged, the helpless plight of the king's cohort marooned in waves of Penda's soldiers, the frustration of his attempted rescuers, the death, the mutilation, the horror and the slaughter were crystal clear to the kneeling Aidan despite his tightly closed eyes. He groaned with anguish as man after man fell, as limbs were hacked and bodies pierced. His suffering at the sight as he watched – as he could not avoid watching – was multiplied by his foreknowledge of it all. Not only did he see it before his very eyes in all it's savagery but, at the same time, he was possessed of a terrible awareness of what was going to happen before any of it took place. The pain of the soldier as the sword bit into his arm was felt by Aidan too but was preceded by another pain of the blow which he knew, with appalling certainty, would surely fall.

The bishop's helpless vision of King Oswald was the most terrible to bear. Blood streamed from a gash across his upper arm, a slash over his forehead and a cut along the side of his neck. The king was fighting desperately but, it seemed to Aidan, that, although in fierce combat with the barbarians, there was at the same time an aura of sanctity not savagery surrounding him.

The bishop knew inevitably and precisely when King Oswald was to die long before he expired. But Aidan's agony was not merely momentary when the fatal blow fell; it lasted from the moment when the king's party launched themselves into the thick of Penda's men. Nearer and nearer came the time of the death – approaching inexorably and becoming more painful every second in Aidan's sure knowledge of the instant the king's life would be lost.

That instant of Oswald's death ended Aidan's vision. The sight, visible with extraordinary clarity a moment before, disappeared in a second as if night had suddenly blotted out the scene. The kneeling man had seen and felt nothing for a long time afterward until he realised he was lying on the floor of the deserted chapel and two monks were beside him.

'My Lord Bishop.'

He could feel a hand patting his cheek, trying to bring him back to consciousness.

'My Lord Bishop, are you alright? We didn't know you were here. You have been missing for hours. Let us help you . . . Come along . . . Sit up.'

Aidan, still numbed by the horror of his vision, allowed himself to be led back to his cell. The brothers wanted to bring him food and drink or to fetch the infirmarian or . . . anything. They were sure he should not be left alone, they said, and much more in the same vein. In the end he persuaded them to leave him to himself. He wanted only to sleep, he said – and eventually they, reluctantly, agreed.

Then the next stage of Aidan's vision began.

It had the same sense of inevitability followed by reality as the first one. Every step was known to him before it happened. Oswald's body stripped, the sound of the downward swish of Penda's sword before he had even drawn it from it's scabbard, the severed arms on the ground yet at the same time still in place, the desecrated torso of a Christian king flung from the ridge onto the harsh rocks below like so much offal thrown to dogs, the three spears on the ground . . . a head and two arms!

Aidan prayed to Almighty God to let the vision end . . . 'But not my will,' he muttered to himself, 'but Thine be done.'

Then mercifully sleep overwhelmed him.

He made his preparations for departure some days later when he judged the messenger might be approaching the palace. He called the brethren together and told them of the death of the king. A requiem Mass was said and prayers were offered continually for the dead monarch's soul. Aidan had seen Brother Alselm, whom he had appointed prior, and given him instructions to begin a novena for Oswald and arrange a constant watch in the chapel night and day until Aidan's return.

Then he had taken up his staff and a tiny bundle of his belongings and seated himself by the waters edge, praying quietly until the tide went out when he could cross the stepping stones and travel on foot to Bamburgh.

A king had died. Now another must be anointed and crowned.

Chapter 9

Down by the harbour Brother Uffa and his two companions, Brothers Wolhere and William, who had come from Bernicia to escort the princess, were patiently awaiting her party before going aboard. Uffa and Wolhere had been in and out of boats all their lives and, for them, the voyage to Northumbria held no fears; but it seemed that everyone else in the party was more than a little apprehensive.

Enfleda had always regarded her mother's stories as so much fantasy that only now, with the ship riding at anchor a short distance off shore, and she herself about to be rowed across in a small boat to board her, did it pass through her mind that the sea trip might, after all, possess an element of danger. The misgivings of her two ladies-in-waiting, however, were so transparent that she suppressed her own and hurried the girls into the boat with a gallant attempt at cheerfulness.

There was room in the little boat for one other person and, after some hesitation, Father Romanus, who had been appointed as her chaplain, agreed to join them. He climbed in with such exaggerated care that, whilst attempting to lower himself onto the thwart without disturbing the boat, he lost his balance and fell backwards off the seat with his legs in the air. The boat rocked violently and one of the ladies-in-waiting gave a scream of fright and clutched her companion tightly who, in her struggle to release herself, made the rocking more violent than ever. Enfleda had found the incident more amusing than alarming and imagined what her mother might have said to reprimand those concerned had she been there.

Father Romanus was pulled back to safety by a perspiring crew member and the boat cast off carrying the first of the party out to the ship.

There were eleven passengers in all – one other priest, Father Remus, one servant each for him and Romanus, Brother Uffa and his two companions and Edric, a solemn elderly man who was to act as Enfleda's chamberlain, completing the party. The captain, a taciturn Bernician called Olda, with three sailors under his command, comprised the crew. They had already waited four days for a favourable wind and, now that they had one, Olda was more than anxious to set sail.

Enfleda was impressed by the size of the vessel and delighted with her quarters confined though these were. The ship was more than one hundred feet in length, or so she had been told, with a commodious well-deck amidships and a raised poop deck aft beneath which was a general living and sleeping area for passengers, one small corner having been curtained off to give the princess some privacy. On the poop deck itself a tiny cabin-like shelter had been constructed, aft of the helmsman, where Enfleda could spend some time on deck and enjoy some protection if she wished. Her mother would have regarded it as the height of luxury she thought, and smiled to herself thinking that at the completion of her voyage she would hardly be likely to be able to compete with her mother's oft-described experiences.

The princess was wrapped tighty in her cloak against a stiff breeze which was pushing them along at what she considered to be a thrilling pace. She choked back a little tear of regret at the memory of her departure from her mother when 'the old girl' had dropped her bombshell. Enfleda had been flabbergasted at the announcement of what she intended to do after her daughter had gone.

'A convent,' Enfleda had gasped, 'You? Going into a convent?'

'Not going into one, dear,' Ethelberga had answered somewhat sharply, 'I shall found one of my own. I've had it in mind for some time now, but of course I couldn't be spared until you were on your way. Once that is accomplished there is nothing to keep me. My nephew, the king, never consults me about anything' how wise of him thought Enfleda to herself. 'Indeed I seldom even see him. So I shall go to my convent to serve my God,' Enfleda had smiled again at this phrase which her mother always used as if the Almighty were her personal property.

'Lyming, that's where my nunnery will be. The buildings are excellent and, before long, I expect we will be a thriving religious community. That's where I shall end my days,' she had then announced without any expression of regret. 'Think of me no more as Queen Ethelberga but as the Abbess – just as the Abbess.'

The princess sighed and watched the prow cleaving the water ahead and glanced back at the broad wake behind them. It was impossible to think of her mother as anything but a queen and that was how she would stay in her daughter's mind. Queen, even before mother, Enfleda reflected sadly. Will it be like that with my children? Will I have any?

She mused on this topic for some time, huddled out of the wind on the lee side, excited by this exhilarating experience. They were almost out of sight of land since the captain had said the he judged conditions so favourable that he was taking a more easterly route than usual. They would often not see land for hours or perhaps not for a whole day. He expected a good journey he had said, as little as six days to reach their destination whilst conditions remained as they were.

Six days before seeing Oswy! Enfleda was a matter-of-fact person but she admitted to some anxiety over what he might be like. Marrying a man one had never seen was what a princess had to expect, of course, just as her mother – the abbess, she giggled – had done, and it usually seemed to turn out alright. Would Oswy have a mistress? Or perhaps several mistresses? Would he keep them after the wedding? If he were experienced would he be gentle? She was not of course experienced but she knew what to expect; her mother, without mincing words, had seen to that. Enfleda sighed again. Everybody seemed to manage 'it' alright, so she supposed she would too. Perhaps even – dare she hope – enjoy it.

Others aboard were less exhilarated by the journey. Edric, Father Remus, their servants and the two ladies-in-waiting were nowhere to be seen and were enduring their misery in as much privacy as they could contrive. Brother William had been told that if you prayed hard enough it took your mind off sea-sickness and he was busy reciting one litany after another and as many psalms as he could remember. It didn't seem to be working.

Brother Romanus too had said some prayers that all might arrive safely but he obtained little assurance of that when, opening his eyes, he saw nothing but the swelling waves and felt only the heaving deck. Brother Uffa, sensing his discomfort, had come to cheer him up and was squatting down beside Romanus with a friendly smile on his face.

'This is the life,' Brother Uffa began on his self-imposed task of reassurance. 'A day or so of this and you'll be enjoying it as much as Brother Wolhere and I do.'

'So you think we will arrive safely? It all seems very perilous to me.' Romanus had to put his lips to Uffa's ear in order to be heard. Uffa took him by the arm and drew him into a sheltered place so that they could talk more easily.

'Perilous,' he queried when they were settled, 'heavens this is nothing. Now, if you're talking about perilous voyages . . .' and he launched out into a description of storms from which he, at least, had emerged unscathed, until he remembered that he was supposed to be cheering up his colleague and, by the look on Romanus' face he was little short of terrified. Uffa decided to change the subject.

'A priest such as you Father, has no need to worry if you put your faith, as I do, in one of the patron saints of seamen.'

'Patron saints? How many are there? Who are they?'

'Bless you, Father, I thought you would have known. Well, there's St Elmo; he's the chief one, I suppose. A bishop he was and a famous preacher as well as a sailor. Once, when he was being chased by persecutors, who were just about to catch up with him, he put out in a little boat and an angel guided him to safety. When there's danger about if you look up there – ' 'up there' where Uffa was pointing was the swaying mast head which made Romanus sick just to glance at it 'you'll see a blue light which sailors call St Elmo's fire. If you see that you'll know that the saint is protecting you.'

Brother Uffa glanced from time to time at Romanus on one side and Wolhere on the other. Romanus had his eyes closed and it was difficult to tell if he was listening or praying but Uffa, now well into his stride, continued with his recital.

'St Nicholas, too, he's a patron saint of seaman. Saved three from drowning off Turkey, they say. He's a great one for patronage is St Nicholas of Myra – children of course, brides, apothecaries, merchants, coopers and I don't know what all else, as well as seamen.'

Uffa paused and scratched his head for a minute.

'Let me see, who else?' he asked himself presently. 'Of course, Brendan. I would have thought you would have known him. Sailed up and down the Irish coast all his life, until he made the famous voyage to his mysterious island in the middle of the ocean. It's a wonderful story. I'll tell it to you sometime.'

Again Uffa paused and looked at Romanus who had opened his eyes and looked a little happier. Then Uffa nodded in a friendly way and said:

'There's one other thing that I'll tell you about later – this,' holding up a little flask which he had produced from the depths of his habit. 'Whilst we have this there's no danger; Aidan said so. Can't tell you about it now though.'

He replaced the little bottle deep inside his clothes and stood up, well pleased with his mission of reassurance. He immediately destroyed it.

'I'm hungry. I must find something to eat. Are you coming?'

Brother Wolhere needed no extra bidding but Romanus turned paler than ever and huddled down out of the wind in his silent misery while the two brothers moved off in search of sustenance.

The wind seemed to the captain to have freshened even more and was dead astern. They were making marvellous time – marvellous.

Aidan awoke with a start as if something had suddenly disturbed him but for a moment he couldn't think what it might be. It was still dark yet it could not have been his servant come to wake him for Mattins. What then?

He said a prayer as was always his custom on waking, then rose from his bed to try to find out what had awakened him. There was still a moon giving enough light for him to see that a heavy swell had built up during the night and the wind had strengthened. But the noise of the storm in his ears was stronger – far stronger – than anything happening outside. He could hear the howling of a gale and the pounding of waves and then another sound. What was it? A ship! That was what it was. He could hear the creaking and groaning of a ship battered by a storm that she was trying to ride out, and the faint cries of those on board at the mercy of the elements.

Uffa! It was Uffa's ship with the princess. It must be. Then why hadn't he poured the oil?

'Uffa. UFFA. The oil. Pour the oil,' Aidan shouted as though he were trying to make himself heard above the shriek of the wind in his head.

'Uffa, pour the oil.'

The bishop sank to his knees to pray for the stricken ship. Why had Uffa not followed his instructions?

Uffa had been struck by a falling spar soon after they were hit by the storm which had come, it seemed, without warning when all but the helmsman were asleep.

Olda had shortened sail just before nightfall, or they would have gone right over when they took the first force of the blast. The captain had sniffed the air and looked round a little anxiously, Uffa had thought, but seeing no immediate reason for concern, let alone alarm, had taken in canvas merely as a precaution, leaving the helmsman to wake him if the weather changed.

The man had not done so and they would, now, never know why. Brother Uffa had been awake when he felt the vessel heel over sharply and shudder when she was struck by a huge wave. He had struggled on deck in time to see the wretched helmsman, who had been clinging desperately to the wheel, lose his grip, as the full might of the second wave caught him and swept him overboard. The monk had the presence of mind to seize the spinning wheel and, with all the force he could muster, try to bring the ship's head into the wind.

He noted automatically, with a seaman's sixth sense, that the wind had backed sharply and was now almost due east driving them towards the shore. He hung onto the wheel tenaciously but it was bucking madly as the gale, now on their starboard bow, was driving the stem round westward and heeling them over at an alarming angle. It was all the monk could do to hold the wheel against the force of the wind and he was all but losing the battle when the pressure on his aching shoulders slackened and he felt someone else throwing himself against the wheel as well.

Glancing quickly round Uffa saw one of the seamen beside him, a huge burly man whose strength was enough to bring the bow round eastward into the teeth of the gale. It was at that moment that Uffa saw the princess.

She was standing on the deck looking lonely and frightened and peering round desperately for someone to help her. As he watched she gripped the mast and tried to hold tight but could scarcely hang on as the wind, streaming out her hair and her garments, all but wrenched it from her hands. A wave broke over the prow and washed over her so that she lost her hold for a moment. She somehow managed to clutch a rope as her feet were washed away from under her and she fell to the deck. Another wave drenched her and then a further one dwarfing the first by it's size. It covered her with a solid wall of water and wrenched the lifeline out of her hands. Uffa, seeing her body careering across the deck, let go the wheel and, half sliding half crawling caught her cloak as she slid towards the edge.

Uffa managed to hook his leg round a bollard and gripped her clothes tighter, praying that they would not tear. She turned her head towards him, calling out in terror and stretching out her arm in his direction. He heaved his body over so that, when he too stretched out, the fingers of his straining hand touched hers but could go no further. They hung there motionless, the monk clutching despairingly with his hand and the princess, her head now hanging well over the side, stretching in anguish for him. Neither could move a fraction further.

It was the roll of the ship back towards an even keel which saved her. An invisible force seemed to lift her body and heave it back on board. In an instant Uffa had her hands in his and was dragging her back to safety. She clung so tightly to him that he had to scream, 'The bollard. Catch the bollard. Your other hand.' She understood enough to throw her left arm round it but would not let go of the monk. Together they clung in a tangled mass, arms and legs intertwined but safe for the moment. They were battered by wave after wave but they stayed locked to the bollard.

Uffa, with no means of moving his position to get the princess to safety below decks, craned his head round forward but saw nothing but chaos. Lines were down and sails in shreds and, while he watched, a cross tree snapped and came down with a crash, trailing a tangle of rigging behind it. Uffa turned his body as much as he dared to look aft. Oh blessed sight. 'Thank our Lord for Brother Wolhere,' muttered Uffa.

The monk, tethered to a rope tightly bound across his waist, was inching towards them over the deck, the rope being carefully paid out by a seaman so that Wolhere himself would not be lost over the side. It seemed an eternity before he reached them and for a moment all three were tangled in a writhing mass as Brother Wolhere tried to loop the slack of the rope around the princess before he could signal that it was safe to drag them back to safety. Brother Uffa watched anxiously as they were pulled, with agonising slowness, to a hatchway over which Enfleda was tumbled to safety.

There had been no abatement of the storm and Uffa almost lost his grip as a wave struck him ferociously. A piece of broken spar, driven by the wind, caught him over the eye and flung him hard against the bollard. At the same moment a heavy box, holding the princess's personal effects which had been stowed on deck, broke loose and slid with stunning force into his side before careering off into the sea.

The blow on the monk's head stunned him for a moment and he released his grip on the bollard to hold his side where the heavy case had caught him. His mind clouded and he put his other hand to the deck to steady himself. For some reason the deck was no longer heaving as though they had resumed an even keel. Why was the wind no longer buffetting them mercilessly, Uffa's confused brain asked itself? Had the storm abated? What was happening? Waves were no longer breaking over him. He moved his hand to a more comfortable position and felt an oily substance which was oozing out from beneath his habit and was dripping over the side into the sea.

He tried to get to his feet but was unable to move. He turned his head and the ship seemed to turn with him, slowly at first and then so quickly that he began to feel dizzy. He looked upwards unable to comprehend what was going on and found that the mast head was spinning in huge circles which gradually merged into each other and became a blur. Uffa knew no more.

The moment Uffa awoke he realised that they were at anchor. Brother William was sitting beside him with his eyes closed, telling his beads. Uffa watched him for a few moments, luxuriating in the calm after the storm with the sunlight streaming in upon him. In the distance he could see the shore line with several small boats tied up against the harbour wall, and what looked like fishing nets drying and men busy on the dock side.

What had happened to him? How long had he been asleep or unconscious? The last thing he could remember was . . . what? The violent rotation of the ship . . . yes. And before that? He was lying there battered by the storm – except that there wasn't any storm although only moments before they were at the mercy of the elements. Why would a storm . . .?

Uffa's mind was crystal clear in a flash. The oil! The flask of oil. Aidan's precious oil which had been given to Uffa with instructions to pour it onto the waves if they were caught in a storm. *When* they were caught in a storm, Uffa remembered. Aidan had known what would happen. It all came back clearly to Uffa's mind which a second before had been clouded and confused.

'When you sail,' the bishop had said, 'you will meet a storm and contrary winds. Remember then to put this oil into the sea and immediately the wind will drop and you will be saved.'

And he had forgotten! The shame of it brought tears to his eyes. Forgotten! It ought to have been the one thing he was ready to do the moment they were in the grip of the storm. Instead, he had tried, by his own puny efforts, to save the ship by bringing her head into the wind, if he had only followed the instructions, Almighty God would have saved them through Aidan's intervention.

Need there ever have been any danger to the princess's life, was brother Uffa's next thought? When had he seen her? Might she still have been washed overboard before he could have produced the flask from his pocket and poured the oil over the side?

'Oh, God help me,' prayed Uffa. 'Blessed Aidan forgive me. Intercede with Almighty God for my forgiveness.'

Forgetting the oil still preyed on his mind and he tried to blot it out by raising himself up to look at the shore line more carefully. His movement disturbed Brother William who came over at once anxious to know if his friend was alright.

'Brother Uffa, what a sleep you have had – and deserved, make no mistake about that. Your rescue must have been dramatic. I wish I could have seen it but I was below confused by what was happening – and terrified too if truth be told.' Then, remembering himself, he enquired, 'How are you feeling? Is your head hurting you – or your side?'

Brother Uffa pushed himself up still further and put his hand to his head and then to his side as if to reassure himself that he was alright.

'I seem to be all in one piece, thank you,' he assured his colleague. 'I think

I am. In fact I know I am. Thank our Blessed Lord for saving us. Where are we?'

Before William could reply they heard Brother Wolhere speaking to them from the door.

'Awake at last? Splendid. And you look refreshed. Is everything alright – head? side? Not troubling you too much I hope?'

'Very little. Let me get up to see how I am. I must go to the head anyway. Even monks get full bladders you know.'

Uffa negotiated the call of nature satisfactorily and settled into a chair on his return.

'Now, Brother William can get me something to eat and drink. I'm parched and starving. Whilst he's bringing them, Wolhere, you can tell me what has been happening. Where are we? Tell me everything.'

'The blow on your head or to your side or both,' began Brother Wolhere, 'knocked you out completely and you were lying on the deck unconscious when I came back for you. With the help of Brother William I got you into this little deck cabin and dressed your head and had a look at your side. There was a big bruise there and some cuts – not many though and very superficial – from some broken glass from something you must have had in your pocket. I expect it was the flask you showed us just after we sailed. At any rate,' Wolhere continued confidently, 'I washed the place clean and there was no bleeding nor was there any sign of deeper injury that I could see. You seemed to come to very briefly at that point, then to fall asleep so we knew you were alright and we left you here.'

Uffa had looked pained when Wolhere mentioned the broken glass but cheered up when the monk continued with his story.

'Well the storm blew itself out in an instant – I've never seen anything like it before. A miracle, that's what it was, a miracle – after you had brought the bow into the wind of course, or we would have gone before the miracle could have saved us.' Brother Wolhere began to smile at the relief they had all felt and then resumed his tale.

'After that it was easy. We had been blown right in towards the shore and it took us only a little while to put in here and assess the damage.'

'And where is 'here?' Uffa asked.

'Here,' replied Wolhere, waving his hand towards the harbour, is Dunwich. It's East Angles territory and we are lucky to be here in more ways than one. Anna is the king here and a good Christian too, who I know will help us. Messengers have gone to him at Rendlesham to tell him about Princess Enfleda being on board so I expect he will be inviting her there before long.'

His account was interrupted by Brother William coming back with the food and a welcome jug of ale. Uffa swallowed a large draught and took a huge mouthful of meat and bread indicating, as he did so, that Wolhere should continue.

'The ship took a terrible battering – cross trees down, rigging in tangles, sails in ribbons and we were taking in a lot of water aft so, if the storm had continued, we would surely have gone down. Lots more damage too so it will take a while until we are repaired.'

'Anyone hurt?' Uffa took a huge mouthful before spluttering out his question.

'Yes several. Let's see.' Wolhere thoughtfully began ticking them off on his fingers. 'Father Romanus is the worst; he broke his leg the instant the first wave hit us. Pitched against the bulkhead, he was, and a chest broke loose and slid across and broke his ankle. Then Father Remus got a nasty blow on his shoulder and it's strapped up at the present. Edric was pierced in the neck by a splinter, from one of the cross trees, I think, and poured blood.'

Wolhere scratched his head for a moment to recall the other injuries.

'Bumps and bruises everywhere, of coure, like these.' He drew aside his cassock and showed Uffa a long scrape down his right leg and a swollen right knee. 'The princess's ladies-in-waiting and the priest's servants are knocked about too – even the captain has a lump on his head the size of a goose egg. Just about the only people unscathed are Brother William here and the princess, despite her narrow escape. And speaking of the princess,' he went on, 'she has given orders that she wants to see you as soon as you are well enough. So, if you've finished with this,' pointing to the remnants of food, 'I'll tell her.'

Brother Uffa had brushed crumbs from his habit, pulled it straight and flattened down his hair by the time the princess arrived.

'Oh, Brother Uffa, are you recovered? How can I thank you,' she started to say before Uffa stopped her.

'No, Your Royal Highness. No. Please, no,' he pleaded, you don't know the story. It was my fault. I'm to be blamed, not praised.' And seeing their astonished faces, he stopped abruptly. Then before anyone could think of what to say he began again.

'I can see I must tell you the whole story or you won't understand.'

Uffa explained at length about his commission from Bishop Aidan to carry the bottle of oil and pour it as soon as the storm hit them. 'But,' he admitted, 'when I came on deck, and the helmsman had been washed overboard, and I could see the wheel spinning, the memory of it went completely out of my mind and, being a sailor, I reacted instinctively. It was the same when I saw you, Your Highness. I could tell you would be gone in an instant unless I did something. I never thought to put my hand into my habit, pull out the flask and pour it on the waves. Never thought. So you see I'm to blame. It was my fault. Only when Almighty God came to my rescue and sent the box crashing into me to break the flask of oil were we saved.'

There was silence after this confession which was finally broken by Enfleda, speaking gently.

'No, Brother Uffa, you are not to blame, you are still to be praised. When I felt the storm I was petrified – all of us were. We were panic-stricken. How can I have been so foolish as to go up to the afterdeck? Because the terror of the sudden tempest blotted out everything else from our minds as it must have done from yours. But you didn't panic. You reacted in a natural way as a sailor would. You *did* seize the wheel and you *did* save the ship and . . .' Enfleda smiled and touched the brother gently on the arm, 'you *did* save me. You reacted, Brother Uffa, naturally, not supernaturally. Almighty God knows our frailities and of what puny efforts we are capable and so He is prepared – or so I have always believed and now know for certain – to work a miracle to help us in exceptional circumstances. But I have never seen a miracle, experienced a miracle, felt a miracle, until today. Have you?'

Uffa shook his head, too moved to speak.

'So are you to be censured because, when you and your companions were in great danger, you acted instinctively . . . and naturally . . . not as if you expected a miracle?'

She paused for a moment and watched Uffa glancing from one face to the other seeking reassurance, and then continued just as gently as before.

'Had the storm blown up over an hour or so you would have been able to act on your instructions. You would not have needed to step so suddenly into the breach as you did. But the storm was on us in a flash. One moment we were running before a fresh wind, the next overwhelmed – devastated in a single instant. Why did that poor helmsman not give the alarm before such a deluge struck us with it's thunder and lightning? It can only be because there was no warning. Even if you had ignored the spinning wheel and wanted to take out your flask, remove it's stopper and pour the oil onto the waves, could you have done that with one hand? Had you not been hanging onto something for all you were worth to stop yourself from being washed overboard like the helmsman? You had to grab the first thing you saw to save yourself before you could save the ship.'

Enfleda looked at Uffa with great compassion.

'And I was there, in all my foolishness, on the deck and, had it not been for you, I should have been in the sea before you could have poured your oil. It is all very well to say that the miracle would have saved us if you had been quicker but that is to speak with hindsight. Now that we have all seen a miracle and felt it and been part of it we believe it. But before that I used to think I believed in miracles but now I'm not so sure that I did.'

Enfleda looked round at the two monks as if including them in her conclusion.

'So Brother Uffa, no matter what you say, I humbly give you thanks on my own behalf and on behalf of all on board. Now you can rest. You have lots of time to recover while the vessel is repaired.'

Oswy was crowned King of Bernicia by Bishop Aidan, in the chapel at Bamburgh Castle, on the Feast of St John the Baptist, twenty-ninth of August in the Year of Our Lord 642.

Aidan had arrived at the castle on the same day as the messenger bringing the news of Oswald's death. His coming so soon afterwards caused little surprise, since his facility for foretelling events, or possessing knowledge of remote occurrences, was well known. Oswy had hardly come to terms with his altered circumstances, however, and was unprepared for the bishop's sudden appearance.

Aidan, suspecting indecision and uncertainty in Oswy, elected to be matter-of-fact. Decisions had to be made and the bishop was prepared to make sure that they were, no matter how much persuasion needed to be used.

'There are a number of matters which require action, Your Majesty, following the tragic death of your brother. First, a requiem Mass must be arranged for him without delay. Oswald was a man noted for his sanctity who was a wonderful example to all his people. If you agree, Your Majesty, I propose we celebrate the Mass here, the day after tomorrow. That will give us time to inform all who are near enough the castle to attend. Then, sire, I would like to suggest that we plan your coronation at the end of the month – perhaps the Feast of John the Baptist would be a suitable day. That will give me time to say several other Masses for the people who live in hamlets further away. If I may beg a horse from you, Your Majesty, I will break my usual custom of travelling on foot in the interests of reaching as many of your subjects as I can.'

Oswy, somewhat bemused by the bishop's incisiveness, muttered, 'Of course. Of course. A horse, yes certainly.'

'Good. You have my thanks.' Aidan spoke briskly as if anxious to pass on to the next item which he did at once.

'Your Majesty will want to spend some time in prayer and meditation, I feel sure. The responsibilities of kingship are heavy ones and require much preparation. Your subjects will expect the same example from you, sire, as they received from your late brother. Nothing less will suffice, as I'm sure you realise.'

Oswy was, in truth, looking rather uncertain as if he were aware of the direction in which the bishop's thoughts were taking him. The king shifted uneasily in his seat and attempted, not altogether successfully, to maintain the frank open countenance of a man with little or nothing on his conscience. Aidan was not to be misled.

'It would be appropriate, Your Majesty, for you to make a good confession so that you will be in a state of grace to receive the Holy Eucharist on that day. Everything must be confessed – I need hardly remind you of that – which will necessarily include any sins of the flesh of which you may have been guilty. Our Blessed Lord is aware of the temptations which the members of the opposite sex provide – after all for man, the product of His own creation, He chose the sexual act as the method of procreation – but the institution of matrimony is the remedy for such temptation and, within the bounds of Christian marriage, physical love may be freely enjoyed.'

Oswy was misguided enough to look up at this point and found himself staring straight into Aidan's eyes, normally benevolent but now harsh and steely.

'So, Your Majesty, should there be such sins on your conscience they must be confessed before you can be crowned a truly Christian king. And that is not all, sire.'

Oswy was wishing profoundly that it was but Aidan went on inexorably.

'An indispensible condition for absolution is a firm purpose of amendment which means,' Aidan seemed to be putting more stress upon the words 'that any man with a mistress must be prepared to put her away, should he not, Your Majesty?'

Oswy nodded miserably and shifted his position again. Aidan, relaxing his stern approach, smiled at the king and continued in a more kindly fashion.

'Your future wife will be here soon, of course, and I see no reason to delay the marriage ceremony for more than a few days after her arrival. It would have been most propitious had she been able to reach us for the coronation and the wedding to have taken place together but I fear she has been delayed by storms. The princess is safe, I am delighted to say, but it will be a month or so before she is with us.'

Oswy, who had ceased to wonder at the sources of the bishop's information, made no reply, perhaps hoping that by not interrupting Aidan's flow the interview might be over more quickly. He was not disappointed.

'So, if someone would be good enough to send a messenger out to inform as many as possible of the requiem Mass, I will go to make things ready. If it pleases Your Majesty I will take my leave. Until tomorrow, sire.'

Chapter 10

Their ship was not ready for sea for two weeks but for all of them it was a time of great interest. King Anna had not merely sent an escort to conduct the princess to his palace at Rendlesham, he had come himself. The king, they learned later, was in the process of stamping out all vestiges of paganism in his kingdom and hoped to capitalise on the presence of a Christian princess and one moreover from Kent, the cradle of Christianity in the island. It had been something of a disappointment, therefore, for him to discover that she was not accompanied by a bishop and that her personal chaplain and his assistants were casualties of the storm and were to be sent to Kent – one on a horse litter.

The presence of three monks of the Celtic Church, however, was a bonus Anna had not expected. Although a Roman Christian himself he had, some time before, allowed a monk from Ireland to settle among his people. The manifest holiness of this man had made Anna determined to find out more about these remote Christians some of whose customs were so different from those of Rome. He rubbed his hands with satisfaction at the thought of the discussions he would have with these new arrivals.

He promptly carried off to his palace, therefore, not only Enfleda, her two ladies-in-waiting and Edric the chamberlain, but Uffa, Wolhere and William as well, leaving only the sailors on board to help his own shipwrights to repair the damage.

Enfleda found King Anna an intriguing study. He was filled with boundless energy and seldom still for a moment – darting here and there, urging on this man or redirecting that one, leaping on and off his horse with remarkable alacrity for such a large man and talking the whole time. His greeting had been overwhelming.

'Your Royal Highness. My dear Royal Highness. What an honour and pleasure it is to have a princess of Kent and princess-elect of Bernicia in my kingdom. I cannot tell you how delighted I am – not of course by the interruption of your journey – very sad, very sad; and so lucky too. Several fishing boats are missing I'm told and one or two that have come back are very much the worse for wear – much the worse for wear. Be careful of that,' he suddenly shouted at one of his men carrying some of the princess's belongings off the ship. 'Here, you,' to another man, 'help him. Good. Good.'

He seems to think it necessary to say most things twice, thought Enfleda and smiled inwardly at this huge man so eager to please and so welcoming to them all.

'Must get going, must,' shouted the king again to no one in particular but, since no one appeared to take any notice the preparations went on as before. They were, in fact, off quite soon and were kept at a steady pace by Anna's repeated urgings. Horses had been obtained from somewhere for the three monks and Edric, whilst a carriage, capable of transporting eight or ten people, had been brought along for the princess and her entourage whose size had been unknown. But Enfleda, being an accomplished horsewoman, had elected to ride and a suitable pony was quickly produced. The king was delighted and insisted that she ride alongside him and Edric with the three monks close behind.

Anna talked for the greater part of the journey often addressing Enfleda first then squirming round in the saddle to include the three riding behind. He had plenty to tell them as it turned out and Enfleda began to look forward to an event, which was clearly going to be of the greatest significance, and due to take place in a few days time, but whose nature became apparent only by degrees since the king's account of it was not a little disjointed.

His first words on the subject startled them all.

'The exhumation and reburiel will be a far more splendid affair now that you, Your Royal Highness, and you reverend gentlemen,' spinning round to the right to address Uffa and William and to the left to include Wolhere, 'will be able to attend. Splendid indeed it will be.'

No one could think of a suitable response to this gambit but none was required since the king was off again.

'He should never have been buried in that fashion. It was a sacrilege – sacrilege is the only word for it. Of course he'd never been a very good Christian – never. Pagan rites and Christian ceremonial mixed up together. It's no wonder the kingdom was in a state of religious turmoil. And then the interrment – well that was a disaster – a religious disaster. Still,' Anna with a beaming smile did his revolving act again to include them all, 'we will put that right in three days time. And you will add to the regal and ecclesiastical importance of the occasion. We'll have him out and reburied with all the rites of Holy Church.'

Anna paused briefly to shout at the driver of the carriage now conveying the ladies-in-waiting in solitary state and before he could resume his account, if account it could properly be called, Enfleda diffidently asked a question.

'Your Majesty, whom are we discussing? And why need he be reburied?'

The king reined in his horse so abruptly that Wolhere, who was immediately behind him, almost collided with the ample rump of His Majesty's enormous steed. The king was clearly puzzled that there should be such doubt in the princess's mind.

'God bless my soul Redwald of course. Redwald, who else? I thought you knew. But then,' he went on, trying to be fair, 'possibly I didn't make myself perfectly clear.'

The listeners tried not to catch each other's eyes to avoid laughing at this masterly understatement. Enfleda was the first to recover and to question the king again.

'King Redwald, who was High King over several kingdoms of this island, is well known to us by reputation, sire, but I fear we were not aware of his religious – peculiarities, shall we say – and certainly not of the details of his burial.' And seeing the look of disappointment on Anna's face at this admission, she continued hurriedly, 'But we would dearly love to hear the whole story.'

The king brightened up at once and immediately began to tell a more coherent tale.

'Redwald became King of the East Angles in the Year of our Lord six hundred and twelve, and not long afterwards he became a Christian following the example of your grandfather King Ethelbert. Well, all I can say is,' the king added, looking very fierce at this point, 'that it's a good job all converts were not like he was. It was the queen of course who led him astray.' Enfleda began to think that Anna too was perhaps beginning to go astray again but he avoided the temptation. 'She was against the Christian faith from the start and didn't see why they should give up their old religion just because they had learned about Jesus Christ.' Anna crossed himself reverently at first and then adopted his ferocious expression again. 'Do you know,' he cried, swinging round as before in the saddle, 'that they actually had a Christian altar for Holy Mass, and a pagan one for sacrifice to devils, side by side. And they saw no wrong in it. No wrong, I ask you,' another revolution, 'and so the whole kingdom got up to some bizarre religious practices as you can imagine.'

The king broke off his story to shout to his lieutenant that they were going the wrong way. After much expostulation and waving of arms they continued as before and the king returned to his tale.

'Well,' he resumed, 'as I was saying, one of the biggest sacrileges of all occurred at his death.' The king took a deep breath as if steeling himself to describe such an outrage. 'He had given instructions to the queen that, when he died, he was to be buried in a long ship underground, after the custom of his predecessors before they came to this country, with a collection of his goods and chattels round him – his helmet, sword, shield, sceptre, ornaments of all kinds, his lyre – he was a great musician – hoards of coins – goodness knows what he thought he was going to buy – bowls and jars and household things and . . . oh I don't know what else. Rich things in plenty there were – gold and silver, beautifully decorated. A treasure, that's what it was, a treasure.'

Anna took another deep breath since his account had been going at breakneck speed and then, with the resumption of his ferocious expression, said, in a disparaging tone,

'Pagan things. Pagan. And right next to them,' he went on, 'was placed a silver crucifix, a copy of the Gospels – although not a very good one – and a jar of holy water. Christian things, you see. Christian things. Not only that, but some of the bowls and jars had crosses on them or the names of saints – St Paul, I'm almost sure was one of them. And right in the middle of these sacred and profane objects the body rested. Oh, it doesn't bear thinking about.'

The king seemed quite put out at the memory of this curious ceremony and Enfleda got in another question.

'And is he to be dug up and reburied?'

Anna, eyes ablaze, almost shouted his reply.

'He most certainly is. Most certainly. Several of my predecessors meant to do it but never managed it. Earpwald, who came after his father Redwald, became a proper Christian but was killed soon afterwards or he would certainly have undertaken it. His brother Sigbert was the next king – he was a Christian too but he also was killed by heathens from Mercia. Then I came along and I've been so busy trying to keep the invaders at bay that only now have I got around to righting this wrong.

'So,' he looked round again in triumph at them all, 'it's to be in three day's time, on Wednesday third September, the Feast of the holy St Gregory who sent Augustine to our island. What day could be more appropriate? The bishop – Bishop Felix, that is – you'll meet him presently – will be officiating but your presence will set off the occasion; truly set off the occasion.'

The Roman bishop and the Celtic monk sat together in companionable silence in the bishop's chambers in the Royal Palace at Rendlesham. The episcopal see had been established at Dunwich but Bishop Felix frequently attended the palace where quarters were set aside for him and where he was very much at home. His companion, Brother Fursey, rarely travelled far from his monastery and only the momentous occasion of the exhumation had brought him now. His Lordship broke the silence.

'You are deep in thought, my good friend. What about?'

The monk smiled but did not immediately reply. When he did so he merely said, 'Just remembering.'

These two had been friends now since Fursey had abandoned his native Ireland and set off to travel in God's service wherever chance might take him. It had taken him to the country of the East Angles where, despite the fact that, at first, he had only a rudimentary knowledge of their language, he had stayed and been accepted and impressed all by his gentle nature and manifest goodness. The king, whom Fursey had met soon after his arrival, had been specially charmed and, when the monk asked for leave to establish a monastery, Sigbert, the then reigning monarch, had granted him land by the coast in the north east of his kingdom beside the ruins of Burgh Castle. There Fursey had gathered a small number of disciples round him, who had built themselves crude huts and a tiny chapel and had cultivated their land and lived a simple frugal existance to the astonishment of the neighbouring villagers. Stories of the kindness and generosity – for they always had something for the poor and sick although they seemed to live off next to nothing themselves – had spread and many villagers came out of curiosity. Some stayed, although not out of curiosity but inspired by their example. More huts had been built and the chapel enlarged.

Then King Anna had made his famous visit. He, like everybody else had been deeply impressed by the sanctity of the community and, despite Fursey's reluctance, had built a larger and finer chapel and a refectory and guest house (much in demand) and granted more land.

'Remembering what?' enquired His Lordship, breaking in on Fursey's reverie.

'Oh, everything – everything that is that has happened here among the East Angles. Do you recall our first meeting?'

It was Felix's turn to smile and to hesitate before answering. He knew that the visit that he himself had made had been even more significant than that of the king. Felix was straight out of the Roman mould and had, at first, been full of misgivings at the stories he had heard about this Celtic monk. Suspicion of the Celtic Church lurked in Felix's mind, as it did in the minds of most of his Roman counterparts but, up to then, this remote Christian sect, as he had thought of them, had been little more than an occasional subject for casual discussion which had usually been dropped as soon as it had arisen. The notion that he might meet it face to face had never crossed his mind until he arrived in Sigbert's kingdom.

Felix was a Burgundian who had been fired with missionary zeal and had travelled to Kent where Archbishop Honorius had given him leave to go north into East Anglican territory to preach the gospel. How he might have fared if Redwald had still been king was a question he had often asked himself as he came to know more of the bizarre fusion of Christianity and paganism which Redwald countenanced. But Redwald was dead and Sigbert had succeeded. Felix could hardly believe his good fortune since Sigbert and he had met in Gaul when, exiled by his brother Redwald, Sigbert had accepted Christianity. And here was that same Sigbert ruling as king and anxious to give Felix, now his bishop, every help.

Felix had thrown himself into the task of preaching Christianity and, for a time, had made many converts. Then came further heathen attacks from Mercia in one of which Sigbert was killed. Moreover many converts apostacised and it looked as if paganism would get the upper hand again.

Fursey's presence had made Felix expect a further rift in the kingdom with two diverging doctrines of Christianity being taught. But, so far from this causing schism, Felix learned that more and more of the people were accepting Christian baptism after the monk's teaching which was reported to be identical to the bishop's own. He decided to visit Fursey at Burgh Castle.

He looked now at his friend who was watching him contentedly as this desultry conversation continued.

'Oh yes, Fursey, I remember our first meeting very well. I was full of – not hostility, that would be too strong a word, but suspicion certainly as if you were certain to profess a faith different from mine.'

Felix leaned forward and pointed his finger at the monk and becoming more animated as the memory of their first meeting came back to him.

'I remember what I said to you too – not at once but soon after our first introduction to each other.'

'What?'

'I said, "Do you think we can overcome the differences between our customs?"'

'So you did. So you did. I had forgotten. What did I reply?'

'You said,' answered His Lordship, very slowly and deliberately 'and I can still remember your exact words, "May we first establish what we have in common before we discuss our differences."'

'That was a wonderful thing to say,' Felix continued presently, 'wonderful, and I've always remembered it. Do you know, Fursey, I've never given our differences a thought since then. We have too much in common to harp on differences. Perhaps we should have sat down together with all our advisers and talked about Easter or your funny tonsure – I'm sorry, sorry,' as Fursey opened his mouth to protest but with, at the same time, a smile on his face; jokes about tonsures were always being bandied about between them. 'I promised I wouldn't talk about your hair style if you didn't talk about mine, didn't I? Let's discuss the exhumation, shall we? Now that the king has brought his royal visitors with him he is determined to make the show even more elaborate than before – and I shall be in the thick of it.'

'And I shall be behind you,' his companion replied. 'I'm not one for big occasions as you know. I'm sure to do something wrong so I'll stick close to you and if you want me to do anything at all, tell me exactly what it is or I'm bound to disgrace myself.'

'Of course you've got three Celtic monks to support you, haven't you,' Felix observed. 'Fortunately we can understand each other so I'm told so we shouldn't have a problem. Have you met them?'

'Not yet,' Fursey answered. 'I'm greatly looking forward to it. By all accounts a miracle saved the ship and I want to learn all about it.'

'A miracle? Seriously? I hadn't heard that.' Felix was all attention at once. 'Let's send for them and we can hear their story. My servant can go and, if we are lucky enough to find them free, we can spend an hour or so together this evening.'

Felix drew his chair round so that he was facing Fursey directly. 'Meanwhile,' he announced, 'you can go on telling me about those fascinating Irish saints of yours whom we were discussing last time we met. Let's see, you told me all about Patrick. Who comes next?'

What a day it was.

A mellow, early autumn morning, with a hint of ground mist, quickly became a warm, cloudless day with a gentle breeze stirring the tall grasses and early turning leaves. King Anna had been out and about early and no one else could lie in bed as a result. Horses were saddled for those who were to ride and a collection of coaches, carts and wagons was assembled for the rest. Anna, himself, was astride his enormous charger, Enfleda had a dainty palfrey, Edric and Bishop Felix staid mares whilst Brother Uffa and his companions were happy with anything on four legs provided the animal proceeded slowly. Brother Fursey said he was no horseman and would walk. He set off about dawn and expected to be at the mound by the time that the others arrived.

In the two days since Enfleda's visit much progress had been made. The tumulus itself had been shovelled aside, leaving piles of sandy soil scattered at random some distance from where the mound had been. No one wanted to wheel it very far, since it all had to be replaced after the exhumation, but the king had been adamant that a large enough area should be kept free for the celebration of Holy Mass at the start of the proceedings. A temporary altar had been erected on the, now, flat circle of the former mound, in the centre of which the ends of protruding planks indicated that the top of the burial chamber was, indeed, just above ground level. Much to Enfleda's disappointment there was no sign of the ship which had been totally covered by the original burial party.

Brother Uffa was looking forward to the celebration of Holy Mass and he and Wolhere and William, with no idea what to expect, had discussed at length whether they would be able to follow the Roman rite and to what extent it might resemble the sacrifice as conducted in the Celtic Church. It had been a surprise to them that Brother Fursey was to assist Bishop Felix along with Father Andrew, the resident priest at the palace, a silent nervous man whose nervousness became markedly accentuated whenever Anna was nearby. The monk's surprise at Brother Fursey's officiation had made Brother William bold enough to enquire whether it was proper that he should do so. Fursey hadn't seemed to mind the question and had given a simple answer.

'You'll see.'

King Anna, Begu, his second wife, two of his daughters and Enfleda the honoured guest sat upon a bench a short distance before the altar with a prie dieu placed in front of each. Enfleda was interested to study Begu for a while since, having greeted them on arrival from the ship, she had retreated so far into the background that they had almost forgotten her presence. One daughter was a nun from a nearby convent who had been given special permission to attend the ceremony but was to return as soon as it was over. The second was a gangling child of twelve or thirteen who kept her eyes tightly closed and her hands firmly joined in prayer throughout.

The remainder of the congregation were sitting or standing or kneeling on the ground in a rough semicircle, to the number, Uffa thought, of some two hundred. Care had been taken to leave an aisle through the centre for the clergy to process in at the appropriate time. There being no vestry a tent had been erected for those officiating, around which the altar boys – Uffa counted twenty – and a man in a cassock, whom Uffa thought might be a sub-deacon, had gathered. The boys were of varying age between seven and fourteen and most were so overcome by the special occasion that they were unusually well behaved since they were under the direct eye, it was to be presumed, of their parents in the congregation. One or two wilder spirits were not above a spot of horseplay, nonetheless, and the sub-deacon had his work cut out controlling them.

Uffa was most impressed with the demeanour of the king. Anna had knelt at once and, despite many distractions around him, had prayed continuously with closed eyes until the ringing of a bell signified the emergence of Bishop Felix and his two priests from the tent.

A palace choir, ten in number, which had gathered over to the epistle side of the altar, began to sing the introit while the sub-deacon, carrying a tall crucifix, led the line of altar boys in procession towards the altar. The three priests came behind, Bishop Felix last of all, wearing his mitre, his most impressing robes and carrying his crozier.

The congregation had risen at the ringing of the bell but all knelt as the clergy arrived at the altar. Father Andrew began to incense around the sanctuary. It was soon all too familiar to Uffa.

'Gloria in excelsis Deo, et in terra pax hominibus'

The three monks were in their element, singing the familiar chant with the choir and many of the congregation and especially with the king who was joining in with gusto. The gospel was St Mark's account of the resurrection which Uffa supposed had been chosen to symbolise the imminent resurrection of Redwald from his pagan sarcophagus to a Christian burial.

Then the bishop addressed them in a brief, moving sermon about the importance of life and death in Christ whether you were king or commoner. King Anna nodded his head vigorously in agreement. The bishop referred to the impossibility of serving God and mammon and urged the congregation to pray for the soul of the king who had died seventeen years earlier but who might, he reminded them, still be in purgatory since time had no meaning in eternity. We had to suffer for our sins for as long as Almighty God thought necessary. Only the prayers of the faithful could reduce this time of waiting before entering eternal bliss. 'Pray for his soul,' the bishop ended, 'as you would have others pray for yours.'

It was a touching homily of which Uffa greatly approved and he began to lose the sense of unease which he had had at joining in an unfamiliar ceremony, and to wonder when, or even if, their differences would become apparent.

'*Credo in unum Deum, Patrem Omnipotentem, factorem coeli et terra . . .*'

The choir and the congregation and the king and Brother Uffa were off again professing their Christian beliefs to God. So far still on well known ground, Uffa thought. The offertory came and went. The consecration was the enactment of the same ineffable mystery that it always was with it's solemnity and awesome significance. It had never failed to move Uffa and it did not fail to do so now. Indeed he was filled with a wonderous thankfulness that this was his Church although the bishop was from Gaul, the country East Anglia and the rite Roman. The universality of it all was as much as Uffa could bear. He felt part of a greater whole than ever before and immersed in the love of God so deeply that he became barely conscious of what was happening before him.

'*Sanctus, Sanctus, Sanctus, Dominus Deus Sabaoth . . .*'

The familiar words brought him back to himself and he began to pray to our Lord to make him worthy to receive His Body in Holy Communion. Almost everybody, except the young, communicated and Uffa, although opposite Brother Fursey, and should have joined the line of communicants going up to receive the Sacred Host from him, deliberately went across to Father Andrew as if moved by an unconscious wish to be more united with the Roman Church.

Uffa knelt for a long time after Holy Communion. Once more he was unaware of his surroundings as he prayed with thankfulness for the experience he had been allowed to enjoy. It was once again singing which broke in upon him although now the Mass was over and the procession was retiring through the standing congregation, the king and his party bringing up the rear. It was an unfamiliar hymn to the monk but it had an easy catchy tune which he soon found himself humming in a goodwill gesture of conviviality.

Brother Uffa wandered idly through the crowds after Mass, revelling in the good fellowship he was aware of all round him. How long he did so he did not know but he suddenly found himself face to face with Brother Fursey.

'Well?' Fursey did not need to elaborate on his query.

'Oh, Brother Fursey.' Uffa was almost speechless with delight. 'You said we would see and we did. It was a new experience, truly it was.' The monk was lost for words but finally managed to say, 'Wonderful. You were so right to assist Mass. I pray that one day I shall have that privilege at a Roman service too.'

'I pray that also,' Brother Fursey replied. 'We will talk about it later. But now you can see,' pointing at the burial site, 'we are nearly at the next stage.'

The exhumation did not prove as moving as the Mass which had preceeded it.

The wooden cover of the burial chamber had been taken off earlier that day and it was immediately apparent that, although the chamber had not been filled with soil, as had the ship and the remains of the trench, some earth had found it's way inside, so that the body, and the objects buried with it, were covered to a depth of three to four feet. To dig down into this would risk damage to Redwald's remains which Anna had insisted must not happen. In any event digging within the confined walls of the chamber would have been difficult and the chances of exhuming the body in a reverent fashion negligible.

Messengers had brought Anna the news as soon as it was realised what was involved and a heated discussion followed. The king had insisted on going over to see for himself but could only agree with what he had been told. It was Ultan, his lieutenant, who provided the most sensible solution.

'If we dig down along one side of the chamber, Your Majesty, it should be possible to get out the wood on that side, so allowing the diggers to remove the soil within much more easily, without damage to the body itself.'

Anna had agreed and there was some delay after the Mass whilst this was undertaken. The royal party retired to the tent formerly used by the priests and refreshments were served. Since they had all been fasting from midnight, to allow them to receive Holy Communion, everyone was ravenous and the food and drink disappeared in double quick time. Brother Uffa came in towards the end and only just managed to get a few left overs before Anna announced that the body of the late king had been exposed and it's removal was about to be attempted.

The populace too had taken the opportunity to feed the inner man and loaves and cakes and chicken and beef and ale appeared like magic and, before long, a carnival atmosphere prevailed. Crumbs and remnants were scattered far and wide, and when the time for the removal of the body arrived, the area resembled that where the five thousand had been fed.

The royal procession formed up again. The sub-deacon once more took the lead, bearing his crucifix, and was followed by the altar boys, bishop and priests, the king and queen and other important visitors. They reached the open chamber where Ultan and four former diggers stood, the latter having hastily rubbed their hands on the seats of their breeches, spat on their palms and slicked down their hair in preparation for the arrival of the royal party. The altar boys shuffled to one side of the chamber entrance and were shushed sternly by the sub-deacon as one or two began to chatter excitedly. Anna bent down and peered into the chamber where the gruesome outline of his ancestor could be made out. Only the central area of the burial chamber had been cleared, the objects above the head and below the feet remaining partly submerged by the soil which had drifted in.

'How can we get him out?'

The lieutenant was prepared for the question having thought of little else for the previous three days.

'We have a sheet here, sire. If we manoeuvre it underneath the body with the help of this man,' indicating the smallest of the diggers, who hung his head and shuffled his feet in embarrassment as the king's eyes focused on him, 'we can take the four corners and lift the body on the sheet.'

'Alright, get on with it,' said Anna stepping aside to let the four diggers move into position.

The little man stepped gingerly forward over Redwald's remains and bent down to take one corner of the sheet that Ultan had manipulated under the heels and then under the skull. He began to pull and the bones rattled as he did so.

'Careful,' roared Anna who was craning his neck over the backs of the kneeling figures to watch every move they made. Ultan burrowed his hand underneath the pelvis and beneath the spine and gradually the sheet was worked into place. He stood back to let one other digger step across the body to take the second corner on the far side. With a man on each corner Ultan moved forward again to assess the situation before giving the word to lift. He was forestalled.

'Altogether,' bellowed His Majesty, 'LIFT!'

It was a premature command. Since more than three quarters of the sheet was still on one side of the body the short side shot up abruptly and rolled Redwald's skeleton onto it's face. King Anna leapt into the air waving his arms franctically. He roared again.

'Careful, you imbeciles. Take it gently, gently.'

The four ex-diggers, bent nearly double, edged out of the chamber drawing the sheet with them just above ground level for fear of disturbing the body further. They laid it down with as much reverence as they could muster at the feet of the king.

Anna stalked round the prone skeleton, peering at it with some suspicion. He bent down to examine the chest area more carefully and suddenly gave a cry.

'Ha. Got it. Sacrilege.'

He reached down into the dust beneath the ribs and, with his thumb and forefinger, lifted out an object heavily coated with grime and silt and blew on it vigorously. Clouds of dust rose round the head of the stooping king, making him sneeze violently and cough and splutter and shake his head and wave his arms to disperse the enveloping miasma. Even that could not dampen his excitement. He rose to his feet, his dusty features bearing an expression of triumph, and held up his prize.

'A crucifix. A crucifix, I tell you. Buried with pagan objects. My Lord Bishop, take this, I must see if there is anything else in there.'

The king spun round to the astonished bishop, handed him the crucifix and darted back into the chamber entrance where he fell to his knees, his enormous rump blocking it completely, and began to sift through the debris which lay on each side of where the skeleton had been. Presently he gave another cry and picked up a second object which he blew on more gingerly and brushed off with his fingers.

'Holy water,' exclaimed the king brandishing what observers could see was an old skin bottle. 'Ultan, give it to the bishop,' he instructed, and thrust his head into the chamber again to resume his search. This time he remained there for some little while without finding any further trophies and eventually he backed out on all fours, cutting a somewhat undignified figure, which convulsed two altar boys who had to be cuffed soundly by the sub-deacon.

Anna stood up, brushed off his knees, squared his shoulders and strutted towards the bishop.

'There you are, my Lord. Just as I thought. A pagan burial with Christian objects included. It's barbaric; barbaric. There are no more sacred things that I can find so now it's over to you. A Christian burial for his remains and may God have mercy on his soul.'

The formalities were clearly at an end as far as the king was concerned. The altar boys, who had found the whole performance rather boring began to chatter among themselves and even the sub-deacon, with a disappointed expression on his face, seemed to have lost the will to control them. Enfleda, with a sense of anticlimax, began to watch the bishop who, bearing the crucifix and holy water bottle, was leading the four sheet bearers away from the scene. Glancing round, and seeing that the other diggers were replacing the side of the chamber, prior to filling in the trench and putting on the roof, she decided to follow Felix and beckoned Brother Uffa to accompany her.

His Lordship and the sheet bearers had, by then, reached the conveyance which was to transport the body back to the palace, and a coffin was being produced to receive it. After some discussion about the best means of getting the skeleton off the sheet and into the coffin, Enfleda decided that the obvious had to be stated.

'Put him in with the sheet round him.'

A circle of heads turned in her direction and then to each other and finally, without a word, they lowered the body and sheet gently into the coffin and tucked in the ends. The coffin was loaded and everyone looked at each other as if uncertain what to do next. The arrival of the king, still in high spirits, brought indecision to an end.

'Come on, all aboard.'

The king was eager that the next stage of the proceedings should begin.

'Horses. Where are horses? Ultan.'

Fortunately the horses appeared at once or the king would have been in danger of creating further chaos with conflicting instructions.

Everyone mounted and waited for the king to give the word. He rose in his stirrups and gazed round to make sure that everyone was ready.

'Forward.'

The procession moved off leaving the diggers shovelling the soil back into place and the altar boys, freed from the control of the sub-deacon, happily fighting.

It had been a long day.

In the solar King Anna, tired but happy, had put his feet up. The reburial had been reverently accomplished and had given him immense satisfaction. He felt that, at last, adequate atonement had been made for the sacrilege of Redwald's burial and he had spent so long saying his prayers of thanks after the ceremony that even his cloistered daughter had left the chapel and was enjoying a substantial meal when he rejoined the party.

His wife and daughters all together made Anna nervous. The queen, distrait when they were married, had become frankly eccentric as the years had gone by. She had spent so much time in her chamber, engaged in Anna hardly knew what, that he generally saw her only on ceremonial or matrimonial occasions. At the former she was impassive and unobtrusive, at the latter passionate and intense. The king's religious inclinations had created in him a certain sexual reluctance which the queen's surprising physical appetite and performance always succeeded in overcoming. Their union had been blessed with only female offspring and those who survived, having inherited their father's religious fervour, had, with the exception of the youngest, taken the veil. The two eldest were in convents too far removed to allow them to attend and the third, having taken every advantage of the festive board which the king provided, had returned within her convent walls, spiritually and physically refreshed. Anna, with a renewed feeling of giving his daughters to God had gone off to the solar for a bit of peace and quiet.

Enfleda too was alone and in pensive mood.
   The interlude with the East Angles had been unexpected but fascinating. King Anna was a delightful character and she had greatly enjoyed studying him as she always did with new people she met. There were so many aspects to his character that he was difficult to categorise. He was charming, kindhearted, ebbulient, endearing, confused and excitable yet, with all that, was a devout, almost saintly man. The princess had been so moved by the miracle that had saved all their lives on the ship that she had become more aware of spiritual matters and found the king both a source of inspiration by his fervour and reproach that she had been less than ardent herself in the past.
   Enfleda sighed. She would have to turn over a new leaf, especially now that she was going to live in a stronghold of the Celtic Church where people would be watching to see what Roman Christians were like. She mustn't let the side down.
   She began to wonder about the new life ahead of her. In particular should she keep to her own Roman customs or conform to Celtic ones. Thinking about it now she remembered that Father Romanus and Father Remus had both returned to Kent and she was without a chaplain of her own. What was she to do about it? It was the first time she had considered it. Her father would send another priest, of course, if she asked for one, but was it a good idea? The notion had only just come to her mind when the solution came also.
   'Brother Uffa.'
   She spoke aloud and smiled to herself as she did so. What would people

say if they found her talking to herself? What a good idea though. She would ask Oswy as soon as they were married if she might have Brother Uffa as her personal chaplain. He could hardly refuse her could he? New wives had to be indulged, or so she thought, so there should be no problem. Would Brother Uffa want to do it though? She did hope so since she had established an affinity with him which greatly pleased her. She would ask him tomorrow before they left to return to the ship. Oh, she hoped he would agree.

Brother Uffa was troubled and was discussing his problem with Brother Fursey.

They had been sitting in silence for some time, Fursey realising that something was on his friend's mind and being unwilling to disturb his musing. Presently Uffa resumed their conversation.

'I was so moved, today, Fursey, when I attended Holy Mass that, for a long time, I didn't realise what was worrying me. Now. Let me see if I can put it into words.'

He hesitated again as if arranging his thoughts before proceeding.

'Taking part in the celebration of Holy Mass today – Mass of course in the Roman rite – I was struck by the realisation that the sacrifice was, in every important way, identical with our own in the Celtic rite.'

Uffa raised his eyebrows in the direction of Fursey as if asking for confirmation. Fursey nodded and then, after a moment, replied, 'Agreed.'

'Alright then,' resumed Uffa, 'in all essentials the same but in some – a few – inessentials not quite the same. Then I recalled that I had noted other differences – minor of course – within our own rite which were sometimes evident in different places. I once went to Ireland,' he continued, as if now telling a story, 'and visited several monasteries there before returning by sea via Hii, right round the north of our island, back to Northumbria. Everywhere I went there were small changes from the last place – nothing of substance but they were there and I began to wonder if it was the same in the Roman Church. Today, after the reburial, I sought out Bishop Felix and spoke for a while to him. He knew the Church in several parts of Gaul and here in England and he admitted that similar differences were evident there too. So I asked him this . . .'

Brother Uffa had drawn his chair up to that of his companion and began tapping him on the knee.

'Suppose, in one region, a fundamental change was introduced. How would that be received by the others and what, if anything, could be done about it?'

'And what was his answer?' Fursey was listening very carefully and he too had leaned forward so that their faces were inches away from each other.

'His answer was that the matter would be referred to Rome for a Papal decree on the validity or otherwise of the new rite. And if it were declared invalid – ' Uffa's finger began tapping again 'those concerned would be told that if they continued the practice they would no longer be considered in communion with Rome – excommunicated in fact.'

'So,' Fursey was simply prompting in his monosyllabic replies.

'So,' went on Uffa taking a deep breath, 'I asked myself what would the position be if the same thing happened in our Church. To whom would such a question be referred? Who would give a ruling? Would we refer to Rome or not? And if not, to whom? And would any decision be accepted by those concerned?

'I think – ' Brother Uffa became hesitant again, as he seemed to be nearing the crux of his problem 'that we need a head – and a single head for the Roman and Celtic Church or there will soon be not one Christian Church but two. The questions about Easter and our tonsure are just examples of how differences can grow up and I believe that unless we give up our position and conform, we will soon be split off and, after that, split up among ourselves. It worries me. The feeling I had at Mass today is because our Faith is universal and as such should be enjoyed by everyone. It would be tragic if anything happened to destroy it.'

There was silence for a long time after Uffa stopped speaking. He himself seemed disconsolate at the threat to Church unity of which he had become aware. Fursey watched him affectionately, realising how fond he had become of this perceptive monk from the north. Finally Fursey rose and laid a hand on Uffa's shoulder.

'You are correct, my friend, but preaching to the converted. You have no need to be concerned about schism here though. Realising as you have, that there cannot be two opposing sects of Christianity in one region, I have been accepting the Roman Easter for some years now. I believe we should all do so and, if you have any influence in the north, you must exercise it if you can. Perhaps not immediately but when the time comes. Remember though that it is not a change that will be made easily – it may take a decade or more. But it will have to be made or else the division of faiths you foresee will come about one day. Perhaps the princess will help you to accomplish it, who knows? Perhaps you and she can do something towards it together.'

Fursey seemed about to stop speaking but after a brief pause resumed his theme.

'It is the Celtic isolation that has created the problem. We have grown to be independent of the rest of Christendom and even independent of each other in our own separate monasteries. Our own customs grew up and we saw no need to change them. What others did had little or no effect on the placid nature of our lives. What we lacked, although we did not realise it, was contact with those whose allegiance to Rome had never been interrupted as ours had. I realised this only too well when I came here and you have realised it too. Now you must try to disturb the Celtic isolation of Northumbria so that outside ideas will impinge upon it as they did on you here. Bring our two Churches together and we will know we are one. Keep us apart and we will grow further and further apart until one day the link may snap.

'Let us pray now,' he ended, 'that this will never happen.'

Chapter 11

King Oswy was standing by the window of his bedchamber where he had stood on that fateful day when the news of Oswald's death had reached him. But, now, he was not watching the angry waves beating on the rocks far below, he was looking tenderly at the unfamiliar form in the bed he had just left.

Enfleda slept peacefully, her head turned to one side, her arm flung upwards bringing her breast into view. The king had not thought it possible that he could have developed such an affection for someone he had seen for the first time only a week ago. Yet here he was wanting to spend more and more time in his wife's presence to get to know her intimately as quickly as possible. He smiled as the word 'intimately' came into his head, realising that it did not merely have a sexual connotation. There was that of course. Oswy had been thrilled by their love-making and had awakened in Enfleda passions she had not suspected – or so she had told him. She seemed happy to discuss their sexual life together in a frank and open manner when, if he had thought about it at all, he might have expected reluctance or embarrassment or even coyness.

Perhaps it was love that he was feeling now, Oswy wondered, instead of the lust that had driven him into other sexual encounters. Certainly the ecstacy he had experienced each time they had come together had some extra dimension to it above the carnal orgasms he had known in the past. 'Thank you' he had said after their consummation. He had spoken without thinking and had realised later, with surprise, that he had never thanked a woman before for the pleasure she had given him.

'A penny for your thoughts?'

He was surprised as Enfleda spoke to him from the bed. In his thoughts he was no longer seeing her although he was looking straight at where she lay. She smiled at him and apologised at once.

'I'm sorry, my Lord, I didn't mean to startle you. You were miles away. What were you thinking about?'

'You.'

This time she laughed aloud in sheer happiness and he smiled back, sharing her pleasure. Their natural ease together had come as a blessed relief to Enfleda. Oswy had been pleasant and understanding from the moment they met but, very soon, all restraint between them vanished and they established a familiarity which she could not have hoped for so quickly. Even in the two hectic days after her arrival, when frantic preparations were being made for the wedding, she knew that she *liked* Oswy. From the moment of their first love-making she knew that, now, there was a much deeper emotion than mere liking. Whether it could be love or not Enfleda did not, then, know but now, only a few days later, she was certain that it was.

Oswy's physical approach to her had been full of understanding and consideration for her feelings. Although she had known what to expect she had no suspicion of her own latent passion, which he aroused so quickly that the need for gentleness was swept away by a mutual surge of violent sexual emotion. She had been almost ashamed afterwards of the flagrant abandon she had shown until Oswy had told her of the excitement her wantonness had created in him and how wonderful his own climax had been as a result.

Her own had astounded her. The nature of the act she had known about but that it's culmination should be such an explosion of pure ecstacy had been a revelation to her. She had clasped him so tightly to her after it was over that her arms had ached and when he had said his simple 'thank you' tears had come into her eyes. For a long time she had lingered in the pleasure of her afterglow and he, realising her fulfillment, had stayed silent, gently stroking and kissing her hair. It had been she who had broken the silence.

'One flesh.'

'What?'

'One flesh – what it says in the bible. Now I really know what it means. That is just what I felt we were, my Lord. One flesh,' and after a pause, 'it was ecstacy.'

And so it had been each time they had been together. Afterwards when they had laid in each other's arms or side by side, unwilling to break the spell they had created, Enfleda had begun to talk, describing her first thoughts when she saw him or relating the terrors of their journey, recalling her childhood and family, amusements and fears or diverting him with descriptions of King Anna. She had felt an urge to share all their life before they met so that she would have no memory that he did not have. Her stories – and she always seemed to have something new to tell – stimulated him to similar confidences although he was, by nature, more reticent than she. Oswy even surprised himself by the things he found to tell her. Enfleda was a good listener as well as a good story teller and her subtle promptings kept up his own accounts of events from his past which he had almost forgotten. Now she spoke to him again, eager for more news.

'Tell me about your brother. It seems so awful, him being killed like that and buried so far away. Somehow without a grave one cannot mourn properly. Do you miss him?'

Oswy came over and sat beside her on the bed. For a moment he put his hands on each side of her face and looked intently into it as if examining her features minutely. Then he kissed her softly, stood up again and began pacing the floor, a habit she was becoming accustomed to. He did not directly answer her question.

'My first thought, when I heard the details of his death, was that I should go and retrieve the body and bring it back here for burial. But you were expected daily,' Oswy smiled at her as he spoke 'and I wanted to be here when you arrived not miles away. Then, as we waited, not of course knowing about your delay by the storm, all kinds of stories were brought to me about strange happenings near where he died.'

'What kind of strange things?' Enfleda was sitting upright in bed hugging the covers round her for warmth.

'Well, miracles, I suppose you would call them. It's hard to know what they were really.'

'Oh, please tell me.' Enfleda was following him closely with her eyes and was squirming with excitement.

'The first was a complicated story about a traveller passing that way on horseback. When he got near to the spot where he knew my brother had died his horse was seized with sudden pains and began foaming at the mouth and rolling its eyes. Finally it collapsed on the ground screaming in dire distress and started to thrash about wildly. One violent movement rolled it right over several times until it came to lie on the exact spot where Oswald was killed. At once it stopped struggling and lay calm for a moment. Then it got up and stood peacefully by as if nothing had happened. The traveller didn't know what to make of it at all but, since the horse was now well again, he rode on. Not far away he stopped for the night at an inn where he told the tale to the landlord, saying that it must have been a very holy spot to cure an animal in that way. Without a word the landlord went to his quarters and returned in a few minutes carrying a girl of about eight or nine, his daughter, who had been paralysed from birth. 'Take me there,' he said to the traveller. 'Now?' asked the surprised man.

'Now, at once,' replied the landlord, 'there's a cart round the back in which we can transport her and we will see if this holy spot can cure her too.'

'And did it?'

'Oh, yes. Completely. She fell asleep as soon as they put her on the ground and, when she awoke the next morning, she could walk properly.'

'Do you believe it, Oswy?'

'I must,' he replied. 'They all came to tell me as king – the traveller, the landlord, his daughter, whom I saw and spoke to, as well as two or three others who swore she had been paralysed since she was born.'

'Well, I can believe it too,' said Enfleda emphatically, 'after the miracle that saved our ship. If Oswald died fighting the heathen he was a martyr and a saint and I'm not surprised such miracle cures occurred. Have there been others?'

'Oh, yes. A lot. Mostly cures of people who took some of the earth, put it into water, drank it and were better at once.'

'From what?'

'The ague, blindness, lameness, possession by devils, fits – all kinds of things. There was one occasion when a man had taken some of the earth, wrapped it in a linen cloth, and hung it on a beam in his house. That night his house burned down and all that was preserved was that one beam with the earth, still in its linen cover, hanging in place.'

Both fell silent for a while considering these wonders before Enfleda spoke again.

'Now I know what you must do, Oswy. You must go and bring his relics back here – perhaps not the whole body, since it would be wrong to deprive that holy spot of it's miraculous power – but some of his bones. You must go and please can I come too? Do say yes. Please?'

Her husband laughed and nodded and said simply, 'Alright, if you want to, of course you can come.'

Enfleda was out of bed like a flash, flinging her arms round him and holding her naked body to his.

'Oh, Oswy, thank you. I do love you.'

For a moment there was a further silence. It was the first time either of them had said it. Oswy stood very still gazing down into her eyes before he answered her.

'And I love you.'

Edith could scarcely believe in her own miracle.

Another month had gone by since the sickness had begun and it was now starting to pass off. She had taken every opportunity to talk to the women around the castle and had asked a number of questions when pregnancy was under discussion, as it often was. She was sure she had aroused no suspicions since they were all used to her childlessness and they had answered her questions sympathetically.

The sickness, they said, often came on between the first and second month and usually disappeared sometime during the fourth, although some women were troubled with it throughout. If she had got it right, and if the women were to be relied upon, which was perhaps in question, she might be almost four months pregnant now.

Four months pregnant! Dare she tell James? Four months pregnant by the end of September might mean a birth about the end of February or in early March. Perhaps she should wait a little longer just to be sure although there was no denying her clothes were tight. Her face too was more rounded, or so James said, although of course he had no suspicion of the reason. He had just thought she was getting a little older and plumper, she supposed, but he seemed to like it and said it suited her.

He was so busy now that she saw him less often and she sometimes found time lying heavily on her hands. There was little need for her skill in the making of church vestments, which had been useful on Iona, and, although she made clothes for herself and James, she had much time to herself. The idle gossip of the other ladies about the palace held nothing for her and she had lately resumed the embroidery which had occupied her as a young lady-in-waiting to Queen Ethelberga. It was while she was so engaged that Enfleda's message reached her.

'Her majesty would be pleased if you would join her in her chamber, Lady Edith.'

She had been surprised by the summons. Along with the other palace women she had met the queen and found her charming and sincere but she had not been singled out for any special attention. Perhaps Her Majesty was inviting several of the women – the older women, Edith thought, smiling to herself – to take some refreshment with her. It would be very acceptable if that were so and she indicated her agreement, put down her work, straightened her gown and prepared to follow the messenger.

Enfleda, looking radiant in a green gown gathered high beneath her bosom and falling in graceful folds to her feet, was sitting by the window enjoying the afternoon sun. She was gracious and charming, putting Edith immediately at her ease and instructing the servant to bring up a stool and place it close beside her.

'Your Majesty.'

Edith curtsied as low as she dared, accepted the seat next to the queen and watched her with genuine admiration. If appearances were to be trusted it looked as if the king were a very fortunate man. Trying not to stare deliberately Edith waited patiently for the queen to break the silence.

'You must have thought it strange, Lady Edith, that I have not invited you much sooner.'

Edith, startled by this unexpected opening scarcely knew what to answer but finally managed to say, 'Why no, Your Majesty, I had no such expectations.'

'It is good of you to say so,' the queen went on, 'but the fact remains that since you were in the service of my mother, I should, in all politeness, have asked you to come sooner. But I have only just learned that you were with my mother – with her literally until the moment of her departure from Northumbria in a leaky vessel bound for Kent. Is that not so?'

'Yes. I was in her service, Your Majesty, even during her flight from York to Whitby and, as you say, it was certainly a disreputable craft she left in – and very full too. We could not all get aboard and I was one of those who stayed behind. A great deal has happened since then and only when I heard of Your Majesty's betrothal to King Oswy – Prince Oswy as he was then – did I know for certain that the ship had arrived safely.'

Edith, who had never forgotten that day when she stood and watched the disappearing craft with James and Father Melchior, fell silent at the reminder of it and of the emotions they had all felt, three lonely figures on the headland.

'I don't think I remember you.' The queen was speaking and Edith dragged her thoughts back to the present.

'You would not, I believe Madam. You were always looked after by the Lady Eldrena and, although the ladies-in-waiting saw you from time to time, there were always several of us together and there is no reason why you should remember me – except perhaps,' Edith added, 'that I was one of the final party to accompany you to Whitby.'

'I can remember little of that I'm afraid. A long boring journey in a jolting cart is about all I can bring to mind – or was until now. Eldrena! Yes, now I recall her. She had been my mother's nurse too and she became ill on the journey, did she not? Do you know, that had gone completely out of my mind.'

'She died, Your Majesty. Perhaps you were not told for fear of upsetting you. It was certainly most upsetting for us all. It was a desperate journey and I think my husband and I were the only ones who remember anything good about it.'

'Your husband. Were you married then?'

'No, not then, Madam. But it was on that journey that we first realised . . . that we cared for each other. We were not to be married for a long time and then in far away Iona where we knew your husband's late brother, King Oswald.'

'Gracious, what a time you must have had. I will look forward to hearing about it sometime.' The queen seemed genuinely interested in what Edith was saying. 'You have every reason for happy memories. But your husband . . . would I have met him?'

'I think not Madam. He was in the escape party, of course, but he acted mainly as a scout, patrolling the area through which we were travelling so he was often far away from the rest of the party.'

'I should like to meet him,' said Enfleda, again sounding as if she was sincere and not being merely polite. 'What position does he hold in the palace?'

'He is what is called the "scriba," Your Majesty. He is establishing a school for the illumination of sacred manuscripts. He is always to be found in the scriptorium. He works too hard, Madam, I fear. I miss him at home.'

Enfleda smiled at Edith's unassuming answer and then, after a pause, made an enquiry which had just come into her head.

'Does that mean that you are alone quite a lot without special duties?'

'I have none, Your Majesty, beyond looking after James and he doesn't need much looking after as a rule.'

Enfleda paused for longer this time and was clearly giving Edith's answer careful consideration. At last she turned round to face her and held out a hand as though seeking to bridge the gap between them.

'The king and I are leaving tomorrow, as you may have heard,' began the queen. 'We feel that the body of the late King Oswald – or at least some of his relics – should be brought home to Bamburgh for veneration by his family and his former subjects. Only a few of us are going from the palace and I will be taking with me the two ladies-in-waiting I brought from Kent and several servants who have been assigned to me here. I don't know exactly how long we shall be away,' the queen went on, 'but when I return, in perhaps three or four weeks time, I hope I will be able to spend some time getting my own house in order.'

Edith smiled and nodded and said, 'Oh yes, of course, Your Majesty,' wondering where all this was leading.

'I have made no appointments yet to my household because, quite frankly, I did not know who was who in the palace and preferred to wait until I did. Until then I could rely on my Kentish ladies.'

Edith, becoming more mystified every moment, made no reply.

'Would you consider something while I am away and give me your answer when I return?'

'Of course, Your Majesty.'

'I would like you to be my First Lady of the Bedchamber, if you feel you could accept. You served my mother and I can think of nothing more appropriate than that you should serve me. I hope you will feel you can.' Enfleda was being her most charming and persuasive while making her offer. 'And furthermore, it would be my hope, that you would consider which ladies in the palace should join my household as ladies-in-waiting. I will not press you now for an answer but I hope – very much hope – that it will be a favourable one when I return.'

Three weeks had gone by and the queen's return was imminent before Edith told James.

She had insisted that he should sit quietly in front of her at the table and promise not to interrupt as she told her story. Several times he had seemed about to break in on her account but, each time, had managed to restrain himself, although with obvious difficulty. Once she had held up her finger to her lips and he had looked abashed and said nothing. He shifted impatiently in his seat as Edith described Enfleda's interest in their departure from Whitby and her failure to recall the journey in any detail. When Edith spoke of their realisation of their feelings for each other he could keep silent no longer.

'You didn't. Surely you didn't discuss that with the queen.'

'Oh James, of course I did. I wish you had been there. She was so natural and easy that we just talked together like any two women in the palace would. And then she told me about the journey to bring back Oswald's relics which you know about . . . and then . . . ' Edith became all hesitation and uncertainty in contrast to her earlier assurance '. . . then she asked me a question.'

'Asked you a question. What question?'

Edith did not answer him and he repeated his query.

'Edith, love, what did she ask you? You're being very mysterious all of a sudden.' He got up from his chair and came round the table to put his arm across her shoulders and said, more gently, 'What was it you were asked?'

'She wants me to be her First Lady of the Bedchamber,' gasped out Edith, burying her head in his chest and holding him tight.

James, not at all understanding what was going on spluttered out, 'But that's wonderful, isn't it. Don't you want to do it?'

'Of course I want to do it. Who wouldn't? But . . . oh dear, James . . . sit down again please. There's something more that you don't know and I want to tell you now. I'll never be able to do it if you don't go back and sit over there.'

She dried her eyes while James, even more mystified, returned to his seat.

'Alright, I'm sitting down. Sitting patiently,' he added.

Edith looked at him and smiled and stretched her hands across the table to take his. Then never taking her eyes off him she told him her news.

'There is one reason why she might not want me now – a reason I never dreamed of or I would have told you before. Oh James . . .' and she let go his hands, slid off her chair and came round the table to kneel in front of him. 'God has been good to us James, I'm going to have a baby.'

His stunned silence made her contrite at once. 'I'm sorry love I told you badly. It's true. Now I know it is. You see . . . '

She got no further. 'A baby? Edith you wouldn't tease me would you?'

'No, my darling. It is true. I am going to have a baby.'

Whatever reaction she might have expected from her husband she could hardly believe what happened. Tears were rolling down his cheeks and he was sobbing like a child. She stood up and came round behind him hugging him and resting her head upon his. Presently he recovered and looked up into her face, his own a mixture of laughter and tears.

'Edith, my darling, I'm so delighted – especially for you. I'm pleased for myself of course but I know how much the loss of our first one meant to you. Just think. After nine years . . . a baby. I can hardly believe it. It's the most wonderful news I've ever heard.'

And he took her into his arms as he spoke, letting her hair dry his moist cheeks and feeling her own tears running down onto his neck and chest. For a long time they remained absolutely still, receiving strength from each other to carry them through this supreme moment. James finally broke the silence.

'When?'

Edith gently disengaged herself from him and looked up.

'What, my dear?'

'When? When do you think it will be . . . the baby?'

'Oh, I'm sorry. We're not very coherent are we? The end of February perhaps or later – a little into March. It's difficult for me,' she reminded him, 'most women have a regular cycle and when that stops they can have some idea when to expect the child.'

Edith looked up at him again, for a moment, and then lowered her eyes in response to his quizzical expression.

'I know that I'm not supposed to be well up in these things but I've been enquiring – surreptitiously, of course – about what to expect without any kind of regular period. It's hard to be sure one's even pregnant, let alone when the baby might come. As you know if I had three or four shows a year I was lucky, so missing didn't mean anything. Then the sickness started and my clothes began to get tight and then the fluid in my breasts which were so tender and, finally, the movements which I felt for the first time about two weeks ago. At first I wasn't certain but then there was no mistaking them and, if you put your hand here . . . ' indicating the lower part of her stomach '. . . there's a swelling which wasn't so big even last time.'

She fell silent for a moment before ending, 'So there you are. I know it for certain.'

James watched her dotingly for some time before speaking again.

'Not that it matters now,' he suggested diffidently, 'but I suppose this is why you think Her Majesty won't want you as her First Lady of the Bedchamber?'

'Of course. Why would she want me pregnant?' was her answer.

'Why not?' was his.

Hulgest was a short insignificant man of so ordinary an appearance that even King Penda had difficulty in remembering him once the spy left his presence. Now the little man stood patiently waiting for the king to give him permission to present his report.

At present, however, the king's whole attention was devoted to a fawning procureur who was displaying naked girls plundered during a raid on the East Angles. There were eight in all, the oldest perhaps seventeen and the youngest . . . what . . . twelve maybe, Hulgest considered. It was rumoured that Penda had a penchant for very young girls but would reveal it only if the queen were absent, as now.

All eight stood in a sullen row before the great king while their repellant owner displayed them as if they were so much merchandise. They were roughly pushed into a variety of postures while his pawing hands displayed a flat abdomen, a swelling buttock, a firm breast or a rounded thigh, always stroking or touching as he did so, regardless of the humiliation of the subject.

Penda left his chair to see more closely and Hulgest watched with some amusement as the king tried to disguise the fact that his chief interest was in the two youngest. Neither, yet, showed full pubertal development – children still, Hulgest thought, and shuddered inwardly as the revolting bargain was struck and the remaining girls led away to be displayed elsewhere. Already one or two of the courtiers present were signalling surreptitiously to him indicating with a jerk of the head or a flick of the eye that they were in the market for the others. Penda passed his tongue over his thin dry lips and was unable to keep an expression of open lust from his face. His eyes followed both girls from the room as his chamberlain led them away. Then he returned to his throne, smirking evilly, unable to forget his two captives. Hulgest wondered, as he often did in Penda's presence, why he served such an abhorrant master. Money of course; there was no other reason.

The king's eyes eventually came to rest on his spy and he pushed himself upright on his throne and rapped out a single word.

'Well?'

'I have much to report, Your Majesty, and all good.' Hulgest knew from long experience how to whet Penda's appetite for revenge. 'There is no military activity of any kind in Northumbria, my Lord. Not a sign of recruitment or manoeuvres or even interest in defence or attack. Your own withdrawal from the field, after the defeat of Oswald, has led them to believe that your forces too, were severly mauled.'

'I know that you fool. They *were* mauled. I don't need you to tell me that. Get on with your report.'

Penda's eyes blazed and his face became suffused with anger. Better be careful though Hulgest. No point in inflaming him like this; there was no telling what he might do.

'But you misled them, Your Majesty. They imagine your losses too great for early recovery – I was told so more than once in as many words – due to your cleverness in giving them that impression.' Hulgest sighed inwardly as he saw Penda visibly relax under his flattery. He hurried on nevertheless. Impatience was Penda's middle name and at any moment he could flare up again.

'The new king, Oswy, is completely taken up with his bride, sire – Enfleda of Kent. Everyone says he is besotted with her and is certainly neglecting rebuilding his army. With winter approaching, Your Majesty – already there is snow on the Northumbrian hills – he has no hope of getting together an army until the spring – April or so at the earliest. With your own preparations so well advanced, by your own perspicacity, you will have a formidable army which can march long before he can summon up any effective resistance.'

Penda's gloating satisfaction was all too plain as he smirked round at his henchmen who smiled and nodded to each other in agreement with their master's brilliance.

'This woman. What is she like?'

Penda often managed to bring the conversation back to the subject of women.

'Passable, Your Majesty. Passable. Not a beauty.' Hulgest was anxious to complete his report without any long discussion of the Northumbrian queen who, in fact, he had never seen. 'And pregnant,' he added, rightly surmising that the king would then lose interest.

'Hm. What else?'

'They are giving all their attention to Oswald's relics, Your Majesty. The king and his wife visited the place of his defeat at your hands and they are spreading false rumours of miraculous happenings which his bones are supposed to have produced. They have dug up his body and taken some of it – the head and arms, I think, which you cut off – back to Bamburgh. They seem to think of little else. Miracles are all they talk about. As I said, Your Majesty,' added Hulgest, who felt that the interview had gone on far too long and who was hungry and thirsty,' there is no military activity of any kind.'

'Good.'

Penda had risen to his feet as he said the word. He waived Hulgest away with an impatient gesture and growled to his chamberlain.

'Now I am going to my private quarters. Bring those two girls and pay this man. But keep him near at hand, I may need him again soon. Go on fool. Go on and get the girls.'

The journey to Maserfield had taken two weeks.

The king and queen had ridden side by side for almost the entire time and had talked in animated fashion for hour after hour. It was plain that they were wrapped up in each other and the mood of the party was jovial and friendly as a result and there was much laughter and gaiety despite the solemn purpose of the expedition. Each night, when their camp had been set up and a meal prepared and everyone had eaten their fill, minstrels entertained them or stories were told and the new queen was regaled with tales of valour from earlier times when Saxon heroes had first landed in these islands and the Britons had been scattered to the west.

As they neared their destination, however, the nature of their undertaking made itself felt and everyone became more subdued and some not a little apprehensive at what might lie ahead. Brother Uffa, now installed as the queen's personal chaplain, and Enfleda herself, were the only members of the expedition with any direct experience of exhumation although the circumstances of Redwald's disinterrment, and those about to be embarked upon to remove Oswald's body, had little in common. Nevertheless Uffa was questioned by several people, including the king, about the niceties that ought to be observed when the remains were exposed and the time for removal arrived.

Three members of Oswald's army, who had been present when the scattered portions of the body had been retrieved and reverently reburied, after the withdrawal of Penda's forces, were in the present party in case of any difficulty in identifying the grave. Not only was there no such problem but there was no shortage of willing locals anxious to guide the king during the last stage of the journey. Word had spread that the royal party was approaching and during the last day's journey, they met little groups of villagers patiently waiting for them to arrive. These would raise a cheer as Oswy and Enfleda rode by and then attach themselves to the rear of the procession or keep pace with it on each side, near enough to see their Lord and Master and his beautiful lady, but far enough away not to be obtrusive.

The king's party made their last camp within a mile of the grave, intending to begin the solemn business of exhumation at an early hour. Brother Uffa had given instructions that an altar was to be erected, and Holy Mass was to be celebrated, before there was any attempt to expose the body. The king and queen, most of the cohort from Bamburgh and many of the locals received the Sacrament and hymns were sung and the area of the grave incensed.

In the three months since the king's death the grave, and the place upon which he had been killed, which was no more than a hundred yards away, had become popular sites of pilgrimage. On the spot where he had died a simple wooden cross had been erected with a plaque attached to it bearing the message

On this sacred spot
His Majesty King Oswald
of Bernicia and Deira
was killed by the heathen while defending Christianity
August 5
in the Year of our Lord 642
aged 38 years.

But the stories of miraculous cures brought about by the earth from such a holy place had spread like wildfire and, where once there had been a flat plain with the cross planted firmly in it, there was now a depression nearly two feet deep and six feet across at its widest point, from which the relatives of the sick, hoping for a miracle cure for their loved ones, had scooped out soil and taken it home. The cross now stood on a small pinnacle of ground in the middle of this cavity and seemed in danger of being undermined if the fervour of the miracle-seekers continued.

It was Enfleda who noticed another curious manifestation of the sanctity of the place where Oswald fell.

After Mass was over, and the diggers were being assembled, she had wandered a short distance from the grave area and had walked up onto an area of elevated ground on which, although she did not know it, Penda's forces had been massed. Looking down towards the scene of activity she gave a little cry of surprise at what she saw. Around the cross and the circle of removed earth was a ring of green grass contrasting sharply with the brown vegetation elsewhere. At first she could hardly believe what she was seeing but, when she looked again, there was no doubt about it. It was now early November and the tufted, withered grass of the plain below her stretched out endlessly all around and there, in it's centre, precisely where the cross stood, was lush turf, green and healthy as though it were early summer. Enfleda clapped her hands in delight and raced back down the hill to Oswy who was standing with Brother Uffa making last minute decisions.

'Oswy, come and see. You too, Brother Uffa. This is another miracle, I'm sure.'

The two men looked at each other in a puzzled fashion as Enfleda stood excitedly in front of them calling, 'Come on. Please come.'

'Come where?'

'Up there. You can't see it properly from here.' And taking Oswy by the hand she dragged him back up the hill with Brother Uffa following.

She turned round triumphantly, when she reached her former position, and pointed downwards.

'There. Look.'

'But what is . . . '

Oswy got no further with his question but stood amazed and speechless as he saw the remarkable greenery before him. Uffa too had seen it as soon as the queen pointed and had crossed himself and fallen to his knees. After a moment Oswy and Enfleda followed his example and for a short time all three prayed in silence. When Brother Uffa stood up he spoke very solemnly.

'There is no doubt, Your Majesty, that your brother was a saintly man. The other stories of miracles – apart from the girl's cure of paralysis whom you saw yourself,' added the priest diplomatically, 'may have been greatly exaggerated or wishful thinking or even – ' he shook his head sadly as he admitted the possibility 'lies. But this grass we have seen with our own eyes, green and fresh when everything else in this inhospitable terrain is brown and autumnal. There is no limit to the power of Almighty God and he reveals Himself in strange ways. Now, in our presence, He has shown us His might through King Oswald, whom I believe we shall soon be calling St Oswald.'

There was silence for a time as Oswy and Enfleda, still scarcely able to believe the evidence of their own eyes, watched the scene below. Then Uffa gave a little cough and spoke again.

'We have been privileged to be here and what we have seen must surely be God's stamp of approval on our enterprise. I think they are ready below. May we return?'

In the three months since Oswald's death a good deal of decomposition was expected but it was still felt that enough resistance would be appreciated to indicate where and at what level the body lay.

Resistance was met almost at once and careful raking soon revealed their first view of the body. Enfleda had been apprehensive about whether or not she would find the smell insupportable but had felt that she should be nearby out of respect for the late king, especially now that his saintly qualities were so evident. Curiosity overcame squeamishness and she edged nearer and nearer, encouraged by the lack of any unpleasant odour. Even those working in the grave, with their faces close to the earth they were removing, seemed unaware of noxious vapours from the putrifying remains which some had thought might be overwhelming. Then as Enfleda was moving closer still, one of the workmen gave a cry.

'An arm! I can see it.'

'Be very careful!'

Oswy stepped to the edge of the grave in his anxiety that no injury should be sustained by the body or it's severed members. As he did so the man who had found the arm gave a strangled cry, turned ghastly pale and looked with staring eyes at the king.

'What is it? What's the matter?'

Oswy, alarmed by the man's expression, which was a mixture of fear and disbelief, stopped for a moment then bent down to see more closely. He and Enfleda and Brother Uffa, as well as several members of the royal party who were close by, were able to hear the man's next words with incredulity.

'It's whole. The arm, it's whole – like mine or anyone's. Not rotten and black, white and healthy as if he had never died.'

The workman, overcome by his astonishing discovery could no longer restrain himself. Leaping to his feet he turned this way and that, shouting all the while.

'The flesh! It's as if he were still alive. A miracle. A miracle. The arm's like mine. As if it had never been in the earth.' Then he sank to his knees, whimpering, 'a miracle,' and became incoherent.

Oswy threw himself prone on the ground and looked intently at the exposed limb whilst Enfleda and Brother Uffa craned over his back to see for themselves. The earth had been removed from the lower part of the forearm, wrist and hand which were clearly in view. There was not a blemish to be seen. Even the individual hairs on the back of the late king's hand could plainly be identified. The skin looked clean and healthy and, when Oswy stretching forward, tentatively touched it he murmured, 'Soft and supple, as if he were alive.'

Gaining confidence, the king brushed aside more soil to reveal the upper forearm, the elbow and the area above it. Then, as they all stared fixedly at the limb, he took the hand and lifted it. The elbow bent as easily as Oswy's own which so startled him that he let it fall again back into place.

'Praise be! Almighty God has used King Oswald again to work another miracle and to show His power,' cried Uffa from behind the king. 'He is incorrupt. Even in death he is preserved by God's hand.'

After that there was pandemonium. Many fell to their knees and prayed as if they would never stop. Others tried to crowd forward to touch the incorrupt remains. The worker who had first discovered the arm rushed from group to group gabbling unintelligible gibberish and laughing and crying at the same time. Oswy clasped Enfleda in his arms whilst tears of joy ran down her cheeks. Brother Uffa had taken a thurible, which had been used at Mass, and incensed the grave before kneeling down in prayer. A few began to cheer and to throw their hats into the air while others struck up a hymn they had been singing earlier before the exhumation. Three dogs, which had come with the locals, set up a clamour of barking. Finally order was restored by Brother Uffa.

With the help of the king's personal guard, which had accompanied him from Bamburgh, the crowd was brought under control and shepherded together so that the monk could address them. Uffa waited patiently until they had all been rounded up and marshalled into place in front of the high ground which Enfleda had climbed earlier. From this vantage point he spoke to them.

'You have all been privileged,' he told them, 'to be present on a miraculous occasion. The preservation, incorrupt, of the body of the late King Oswald, after three months in the grave, is a manifestation of the power of Almighty God. King Oswald was slain by the heathen King Penda but God preserved his mortal body intact to show us that no pagan can ever overcome God's people. Any brief victory of the enemies of Almighty God in this world is as nothing compared with the reward of everlasting glory in the next. That glory will one day come to all who hear the word of God and keep it. Learn from this saintly body preserved in the earth that true riches do not come to the victor in this life but to those who inherit God's kingdom in the next.'

Uffa stopped speaking for a moment and gazed over the heads of the crown assembled before him. Then turning to the king and queen, he continued.

'Your Majesties have enjoyed the supreme experience, as we all have, of taking part in a miracle – a miraculous event which, by the power of Almighty God, defies the laws of nature. It is now the duty of us all to show ourselves worthy of God's goodness in permitting us to be here. This is what I propose, with your Majesties consent.'

Again Uffa paused to get the complete attention of the crown before him.

'I want five men – come forward . . . you and you . . . come along, any one will do. Right,' when five had shuffled forward, 'you will each form a group from those who are here and you will organise a relay of constant prayer whilst these diggers,' gesturing to those who had been working in the grave when the arm was found, 'gently and reverently expose and remove the rest of King Oswald's body. Then his limbs and trunk will be carefully washed and dried and, when the complete body is exhumed, it will be venerated and Holy Mass will be said again. Until then, I want constant prayer to God in thanksgiving for the honour of being allowed to be here. When one group finishes its prayer the next will take it up and then the next and so on. When the fifth group have prayed aloud the first will begin again until the body is laid out for us all to see. I have no doubt,' he concluded, 'that we will find the entire body miraculously preserved. When we have venerated these holy relics the head and arms, so brutally severed by Penda, will be carried by us back to Bamburgh, while the trunk will be reburied here in this hallowed spot.'

Edith had rehearsed over and over again what she was going to say when the queen returned but, in the event, was curiously tongue tied and incoherent so that she felt sure she was not making herself understood.

'Your Majesty,' she finally exclaimed, 'I'm sorry. I'm not saying it properly. What I am trying to tell you is that I am pregnant.'

'So am I,' replied Enfleda.

Enfleda had been more than thankful to be home again. The journey back to Bamburgh with Oswald's relics had been difficult. The cold seemed to descend on them without warning and a mild, late autumn was suddenly turned into fierce winter. The wind blew piercingly out of the north east straight into their faces as they struggled along. Snow and sleet showers blinded them and made their progress perilous. Only when they made camp, which now was becoming increasingly early in the shortening days, and huge fires were lighted, was there any comfort. Then, just as the queen was beginning to be troubled by her nausea, and was wondering how she was going to complete the journey, there was a brief respite and for three or four days a return of the milder weather allowed them to press hard for home.

It was November the 28th, and advent was almost upon them, when their tired horses limped through the castle gates to an enormous welcome. Word of the miracle had somehow preceded them and every man woman and child who was able was there to cheer as they made their entrance. Bishop Aidan had appeared that very day as if from nowhere and had donned his episcopal robes to receive the arms and head of the late king with due ceremony. Holy Mass was celebrated that evening and the relics were displayed for the veneration of the inhabitants of the castle and town. The master silversmith had already begun on the task of preparing reliquaries for such sacred objects.

James had been keen to watch the construction of the caskets. He had sought out Bertram, the silversmith, whom he knew slightly, and asked if he might see them being made at the different stages. It had been a fascinating spectacle and James had marvelled at the skill and artistry Bertram showed. He seemed to make few measurements or plans but knew instinctively what was needed at every step. When the two majestic caskets were complete James was lavish in his praise.

'Magnificent,' he exclaimed, 'truly magnificent.'

Bertram, who was a tiny man with a humped back from a childhood illness, glanced at his observer with a little smile whilst checking his work for the last time and giving it a final polish.

'I might say the same about your own work,' he said finally. 'I've seen some of it you know. It's as good as mine in it's own way – perhaps better.

You're an artist just as I am. Oh, I don't mind saying it,' as James seemed surprised. 'I know I'm an artist. We both are and for all I know there may be better ones somewhere – but not in Northumbria,' he added with a sly grin, 'not in Northumbria although one day I expect there will be.'

'Where did you learn and who taught you,?' enquired James.

'I had the most marvellous teacher,' Bertram answered. 'Eloi was his name and he was such a good man that he'll be St Eloi one day or I shall be very surprised. He lived in a part of France called Haute Vienne, near where I was born, and he was in the service of King Clotar the Second and later King Dagobert the First. I was lucky to work under such a man. He decorated shrines and tombs and made crosses and plaques and chalices – mostly in gold but also sometimes in silver.' Bertram stood quite still for a moment gazing into space before continuing. 'One of his finest pieces was for the altar of the Church of St Denis in Paris. I was with him when he made it and he took me with him to see it put in place. And do you know,' Bertram went on becoming quite animated, 'he never took the tiniest bit of precious metal for himself like so many did. There was one occasion,' the little man began chuckling at the recollection 'when King Clotar asked him to make a gold throne and provided the amount of gold which had been asked for before. Eloi made two thrones out of it and that's when the king took him into his service. Eloi became a priest later and finally a bishop. So you see,' Bertram grinned, bringing his story to an end, 'I had the best possible teacher a man could wish – best possible.'

James was not alone in his admiration of the reliquaries. The king and queen and Bishop Aidan were delighted with them when the two gleaming caskets were displayed for them before Holy Mass. They were now lined tastefully with purple cloth and the arms were laid reverently in one and the head in the other. The former were to be kept in the castle chapel of St Peter but the head was to go to the Monastery of Lindisfarne at the king's insistance. It was an impressive occasion at which Aidan presided and Brother Uffa was the celebrant. At the conclusion of the sacrifice the relics were borne in solemn procession round the chapel before the arms were deposited, in their casket, in a specially prepared alcove behind the altar.

Afterwards there was a splended banquet to celebrate the great occasion and to welcome back the king and queen. Enfleda, still suffering from nausea, did her best to eat some of the food put in front of her, for appearances sake, but did not find it easy. Edith, who knew exactly what the queen was suffering, was assiduous in her duties and hovered close by throughout the long meal. Bishop Aidan, sitting between the king and queen, ate sparingly despite Oswy's urging. The food during the journey from Oswald's grave had been adequate but not exciting and the king ate and drank with relish until a quiet cough from the bishop attracted his attention.

'Would your Majesties care to hear of a prophesy which has now been fulfilled?' Aidan enquired.

Oswy, about to drain a fresh goblet of wine, paused with it half way to his lips as if arrested by something in the bishop's tone, and nodded. Enfleda, anxious for anything that would divert her from the food and her nausea, was more emphatic.

'Yes, very much, my Lord Bishop. Do tell us.'

'It was, I believe, a year or two after I had come to King Oswald's court, from the Island of Hii, which you would know as Iona, Your Majesty,' he added, seeing the puzzled look on Enfleda's face. 'It was Easter time and, after hearing Holy Mass on the morning of Easter day, the king and I with many nobles sat down to dine here at this table just as we are doing now. The king was seated where you are Your Majesty,' the bishop continued nodding towards Oswy, 'and I was in the same seat I occupy now. A silver dish piled high with rich food was placed before us and I was about to bless it before we ate when one of the king's servants entered in some agitation. He was a man who had been specially appointed to relieve the poor and needy of the kingdom. He was a good man but I cannot now recall his name,' Aidan added regretfully.

A silence had fallen on those close to the royal couple and they had stopped eating to give more attention to what was being said.

'The servant reported to the king that a large crowd of poor, sick and lame people had gathered on the road outside the palace and were begging alms from the king. King Oswald did not hesitate one moment,' went on Aidan in a more incisive tone. '"Take all this food here" he said, pointing to the dish before him, "and give it to them at once. Then weigh the dish and give it's value in money to them also, distributing it equally to all. We have more than enough left for ourselves on these other tables so that we can all eat our Easter meal together, poor and rich alike."'

Aidan reached over and took King Oswy's right hand before speaking again. Then holding it up in the air he continued:

'I was so moved by the enormous generosity of the king that I took his hand, Your Majesty, as I am now taking yours, and I exclaimed, "May this hand never wither with age." Well, Your Majesties, my Lords, you have seen today that it did not wither with age nor even with death and buriel. I had no knowledge then of what would one day happen but now I have seen, as you all have, God's prophesy, uttered through his most unworthy servant, come true.'

All around the nobles and their ladies were laying down their knives and pushing away their platters. Everyone seemed suddenly to have no appetite any longer. There was a shuffling of feet and some downcast eyes and the king looked distinctly uncomfortable and quite uncertain what to do next. It was Enfleda who prompted him.

'Was that not a generous gesture, my Lord – a gesture to emulate?'

'Oh, indeed,' Oswy responded immediately, clearly relieved that the embarrassing silence had been broken. 'We have all eaten our fill already, I am sure. Let us, like my saintly brother, send all that remains of our food to the needy whom I am certain we will have no difficulty in finding even though they may not be outside the castle gates. Wilbert,' he called to his chamberlain, 'have all this food collected and see that it is distributed to those most in need of it. We will withdraw to allow the servants to get it all together. When all is done report to me again.'

Grace was said and the company rose, those near Their Majesties standing deferentially aside to allow them and Bishop Aidan to leave the banqueting chamber first. Oswy walked over to a huge fire blazing at the far end of the audience chamber and began to warm his hands. Aidan followed and, after a moment when the king turned towards him again, asked a favour.

'Your Majesty, may I be so bold as to ask if I might be permitted to see the Gospels which Her Majesty Queen Enfleda brought from Kent as a wedding gift? When I was here on the occasion of your marriage I was obliged to return to Lindisfarne soon afterwards, you may recall, without seeing them. Brother Uffa had spoken to me of their great beauty and, before I leave this time, I would dearly love to see them.'

'By all means. Of course.' Oswy, clearly delighted that a new subject had arisen to free him from his former embarrassment, could not agree too quickly. 'My chamberlain has gone on . . . other duties,' Oswy went on hastily, 'but Brother Uffa knows where they are in my private quarters and I'm sure he will bring them. Brother Uffa,' raising his voice to attract the monk's attention, 'would you be so good as to help us by bringing the Kent Gospels here for his Lordship? Thank you,' as Uffa, only too happy to please gestured to two servants to accompany him and left the room.

'Let's see . . . here I think,' exclaimed Oswy jovially. 'Clear this table by the window. The light is good here and you will be able to appreciate them. You will be amazed at their beauty, my Lord.'

Only a short time passed before Brother Uffa led the two servants back into the room carrying a large volume.

'Here, put it here,' called the king, now quite free from any restraint. 'My Lord, come and see. Did you ever see anything so beautiful?'

Aidan poured over the St Matthew Gospel for a long time, gently turning the pages to admire the wonderful regularity of the script and the resplendant beauty of the great decorated pages.

'It is truly magnificent,' he said at last. 'With one exception the most excellent example of sacred embellishment I have ever seen. But the style of writing is unfamiliar to me. Do you know what it is called, Your Majesty?'

'Sadly no,' Oswy answered. 'The queen may know . . . do you, my Lady,' addressing Enfleda who was feeling somewhat better now that she was not plagued by the sight nor smell of food.

'I should my Lord, but although I have seen them many times I have never had the script explained to me although it was in common use in Kent. But surely,' she suddenly cried, clapping her hands in excitement, 'our "scriba" will know, will he not, Edith? She turned towards her Lady of the Bedchamber to continue her question. 'Can we not . . . Edith, whatever is the matter? Are you alright?'

Edith, who had been watching Enfleda closely from a distance which had not permitted her to see the open book, had moved forward as the queen addressed her and saw the initial page of the St Matthew Gospel with the great decorated page beside it. She was standing quite motionless and was gazing at the two pages as if transfixed by what she saw. Her mouth opened and closed but no sound emerged. She moved closer and became oblivious of everything but the volume on the table. She reached out her hand as if to touch but then withdrew it quickly. She turned her head towards the queen and was about to speak before Enfleda broke in again.

'Edith, you look as if you have seen a ghost.'

But it was clear as she was speaking that the colour was returning to Edith's cheeks and once more she was aware of her surroundings. With a penitent gesture she curtsied to the king and then to the queen and remained in her deep curtsey as she addressed them.

'Your Majesties, my humble apologies for my behaviour. How can you forgive my presumption. I had a great shock, sire, my Lady – so great that I was unaware of everything but this Gospel text on the table. Please forgive me Your Majesties.'

'Of course.' Oswy was quick to forgive and smiled kindly at Edith while Enfleda helped her to her feet.

'We could see you had had a shock, Lady Edith,' said Oswy speaking gently, 'but what caused it. You did indeed, as the queen said, look as if you had seen a ghost.'

'I had, Your Majesty. That ghost.' Edith was pointing at the Gospels as she spoke.' They went with Queen Ethelberga to Kent, years ago, soon after King Edwin was killed, and I never thought to see them again.'

'Of course, I had not realised that, since the Gospel's came with my mother, you would know their history.' Enfleda was again clapping her hands in excitement as she spoke. 'But,' she continued, with a puzzled frown on her face, 'what I don't understand is how you can be so sure that these are the same Gospels. Can you be certain?'

'Quite certain, Your Majesty,' answered Edith quietly. 'You see, my husband made them. They are all his work. I would know them anywhere.'

'I still can't believe it.'

James and Edith had returned to their quarters as darkness fell and had lighted the lamp and sat down at the table to go over again the events of the day. James was shaking his head from side to side and looking so bemused that Edith placed her arms around his shoulders and rested her head upon his.

'When I saw those Gospels lying on the table I couldn't believe my eyes. To see them again after all this time – more than ten years and they appear like that.' They were now sitting close together holding each other's hands.

'What did you think, my love, when you saw us all waiting there – the king and queen and Bishop Aidan and the court all looking at you?'

'I didn't know what to think. I just looked from one to the other and then at you and . . . then . . .' James took a deep breath '. . . at them – the Gospels – lying there on the table. Everything else went out of focus and I had eyes for them alone. It was the king's voice that brought me back to my senses. "Go on," he said, "have a good look and then tell us all about them."' And James shook his head again at the wonder of it all.

The king and queen had wanted to know everything. James had told them about his early training with Father Birinus, described his conception of the new designs which he had shown to Bishop Paulinus and then perfected in the two Gospels before them. The king had asked about the animals and birds and if they were based upon reality. Enfleda had marvelled at it all and had squeezed Edith's arm in encouragement at her husband's triumph.

Bishop Aidan had not spoken for a long time until the king had deliberately turned to him to bring him into the conversation. The bishop had been very gracious in his comments.

'You may recall, Your Majesty,' he remarked, 'that I said earlier that only once before had I seen such excellence. The other occasion was on Hii and the artist was the same – our friend James here. I would like to ask him if I may about the script.'

Oswy nodded and the bishop continued.

'The script you use here James, and used on Hii, is quite different from this. What is this one called?'

'This is uncial, my Lord. The one you are familiar with, which is used on Iona, is called Irish Majuscule. Perhaps if you would do me the honour, one day, of visiting my scriptorium, Your Majesties, my Lord, I will show you a comparison.'

It was Enfleda who answered.

'Thank you, Master James. I would love to see your present work and how it compares with this. I will come soon and I am sure the king will also.'

After that it had become a happy occasion. Spirits had been high when the bishop made his so important suggestion to the king.

'Your Majesty,' Aidan had said, 'it is clear that we have in Master James, an incomparable artist whom we have not utilised to the extent we should. May I suggest that we establish here in Northumbria a school of sacred illumination which will be pre-eminent in the whole country. Since the principal home of such decorated scripts should be a monastery I hope you will allow James to teach not only here and on Lindisfarne but at other monasteries also. He must seek the most apt pupils to take charge of each branch of the school under his overall direction. He has no equal of whom I am aware – in this country at any rate – so let us give him every support – every chance to create such beauty for Almighty God that all with artistic aspirations will want to come here.'

'You must be very proud,' said Edith later.

'Not proud,' he answered. 'Father Birinus would never have countenanced pride but I will admit to enormous satisfaction.

'Now,' he added, 'all we need is the baby. If he's a boy I will teach him.

Chapter 12

The celebrations marking the return of the relics ended quickly with the start of advent. Aidan went back briefly to his see but returned again soon afterwards with six monks who were to accompany, in solemn procession, the late king's head on it's journey to Lindisfarne. Despite the lateness of the year James went with them to decide what might be necessary to improve the facilities at the monastery to allow more copyists to work and to permit the training of others. Though he was anxious to make a start on the establishment of a school on the island it was evident that as yet there was no suitable person to be left in charge whilst James was at the castle. Paul was making excellent progress and was advancing quickly but was not yet ready for the responsibility. James foresaw a busy period ahead.

It was well into the third week of advent when he returned to a delighted Edith. Since his earlier journeys with Aidan James had seldom travelled abroad for any period of time and she had missed him greatly, although her attendance on the queen kept her busy. Her pregnancy was making smooth progress and she had developed the bloom of impending motherhood. Her face was now a little rounder, her hair thicker and more glowing, her skin texture smoother and tinged with the faintest pigmentation of pregnancy which enhanced still further her physical attractions.

Edith enjoyed her official duties and had developed an easy and friendly relationship with the queen whose early pregnancy had been less troubled than her own. The sickness, which had affected her so much during the ride back to Bamburgh, and at the celebrations following their return, had passed quickly and Enfleda was revelling in her pregnant state and hoping fervently for a son. It was a matter she brought up with Edith.

'Oh dear, I have had so much advice about how to tell if an unborn child will be a boy or girl that I'm hopelessly confused. Do you believe there is any way we can know?'

Edith smiled, remembering her own thoughts on the subject so long ago.

'I have little experience, Your Majesty, although perhaps more than you know about. Some years ago – around ten years ago in fact – when I was in Iona I had a terrible miscarriage. I was so ill that I'm told I nearly died and, even when my life had been saved, my return to health took many months and was only complete as a result of the help I received from Biship Aidan.'

The queen was at once interested and wanted to know more and, although it was years since Edith had ever told anyone the story, she found herself describing it all to Enfleda without concern. When the tale was done Enfleda was immediately contrite.

'Oh, Edith I hope it didn't distress you telling me your story.' Edith shook her head and smiled. 'It must have been terrible to lose a baby like that. I would be devastated. You don't think there is any chance that I will miscarry, do you?'

Edith, alarmed by the direction the conversation was taking tried to be as reassuring as possible.

'Oh no, Your Majesty, I'm sure there can't be. Why, you have been so well; better than I was then,' she lied hoping that the queen's fears would be allayed. 'As to telling the sex of the child, madam, I have to say that I doubt if any method is accurate. And if *you* were to ask, Your Majesty, in your position, they would be sure to say you were going to have a son for fear of disappointing you. Do you know yet when the child might be born?'

'Well,' answered Enfleda, looking happier again, 'I was married in early October and since then I haven't seen anything so I suppose I must have conceived almost at once and that should mean a baby in perhaps July. I'm glad it will be summer and we shall be able to leave him – you see I'm still talking about him – kicking around in his cot with few clothes on and not bundled up against the cold. I love bare babies with their chubby little legs and arms waving about freely. Oh Edith, I'm so looking forward to it and so must you be.'

And so Edith was and James too.

He had been intensely interested in the course of her pregnancy and had asked countless questions about it especially after his absence on Lindisfarne. There had to be a formal inspection of her enlarging abdomen and James made several attempt to feel his unborn child, as he had seen old Marge do, but could make out nothing.

It was she who had brought Enfleda herself into the world as well as Queen Ethelberga's older children, Ethelhun and Ethelthryd, who had died. It was said that she survived a series of spectacular adventures after the fall of Edwin's kingdom before reappearing at Bamburgh under King Oswald's reign and carrying on where she left off, looking after the ladies of the court.

Old Marge radiated confidence and never once frightened Edith with tales of previous accidents when everything had gone wrong, as some other attendants did, and she always scolded any lady who began to tell similar stories.

'Of course things can go wrong sometimes, dear,' she commented, 'as you know from experience, but there's no use in dwelling on the matter and they are far more likely to go smoothly. You have had a labour, although a very early one, and that should help you. I don't expect any problem with you, my dear, nor, for that matter, with the queen. She is young, which is a good thing, but not too young which is even better. The really young ones – thirteen and fourteen – do suffer a lot sometimes but, when they get to eighteen or nineteen like Her Majesty, that's the best possible time. So I doubt either of you will worry me.'

By the end of February Oswy felt that he could bear the restraints of winter no longer.

December and January had seen hard frosts and piercing winds. Children had made long slides on the ice and youths had bound their feet in greased wrappings and slid around dangerously on frozen ponds and shallow rivers. Games were played with a flat stone which was kicked or beaten with sticks from one member of a team to another whilst the opposing team tried to get possession of it and keep it as long as possible. Oswy had tried the game to work off his suppressed energy but he had little aptitude for it and growled in protest, becoming more disgruntled than ever.

Then the killing frost eased a little and snow fell and, with some of the ice becoming precarious, three youths were drowned while attempting to cross a lake which a little earlier had borne them easily. More snow fell and still more. Snowmen were built and snowball fights conducted in earnest and there was great hilarity among the young. But food was scarce and trudging through deep snow exhausting and old people shivered and coughed and died and everyone prayed that the weather would change.

Oswy was disturbed too because he disliked the changes pregnancy had produced in Enfleda. Where Edith developed a bloom of elegance, Enfleda became coarsened and sallow and, for Oswy, she lost much of her former attraction. She complained of heartburn and swollen feet and, although every kind of food was put before her, she always seemed to crave something that could not be obtained. Old Marge said that such vagaries of appetite were common and were not to be taken notice of and would pass, but the queen found them annoying, and Oswy had little patience with her, and each began to get on the other's nerves. Oswy took to flirting with the prettier ladies-in-waiting which produced their first real quarrel. Temporarily they had lost some of their early closeness and, although both were saddened, neither wished to be the one to make the first move towards reconciliation.

The long winter was upsetting them all thought Oswy. If only the weather would break and some signs of spring would appear he was sure everything would be alright again.

By the end of February Bishop Aidan's need to commune with Almighty God in total solitude had become overwhelming.

At such times it had been his custom to leave his monastery in the hands of the prior, Brother Eddius, and go along to one of a group of tiny rocky islands which jutted starkly out of the sea to the east of Bamburgh Castle. The nearest of these was some two miles offshore and it was this one which Aidan selected for his lonely worship of God without the possiblity of distraction. He had called the island his retreat, or 'fahren' in his Celtic tongue. Locally the word had been corrupted to 'farne' by which the group of islands became known.

Aidan's inner 'farne' was lashed by storms and pounded by towering waves. It was a wild and desolate place, a paradise for seabirds and seals, inhospitable to man but as near heaven for Bishop Aidan as any place on earth. Here despite unimaginable privations he achieved blissful unity with his God.

This year he knew that his prayers would be more than ever necessary to sustain his people in their forthcoming ordeal which only he forsaw.

By the end of February Penda had almost one thousand men under arms.

He took care to move them out with as much stealth as possible. The first detachment set out from the north west corner of his kingdom moving directly northwards along the eastern border of Wales. Penda had been at pains to prepare the ground carefully to prevent their progress being opposed through misunderstanding of their purpose. Emissaries had visited the Welsh kings to express Penda's reassurance that their kingdoms were in no way threatened, and bearing gifts to emphasise his goodwill. Some troops were certainly moving northwards, it was admitted, since King Penda was disturbed by certain developments – unspecified – in that area but there was no suggestion of any attack on the integrity of a Welsh kingdom. Relations had been good between them for many years, it was emphasised. King Penda was delighted that such peaceful coexistance should continue, as these costly gifts showed. The troop movements should be completely disregarded since the Mercians were merely taking precautionary steps. No immediate assault on anyone was planned etc, etc.

At the same time other emissaries visited the court of King Oswin of Deira again bearing gifts but this time telling a different story.

Oswin was the nephew of the late King Edwin and had been converted to Christianity along with him by Bishop Paulinus. He was known to be an exceptionally devout man with no warlike tendencies of any kind. The animosity which had existed for so long between Bernicia and Mercia was believed to sadden him and it was this feeling that Penda sought to exploit.

The emissaries admitted the antagonism but stressed that King Penda wearied of this belligerence and would willingly bring it to an end. Direct negotiations with Bernicia had not been promising so was it too much to hope that King Oswin might be able to influence his cousin, King Oswy, to take a more favourable view of Mercia? King Penda, it was implied, had recently been impressed by his contacts with Christianity and might, it was hinted, be prepared to seek further instruction in that faith in which case who could say if he might not decide to accept it. King Oswin's sanctity was well known, it was agreed, so what better than to arrange a state visit of Oswin to Penda perhaps in the early summer and, if several of his monks were to come as well, a further examination of the Christian Faith would be possible.

It was an overture King Oswin was unable to resist and agreement was reached that such a visit would take place in May. Meanwhile there was, surely, no purpose to be served in letting King Oswy know, was there, since he might misunderstand the purpose of the meeting and further conflict might be precipitated.

Meanwhile detachments of Mercian soldiers continued to move inexorably northwards. Soon they were moving in an almost continuous line along the Welsh border and, had the Welsh kings been minded to warn any potential victim, few if any scouts would have penetrated this line. The kings decided to accept Penda's presents and say nothing. The destination of the troops was no business of theirs – yet.

By the third week of March Penda's entire army had crossed the River Ribble and occupied the old Kingdom of Rhegad to the south of the Britons of Strathclyde. The intense winter the east had experienced had not affected these north western regions to the same extent although the mountain chain, which now separated the Mercian army from the Bernicians, was still covered in deep snow. Penda spent an anxious week waiting for the weather to change to allow his men easy access to his enemy over the hills. By the end of the month the thaw had come and his troops poured into the ancient Kingdom of Bernicia devastating everything in their path.

Opposition was merely token. Only rarely were casualties suffered and progress slowed. For the most part they swept uninterruptedly eastwards and northwards with the destruction of Bamburgh and King Oswy as their goal.

One week after crossing the mountains they had laid waste to all the country north of the rivers Tyne and Wear. Hartlepool, Jarrow and Hexham were razed and a victorious army was advancing rapidly on the capital. Atrocities were manifold. Captives were massacred with extreme ferocity. Families were herded into their own homes which were then set alight. Armed resistance had been answered by mutilation or crucifixion or impalement. Women, and sometimes children, had been raped before assassination. Old people were eliminated by the readiest means available, thrown into ponds to drown, run through, garotted or clubbed to death with brutal deliberation. Penda was provided with a stream of young girls for violation or involvement in his practices of sexual perversion.

A few Northumbrians escaped, mostly fleeing northwards where they reasoned the Mercians would not follow. But, as the advancing forces approached the north eastward parts of the kingdom, more of the escaping peasants headed for the coast in the hope of getting away in boats. It was some of these who first brought the news to Oswy.

The thaw had been a blessed relief to Oswy. Horses were saddled and hunting expeditions mounted almost as the snow melted in front of them. Fitful sunshine broke through. Snowdrops and crocus were uncovered and the earliest buds appeared. The king and his party revelled in this freedom and rode further and further afield, returning later and later in the day. It was on such an expedition that the first of his fleeing subjects was encountered and the danger realised.

The meeting was almost a fatal one for the king.

A spearhead of Mercians, under orders to capture the desperately escaping peasants at all costs as they neared Bamburgh, had ridden far ahead of their front line. Some of the party had been outdistanced by the faster horsemen so that it was a small detachment of only eight men who finally caught sight of the fleeing Northumbrians. The pursuers bore down on the wretched fugitives at the gallop and were all but upon them when Oswy's party breasted a hill and ran straight into them. After a brief moment of surprise Oswy was the first to grasp the nature of the encounter. He shouted a terse command.

'Get them. Let none escape.'

Putting spurs to his horse and wrenching his sword from its scabbard he leapt forward to impale the astonished leader who, with the need to overcome the escapees in mind, had as yet drawn no weapon. Oswy let his first charge carry him right through the group before he wheeled his horse and attacked from the rear. The Mercians, trying to rein in their horses, had lost their impulsion and were temporarily at a disadvantage as well as being outnumbered by the twelve members of the hunting party. Well aimed arrows struck down three and a fourth was unhorsed by a swinging broadsword. The rest were attacked in earnest and a bloody battle ensued. Three of Oswy's men and two of Penda's fell before the last man turned his horse and tried to make his escape.

Oswy and two of his officers set off in quick pursuit. They had the advantage of fresher horses, for the Mercians had been riding hard for some hours, and it was Oswy himself who overtook the fleeing horseman first. He parried a desperate backward thrust from his opponent and, as he came alongside, launched himself bodily from the saddle carrying his enemy to the ground. Both were rolled over and over by their momentum but it was the Mercian who recovered first. He had somehow managed to retain a grip on his sword and was staggering towards the fallen Oswy, who was temporarily stunned by the force of his fall, when he was run down by the other two horsemen and felled by a slash deep in his neck.

Oswy pushed himself painfully to his feet and gasped out his thanks.

'My gratitude to you, Ricbert. He would have had me I think.'

Then, shaking himself to clear his head, he looked around for his sword as the third man returned with his horse.

'Now,' Oswy panted, getting back into the saddle, 'to find out what all this is about.'

The news appalled him.

The small party of fugitives who had been saved from the Mercians lost no time in telling him the position as they knew it and Oswy quickly realised the seriousness of the situation. The peasants could give no idea of numbers but they knew enough to convince the king that this was no small scale operation. For armed Mercian soldiers to have penetrated so far into his kingdom a major invasion must be in progress. Oswy hesitated only a moment.

'Ricbert, Alban, Peter – you three ride west and south and find out what you can. Take extreme care but get me some information. Be back by dusk tomorrow if possible. We must return and do what we can. It looks as if we will never raise an effective force in time to mount an attack if, as I think, there is a large army against us. We should have captured one of these,' gesturing towards the dead Mercians, 'and perhaps we would have learned something but it is too late to worry about that now.'

He stopped for a moment and looked drawn and pale. Then shrugging his shoulders he remounted his horse.

'Farewell, Ricbert, and good luck. We will ride as hard as we can for home with the bodies of our three friends. If we cannot attack we must defend. A siege it must be.'

The town of Bamburgh nestled at the foot of the towering rock upon which the castle stood. The ground sloped upwards towards the base of the rock giving the inhabitants a measure of protection which they had increased by constructing a high perimeter bank with a pallisade fence on top and a deep ditch on the landward side. Entrances through the bank were few and heavily guarded by towers on each side of massive gates. It proved to be a defensive wall which Penda was unable to breach.

In the breathing space they had been granted by the king's intelligence of the Mercian advance all defences had been strengthened. Weapons had been mobilised and lay at numerous strong points around the wall. Arrow stocks had been replenished. Projectiles were stacked ready to be launched upon the heads of the Mercians below. Foodstores had been hastily augmented by bringing in whatever could be transported from nearby farms, and much of what could not be moved was destroyed to prevent it falling into enemy hands. Their water supply was secure from two deep wells. Fish could always be obtained since the outlet to the sea was protected and the Mercians were not sailors.

They had delayed Penda for two weeks and there was every prospect that they could hold out for far longer. With supplies from further afield coming in by boat it was not too much to hope that they could last out almost indefinitely.

Initially Penda had launched attack after attack in his frenzy to beat down the defences but all had been repulsed with considerable losses to the attackers but few to the defenders. Night attacks had been tried but the men of Bernicia had expected them and, in the dark and confusion below, the assault never achieved momentum and the experiment was not repeated. Penda raged and cursed his commanders, called his men cowards and inflicted savage punishments for trivial offences. Morale became low and there were desertions and, to add to their problems, their own food supplies became precarious. The devastation of the countryside during their advance, and the destruction by the Northumbrians of what they themselves could not bring into the town, meant that rations were short and foraging parties were obliged to go further and further afield for little return. If the town did not fall soon retreat was inevitable.

Then almost simultaneously two things happened. The first involved Coenred, one of Penda's senior commanders, the second Tynbert, one of his rawest recruits.

Coenred was from a noble Mercian family and had waged war all his life. The campaign against Oswy was to be one of his last – probably *the* last since the journey northward and the trek across the mountains had taxed him more than he cared to admit. The stout Northumbrian defence was infuriating and seemed likely to spell failure for his ultimate expedition.

Coenred sat apart from his own troops enduring, not for the first time, the hardships of a long campaign but, now, finding them barely supportable. He raged inwardly as he watched the smoke from the cooking fires drift gently away to his left and he heard the occasional guffaw of laughter or angry exchange or bellowed command.

The wind was gusting and the smoke was now being driven in his direction and he growled in irritation as it began to increase his discomfort. He stood up in annoyance, reluctant to return to his quarters but obliged to move by the drifting smoke. Drifting smoke . . . He turned instantly and watched the fires. Little showers of sparks were, now and again, being blown by the wind towards where he was standing so that the men who had been gathered around that side of the line of fires had been obliged to move away as he had.

He spun round quickly in the opposite direction to gaze intently at those buildings of the town of Bamburgh which were visible above the bank and pallisade. Wood! Wood every one of them and even parts of the castle itself above them. Could his men get together enough wood to fill the ditch to a level high enough for the sparks and flames, when set alight, to be carried into the town by a favourable wind. Favourable wind! Favourable for Penda but not for Oswy. Coenred slapped his thigh in delight. That must be it. They would burn them out.

Penda needed no convincing but grasped the notion with wild delight.

'Burn them. Yes, burn them of course. And none of you so called commanders thought of that,' he snarled angrily rounding on the others assembled there. 'You with your military theory and new ideas; none of you came up with that. It took a veteran like Coenred to show you up. Well done. Coenred my old friend. Well done,' and Penda slapped him on the back and pummelled his arm in his excitemnt. 'Now listen all of you. Tomorrow I want every available man scouring the countryside for fuel. Break down every dwelling you see and bring the wood back here. Collect brushwood for kindling. There was a sizeable wood to the north as we came in; cut down anything that will burn – anything dead or blown down already. Get it here as quickly as you can. Have wagons available to haul back what cannot be carried.' Penda was delirious with delight and could hardly issue orders quickly enough. 'Every man remember, every man. This is our chance. We've got them; we've got them.'

James was not alone in his alarm at the mass of Mercian soldiers ringing Bamburgh. From the heights of the castle he could see many details of the activity in their camp. Their numbers alone were alarming and James with little military knowledge at his disposal did not see how the town could possibly hold out. He had been included, as every able bodied man and boy had, in the preparations for the assault, going out with foraging parties, helping to stockpile weapons and reinforcing any point of the bank or pallisade which showed any sign of weakness. If necessary he would fight but if things reached that stage there would be little hope left.

His absence from Edith worried him. She had been able to do little but remain in the castle itself, mostly in the royal apartments with the queen, who, after an initial frightened reaction, had become a tower of strength among the women. Edith and Enfleda spent much time together making what preparations they could if the outer defences were breached and the king and queen were obliged to leave by sea. Everything was now ready and they waited as patiently as they could. Brother Uffa, in the absence of Bishop Aidan, who had surprisingly not appeared, held exposition of the Blessed Sacrament every day until dusk and elaborate preparations were made that, in the event of the town falling, no sacred hosts would get into the heretics hands.

The dreadful threat to their safety had brought the king and queen instantly together again. Oswy, although busily engaged every day in supervising the defences, was his old caring self the moment he returned to Enfleda who could not do enough for him. He had been urged by his advisers to leave at once and run no chance of his apprehension by Penda but the king refused and was determined to oppose his enemy for as long as possible. If the worst came to the worst he would finally leave by sea with the queen and a small group of retainers and hope to find safety either north with the Picts or south with Oswin of Deira, if *he* could still be relied upon. Oswy had raged against his cousin and had refused to believe that Penda's forces could have reached Bamburgh without Oswin's knowledge. A ship had already been sent south to determine if Deira were still a safe place for Oswy's escape if, in the end, it came to that.

Edith herself had now reached the time when Old Marge expected her labour to begin. There had been one false alarm already a few days earlier when, for three hours, pains had come every fifteen to twenty minutes before disappearing completely to everyone's disappointment. A worse time for a child to be born could hardly be imagined.

Would all this trouble have an effect upon the baby, James wondered? Might it be abnormal as a result? Old Marge was reassuring but Edith looked frightened and strained and James knew how worried she was.

The Mercian camp was slowly settling down for the night. At dawn tomorrow details would be sent out with hatchets and swords and even spades and clubs for smashing the crude houses of the locals. Now the wise ones were getting what sleep they could before what looked like being several days of intense activity. But others were gambling, or scavenging for what food they could find, or waiting in an impatient line outside one or other of two makeshift brothels set up with captured Northumbrian women.

In the far corner of the camp a gambling game of a special kind was in progress. Tynbert, a lad of no more than eighteen years of age, was on his first campaign but it had not taken him long to realise that soldiering was a greatly over-rated pastime. The fact that he had avoided any service in the Mercian army for as long as he had, when his contemporaries were conscripted at least two years earlier, was a tribute, if such was the right word, to his capacity for avoiding what was likely to be uncongenial or unrewarding. Furthermore, his ability to make himself scarce, when there was either fighting or work to be undertaken, was almost unlimited and he could devise profitable enterprises even under the noses of his officers. He was engaged on one now.

On a foraging party a week earlier Tynbert had separated himself quickly from his companions, as was his custom, and was sharply on the lookout for anything he might turn to his advantage. It was then that he had found the rats.

They were large and surprisingly dark in colour – almost black in fact – and it took him some time to catch the first. Had he not almost smothered it in a dirty, ancient coat, he found almost rotting behind the door of the hovel he had entered, he might have been bitten severely. As it was he stuffed the animal into an old sack and set about catching more. He caught five in all and was bitten only once – at least by the rats although the rat fleas gave him an unpleasant time.

Tynbert was now briskly making a book on which of several dogs, adopted by some of the soldiers during the campaign, could kill a rat first. A rough, round enclosure had been constructed some ten feet in diameter and, when sufficient bets had been placed on two dogs to be matched against each other, a rat was released into the circle and the two dogs after it. The winner was the one that killed it.

Tynbert had gone each day to the house where rats seemed to abound. It had evidently not been found by the troops during their scouring of the area since the two dead bodies it contained had not been killed, as far as Tynbert could determine by a hasty examination of their putrifying corpses, but had died of natural causes. That was no concern of his but the rats were and he collected several each visit and a contest was held each night.

But tonight he was feeling the contest trying. His head ached and his eyes burned and he had developed a hard rasping cough which racked his burning body. One of the flea bites on his leg was angry and swollen and three large lumps had appeared in his groin. The gamblers cursed him for his slowness, and his fingers became so fumbling that he let one rat go before it was put into the circle.

That night Tynbert was barely able to crawl into his blanket before his head began to swim and his senses left him.

In the morning he did not move when his troop was roused and when the officer who found him tried to kick him awake he found he was kicking a dead man.

In the three days which were needed to collect sufficient wood to burn Bamburgh sixty of Penda's men died from the plague.

All of them had been at the rat killings. The rat fleas had spread not only to Tynbert but to the spectators and dogs alike. The deterioration in the condition of those infected was dramatic, some victims dying within a day or less. None so far who had contracted the disease had survived and its manifestations had been similar in all – swollen glands in groin or armpit or neck, headache, shivering and sweating, burning eyes and then lethargy, coma and death.

Not all developed the harsh painful cough and difficulty in breathing which had troubled Tynbert but those who did, although they did not know it, were the more dangerous ones – to others. While the fleas gave the plague to those they bit, the cough spread the pestilence widely and those who breathed it in succumbed to it. It was this that proved the scourge of the Mercian forces.

The sixty who died in the first three days became one hundred and sixty, two days later and still Penda was waiting for the wind. There was, now, no escaping the fact that a serious epidemic was amongst them. Penda ordered the dead to be thrown into pits of lime but forbade anyone to touch the bodies. They were to be impaled on swords or forks and pitched into the pits but these filled so quickly that the bodies had to be carried on carts outside the lines and burned on grisly bonfires.

Retreat was staring Penda in the face when in the evening of the sixth day after Coenred's plan had been devised, a west wind began to blow. In a last desperate attempt to destroy the town before the plague destroyed him Penda ordered the fires to be lit at dawn.

When the filling of the ditch began its purpose was not immediately apparent to Oswy nor his men. Could it be, one suggested, that an attempt was to be made to construct a long ramp sufficiently high and strong to bear the weight of Penda's men and allow them to attack over the top of the bank and fence? But as more and more wood was brought, and the ditch was filled along nearly all its length, its real purpose became clear.

'Fire. That's what it means, sire. Fire,' reported Martin, one of Oswy's commanders. 'They mean to burn us out and they may succeed,' he added, 'if they can build high enough up the bank and if they wait for a strong west wind. The flames will destroy the fence and spread to the roofs of houses some of which will flare up in an instant. The smoke will be thick, I'm sure, and we won't be able to see to defend if they bring ladders and scale the bank. It is serious, Your Majesty, very serious. I fear we may not be able to hold them off.'

The realisation of the Mercian plan had a profound effect upon the town. Morale had been high before but now everyone was plunged into the deepest gloom and many were in despair. The first day of the filling of the ditch with inflammable materials seemed to have produced enormous quantities. A day or two more and all hope would be gone. When the pyre had assumed gigantic proportions along the whole length of the perimeter defences everyone knew that all they were waiting for now was a west wind.

On the night of the second day after the holocaust had been prepared the wind came.

On the same night Edith's labour began.

James had been watching the branches of trees and bushes bending in the wind when there was a crash from behind him. Edith had been picking up a dish which now lay shattered at her feet while she was leaning forward clutching the edge of a table for support.

'Jamie, the pain. Oh, the pain.'

He ran across at once to help her to a chair, watching her white face anxiously.

'Marge. Shall I get old Marge?'

'In a minute; just let this pain pass first.'

In a moment she looked calmer and blew out her cheeks as the pain went and smiled bravely at her husband.

'That was a strong one,' she admitted. 'I've had one or two little ones over the last hour but nothing like that. Oh dear, I don't remember them as strong as that last time but I suppose they were. You can help me to the pallet in a moment but you had better put those old clothes onto it first, my dearest, because I think I shall make a mess if you don't. I can feel the wetness on my legs so I suppose the waters have gone.' She broke off, caught her breath and gasped quickly, 'Here's another.'

The second was not so strong, nor the third and there was almost ten minutes between them. James helped Edith to the bed and laid her gently down, trying, at the same time, rather ineffectually, to dry her dripping legs.

'Leave them, Jamie, I shall be alright for a few minutes. Run for Old Marge as soon as this pain has gone which is coming no . . . w . . . ' She stopped suddenly and gripped her clothes with both hands until the pain had gone. After a moment she gave a brief mocking laugh and said, 'Relax, they told me. Don't fight the pains. Well it's easier said than done, I can tell you. Go now, dear, and come back with Old Marge as quickly as you can.'

Old Marge came as fast as her, now, ample bulk would permit and, after a quick examination to satisfy herself that Edith was alright, she pushed James out with instructions to bring one Neta, who helped Marge with her more influential patients.

'But don't go far away mind,' said Marge as he was disappearing on his mission,'I shall want you handy – just in case.'

But 'just in case' had not materialised and neither, come to that had the child. James waited and waited, pacing the passageway outside the room. Whenever Marge emerged with demands for more water or more blankets or to fetch a mysterious little flask which she said would help to take away some of the pain, James asked was his wife alright and was everything going well and . . .

Marge always stopped him though before he had asked half the things he wanted to know and what she said was difficult to understand.

'She's only early yet,' she said once. 'Can't expect anything yet,' adding mysteriously, 'still only three fingers.'

Three fingers. It was incomprehensible to James. Surely three fingers weren't the only parts that had come out; or the baby didn't only have three fingers? There was no way she could know that, was there? It was too late to ask more because Marge had disappeared into the room again and he was left standing outside wondering.

At one point the queen came and he scrambled to his feet in embarrassment but she was gracious and kind and she asked very politely if she might go in.

Emerging some time later, she too was anxious to stress that the birth would not be for some time yet. 'You see,' she explained, 'she is not much more than three fingers.'

James looked so confused when she said it that Enfleda felt she should explain.

'I'm afraid I've puzzled you,' she remarked. 'I thought you might know. It isn't so peculiar as it sounds. It's the neck of the womb, you see; it has to open for the baby to come out and, so far, it has only opened about so much,' holding her left thumb and index together in a little circle and placing the tips of 3 fingers of her right hand into it. 'It has be be fully open before the baby comes,' Enfleda went on, 'so you can see it will be a little while yet. I should try to get some sleep if I were you. I fear it will be a terrible night for us all.'

James watched her retreating form miserably. Terrible night it would be. Even if his child was born safely, would any of them survive? If those fires were lit in the morning they were doomed. In a fit of depression he wandered over to the window to look down on the Mercian camp below.

There was a lot happening evidently but it was hard to understand what it all meant. Why were there three big fires – dying down now he had to admit – outside the periphery of the camp. Surely they could have added that fuel to the rest in the ditch. A shower of sparks and a sudden blaze of flame reminded him that wind was getting stronger. They would soon be lighting the fires. Very soo . . . so . . . He sank to the floor in black despair. His wife was in labour, his baby was being born, yet all of them were on the brink of annihilation.

The next thing he was aware of was a cry from Edith's room. She was shouting out in pain and he was not there to help. Struggling to his feet he was about to enter the room until he remembered Old Marge's instruction and stopped. But there was a lot of shouting in the room still and another cry from Edith.

'I can't. I can't.'

'Yes you can. You must.' that was old Marge. 'Hold your breath with the next pain and push . . . and push . . . PUSH. Harder, come on. You can do it if you try really hard.'

James, rooted to the spot, listened horrified. What could he do? It must be nearly time for the birth. 'Push,' Marge had said, so the child was actually coming. Would Edith have the strength though? There it was again.

'Once more, dearie, push . . . and again, harder. Take hold of your legs behind your knees – good – now put your chin on your chest and push right down to the back.'

Unable to bear to hear more James turned suddenly to look out over the town again. He must have fallen asleep because now it was nearly dawn, he realised, and they would soon be lighting the fi . . . dear God, they had lit them. Thick black smoke was billowing out over the town and darting flames were shooting up to the sky along the whole length of the ditch.

'Oh, God help us,' prayed James. 'Don't let us perish. Let my child be born, at least, before we all die.'

There was a brief moment of silence during which he mumbled incoherent prayers and then there was the sound of a baby crying.

A baby. Crying!

The child must be born. Would he be alright? Would Edith . . . 'Oh God,' James prayed again, falling to his knees, 'let them both live? Let my child be whole? Let . . . '

He opened his eyes to see Old Marge standing in front of him holding a little bundle in her arms and she was beaming all over her big round face.

'What,' James began but got no further when he realised that Marge was holding the bundle out to him.

'Your son,' she said. 'Take him. He's fine and so is your wife. You can come in now.'

Bishop Aidan was nearing the end of his month of solitary retreat on the Inner Farne when he saw the smoke.

It was moving steadily, driven by the fresh wind, and it came into his view as he knelt in a small, circular cavern in the rock which so surrounded him that he could see nothing about him but the heavens above. He had prayed since long before it was light with his head bowed and his eyes closed. As he opened them to gaze upwards towards his God the first wisps of smoke passed across the sky.

'Almighty God,' prayed Aidan, 'what wicked men these are who do the work of the devil. Dear Lord, protect your suffering people of Bamburgh that they may not fall into the clutches of the heathen. Lord, hear my prayer.'

And bowing his head again Aidan prayed without ceasing for a long time. When he raised his head once more the sky was clear and a steady easterly wind was blowing. He rose to his feet and emerged from his tiny rocky cell and saw that Bamburgh Castle was plainly visible but beyond it to the west the mainland was enveloped in dense clouds of smoke, pouring back onto those who had started the fire.

The Lord God who created the earth had commanded the winds to do his bidding.

With the change of wind the devastation in Penda's camp was total. The lines of soldiers, waiting with ladders and grappling hooks to scale the defences, were blinded by the returning smoke which enveloped them completely. Its thick clouds were driven straight into their faces, and searing eyes, making it impossible to see anything. Men cannoned into each other in their desperate attempts to escape from the stifling fumes. Horses plunged and strained and trampled the fallen underfoot, felling others with flying hooves. Soldiers abandoned their equipment in their attempts to get away more quickly. All thoughts of attack were forgotten in their desperation to flee the field.

Penda was caught in the thickest smoke of all. After a moment of incredulity he went into a towering rage at the failure of his last throw and, drawing his sword, he swung wildly around him to clear a path as he too turned and plunged headlong back through his camp and to the open country beyond.

The fires were now burning so fiercely that none could withstand the dense billowing smoke. In no time the entire camp was abandoned but for the dying victims of the plague.

What the smoke and flames had begun the plague ended. Many who had waited to take part in the final assault upon Bamburgh were already infected. Had their attack succeeded they would have died within the walls of the conquered town; as it was they collapsed in their headlong flight away from it. The Mercian forces were hopelessly scattered over a wide area and those who had escaped the panic and the pestilence had neither the will nor the ability to regroup as an army. In ones and twos and small groups Penda's men retreated, overcome by Almighty God and the plague.

The Northumbrians were transformed from black depression to wild delight.

They had, at first, no means of knowing the extent of the disruption to the Mercian forces but thought that it was likely to be great – at least for a time. Whilst the wind blew and the smoke poured westward they were safe but what would happen when the fires burned themselves out? There was much concern about the Mercian's regrouping within the next day or two and returning to resume the seige, but gradually, as scouts were able to penetrate deeper and deeper into the abandoned camp and beyond, to discover that their attackers had completely fled, they were at last able to comprehend their salvation.

A report on the plague victims had fortunately been brought back immediately after the first carcases were discovered. Physicians were quickly despatched but only a cursory examination was necessary to reveal the tell-tale signs of the infection. A number of small epidemics had occurred from time to time in Northumbria and the effects of the disease were well known. There was only one thing to be done. While the east wind still blew, everything in Penda's camp was burned to eradicate the pestilence completely.

The town simply could not believe its good fortune. Everywhere there was jubilation and a tremendous feeling of release from the very jaws of death. Brother Uffa celebrated a Mass of thanksgiving and, on the next day, when Bishop Aidan arrived, having been brought out of his retreat by his monks as previously arranged, High Mass was sung, a banquet was held in the castle and there was feasting throughout the town. The king and queen went everywhere, congratulating their subjects on their escape and praising them for their bravery during their ordeal.

It took a long time for the excitement to die down but gradually things began to return to normal and the castle was able to look forward to its next big event – the birth of Enfleda's child.

James and Edith, the birth of *their* son almost forgotten in the excitement, named him Eadfrith after James' father.

Chapter 13

Enfleda, Queen of Bernicia – and perhaps of Deira too if her husband's ambition could not be held in check – shifted in her chair in a vain attempt to ease her discomfort.

She was irritable and out of sorts. Her first three pregnancies put together had not been so troublesome as this fourth one. The early vomiting had no sooner subsided than heartburn followed. Goat's milk had been prescribed by Neta as an infallible remedy but it was so nauseating that Enfleda was hard put to know which was worst, the disease or its remedy. Old Marge – God rest her soul – would have found something better to relieve it, she was sure, but the poor old lady had coughed herself into the grave two winters ago and, now, Enfleda was left with Neta who was alright she supposed but it didn't seem the same without the old midwife.

It had been Marge who had delivered her of her son Egfrith, in the summer after the town had almost fallen during Penda's seige, and Marge again who was there – but only just in time Enfleda remembered – when her daughter Alchfreda had popped out like a cork the following year. A son and a daughter in two years was enough for the queen for a while and the folk remedies Old Marge had recommended had postponed a third pregnancy for nearly three years. The next child, Ostryd, had been an enormous baby whose shoulders had stuck fast until the old midwife had heaved herself onto the bed and pushed with all her might to get one shoulder through. The queen's belly had been sore for a week afterwards, and Ostryd had been purple in the face at birth with one bloodshot eye but, surprisingly, had turned into a very pretty little girl with fair curly hair like her father.

Enfleda smiled to herself at the memories of the last eight years – good years by and large she had to admit. Oswy, in his own way, had been a good husband and he never gave her a moments anxiety until she began to look gross and ugly when carrying one of his children. Those months, when her pregnant state had robbed her of her natural elegance, had been the only times they had quarrelled. Well, almost the only time!

There had been the disclosure of the son whom Oswy had sired before they were married which had so incensed Enfleda when she found out about his existence. Strange, really, she mused, trying to keep her mind off the pain in her back which had come on after the heartburn, how she could accept that he had had mistresses before their marriage but the notion that he had a son who was not hers infuriated her. He hadn't of course chosen the most helpful time to let it slip out.

'It makes me so proud to have another son,' he had said when he came to visit her during her lying-in after Egfrith. He had realised his slip of the tongue at once but by then it was too late. He had been all contrition when Enfleda upbraided him in a fury until he was finally obliged to tell her the whole story.

There had been an Irish princess from the north called Riemmelth or some such – Enfleda never seemed to get the hang of foreign names – and Oswy, who had then been nineteen or twenty was no match for the skillful seduction of an older woman, or so his story went.

'How much older?' Enfleda had enquired?

'Five or six years,' Oswy had replied airily, adding, 'and a widow too of more than six months, so you see when she knew that I was over in Ireland for a visit, and would be returning to Northumbria in a month or two, she thought we could have a nice little affair which would be over and done with the moment I departed.'

'But it wasn't, was it?' Enfleda had commented bitterly.

'Well,' the shamefaced Oswy had muttered, 'it was for me and neither of us thought of a baby but that's what happened. She refused to marry,' he had continued, feeling that he had better make a clean breast of things now that the matter had come out into the open,' and the boy was born four years ago. Alchfrith, she called him,' he ended unhappily.

He had looked so miserable, Enfleda remembered, and had been so delighted with their son Egfrith, that she had forgiven him and put the thought of the boy out of her mind until last month when Oswy had mentioned him again. He had been hesitant at first, but was obviously raising something which had been in his mind for some time.

'Enfleda.'

She had been wriggling about to find a comfortable position, she remembered, and hadn't heard him the first time.

'Enfleda, may I talk about something – something I'm sorry to bring up but it's been bothering me. Please don't mind too much when I tell you what it is.'

Puzzled, she had agreed, and tried to concentrate on what he began to tell her.

'I have thought a lot about what I am going to say, my dear, and if there were any way not to say it no one would be more pleased than I. But, if a certain thing happens when our next child is born, there may be no escaping it.'

What was he getting at she had wondered and why might it upset her? Before she had thought of any suitable reply he was speaking again.

'King's need heirs, my dear, you know that. Oh I know we have Egfrith who is a fine boy but he's our only one and if anything should happen to him' he had shaken his head at the appalling thought' we have just two girls, unless . . . ' he had hesitated again and then gone on in a rush ' . . . you bear another son this time.'

'Oh.'

It had been then that she had begun to realise what he was going to say. There had been absolutely silence between them as if neither wanted to be the one to bring the subject out into the open. Oswy had looked so miserable that in the end she had been the one who had done so.

'Alchfrith?'

He had nodded before saying quietly, 'Would you mind so much if we were to bring him over if you were to have a third daughter?'

Would she? Enfleda had been uncertain then and was uncertain now and, being essentially a fair minded girl, she could see his point of view at once. With only one son the succession was not secure. Children died of fever, or accident, or war . . . or any number of things, and without another heir there would be no shortage of contenders to the throne if Oswy . . . if Oswy . . . died. She had agreed finally to Alchfrith being brought over if their next child was a girl – but only on that condition.

Now all she could do was wait and hope.

Oddly enough she hadn't minded the suggestion as much as she had expected she would, probably because of her distress at the king's other plans. She had pleaded with him to abandon them and so, she was sure, had Bishop Aidan but he had been adamant and had marched into Deira at the head of an army.

Although she could generally persuade him to her way of thinking, in this he would not be swayed. Oswin had refused to join forces with him in opposition to Penda and as a result the Mercian king repeatedly gained easy access to the south and west borders of Bernicia which, over the years, he had harried mercilessly. After the last such raid, Oswy had decided that if Oswin would not be with him he must be against him, hence the invasion of Deira with the intention of removing him from the throne and uniting Deira with Bernicia under one ruler – Oswy.

'Please God,' prayed Enfleda, 'keep him safe and let him not do anything he will regret.'

Throughout the years of his bishopric Aidan had made many journeys across Northumbria, carrying the word of God to even the remotest parts of the kingdom. The response to his teaching had been overwhelming. Few did not profess Christianity and nearly all who did, influenced by the example of the king and his court, followed its teaching faithfully. More priests had been ordained who travelled the province far and wide to make the sacraments available to all. There was no need for the bishop to undertake another missionary journey but to the great surprise of all he announced that this was something he must do. There was a reason, he explained – a special reason which had not yet been made plain to him. It did not need to be made plain. God had told him that he must go. That was enough. He took just one companion, Brother Oda, and at the end of July they set off from Lindisfarne heading north west.

It was during the second week that they met the young man.

He was clearly a shepherd with a substantial flock which was grazing a long stretch of fertile grassland rising from a winding stream in the valley below them. The young man scrambled to his feet as the monks approached him and gave a little bow of welcome and with an outstretched hand indicated some low rocks beside where he had been sitting and said politely, 'Good day to you both, brothers. Will you not join me for a while. It is almost noon and the sun is hot. I have water here from the stream below and a little bread and cheese – quite enough to share with you.'

Aidan did not reply immediately but, for a few moments, never took his eyes off the young man absorbing every detail of his appearance. Brother Oda, sensing the bishop's interest, remained silent and waited for his superior to speak.

'Thank you,' the bishop said eventually. 'My friend and I have come a long way and, although we still have a distance to go, a rest will be welcome; the water too,' he added, 'although I must ask you to excuse us from accepting your offer of food. It is not our custom on this day, Friday, to eat before the evening. But we will sit here and talk. I think you and I may have something important to discuss.'

The youth seemed startled by this curious response but handed his water bottle to his visitors and waited until each had drunk before speaking again.

'What can we have to discuss Father,' he enquired. 'We have only just met. What can you know of me and I of you except, as I can see from your habits, you are holy monks.'

'Monks certainly,' Aidan replied smiling, 'and I am certain Brother Oda here is a holy man. But you are wrong in thinking I know nothing about you and that we do indeed have important business together.'

Aidan took a little more water and passed the bottle back to Brother Oda before speaking again. When he did so it was the monk he addressed.

'Would you be so good as to take the bottle to the stream, Brother Oda, and refill it while Cuthbert and I have our talk?'

Oda took the bottle, got to his feet and without a word descended the gentle slope down to the water.

'How did you know my name, Father? Have we met before? I do not remember it; when did we meet?' The youth was beginning to be uneasy under Aidan's steady gaze and his voice tailed off doubtfully.

The bishop however did not answer the questions but instead asked another and more curious one.

'Do you recall any event which took place on the road to Damascus?'

After a startled pause, Cuthbert answered confidantly.

'Of course, Father. Our Lord sent a bright light from heaven which struck St Paul – Saul as he was then of course – and knocked him from his horse'.

'Why do you think Almighty God did that?'

This time there was a longer pause before the young man replied and before he did so Aidan spoke again.

'Was it merely to stop Saul persecuting Christians do you think, or might there have been another reason?'

'I think, Father,' Cuthbert answered, speaking slowly and deliberately, 'that God was calling Saul to His service – selecting him to do work for Him, not against Him.'

'Very well then; when Almighty God reveals himself to a human creature in this way would you not expect that such a creature would accept the Lord's bidding?'

'Most certainly, Father,' answered Cuthbert without hesitation.

Aidan looked steadily at his young companion for some moments before asking surprisingly.

'How is your knee?'

'My knee,' began the puzzled Cuthbert before realisation seemed to dawn and he uttered just a single word. 'Oh.'

'I seem to have heard –' Aidan was no longer looking at Cuthbert but seemed to have his eyes on Oda down by the stream 'that your knee was much swollen some years ago – so swollen and painful in fact that you could scarcely move it at all and certainly not walk on it so that you had to be carried by your father's servants. Until, that is,' the bishop went on turning back to Cuthbert again, 'a man in dazzling white robes, riding a fine horse, came by and applied a simple remedy which cured you almost at once. Is that not so?'

Cuthbert did not speak but nodded silently.

'And did it not occur to you, after you were well again, that what had happened was like the cure of the blind Tobias by the Archangel Raphael, who indeed your figure in white resembled? And were you not reminded of the angels who came on horseback to defend the Holy Temple and Judas Maccabeus?'

This time the nod was scarcely perceptible.

'I have owned but one horse in my lifetime,' said Aidan surprisingly, in another remarkable change of subject, 'but little though I know of these animals I find it surprising that one should pull the straw from the roof of a shepherds hut to reveal a secret store of food to sustain a hungry man as I believe,' the bishop stressed, 'yours did.'

There was no movement at all from the young man before him until Aidan asked again, 'Did your horse not do that?'

'Yes.'

The answer was so quiet as to be barely audible although Aidan had no need to hear it.

'Then why do you hesitate to enter the religious life if you know God is calling you in these ways? Think about your answer and remember you are not answering me but our Lord.'

Neither spoke for some time and then the bishop took up his staff and both his bundle and Brother Oda's and went down the hill towards the stream leaving a silent youth sitting with his head buried in his hands.

Eight miles to the north west of the town of Catterick, in the Kingdom of Deira, lay the village of Gilling, sometimes known in the local tongue as In-Getlingum. Not far from the village itself, in wooded country to the south, was the estate of Hunwald, nobleman, member of the Court of Deira and friend and confidant of King Oswin. In Hunwald's private quarters, behind closed doors, away from the prying eyes of servants, these two men faced each other across a table.

On state occasions few kings fitted their role so well as Oswin – tall, broad shouldered, erect and handsome. But now his face was drawn and lined and a trickle of blood from a wound on his cheek had congealed into a dry, reddened line running down past the angle of his mouth onto the neck of his tunic. His normally upright figure was slumped in a chair and his usual air of confidence and authority was replaced by one of utter dejection. In his weariness he had even forgotton a goblet of wine beside his elbow.

Hunwald, concealing his anxiety, waited for the king to resume his story.

'I couldn't fight a pitched battle with Oswy,' he croaked after a moment. 'My force was too small; nothing like his. We were heavily outnumbered. We had been surprised you see. Given earlier warning of his approach I could have raised more men. My true supporters, like you, would have rallied round.' Hunwald shifted his feet uneasily beneath the table and remained silent, waiting for the king to continue. Oswin had remembered his wine and was draining it eagerly.

'Oswy was advancing along the north bank of the River Tees before we were aware of any danger,' Oswin went on. 'We had a paltry force beside his and all we could do was to harry the fringes of his army in a series of rapid strikes, retreating the moment we had inflicted some casualties in the hope of delaying his progress.'

The weary king ran his hands through his hair, normally fair and imposing, but now dirty and unkempt and, like his face, streaked with blood. He shifted painfully in his chair as his left thigh began to throb where a spear had sliced through his clothes and bitten into his flesh.

'They caught us eventually at Wilfar's Hill, north of Catterick,' he explained. 'We had no hope. A few of us fought a rearguard action while the main body of troops escaped and then we fled too as best we could. Most came south but I thought to mislead them by riding west and turning north to come here where I knew you would help me.'

Hunwald again seemed anxious for a moment before answering, 'Of course. You know you are safe here.' Then he added, 'My men are so few and scattered I could not get them together in the time or we would have been with you.' He rose from his chair and walked to the window to peer out nervously. He turned back into the room to face the king and asked, 'Are you alone?'

Oswin, who had seemed almost asleep, roused himself. 'No, not alone. I have one man Tondhere with me whom I can also trust. He too will need hiding.'

Hunwald was silent again for a while as if considering the best way of hiding the king and his servant. At last he took up a cloak which was draped roughly across his chair, threw it round Oswin's shoulders, and taking the stricken man by the elbow raised him to his feet. 'I know the best place for you,' he remarked as he helped the king away. 'A place only I know. They won't find you there. Tondhere we will hide separately; it will be safer that way.'

'No one will find either place – unless I tell them.'

It was still dark and Oswy was asleep when the messenger arrived.

He was stopped first by one of the perimeter guards and brought before Ricbert who was at once suspicious of the man until he heard his story. Ricbert hesitated only a moment, looked at the still-dark sky, but decided that this news could not wait. Catching up his cloak he hurriedly barked, 'Bring him,' and set off to King Oswy's tent.

The king, loath to be disturbed, was angry until he saw his captain and, behind him, the cringing messenger held by two guards.

'Ricbert.'

Rubbing sleep from his eyes and struggling upright the king shivered as the cool, morning air caressed his naked body. His servant, ever to hand, held out a fur wrap which the king wound quickly around himself before fixing Ricbert intently with his eyes.

'Well! This must be important. Who is this wretch?'

'Sire, he says his name is Ruda and he serves a master called Hunwald. What he has to say is vital to Your Majesty. May he tell it?'

Oswy nodded and indicated to the guard that they should bring him forward.

Ruda, sinking to the floor, as he found himself in the presence of the king, licked his lips and made some incoherent sounds before Oswy spoke again.

'Listen, Ruda, or whatever your name may be. If your message is important I want to know it. If it is not may the Lord God help you. I will sit here; you will kneel there. Tell me what you were sent to say NOW.'

Ruda, kneeling as directed, began haltingly. 'Your Majesty, my master is the Lord Hunwald whose estate is some eight or ten miles from here to the north west. Sire, I have been sent to say that he has King Oswin in his house and awaits your command.'

'Oswin!'

Oswy had leapt to his feet as his cousin's name was spoken and was gazing fixedly at the messenger. Then throwing himself down on one knee before the cowering creature he seized him by the neck of his tunic and hissed again, 'Oswin. How did your master find him? How?'

Ruda swallowed once or twice before gasping, 'I think the king came for shelter, sire, which he thought my master would give him . . . thought he would . . . ' the man faltered lamely, before ending, 'but my master says I must tell you that he is loyal to you and if you will send men he will deliver King Oswin to you.'

'Does he?' Oswy released his grasp from the messenger's clothes and stood upright again. 'Does he,' he repeated, adding, 'a traitor to his king but useful to us. Ricbert!'

'May it not be a trap, sire,' warned Ricbert quickly. 'Can we trust this man?'

'Oh no. No Ricbert. We can trust neither this man nor his master but I do not think it is a trap. They would know I need not go myself but someone must. We must take Oswin.'

'Prisoner sire?'

Oswy did not reply but a look of concern replaced the expression of elation on his face.

'Oh, Dear God,' he whispered almost to himself. 'If I take him prisoner I can never regard Deira as mine. He will always be there. People will rise in his support. Dare I risk that?'

There was silence for some time in the tent, the only audible sound being the harsh breathing of the messenger cowering on the ground between the king and his officer. Oswy turned from the others and fell to his knees in prayer while the guards and Ricbert, and even Ruda, looked questioningly at each other. At length Oswy rose and turned to address Ricbert in such a low tone that the captain had to crane forward to hear what was said.

'No, Ricbert. Not prisoner. He . . . must . . . die,' and raising his voice again to it normal tone Oswy repeated the order.

'He must die. Send Ethelwin to do it. And Ricbert,' as the officer turned to leave the tent, 'Tell him to take a priest with him. He must not be killed before he has been shriven.'

Aidan was 100 miles away to the north yet he knew of Oswin's death the instance it occurred.

The bishop, on foot as always, was moving slowly through rolling moorland up a steep slope which would lead him to the next hamlet. Brother Oda, was well ahead, reaching the brow of the hill, when he heard a muffled exclamation behind him. Turning he saw his bishop standing motionless, holding a clenched fist to his forehead and screwing up his face as if suddenly struck by pain. Oda dropped his bundle of belongings and ran back down the hill as quickly as he could, sliding on the loose stones of its rough surface and calling out, 'I'm coming, my Lord, I'm coming,' as he raced along.

Aidan had let fall his staff and had dropped to his knees by the time the monk reached him. Oda stretched out his hand and was about to touch the old man upon the shoulder, and was bending to ask if he was alright, when he realised that the bishop was praying fervently with his eyes closed. There was such calm in the expression on the face of the kneeling figure that Oda drew back his hand, feeling that the other could not have been struck by illness. In the stillness of the afternoon the only movement seemed to be the steady beat of an artery, plainly visible in its tortuous path across the almost transparent skin of the bishop's temple, and the imperceptible flicker of his lips.

Oda, who had been the assistant to the infirmarian for a time, counted the beats through force of habit, unwilling now to disturb the master who moments ago he had feared stricken. One, 2, 3, 4, . . . Not a fast rate and certainly strong too if the pulses in the vessel were anything to go by. Then Oda remembered the bishop's great powers of perception of things hidden from others and, after a moment, he too knelt down beside his superior and began to pray.

When Aidan opened his eyes the young monk was still praying peacefully beside him. The bishop rose and touched his companion gently. Oda scrambled up also but could not refrain from questioning Aidan.

'What has happened my Lord? Something serious I fear? So, when I saw you in prayer, I prayed too although I knew not for what.

'You prayed for a man's soul, Brother Oda, – the soul of a king, a Christian king, and a man of God. He was murdered a long way from here only a short time ago at the very instant that you heard me cry out and came rushing to help me. Thank you,' the bishop added, 'for your solicitude.'

Oda did not speak for some moments but crossed himself and murmured a 'de profundis' for the soul of the dead man.

'Do I know the victim, my Lord?' he asked at length.

'Perhaps, who can say,' answered Aidan. 'We of Lindisfarne, and of other monasteries in the north, are not of this world so I think perhaps you do not. He was a good man – Oswin by name – descended from Iffi through his father Osric of the Deiran royal family. He had been King of Deira since the holy St Oswald met his death so tragically at Penda's hands. We have prayed for his soul, now we may talk of his life.'

But strangely, Aidan said nothing for some time although, judging by the faraway expression in his eyes he was remembering the late Oswin and former times.

'He gave me a horse once,' the bishop said so suddenly that Oda was quite startled. 'It was perhaps the only time we disagreed – strange that I should think of it now at such a time.'

'Did you own the horse for long, my Lord? Was he a good animal?'

Aidan smiled a slow gentle smile and then, looking at Oda, shook his head from side to side.

'I never found out if he was good or bad, Oda. I owned him for less than a day. Then I met a poor man who had next to nothing – a few rags to clothe him and a few scraps to eat. So of course,' the bishop remarked as if describing the most natural thing in the world, 'I gave him the horse which was richly caparisoned since the king had chosen him specially for me.'

'Was His Majesty displeased, my Lord?'

'Yes, Oda, I fear he was – at first at any rate.'

'Whatever did you say to explain what you did?'

'Oh, there was no difficulty about that,' laughed Aidan. 'I just asked the king a simple question: – "is the child of a mare more important to you than a child of God?"'

Neither man spoke for some moments until Oda said, eventually, shaking his head as he did so, 'You are a clever man my Lord. I would like to think I would be half as clever one day. Put like that there was only one answer was there not?'

The two picked up their belongings and resumed their ascent of the path. At the top they paused to contemplate the tiny hamlet in the distance for which they were making. Oda looked several times at the bishop in a worried fashion and then asked another question.

'My Lord, if King Oswin was a good man – a really good man as you say – why were you so stricken at the time of his murder since he is surely destined for heaven?'

'Can you not guess, Oda? Can you not guess? I was stricken, not by what had happened to Oswin, but because King Oswy, his cousin, had ordered the blow struck. I grieved for the soul of the murderer, not the victim.'

'Plague!'

Oda had uttered the single word the moment they entered the village. The first house contained three corpses, dead for days judging by the stench of putrifaction, the next four and the one after that three again. Oda stooped to examine one who looked as if he had died more recently, perhaps that day or the previous night. He seemed about to speak after his cursory examination but then shook his head and moved across to a second body. This was a shrivelled, emaciated figure, clad only in a few rags, so sparse and torn that the mass of swollen buboes in his groin were visible the moment Oda lifted the thin covering aside.

'It is the plague, my Lord. There is no doubt of it. I have seen it before and these poor creatures show unmistakable signs of being its victims.'

Oda, kneeling by the body, looked up at the bishop who, with an expression of anguish on his face, had closed his eyes in prayer.

'Eternal rest give unto them O Lord and let perpetual light shine upon them. May they rest in peace.'

'Amen.'

The two clerics looked at each other in silence for a moment. Aidan was clearly deeply moved by what they had found and Oda, realising his master's mood, remained silent until the bishop chose to speak.

'Will there be any left alive?'

'Perhaps, my Lord. Who can say. Some have been dead for days – maybe as long as a week – but these two are recent victims and there may be others who have not yet succumbed.' Then he added as Aidan still said nothing, 'If any escaped the infection I think they will have fled. If we find any alive it will be because they *could* not leave.'

'We must search for them,' Aidan was suddenly determined. 'You, Oda, take those few huts on that side. I will take these over the way. Any who are alive must have the last rites. Go now and search thoroughly.'

Oda scrambled to his feet and brushed dust from his habit. He turned to leave the hovel then paused in the doorway, almost blotting out the light completely.

'I will go at once, my Lord, but I beg of you, when you are searching, be careful. The plague strikes swiftly like an arrow. Everyone near is in danger. Take great care my Lord.'

He peered inside as he spoke to the bishop, now almost invisible within the gloom of the hut until Oda moved aside to allow shafts of sunlight to pour in again. The old man took up his bundle and staff and as he emerged he touched Oda lightly on the forearm.

'I know the risks, Brother Oda, but I am grateful for your warning. But it is not death, which is inevitable, that matters. What matters is that all who die should be in a state of grace so let us find them and administer the last sacraments wherever we can.'

They found four, one moribund and three plainly so severely affected that they were beyond recovery. One was able to tell them that a few – five or six perhaps – had fled the village in an attempt to escape the pestilence, but a village to the north had also been stricken and one to the east in the valley so where would they go? The man looked with hollow, haunted eyes at Aidan. Was it God's punishment for their wickedness? Would he forgive their sins or condemn them to hell. Would the good fathers pray for him?

This man was the last to die on the evening of the following day. The bishop had refused to leave until then but, by the time the man expired it was dark and too late to continue their journey, so they spent a second night in the deathly town. Between praying for their souls and giving what solace they could they had buried twenty-one men, women and children in four places. For fear of contracting the contagion themselves they lifted the bodies of the more decomposed on two spades or rolled them over into shallow graves dug as close as possible to where they had died. On Brother Oda's advice the few thin blankets they found, and any garments which were not on the bodies of the dead, were burned since, he explained to the bishop, no one knew how the disease was spread and anything they handled could be contaminated. They prayed together to the holy St Sebastian, protector against death from plague, that they might not already have been infected.

Oswy, leaving most of his army to complete the subjugation of Deira, returned home soon after Ethelwin reported Oswin dead. Although now, by conquest, King of both provinces of Northumbria he gained no pleasure from his victory and he brooded ceaselessly on the murder of his cousin. The reaction of his queen and his bishop, he realised, would be predictably sharp and critical and, now that the deed was done, he found the prospect of facing them grim. Oswy, hunched in his saddle, rode silently and alone, endlessly churning over in his mind his decision to order the killing. Time and again he regretted what he had done and fervently wished it undone. The sight of Ethelwin, the instrument of the crime, was anathema to him and the lieutenant, having been berated soundly, on more than one occasion during the first day of their return journey, kept well away so as not to provoke further outbursts.

Bamburgh was reached eight days later and, as chance would have it, only hours before the return of the bishop and Brother Oda.

They had spent two more days at the next hamlet where Aidan had given the last sacraments to three peasants who remained alive and had sat patiently with the last to die – a mother holding an already dead infant in her arms. Then the monks, finding no further evidence of the plague in the neighbourhood, set off directly south east to confront the king.

At first their journey had been easy and they had made good time, neither having any inclination to delay after their harrowing experience. Then the bishop had begun to show signs of fatigue and his face had taken on a haggard, drawn appearance, whilst his pace became slower and slower. He made various excuses. The month away had sapped his strength, he told Oda, and he was – don't forget – not so young as he once was. But the brother had feared the worst and, desperate that the bishop should complete the journey, had finally commandeered a donkey in the king's name. It was a measure of the bishop's malaise that he agreed to ride it.

Oswy, uncertain how to face his wife entered her chamber quietly and stood before her looking shamefaced and hesitant. He did not have long to wait for her reaction.

'Murderer!'

Enfleda was beside herself with rage as she had seldom been before. Only her inability to rise from her couch, because of her swollen belly and the pains in her back, stopped her from flinging herself upon him. Oswy edged nearer trying to be placating and hoping to ride out the storm of her anger which was seldom prolonged. He muttered a pathetic justification.

'There was no other way. If I'd left him alive his people would have risen against me. I *had* to do it,' he repeated plaintively. 'There *was* no other way. We were at war and in war,' he ended defiantly, 'people die.'

'People are killed in just wars, but murdering your captive and your cousin isn't war.' Enfleda was venting all her frustration in her own helpless position on her husband. 'It's assassination, that's what it is. And in any case,' she continued after a pause when Oswy made no response, '*You* were at war; *he* wasn't. *You* were the invader. Did he attack you? Did he even oppose you, army to army? Well,' since the miserable Oswy still made no reply, 'did he?'

It took a long time for the king to answer. Several times he opened his mouth to do so without any sound emerging. Then he seemed to draw himself upright as if about to be defiant before turning away again but still saying nothing until the queen prompted him.

'Well!'

'No,' he admitted. 'No he never openly opposed us. He harried us of course,' Oswy was more confident now, speaking in factual terms as a soldier describing his campaign 'but he was never able to raise enough troops to fight a pitched battle. In the end,' he went on miserably, 'we caught up with him near a town called Catterick. His forces – at least some of them – fought a rearguard action whilst most escaped, including,' he almost whispered, 'Oswin himself.'

Then as Enfleda was about to rate him again, he rounded on her fiercely.

'Go on. GO ON. Say what you like. I'm sorry I did it. I've wished a thousand times I could undo it but I can't. I did it as a soldier but I wish, by all that is holy . . . ' he choked for a moment on the words ' . . . that as a Christian I had spared him. Spared . . . him . . . spared . . . ' His voice tailed off into incoherance.

There was no sound between them for several minutes. Oswy looked up, searching it seemed for some hint of forgiveness in Enfleda's eye. She stared at him stonily before gesturing to a chair and indicating that he should bring it to her side.

'Are you really sorry?'

The two moist eyes that he turned towards her were, she felt, the saddest she had ever seen.

'Sorry? I have never been so sorry for anything in my life. One part of me seemed to have to do it and one,' he shrugged breifly, 'knew what a sin it was.'

He moved his chair beside her yet remained half turned away as if unable as yet to meet her gaze. Then he began to talk quietly as if to himself.

'It isn't easy to be a good king. God knows I've tried to do it well, as He would have wished, but, although I'm king to everyone, I'm just a man within myself with all the weaknesses other men have. I have sexual weaknesses – you know that – but I hope I keep them under control. And what's more I've been faithful to you – tempted once or twice perhaps but no more than that, and I don't know that any other man would be different.'

Oswy turned towards her before continuing and this time it was she who looked away.

'Penda – may he rot in hell – has been a thorn in my flesh for years, just as he was in Oswald's. We never seemed to beat him off for long no matter how hard we tried. With Oswin's help I thing we could have done it – taken the fight to him; crippled Mercia so that it would take years to recover if ever. But my holy cousin,' the words were spat out viciously which he at once regretted 'No. He is dead and I mustn't speak ill of him. My cousin anyway,' he went on after crossing himself, 'would never join me in this plan or even put difficulties in Penda's way. So we had to suffer attack after attack of which, as you know full well, one was only beaten off by God's grace and the pestilence.'

Oswy stood up and walked over to the window. Enfleda remained silent, reluctant to disturb him and, in truth, finding her anger at him melting away as it always did when his humility came to the fore; but followed him with her eyes. Presently he came over to sit down again by her side and after a moment took her hand.

'I had all these frustrations,' he resumed, this time meeting her eyes and holding them in his serious gaze, 'but that still doesn't . . . doesn't . . . justify what I did. I will make the humblest confession possible when the bishop comes and will carry out whatever penance he may impose, however humiliating. I will ask . . . have already asked . . . God's forgiveness and I must ask yours too. Can you forgive me?'

'Oh Oswy.'

That was all Enfleda was able to say before dissolving into tears. Oswy left his chair and knelt before her, taking her in his arms and making soothing noises. For several minutes she held him tightly as the tears rolled down her cheeks. Gradually her sobs became softer and she raised her head to look into his face. They both smiled, and Enfleda began to dry her tears while Oswy sat back on his heels on the floor in front of her. She laughed again and rumpled his hair playfully.

'I could never be cross with you for long could I? Oh dear, Oswy, I can't endorse what you did but I can't go on holding it against you. Of course I forgive you but,' she added, taking one of his hands and smacking it as though he were a naughty boy, 'I hope that when Bishop Aidan comes he gives you a thumping great penance. You deserve it.'

Edith had made one of her rare visits to the scriptorium to see for herself the spectacular progress her son was making under his father's guidance.

James of course could hardly wait to begin teaching Eadfrith the art of sacred illumination, but even he had been astonished at the boy's ability. So adept was the lad becoming that James was conscious all the time of the risks of pushing him ahead too quickly. But no matter how slow and deliberate James attempted to make his teaching Eadfrith raced ahead, assimilating his instructions with lightening speed and even – and James could scarcely contain his excitement – showing originality of design when given a free rein.

Just now Edith was watching Eadfrith complete a task he had just begun when she came in. It was an exercise in knot work which, he proudly told her, he had already done many times. After carefully spacing his points he began to construct a variety of patterns from the one basic design.

Eadfrith stood up obediently but as Edith turned to go he whispered urgently to his father, 'Can I show mummy some beasts? Please?'

Hearing the whisper, and wishing more than anything to stay longer, Edith paused by the door and came back a few steps into the room. She must have looked as expectant as her son for in a moment James stern expression relaxed.

'Very well. Just two. Nothing elaborate mind. Perhaps a double reptile and – what else – two dogs heads like you did yesterday. But carefully mind,' as the boy returned gleefully to the table.

'These are new,' James explained to his wife, 'and he hasn't been doing them for long, but the idea is to give the design an animal association for greater excitement, so at this stage the designs he does are very simple as of course are the beasts as you can see,' pointing to the two simple heads of a reptile like creature at the ends of curving bodies suggested by simple lines.

'That's quite good Eadfrith,' he added. 'Now the dogs, just as simply.'

They soon emerged.

Edith overcome with surprise at the rate of the boy's progress thought she must support her husband's caution in praising him.

'Very clever, dear,' she said 'although,' she added, 'I perhaps wouldn't have known they were dogs – especially that on the right. Still you are doing well.'

And fearful that she would start to weep in her pride for the lad she turned hastily to the door, calling over her shoulder, 'I will leave you. But it has been very interesting and I will come again if I may. Thank you both.'

There was silence in the scriptorium after her departure as James gazed at Eadfrith and Eadfrith, just a little deflated by the criticism of his dogs, gazed at them.

'Well,' James broke the silence, 'back to the spirals. We will come to beasts again later.'

The bishop was weakening fast by the time they reached Bamburgh. Oda had been anxious to seek help at once but Aidan would not permit it and had insisted that when they arrived they were to go straight to the chapel and speak to no one.

The donkey came to a halt beside the door and Oda was easing the frail figure off its back when he heard an exclamation of surprise behind him, and realised that a woman he did not know, who had just emerged from the chapel, had run forward to help.

On leaving the scriptorium Edith had gone immediately to say a prayer of thanks to God for the artistic gifts with which He had blessed Eadfrith. She had stayed longer than she intended, half praying half dreaming in the quiet of the chapel in the still summer evening. She had not heard Brother Oda and the donkey approaching and, at first, when coming out from the shadows into the bright sunlight, had not recognised the bishop nor realised what was happening. When she saw who it was, and the illness reflected in his face, she was appalled.

'It is Bishop Aidan. He is sick. What is the matter with him Brother? What is wrong?'

Oda glanced at her quickly, uncertain whether to accept her help now that the nature of the bishop's illness was so clear. She gave him no chance to decline, however, since she had already wound the old man's arm around her shoulder and was beginning to move with him towards the church. Oda started to answer her but a series of violent coughs from the sick man left his words inaudible and he had to repeat them.

'This is the plague, my Lady. I fear the bishop is seriously infected and is declining rapidly.' Oda stopped and grunted with exertion as they dragged the, now, limp figure of Aidan along. 'Can we lay him gently down with his back to this buttress? That way he can see the altar and say his last prayers to God for I fear he is not long for this world.' Then Oda began coughing too and added softly, after he regained his breath, 'nor perhaps am I.'

Edith looked sadly at the wasted figure of His Lordship the Bishop. His eyes were closed although his lips were moving almost imperceptibly. A bout of coughing racked his frame again and, when Oda moved the collar of his habit to allow him to breathe more easily, Edith saw a massive swelling down the side of his neck and behind the angle of his jaw. These were the buboes of the plague without a doubt.

When she saw the terrible evidence of the disease the implication of her own position struck her immediately, and instinctively she drew back a little from the still form. Oda, noticing her movement, turned towards her with a warning.

'Leave us now, my Lady, I beg you. He . . . we . . .' he corrected himself, 'have contracted this disease from infected villages in the north west. It was rampant there and many died. I was assistant to an infirmarian once and I have seen it before. It is very violent for a while and then fades away so more and more of those affected begin to recover. We . . . ' he broke off as he turned his eyes towards Edith and saw how white she had become and that she was watching him with staring eyes.

'How . . . how is it contracted, Brother?'

'We do not know, my Lady. From person to person, certainly, but how we cannot tell. It seems to spread most readily when the lungs are affected as are His Lordship's and . . . ' again Oda hesitated before making the admission' . . . 'are mine.'

'May I . . . have I . . . do you think I have become infected from my contact with the bishop? Oh Dear God!' exclaimed Edith.

'I cannot say mistress, but the longer you stay with us the more likely it must become. Let us pray you have not been affected so far but leave us, I beg you, and . . . ' Oda stopped speaking but raised his hand to halt Edith who had begun to turn away. 'And,' he resumed when he had her attention again, 'tell everyone that, on the bishop's instructions, no person is to come to him. If they do all may catch the plague. Before he became so ill as you see him now he was adamant. "Take me straight to the chapel," he insisted, "but let no one in. I give them all my blessing but they cannot come to me for fear of the contagion," that is what he said.'

'Yes, that is what I said and I say it again.'

They both looked in surprise at Aidan who had opened his eyes and, in a feeble voice, barely audible even in the stillness of the chapel, confirmed his order. Edith and Oda looked back to each other without speaking, waiting to see if he would say anything further. The bishop closed his eyes and they thought he had lapsed into unconsciousness until he said, in little more than a whisper, 'No one was meant to be here, and, if they were, Brother Oda was to insist that they left the chapel before we entered it.' After a pause when his breathing was laboured from the exertion of talking he continued, even more faintly, 'You . . . you were . . . not supposed to be here.'

Oda gently adjusted the old man's position as he finished speaking, and Edith waited uncertainly, not knowing whether to leave or remain. After some time Oda ceased his attentions to the bishop and addressed her again.

'You had best leave us, my Lady. We are in God's hands here and we could be in no better. Please go.'

Edith, looking over her shoulder at the two stricken monks, reached the chapel door. Silence fell. Oda looked with affection at the old man who was, it appeared, at last peacefully asleep. Then the younger man heard a sound and he turned to find that Edith was again standing close by, tears streaming down her cheeks. The monk made to rise but she shook her head and he resumed his place by the bishop's side. Edith too sank to the floor beside them and in a few moments spoke in halting tones.

'If . . . if . . . no one is to come to you . . . for fear of contracting the disease . . . may . . . may . . . they not perhaps . . . contract it from me?' And when Oda did not answer she repeated the question.

'May they not?'

Oda, with reluctance, was obliged to reply.

'If you have already become infected from us . . . yes, my Lady, they may.'

Tears were again pouring down Edith's cheeks as she realised her peril. Aidan slept on and Oda could think of nothing comforting to say and had turned back to the old man when he heard Edith speaking again but this time it seemed to herself.

'My husband . . . my son . . . they could both catch it, would be almost certain to do so by being with me so much. They might . . . die like Penda's soldiers did. Or the queen or . . . the king might die and perhaps . . . their child when it is born. Dear Lord Jesus, what am I to do?'

Oda was about to speak until he realised that the bishop had opened his eyes and with a tiny shake of his head had indicated silence. After a moment it was His Lordship who answered.

'My daughter,' he began, in a voice stronger than before, as if summoning up all his reserves of strength, 'my daughter, you are a brave woman to face your predicament so squarely. If you have contracted the plague from – may God forgive us – one of us, and you return to the palace anyone might contract it also. If you do not have it, nor acquire it, all will be well but you cannot know which it is. Do you feel that you have the strength to stay here – not close to us of course but here in this chapel, or better still in the sacristy where you could be separate from us – until you are, please God, safe or, if that is His Holy Will, you know you are not. That way my child you will infect no one you love and their deaths will never be laid at your door? Do you have that strength? You are in God's house here and He will sustain you throughout your ordeal.'

Edith looked from one to the other of the two men as Aidan stopped speaking. She turned towards the altar and crossed herself and seemed to be praying. At one point she seemed about to approach the bishop but stopped after one or two steps in his direction. She stood with closed eyes for a long time as if pondering her problem. Tears continued to roll down her cheeks without any effort on her part to dry them.

Finally she turned and moved back down the aisle towards the daylight stopping several times along the way as if still in doubt. Oda watched her fixedly, waiting for her to disappear through the chapel doors.

Then he saw that she had closed one door followed by the other before lifting, with some difficulty, the heavy wooden bar and dropping it into place to lock them in.

An hour later Enfleda's pains began.

Edith and Neta had been sent for at once but, although the midwife had come promptly, Edith could not be found. Messengers scoured the palace but to no avail. The queen, at first distraught by this, was so quickly in the throes of a strong labour that she became oblivious of anything else.

In an hour the queen had given birth to her third daughter.

In the gloom of the chapel Aidan lay inert his life apparently ebbing away.

His body became wraith-like, his eyes deeply sunken, his skin transparent, his hands skeletal, yet he still lived. The massive buboes in his neck appeared also in each armpit. His cough racked his frail form and the rasp of his breathing filled the tiny chapel. Scarcely able to make any movement for himself it was Brother Oda who nursed him attentively, gently easing him into new positions to relieve the numbing pressure of the earth floor on his buttocks and the buttress on his back.

It was Oda too who communicated with those outside. In the side wall of the chancel there had been cut an oblique aperture through which sufferers from leprosy could see the Holy Sacrifice of the Mass yet would not infect the faithful in church. Oda had spent some time by this leper squint and had finally attracted the attention of someone outside. Brother Uffa had been summoned to the squint, first to be told about the bishop's critical state, then of Oda's infection and, finally, of Edith's voluntary incarceration to protect them all.

The two monks had spoken for a long time although Brother Uffa had made no attempt to make them change their plans. It was arranged that food and drink would be brought to the sacristy entrance which would be strictly barred except when opened to allow the prisoners to take the provisions inside. The king and queen were to be told but they were not to come, not even to the leper squint since even that contact with those in the chapel could be dangerous. Oda was insistant that as few people as possible should talk to him in this way – perhaps it would be best if Uffa alone were to do so.

'On no account Brother,' emphasised Oda, 'are master James and his son to attempt to come. The Lady Edith is distraught as you can imagine but she insists that they do not try to come and if they do she will not see or talk to them. I think she may feel,' surmised Oda sadly, 'that if she should catch a glimpse of either of them she would weaken in her resolve and would want to rejoin them so that they too might become infected – if she has caught the disease.'

Edith's sacrifice in the interests of them all affected James profoundly. Brother Uffa spent hours with him in an attempt to convince him of the rightness of her decision. Suppose she had caught the disease, he had pointed out, and James and Eadfrith had caught it from her and died? Suppose the king and queen and their attendants in the palace had died and hundreds more in the town too. Another epidemic, like that which affected the Mercian soldiers a few years ago, could wipe out Bamburgh completely and leave Northumbria without king or heir. Surely Edith had been right and James, when he came to see things clearly, would accept that.

'But why won't she see me and talk to me? You have spoken to Brother – whatever he is called – through the squint. I could talk to her like that, comfort her, sustain her, help her. Surely Brother, I could do that. There can't be any risk of catching plague just by talking? Can there? Answer me.'

And Brother Uffa had at length answered with the truth which was the only answer he knew how to give.

'No. I do not believe there can. But,' he went on quietly, moving his stool nearer to the desolate James and laying a hand gently on his arm, 'I do not believe that fear of contamination is the real reason she will not see you.'

James looked up in a puzzled fashion, clearly unable to comprehend what was in Uffa's mind.

'The real reason,' the monk explained, 'is that she knows that, if she were to see you just once, she would be unable to maintain her resolve and would want to open the doors and throw herself into your arms. And if she did that . . .' Uffa shrugged and realising that James, with downcast eyes, was no longer looking at him, completed his words '. . . the risk of infecting us all would be there again.'

James seemed to accept this for a time but then they had to go over it again and yet again until both scriba and counsellor were exhausted.

After the monk finally left James sat for a long time. His abject desolation at her exposure to such danger, without him being able to help her, remained but, gradually, he began to accept that what she was doing for them all was right. The thought of not being able to see her, however, hurt most of all and went round and round in his brain. Time and again he had remembered the last occasion they were together in the scriptorium with Eadfrith. If only he had known then that he might never see her again he would . . . would . . . would what? More rational now, he realised that, even had he known then what was to happen, he could not have convinced her any more strongly of his love for her than he had done when they shared their mutual pride at their son's achievements.

Perhaps there *was* nothing he could have said. Perhaps the realisation that he might never see her again *would* have been harder to bear than this sudden deprivation he had had to endure. He held his head in his hands in misery, endlessly churning over in his mind . . . 'never see her again . . . never see her . . . '

He sat up with a jerk. Perhaps he could see her again. Perhaps there was a way if only for an instant. What had Brother Uffa said? She was to separate herself from the other two in the chapel by going into the sacristy, and each day food and drink was to be put outside that door. *She* would bring it in; she would *have* to do so. The others were to remain in the nave so Edith was the only one who could open the sacristy door and lift the provisions inside. It would give him a glimpse of her – little more – but anything . . . anything was better than never seeing her again.

A niche in the angle of a building behind the chapel gave him a clear view of the sacristy door from a distance of some fifty yards. He could see at once that there was nothing outside the door. Was he already too late? Looking up at the sky he saw that it was lightening in the east but was still dark to the west behind him. They would not have come yet; he must be in time.

They came when it was almost full daylight. One man carried a basket covered with a cloth and another a large skin of water. They placed their burdens hastily two or three feet away from the door and were gone in an instant, fearful no doubt that their mere presence so close to the chapel might expose them to danger. James remained at his post, never for an instant taking his eyes off the door, willing it to open so that he could see her.

An hour or so went by before the door opened slowly. For a moment no one emerged, as though whoever was within was anxious to ensure that they were alone before coming outside. Then she came into view.

Her hair was tousled and her dress awry and she looked so small and vulnerable that he needed to exert all his will-power to remain in his hiding place and not give himself away. She looked from right to left, as if fearing someone might be near by, before taking the skin and lifting it inside.

Seconds later she returned, tried to lift the basket, but, finding it too heavy, took hold of one of the handles and walked inside backwards dragging it after her. The door closed James was alone again.

He had seen her. Even if he were never to set eyes on her again in this world he had watched her in the knowledge of that possibility. Feeling absurdly cheered by this brief glimpse of his wife he rose from his cramped position determined to be there again the following morning.

If he were to sprint across the fifty yards to the door as soon as she had gone back inside with the basket or skin, whichever she took first, he could get into the chapel too and if one were to die so would the other. But that would leave Eadfrith alone.

'Dear Lord Jesus Christ,' he prayed, 'what am I to do?'

It was soon plain that Edith too had become infected.

It was during the second night that Brother Oda, who had been dozing beside the sleeping Aidan, heard her coughing from within the sacristy. Edith had retired there at their insistence. She had stationed herself by the door leading from there to the sanctuary so that she could see the altar and tabernacle with its crucifix on top and gain what comfort she could in her enforced isolation. She had propped open the door into the church so that she could just keep the bishop in sight and Oda could speak to her.

Her loneliness was barely supportable. Time and again she imagined the disease working its way through her body. Oh Dear Lord, was that ache in her groin a sign that the buboes were forming? Now it had gone; perhaps it had only been the position in which she had been lying. She thought she felt hot then cold. She shivered violently and had to search around for some covering to obtain some warmth. A bundle of cassocks was all she could find and she piled these on top of her and lay with her knees bent up and her head tucked down like a child in the womb.

In her confusion, half sleeping half waking, she imagined at one moment that she was pregnant with Eadfrith – no not with him but with the son who miscarried – no that was foolish since she was not yet married to James but was sitting at his feet with her head on his knees by the banks of a river. They were on a journey. Where were they going? Catterick? No they had been there. Whitby? If they were going there where was Queen Ethelberga and where was Bishop Paulinus? But Ethelberga wasn't the queen; the queen was Enfleda and Aidan was the bishop. Aidan; something had happened to him; what was it? Everyone seemed to have changed except James. Oh Dear God protect James and protect her son. If she were to die, at least let them live. Let what she was doing now not be in vain?

She slept for a while after that until a sound from the chapel disturbed her again. James was coming for her to take her out of this prison and back to her son. No, NO. Don't James. Stay away. Keep the boy away. Leave him in his scriptorium with his designs and his beasts . . . Beasts; she seemed to see them on all sides. They looked like dogs; no they didn't she had told Eadfrith that they didn't. Reptiles! . . . Yes but horrible ones, not the ones he drew. Go away. Snakes. Please God not snakes . . . and she cried out in alarm in her sleep and sat up suddenly.

She was breathing with difficulty, taking big gasps at first and then the coughing began.

Oda heard her and managed to get to his feet which was so difficult to do that he only succeeded after a long time. He had lost his bearings and thought he was shuffling towards the sacristy door in case he might be able to help. But he was misled by the sanctuary lamp, gleaming red in the dark of the church and he turned towards it, stumbled at the altar steps and lay still, unable to move, listening to the coughing echoing round the walls of the chapel.

When it was full daylight Edith managed to stir herself and brought in the provisions from outside the sacristy door. She carried some of them through to the entrance to the nave where she saw that Aidan was alone propped up against the buttress. Where was Brother Oda? She steadied herself on the lintel until her own fit of coughing passed and then edged slowly into the chapel until she caught sight of the monk's body stretched out motionless across the lowest two steps of the altar.

Was he dead? May God have mercy on his soul if it had already left his body? And was Aidan still alive. He seemed not to move but . . . perhaps. She edged nearer to him and could just make out the faintest movement of his chest wall and then saw his eyelids giving the merest flicker. If Oda were dead who would look after the bishop in his few last lingering moments. She could not or she might contract the disease.

'Might!'

She realised that she had spoken aloud and instinctively turned to the two monks to see if either had shown any response. She held her lower ribs tightly to control the pain as she began to cough again. It was a long spasm and it left her so breathless that she had to support herself once more on the buttress against which Aidan was lying. She had not realised that she had moved so close. Surely she ought not to be there? She might contract . . .

In a brief spell of clarity she realised that it was no longer 'might'. She had the plague and the certainty of it gave her more comfort than anxiety.

No more agonising doubt. Her shivering, her heat and cold, the pains in her limbs but above all her cough . . . just like the bishop's and Oda's. She turned to look at Oda, stifling another cough as she did so and remembering that she had not heard him cough nor make any other sound since she entered the chapel.

Moving away from the buttress Edith slowly approached the prostrate Oda. There was no movement – none. Could she be sure? Dare she touch him? What did it matter now. She placed her hand on his outstretched arm; cold. She moved her fingers to his wrist and felt for a pulse; none. Was that the right place though? None on the other side of the wrist either nor in the neck. His other arm was doubled beneath him but she had no need to try to feel a pulse there. 'Eternal rest give unto him O Lord, and let perpetual light sh . . . '

She began to cough again before she came to the end of the prayer and she almost choked as she felt warm fluid well up into her mouth. What was . . . ? Then she saw that the hand she had held to her mouth during the spasm was bloodstained. She leaned forward and let the red blood in her mouth spill out into her hands. With a kerchief she dried her mouth and chin and dabbed her hands to clean them also.

A movement caught her eye and she saw that the bishop had opened his eyes and was looking vacantly in her direction. She must tell him about Brother Oda and they must say what prayers they could.

He had closed his eyes again when she reached him but seemed to understand when she told him that the monk had died. Aidan focused his eyes on her for a second and said in a whisper, 'Pray for him and . . . I . . . will pray too.'

Edith said all the prayers for the dead she could remember her recital punctuated by bouts of coughing although this time with only a tinge of blood. Aidan made no sound but the movement of his lips showed that he was joining her in prayer for Oda's soul.

After a long silence the bishop stirred and spoke very softly to Edith.

'I have been listening to you my daughter and I know that our worst fears are confirmed.' The effort of talking seemed to tire him and after a moment Edith replied, 'Yes my Lord. I too have the plague. My . . . chest . . . burns and my cough . . . ' It was the cough itself that stopped her speaking and when the fit was over she lay almost exhausted by his side. When she was breathing more easily she heard the bishop speak again.

'My daughter, you and I are not long for this world. I believe you to have lived . . . ' his voice tailed off for a moment but presently he continued . . . 'a good life; but we know from our Lord Himself that a just man sins seven times a day. Make your confession and while I still have strength to do so I will give you absolution.'

'*Bless me Father for I have sinned.*'

Edith began the familiar formula but her breathing was so harsh and difficult and the rasping cough so painful that it took her a long time to complete the recital of her few sins.

'Are you truly sorry for them?'

'Yes my Lord and for any that I can no longer remember.'

The bishop said nothing for a long time then with infinite slowness turned his head towards her and said, 'Make a good act of contrition whilst I give you absolution.'

'*Oh my God, I am sorry . . .* '

'*Dominus noster Jesus Christus te absolvat . . .* '

' *. . . and I firmly resolve never to offend thee again . . .* '

'*Deinde ego te absolvo a peccatis tuis in nomine Patris . . .* ' The bishop's hand barely moved as he attempted the sign of the cross.

' *. . . et Filii et Spiritus Sancti*'

' *. . . firmly to avoid the occasions of sin.*'

It was done thought Edith. She was shriven and there could now be no more occasions of sin. 'May Almighty God help my dear husband and chil . . .'

The cough which disturbed her prayer was mild but the haemorrhage which accompanied it was profuse. Her mouth filled with warm sticky fluid. It poured out down the front of her dress as she tried desperately to take a breath. The chapel was fading and spinning. The altar was . . . where? She tried to turn towards the tabernacle but could make no movement. Her hand made a faint helpless gesture as she choked in her own blood, slid over onto her side and lay still.

Aidan survived until well after dark, drifting in and out of consciousness, praying in his lucid moments to ask God's blessing on the two faithful departed who lay beside him.

His last thought was that his death was as he would have wished it – Almighty God and he alone.

It was the 31st of August in the year of our Lord 651, eleven days after the murder of Oswin.

On the Lammamoor Hills that night the young shepherd Cuthbert, in an agony of indecision about his future, paid little attention to the sheep he was supposed to be attending.

'Was Almighty God really giving him these signs? Should he enter the religious life? Why would *he* be chosen? *He* was no St Paul; the comparison was blasphemous. How would he decide? Would God give him one more sign?

He was sitting in a little hollow with his back to a boulder to protect him from a cool east wind. Worn out by indecision he almost slept until a sound disturbed him. Music? From where? It couldn't be music yet, by all that was wonderful, that was what it sounded like. It must be a trick of the wind in the early dawn which he could just see breaking in the far distance.

But that light could not be the dawn. He was looking west not east. He scrambled to his feet and climbed round his boulder to look eastward. Dark! No sign of dawn yet. So what was he seeing?

Cuthbert turned more slowly this time since the sound of music was unmistakable. Why did it not awaken his companions whom he could see huddled together in a hollow further away wrapped tightly in their cloaks? How could they possibly sleep through that wonderful overwhelming sound? It was heavenly!

Cuthbert fell to his knees as he said the word. It *was* heavenly. Almighty God was giving him another chance.

'Oh my Dear Lord Jesus Christ,' Cuthbert prayed with tightly closed eyes, 'forgive Your doubting servant and accept him to Your service for the rest of his mortal life and by Your grace may he come to live with You always in everlasting happiness in the next.'

Cuthbert opened his eyes. The light was streaming down from the heavens in a series of powerful beams directed, it seemed to him, to the south, towards the island of Lindisfarne and the Palace of Bamburgh. Now thousand upon thousand of heavenly figures were moving down the beam as if propelled by some mysterious motive force. And here they were returning – triumphantly returning he could tell. He did not know how he knew that this was a wondrous celebration, but know it he did for certain. Instantly he knew why. They had all come – there could be no other explanation – for a human soul to bear it in glory back to heaven and he – poor miserable creature that he was – had been priviledged to see it.

Cuthbert closed his eyes again unable to look at the light so bright had it become. There was something now in the centre of the beams moving upwards which was brighter still – without form, without human shape and yet there *was* a shape; no three shapes. These were three souls being borne to heaven by countless numbers of the heavenly host. He watched spellbound as this piercing radiance moved steadily upwards. Now it was less bright and he could perceive something about one soul which he could, for the first time, recognise. He could hear that same soul, in its human form, speaking to him on that very hillside.

'Then why do you hesitate to enter the religious life if you know God is calling you in these ways,' was what he had been asked.

This was the monk whom Cuthbert had met who had seemed to know everything he had done – who had known that God was calling him and that Cuthbert had been reluctant to go.

He had no reluctance now.

In the morning when his friends awoke he was nowhere to be seen but was miles away striding out towards Melrose Abbey.

As James crouched by the wall on the third morning he was in no doubt what he would do.

He had spent as much time as he could with Eadfrith on the previous day. The boy had asked innumerable questions of course but James had been encouraging. He had stressed what a wonderful thing it was that Edith was doing for them all, urged Eadfrith to pray to Almighty God for help, shown him many new and beautiful designs and colour schemes in the scriptorium. They had enjoyed themselves as much as they possibly could with such a threat hanging over them. James had taken a horse and with Eadfrith mounted in front of him they had ridden out onto the moors and not returned until dusk was falling. They had eaten a special supper together, with several of the boy's favourite dishes, and finally James had kissed him goodnight looking long and endearingly at him knowing that he might never see him again.

But now James' position in the niche was proving uncomfortable. Keeping himself poised for the dash across the open ground was tiring the muscles in his legs which ached abominably. Several times his eyes became blurred as he fixed his intense gaze on the sacristy door. He had expected it to open long before this. Surely it would open any moment now. The food had been there . . . how long had the food been there? Much longer than yesterday or the day before. He looked up at the sun and found it high in the heavens. In alarm he scrambled to his feet. What was happening? Why hadn't Edith come for the food? She couldn't . . . 'Oh Dear Lord,' he prayed 'let her not be plague stricken.' Perhaps she was too weak to raise the bar. How much longer should he wait?

Once he walked to the door and even raised his hand to knock but could not bring himself to do so. Perhaps he should shout. But if she were ill and unable to get to the door that would only cause her greater distress if she recognised his voice.

It was past noon when he finally went in search of Brother Uffa and poured out his story in a near-incoherent fashion. The significance of the food, which had not been taken in, however, was clearly evident. Uffa too had disturbing news.

'This is bad, very bad. I fear I was unable to get anyone to speak to me through the leper squint either. Before today Brother Oda came quite soon when I called but twice this morning I got no answer, although I was there a long time on each occasion.'

'Are they dead?' James was desperately clutching at Uffa's habit as he gasped out the words. 'Let us break in the door and see.'

'It is possible that they are dead, my son, but we must not yet break in. If all have been infected we must wait until all are dead before we dare try to remove the bodies for fear of contamination. To enter whilst one still lives would immediately expose us all to risk again. We have prayed to God constantly, as you know, asking him to give them absolution in their last torment, even though I have not been able to administer extreme unction in the approved fashion. But God is merciful, my son. His servants are good people who have faithfully obeyed His Holy Will and, if they have died, they will have spent their last hours on earth in His house. He will not allow them to suffer because we cannot fulfil the letter of the sacrament but have enacted it in spirit.'

'But aren't you going to break in? You must!' James was shouting now. 'Perhaps even if the monk's are dead she can be saved. It is only two days.'

Uffa was adamant however. If by noon tomorrow, food was not brought in, and no one answered at the leper squint, they would break in. James pleaded but the monk would not be moved and James distress became acute and he broke down in tears.

Soon after noon on the fourth day after the Chapel had been sealed the sacristy door was forced.

There were many who feared for their lives if they entered such a charnel house. Bishop Aidan had been near to death that first evening; if he had died then, or during the night, almost three days would have elapsed and, in the still warm weather of late August, decomposition could be advanced. Even without the plague the stench of death and putrifaction might pervade everything. It would be distressing work for certain and perhaps dangerous.

A volunteer party of three had agreed to batter down the door. Brother

Uffa had insisted he must enter first in God's name to establish if it was safe for others to follow him and to pronounce a blessing at the outset and say prayers for the souls of the faithful departed.

The force of the final blow with the battering ram which was needed to break down the barred door, took the first two men who wielded it across the threshold and part of the way into the sacristy. They stumbled to the ground as resistance was suddenly overcome when the door gave way. Finding themselves inside the plague-infested building they made to scramble to their feet anxious to retreat from any possible danger.

The watchers outside gasped as the crash came and waited for their colleagues to extricate themselves with utmost speed. The last man, who had barely passed beyond the door frame, was turning to come out when he suddenly stopped and, to the surprise of all, turned back and went in again. Neither of the others appeared and Brother Uffa had to squeeze past the three men, all of whom were standing quite still in amazement at something inside.

The monk was instantly aware of it too. Instead of the awful stench of putrifaction, the sacristy was pervaded by a delicate perfume unlike anything he had experienced before. Within the chapel itself the fragrance was stronger still and infinitely pleasing to the nostrils. Uffa quickly crossed the few yards to the body of Bishop Aidan from which some of the perfume seemed to be exuding. Beside his body lay that of Edith, half face down in a mass of congealed blood. Both corpses showed the lividity of death in their dependant parts and skin was evidently beginning to peel from several places which were exposed to their gaze. No odour of decomposition was perceptible from either, however, only the wonderful aroma that filled the entire chapel and was now beginning to be appreciated by those outside who were nearest the sacristy door.

That they were in the presence of a miracle none doubted. More and more of the bystanders were attracted inside by the aroma. One of them opened the front doors of the church and beckoned the remaining watchers whilst Brother Uffa, turning aside from the bodies of Aidan and Edith, went across to that of Brother Oda to find the same stark evidence of death but the same fragrance of paradise.

Before long the chapel was filled, the infinitely appealing perfume overcoming all fear of the pestilence. The three bodies were rolled inside cloths which kept the decomposition from view yet in no sense diminished the wonderful aroma. They were carried onto the sanctuary and placed carefully by the side of the altar to await the requiem Mass to follow.

Messengers were sent for the king and for James and Eadfrith that they might experience the wonder of the miracle with the rest. During the Mass Brother Uffa preached about the experience all had enjoyed.

'You have been privileged,' he announced, 'to be the witnesses of a miracle which Almighty God has worked to testify to the holiness of His three servants who have departed this life. What you have been aware of,' went on Brother Uffa to the silent congregation 'is quite simply called, "The Odour of Sanctity." From time to time it has pleased God to testify to the holiness or sacrifice of one of His subjects by overcoming the stench of decay in their decomposition and replacing it with the supernatural fragrance of heaven.

'By the holiness of these two Christian monks and the sacrifice of one good woman we have been privileged to enjoy an experience which is given to few. Let us remember the sanctity and example of the bishop and offer up the Holy Mass for his soul and that of his companion Oda. Let us remember also – always remember – the sacrifice of our sister in Jesus Christ, Edith, which, I have no doubt, saved this community from disaster. Pray too for the husband and son she leaves behind her so that sustained by God's grace and this wonderful miracle they may overcome their grief in their absence from her and may one day be reunited with her in heaven.'

James and Eadfrith knelt side by side in the fragrant chapel long after everyone else had gone. Neither could have explained the peace of mind they had regained by the miracle of the odour of sanctity for when God has worked a miracle no explanation is possible. They walked out into the early evening and went home contentedly hand in hand.

Chapter 14

In the scriptorium at Melrose Abbey Eadfrith was doodling.

He laughed out loud as he often did when he knew his design was right – not perhaps as he had intended it since he was often uncertain about what he intended – if anything. 'Things just happen on the parchment if you let them,' his father had taught him early in his tuition and how right he had been.

Eadfrith missed his father who had been away in Iona and Ireland, at the invitation of sundry abbots, for too long for his liking. Almost three years now it was and, although Eadfrith had been fully trained before his father left, there were ideas which the younger man had developed since, about which he wanted advice – expert advice which only his father could give. Well, it wouldn't be long now before they would meet again. James' last letter had indicated that the gospels he had been working on in the Monastery of Durrow were almost complete and he would soon be back.

Eadfrith's eye caught the letter L again as his thoughts turned to his father. There was a technique which James, and some others including Eadfrith, had used to accentuate letters – red lead dots neatly placed in two or three rows around the margin.

Yes indeed; the tail, even with its bird's head decoration, looked less complete than the outlined stem of the letter. He would . . .

Eadfrith stopped suddenly. Suppose, just suppose, he extended the idea and instead of outlining a single letter he put a whole word into a complete frame of dots. That might give greater accentuation still.

He continued to muse. The four gospels dedicated to Cuthbert. Now that would be something.

'Turned you out . . . out of your own Monastery? My Lord Abbot can you be serious? It defies belief.'

Brother Boisil, the prior of Melrose Abbey, had started to his feet at the news he had just learned from the two travel-stained monks before him. The elder, Abbot Eata, sat with downcast eyes, as if equally unable to grasp the enormity of what had happened to him and to his companion, Brother Cuthbert. The uneasy silence was finally broken by the younger man.

'I fear it is true, Brother Prior. And it affected the Lord Abbot deeply,' he added, glancing at Eata, sitting miserably beside him. 'It is a long story, Brother Prior, but if you, my Lord Abbot, wish it,' turning in the direction of Eata, 'I will gladly undertake the task of telling it.'

Eata made no reply and did not even raise his eyes from the floor, but a brief gesture of his arm indicated that Cuthbert should continue.

'Perhaps you should know first, Brother Prior, that Alchfrith, the illegitimate son, whom King Oswy made Sub-King of Deira some time ago, has, in the opinion of many, designs on his father's throne. Alchfrith therefore takes such opportunities as present to embarrass the king, put him into difficulties, cause problems whenever he can. One difference between them, which Alchfrith has begun to exploit, is that the father supports our own Celtic Church and the son the Roman one. The differences between our churches are small. Alchfrith would make them loom large.'

Cuthbert looked at Eata for approval to continue but there was no response. Presently Boisil said, 'Go on. Tell it all. I am calmer now and I would like to hear everything.'

'Well,' continued Cuthbert, 'when we accepted, from the sub-king, twenty hides of land at Ripon to found a monastery two years ago, we did not know that we were, so to speak, being used like the pawns in the game of chess, of which our beloved abbot here is such an acknowledged master.'

At last Cuthbert got a response from Eata who waved his hand as if to dismiss the notion of his expertise, and, giving a little smile for the first time, said, 'Spare my blushes, Brother Cuthbert. You are explaining it well. I think I have been too upset to follow all the intricacies before. Pray continue.'

Cuthbert nodded in reply and drawing his chair round to face the abbot and prior, resumed his account.

'As I was saying, then, when we accepted Alchfrith's offer we were, in the words of some of the younger people I used to meet, being "set up". Cuthbert's lighthearted approach was having its desired effect and both Eata and Boisil looked more interested and less unhappy.

'Alchfrith's strategy was, I believe, evolved when a young monk from Rome came into his kingdom. This monk was Wilfrid, a native of Northumbria, a man about my own age who had been recently tonsured – in the

Roman fashion of course,' added Cuthbert with a twinkle in his eye, 'in Gaul at the city of Lyons. Some years before he had been breifly at Lindisfarne but, wishing to extend his knowledge of the world, possibly more than his knowledge of our Saviour . . . and if I am unkind I ask Almighty God's pardon,' Cuthbert interjected more humbly as he caught a look from Boisil. 'Wishing to extend his knowledge, anyway, he went to Rome. Our gracious queen, Enfleda, helped him by sending him first to her kinsman in Kent who arranged his onward journey in due course.

'By all accounts,' went on the monk '– and of course as guest master at Ripon I was given more information about the outside world than I ever sought – he stopped at Lyons, once on the way to Rome and again on his return. They say the archepiscopal court there is both rich and powerful. The archbishop lives in considerable opulence rivalling that of the governor. The governor was greatly attracted by Wilfrid and even offered him his daughter in marriage. But Wilfrid had his heart set on a career in the church and it was during this second visit that he became a monk.'

Cuthbert paused briefly to shift his position in his chair before resuming his tale.

'On Wilfrid's arrival, then, in Deira, with such a strong Roman ambience – he had been, I am told, in great favour with Boniface, the Archdeacon of Rome, and had an audience with the Holy Father himself,' put in Cuthbert in parenthesis 'he was water upon Alchfrith's wheel. We, in the monastery at Ripon, were told that, unless we were prepared to accept the Roman practices of the calculation of Easter and the style of tonsure, we would have to leave. Alchfrith visited us himself and had a most forthright and unhappy interview with Abbot Eata here which upset him profoundly. Is that not so my Lord?'

'Profoundly,' agreed Eata, heaving a great sigh. 'It was very unpleasant. Do you know, Brother Prior, he even went so far as to suggest that our ordinations were invalid.' Eata looked miserable again and lapsed into silence.

'How could they be invalid?' Boisil had been listening quietly for a long time, taking in Cuthbert's account, but this stung him into a response.

Brother Cuthbert waited politely to see if the abbot would choose to answer before doing so himself.

'The argument, Brother Prior, is this. Despite our traditions and our faithful preservation of God's teaching for so long in our isolation, we have not, for example, been able to consecrate bishops as some say – Wilfrid certainly says – Canon Law lays down. It is customary, I have been informed, for a bishop to be consecrated by an archbiship – metropolitan is sometimes the word used – together with two or more other bishops, or, if not an archbishop, three bishops at least. We, in our church, had no archbishops, and to bring several bishops together at one time was often difficult. Hence our practice of consecrating bishops somewhat differently.'

Cuthbert frowned and looked troubled before, with a shake of his head, continuing.

'But what is now being suggested – at least by the sub-king – is that, if the consecration of the bishop is invalid, his ordinations of priests are invalid also. I use the word "suggested", Brother Prior, for that is what it was – a suggestion from Alchfrith. He was merely implicit not explicit but he was threatening nonetheless.'

'Well,' Cuthbert shrugged and rose to walk towards the window, 'we were, of course, not prepared to change our customs and we left Ripon – quickly too; Alchfrith left us in no doubt about that. He actually came back to make sure we went. So here we are.'

There was silence for a long time after Cuthbert's account as the others pondered on the unhappy episode. It was Boisil who finally spoke.

'Will this be the end of Alchfrith's attack on us? Is he planning something else?'

Again Cuthbert gave the abbot the opportunity to speak before answering the question himself.

'To be sure he is planning something else. It is my belief that he will install Brother Wilfrid as Abbot of Ripon and will be prepared, should Wilfrid wish it, to strengthen the temporal power of the monastery by further grants of land and money. That will be, I believe, to Wilfrid's liking. After that I am not sure what the plan will be. They tell me,' Cuthbert surmised, looking unhappy himself now, 'that attempts have been made to influence Queen Enfleda to resume her practice of keeping the Roman Easter. Were she to do so in, for example, two years time, in six sixty-three, the king, keeping our dates, would be celebrating Easter Day whilst she was still observing Palm Sunday. And in six sixty-five,' he added, 'I calculated that the divergence would be greater still.'

Again neither man responded to Cuthbert's remarks and presently he rose to his feet and asked the abbot's permission to retire.

'May I be excused my Lord Abbot? I find consolation at such times only in the presence of the Blessed Sacrament. My time as guest master brought me more into contact with the world than I found congenial. How fortunate we are that our eyes are turned always to our Lord Jesus Christ and that the machinations of this world are seen for what they are – mere triviality compared with the glories of the next. May I leave you my Lord?'

Eata finally roused himself from his inertia. 'Very well Brother Cuthbert; pray to God for us all and presently I will join you. But do not be too long. In perhaps an hours time, after Vespers, I must gather together all the monks and tell them what happened. I will need you then along with the prior. Until after Vespers then.'

The sub-king of Deira was rubbing his hands with glee.

Why had he not thought before about the possibility of using religion as a weapon? When he had offered the Melrose monks Ripon he had no other thought in mind than to embarrass his father. Bring them down into the new monastery, let them settle in nicely then bring pressure to bear. Either they would conform to Roman practice, in which case he had gained a victory over the Celtic Church which his father firmly supported, or they would refuse and he would throw them out with ignomony, so cocking a snook at the old man and infuriating him once more.

But now Alchfrith was beginning to see how he could use the Roman Church much more effectively to his own advantage. Oswy and the Celtic Church had had it all their own way for far too long. It was plain to Alchfrith that, although Northumbria and Iona and remote parts of Ireland were strongholds of that Church, they made up a tiny minority compared with the whole might of the Roman one which had spread virtually throughout the whole world. All he needed to do was to get Rome on his side and he would wear Oswy down, and, in due course, the whole of Bernicia and Deira could be his.

Alchfrith yearned for power even more than he did for riches but, as he often said to himself, if you gained all the power the wealth would be yours anyway, and once he had met Brother Wilfrid, he realised how powerful he could become.

Alchfrith had hung on Wilfrid's every word when he was describing the power and might and opulence of Rome. It was almost as though an angel had been talking.

'The grandeur of Rome, Your Majesty,' (Wilfrid had quickly learned to flatter if flattery was called for; Alchfrith loved to be called 'Your Majesty'), 'cannot be imagined unless one sees it with one's own eyes.

'It is as if one were gazing into the still waters of the well of history itself. Imagine, sire, this cradle of our Christian Faith with St Peter, the Keeper of the Keys of Heaven, arriving there in the year forty two, and the courageous

St Paul about the year sixty. Can you not visualise, Your Majesty, Paul writing, what everyone there calls, the captivity epistles whilst in the city – those to the Phillipians, the Colossians, the Ephesians and to Philemon. Consider his stirring words to the community of Phillipi in Macedonia, the first of the churches he founded outside the Holy Land. It is an epistle of transcendant beauty, sire, containing within it passages of great Christological significance.'

Wilfrid had paused there and looked at Alchfrith who, mesmerised by the eloquence pouring over him, had waved him on saying, 'Continue, continue, I want to know it all.'

'It was the Archdeacon of Rome himself, Boniface, who made me fully aware of the significance of the saint's words in those memorable passages, Your Majesty – passages in which St Paul reminds us that, before the Incarnation, Christ existed already as the son of God, of the same nature as God, with all the glory that belongs to the grandeur of God. At the Incarnation He assumed the human nature without diminishing His Glory as God,' (Wilfrid had paused there, briefly, and Alchfrith had remained unaware that the monk had thought it best not to stress the assumption of humility which accompanied the human nature which the saint had commended so strongly to his Philippian readers. He had quickly continued). 'Christ was exalted after the resurrection with all the splendour of the Godhead which is His by right from bearing the Name that is above all other names.

'Does it not stir you to think of the foundations of our Faith being laid in the majestic city? And not only laid but kept pure and untainted by any suggestion of heresy. It is no coincidence, sire, that the heresy that comes first to my mind is that of quartodecimanism – the custom of observing Easter on the fourteenth day of Nisan, as the week of the Jewish passover was called, whether Sunday or not. His Holiness, Pope Victor the First, who occupied St Peter's chair for a decade from the year one eighty-nine, stamped firmly upon that practice, even excommunicating Polycrates of Ephesus, one of its leading protagonists. The Celtic Church are not quartodecimans, of course, but they are misguided nonetheless. Their practice must soon be challenged as have so many other irregularities over the centuries. The names of those illustrious Popes who fought heresy make stimulating hearing, Your Majesty – Julius the First and Liberius, who condemned Arianism, Damasus the First, who destroyed Apollinarianism, Innocent the First – Pelagianism. Celestine the First – Nestorianism, and Leo the First, whose famous letter to Flavian, the Patriarch of Constantinople, in four forty-nine, undermined Eutychianism.

'Faced as we are in; the northern parts of these islands with another schism concerning the celebration of Easter, is it not salutary to remind ourselves of the many other attempts to adulterate our Faith which Rome has resisted, as it will resist this one. Do you not agree, sire?'

Alchfrith had agreed alright. He sometimes thought that Wilfrid could convince him black was white, although of course Wilfrid's theology was sound, of that there was no doubt.

But what was important, mused Alchfrith, was that he could quite easily get the might of Rome behind him and who could withstand that; Oswy? Never; not in a thousand years. To hear Wilfrid tell it Rome was the most powerful city in the world and of unsurpassed beauty, its churches too magnificent to imagine, the monk had said.

'When the Edict of Constantine was delivered in the year three twenty-one, the Church was enabled to accumulate immense estates – the Patrimony of St Peter, is how these are sometimes known. They are opulent beyond belief, both in Italy and in other countries. And what majestic churches and historic sites – The Basilica of St Paul Outside the Walls – San Paolo Fuori le Mura, as the Romans say . . . ' Wilfrid rolled the words round his tongue in a fashion which fascinated Alchfrith ' . . . erected by the Emperor Constantine on the site of the relics of St Paul himself. Then there is the Lateran Basilica, dedicated to St John the Baptist, given to the Church by Constantine to be the official residence of the Popes. And perhaps the most majestic of all, in the opinion of many, including myself,' Wilfrid added with an appearance of modesty, 'St Mary Major – Santa Maria Maggiore,' he had tripped off his tongue again 'built by one Pope, Liberius, and magnificently extended by another, Sixtus the Third, in four thirty-five. It is built,' Wilfrid intoned solemnly, 'where, one August night, the Blessed Virgin Mary left her footprint in a miraculous fall of snow.'

There was silence for a time as both men contemplated the phenomenon of a fall of snow at the height of the Roman summer.

'I mention but a few,' Wilfrid had gone on quietly, adding after a pause, 'has Your Majesty seen the church dedicated to St Peter, here in York?'

'But it is virtually a ruin.' Alchfrith was clearly surprised at the question and unable to see what was in Wilfrid's mind to ask it.

'Just so, Your Majesty. Just so. But you will recall it was a church originally built by the Roman Bishop, Paulinus, who evangelised this entire region. It was always a modest structure,' the monk admitted, 'built at a time when it was not possible to construct a more elaborate one. But modest though it was it was, nevertheless, the house of God when the Celtic Church brought the Faith back again to the province, as it must be acknowledged they did,' Wilfrid put in somewhat grudgingly. 'Was God's house restored? By no means. It was left to rot. The roof began to leak, its walls became damp, birds flew in and out of the windows which had never been glazed, and they nested in its crevices. Never should a House of God been allowed to decay in this way. When I saw it recently and compared this sordid ruin with the glorious constructions of Christian Rome and Gaul I was saddened.' Wilfrid paused for a while as if collecting his thoughts before continuing, although he had scarcely hesitated over a word up to that point. Alchfrith remained silent waiting for what would come next.

'Almighty God has given us intelligence, sire, and the ability to design and construct beautiful things in His honour. Nothing we can build on earth is worthy of Him of course, but whatever we do in His name must be done to the utmost of our ability. Instead of allowing this church, here in York, to deteriorate it should have been rebuilt by Celtic monks using all the skills they had available to them . . . modest though these may have been,' added Wilfrid as an afterthought. 'But that is not their way, sire. Have you,' asked Wilfrid, in another apparant change of direction, 'visited Lindisfarne?'

'Lindisfarne? No, why no. I haven't. Ought I to have done so?' Alchfrith again spoke in some surprise at the remark.

Wilfrid smiled to himself and appeared to be considering the question. After a few moments he replied.

'It would depend upon what you were looking for, sire. You would find holiness – let that not be in doubt. But you would not find a community which had built a House worthy of our Lord. Humble dwellings of simple, wooden construction. An ordinary chapel – this may have been improved now,' he added, 'since when I left the new Bishop, Finan, who was successor to Aidan, had begun the construction of a larger one. It was nevertheless to be merely of hewn oak and to be thatched mainly by reeds.' Again Wilfrid appeared to be lost in thought until he suddenly proceeded. 'As I'm sure you can appreciate it is all so mediocre, Your Majesty, when as I have said we should be offering to God only the best that we can devise and build, like those splendid churches I was describing only a little while ago. If only I could replace it with a worthier temple to the Lord. Even the site is so unsuitable. How can such a tiny island, half attached to the remotest edge of the kingdom, properly represent the Church of God in Northumbria. A central position with easy access for all is necessary – here for example. That would be ideal. Do you not agree, Your Majesty?'

This time Alchfrith had no difficulty answering Wilfrid's question
'Oh yes,' he replied. 'Ideal.'

And so it would be he thought again – ideal. He was beginning to see how it could be done too. The queen was a product of the Roman Church, wasn't she? Of course she'd been surrounded by Celts ever since she married Oswy and had had little chance to follow her earlier customs. Nevertheless she had been intrigued when Alchfrith had – half jokingly of course – brought up the matter of the king and queen observing Easter at different times. If he were to take this suggestion further as he had a mind to do, he would have to go carefully, of course, since his relations with her were still uncertain. It had taken all his diplomacy to get her to take a favourable view of him at all. Not surprising either, he considered since he was, after all, Oswy's bastard son . . .

Alchfrith always had to steel himself to say the word 'bastard', yet he never said illegitimate. His birth out of wedlock still rankled, although he never forgot that he was of Royal Blood, his mother a princess in her own right. And he meant to be a king in his own right too, ruler of the entire kingdom, perhaps even High King with authority over other kings as Oswy had.

Alchfrith loved planning the acquisition of power and with Wilfrid's help he meant to get it. Wilfrid had a different purpose in mind, but if he overcame the Celtic Church, and the Roman Church became the power in the land, with York as its episcopal see – archepiscopal see perhaps – Alchfrith's importance would grow all the time until, one day he would overthrow Oswy or oust Egfrith, whichever was then in power.

The first step was to put Wilfrid in as Abbot of Ripon, increase it size and its endowments at the same time and then, when the opportunity presented, have him consecrated bishop – but of York, nowhere else. York.

Enfleda strongly suspected that Oswy was up to something.

He had been away from Bamburgh several times in the last few months and had given evasive answers when she had enquired what he had been doing and who he had seen. In the past he had been keen to tell her all the details of his visits, sharing the amusing parts with her or blowing off steam when some petty official or other had particularly annoyed him.

She hadn't thought much about it at first, thinking perhaps that he was getting a bit older and the journeys were tiring him more. But once, when he had said that he had been to Hexham, and she had asked about Frida, one of her former ladies-in-waiting, who had gone to live there with her husband, he had said they were both fine, when Enfleda subsequently learned that Frida had been very ill and was still not fully recovered.

Why had he misled her? If he had forgotten to ask about Frida why not say so? Then the thought occurred to her that perhaps he hadn't been to Hexham at all but to somewhere else. She began to keep her ears open when her ladies were gossiping. She was careful never to ask direct questions but she led the conversation into channels which, once or twice, had confirmed her suspicions.

Oswy was lying to her about where he was going on his trips. There could only be one explanation for that – a woman. Perhaps he was getting older but he wasn't too old for that. If he was coming home tired it wasn't the journey that was doing it.

Enfleda decided to bide her time and make no accusations she couldn't substantiate. In any event she must keep on the right side of him for the moment or he might decide not to take her to see her youngest daughter, Elfleda.

The queen's fifth child had been another girl. Why had she been able to produce only one son, Ecfrith, followed by such a succession of females – Alhfleda, Osfryth, Edith, who was born at the time of the miracle and died soon after being named after her attendant, whose sacrifice had saved them all; then nearly five years without anything until Elfleda had come along early in the year 656 during the final preparations for Oswy's battle with Penda by the River Winwaed. She hadn't wanted another girl, heaven knows, but she hadn't wanted to give the child away either. Of course she could understand that Oswy wished to give thanks to Almighty God for helping him, once and for all, to crush Penda; but she would have preferred if he had thought of some other way of doing it than giving the infant into the charge of Abbess Hilda, in the nunnery at Whitby, to be devoted to the religious life. Not that she begrudged Almighty God her daughter, but she just wished there could have been some other way to thank Him.

Now she was allowed only one visit a year and for no time at all – a day or two at the most. Well she could put up with it, she supposed, but, if Oswy really was up to no good with some chick or other, perhaps *she* would enter Abbess Hilda's nunnery too to spite him. No, not to spite him, Enfleda admitted to herself. If you gave yourself to Almighty God it was because you wanted to, not to spite someone else – because you loved Him more than all the other things in life, even Oswy! She *did* love Oswy still, she had to admit, but if he was leading her a dance with another woman, she'd show him. She wasn't going to take it lying down.

Enfleda's sense of humour was never far below the surface and she giggled to herself at the inapt phrase. She wasn't the one taking it lying down; that was the trouble. She'd put a stop to it though never fear.

Eadfrith was unable to see his father as soon as he had hoped since James' stay in Ireland became unexpectedly prolonged.

His work on the gospel book for the Abbot of Durrow was well advanced, and he had reached chapter twenty of the gospel of St John, with Mary Magdalene weeping by the empty tomb, when he was overcome by a deadly lassitude. He struggled on through the whole of the day and part of the next until Brother Desmond, one of his pupils, pointed out, with great diffidence, several errors which James would never normally have made but which, on this occasion, he had not even noticed.

Realising that he was ill they sent for a physician who took one look at him and said, 'Jaundice. No more work for you for some time. Your eyes are yellow already and by tomorrow you will look like one of your own pigments. It's no use trying to go on. You'll tire yourself out and probably collapse and only delay your recovery. It's into the infirmary for you. You need a simple diet, lots of fluid, plenty of rest and, in a month perhaps, you may be back at work. Try to come back sooner and I won't answer for the consequences.'

It had been longer than a month – almost six weeks – before work began again and then for only two or three hours each day. By the time John's gospel was finished it was nearly advent, and too late to attempt the crossing to Iona with safety. James had remained at Durrow, enjoying an enforced, but much needed, rest whilst the pupils from the school he had established went back to their own monasteries.

His task completed, he decided to involve himself in the affairs of the monastery to an extent that had never been possible before. After Edith's death, at the suggestion of the king, and with the agreement of the abbots of various monasteries in the kingdom, he had travelled widely, setting up scriptoria where previously none had existed. Taking with him an advanced pupil, he would spend a few months at a time in one establishment, before leaving his assistant to continue the supervision and repeating the exercise elsewhere. His total absorption in the task gradually dulled the pain of Edith's loss which was also greatly helped by the huge pleasure he had obtained from Eadfrith's astonishing progress.

For the first few years, wherever James had gone Eadfrith had gone too, steadily assimilating all his father's skills and revealing an originality which James could never have hoped for. Had it been in his nature he might have envied his own son whose ability, he could clearly see, would one day surpass his own.

With some diffidence, the young man had said, 'There are two things I want to do, father. One, of course is to use my artistic ability to the full, to God's greater glory; the other is to enter His service completely and become a monk. Whenever we have been at the Abbey of Melrose – and we have been there several times you will recall – I have been particularly impressed by one of the monks, Brother Cuthbert by name. Perhaps you remember him? Each time we went there I felt more strongly that I wanted to be a monk like him and now,' he had ended smiling, 'I'm sure.'

And that had been that, James recalled. Eadfrith had been accepted at Melrose and then, not so long afterwards, he himself had been invited to visit Durrow. Then the king, who, James had thought, had been in a strangely unpredictable mood since the final defeat of Penda, had decided that he wanted to see Iona, which he had heard such great things about, and would travel with James on the first stage of his journey.

All that had been nearly three years ago. His son was a monk and he was living in an Irish monastic community. Perhaps he too should enter the religious life?

James decided to apply himself as closely as possible to the monastic routine until the time came for him to leave. By then he should know if complete dedication to God was for him or not.

He wondered several times why different men came to the monastery, before realising that he was not asking himself the right question. They may have come for one of any number of reasons, he acknowledged – after all he had come to illuminate the gospels. What was important was why they stayed. After turning this over and over in his mind he decided that there could be only one reason – that they believed they could serve Almighty God better in that fashion than any other. Did that apply to him?

Did it?

One day when he was absorbed in his work in the scriptorium, he realised that he had missed Sext – missed it by so much in fact that it was almost time for None. He packed up his materials as rapidly as he could and made his way to the chapel. A week later the same thing happened again. What was the matter with him? He had followed the monastic routine religiously for months; why was failing in it now?

Quickly he began preparing to leave when he suddenly stopped. These omissions could only mean that he was less than wholehearted in his committment to the rule. He laid down the styli, which he had been collecting together, and sat back to think about his problem. After a while he rose to his feet and began examining the completed parchment sheets of the gospel. There was no escaping it! This was what he wanted to do in the service of God, not to follow the monastic routine, however praiseworthy this was for some – including, he remembered, his son. Well, it had been an important question to decide but now it was answered beyond any doubt.

Bishop Aidan's successor, Finan, a hot tempered man, who put James in mind of Bishop Gobban, had died and King Oswy had appealed again to Iona to send another bishop for Lindisfarne. Brother Colman, from within the Iona community, had been elected the day before James' arrival and, with such an opportunity presenting, the new bishop was anxious to learn as much as he could from him. James was immediately involved in long discussions about Northumbria.

What was King Oswy like, Colman wanted to know. Did he staunchly support the Celtic Church?

James had not considered the first a very easy question to answer but found himself stressing Oswy's good points to a far greater extent than his failings. As to did he support the Celtic Church, the answer was yes, very strongly. The king was a good Christian who loved Almighty God, James was certain. Had he not given his youngest daughter to God in thanks for his victory over Penda?

Did the Roman Church have a strong presence in Northumbria?

No, scarcely any, in reality, although the Archbishop of Canterbury, Deusdedit, did regard himself as the metropolitan with jurisdiction over all the country.

Was the queen a good woman?

That had been an easy question to answer. Yes, a very good woman whom his wife had adored and served faithfully until her death ten years ago.

Colman was sorry to hear of James' wife's death. He would pray for her soul. How had it happened?

That had led to a long account of the incarceration of Aidan and Oda and Edith in the chapel and of the miraculous events that followed. James had sensed a grudging feeling of respect for Lindisfarne and Bamburgh after his story was told, and Colman's questions, which if not brusque had been certainly direct, took on a more considerate tone. He returned to the subject of Northumbria.

A map seemed the only solution here and James drew one showing the huge expanse of the two territories which had now been extended, by

Oswy's conquests, to include an area in the north west previously occupied by the Britons of Strathclyde, and an uncertain area of Pictland farther north. As to influence, Oswy was regarded as High King – Bretwalda was the term sometimes used – by the Mercians, the Middle Angles, East Saxons and South Saxons – in fact a considerable area of the country.

Colman had considered for quite a time after this reply, then repeated quietly to himself, 'Mercians, Middle Angles and East and South Saxons,' orientating himself on James' map as he did so. After a further pause he looked very deliberately at James and addressed him slowly as if clearing his mind as he spoke.

'My own new see will be that of Lindisfarne which covers all Northumbria. Northumbria itself occupies a large part of the country and its king holds some sway, you tell me, over other kingdoms. Correct?'

'Yes, that is correct, my Lord.'

'These kingdoms under the authority of King Oswy, do they have bishops?'

'Some have certainly, my Lord, but I will have to think carefully to tell you which, and who the bishops are – or were, since my information is three years out of date. Let me see – the Mercians and Middle Angles share a bishop, I'm almost sure. He is . . . ' James tapped his knee in irritation as he tried to remember the name '. . . Durnian,' he suddenly said. 'No, wait a minute, he died, and was followed by . . . someone I didn't know and after him came . . . Trumhere. Yes, that's right. Bishop Trumhere. Now,' he began scratching his head as he tried to recall the others, 'the East Saxons have Cedd and the South Saxons . . . they don't have a bishop at all so far as I know. So there are just two bishops, my Lord, in addition to yourself – Trumhere and Cedd.'

'Celtic Church or Roman Church?' The question was again peremptory as earlier ones had been.

'They were both consecrated by Bishop Finan, your predecessor, so they owe allegiance to the Celtic Church.'

There was a further period of silence from Colman before he began speaking again in his half musing fashion which left James wondering whether he was being questioned or not.

'King Oswy holds sway over nearly all England. I hold sway over Northumbria and the two other bishops, in territory under Oswy's authority, are Celtic. Then why,' he suddenly asked abruptly, staring hard at James, 'does Archbishop Deusdedit consider he has any influence over us. The Celtic Church is far more widely distributed than the Roman one. Perhaps they have more bishops. Do they?'

That made James ponder again and search back far into his memory.

'Canterbury has its archbishop,' he began 'Deusdedit. London has a bishop, that's two but I don't know who he is. The see of Rochester is three and that bishop I think is called Damian. There is a fourth with the East Angles, who was Thomas who died, and I think it is now Bishop Bertgils. So there you are my Lord – one archbishop and three bishops.'

James sat back after his answer surprised that he could recall so much after so long, but Colman was not finished.

'And the archbishop's authority – or supposed authority. From where does that derive if we are territorially so much larger?'

James chose to regard the question as rhetorical and said nothing but he wasn't going to be allowed to avoid and answer.

'Well?'

James sighed, realising, that he was going to have to answer. He tried to pick his words carefully.

'You must know the answer to this better than I my Lord. From Rome. Christ gave the care of His Church to St Peter who has passed it down through all his successors to His Holiness, Pope Vitalian, whose election was shortly before I left Northumbria. It is the view of the Roman Church, as you are aware, my Lord, that all bishops and archbishops are answerable to His Holiness, even those in your Church.'

'My Church?' Colman's response was instant. 'Not yours?'

James sighed again seeking another diplomatic response which would avoid confrontation.

'I was brought up in the Roman Church, my Lord, in Kent. As a young man I took part in the evangelisation of Northumbria with Bishop Paulinus of the Roman Church. Ever since I came here, my Lord, in the year six thirty-three, twenty-eight years ago, I have lived among adherants to the Celtic Church whose customs I have naturally followed. How could I celebrate Easter alone on a different day from everybody else? But, my Lord,' James went on rising to his feet and stimulated by the bishop's acerbity, deciding to abandon diplomacy, 'if you ask me to say if the Celtic Church is mine I must answer no. The existence of two Churches disturbs me. There should be only one. You will ask me my Lord,' James continued quickly seeing the bishop about to speak, 'which one that should be – which Church should conform to the customs of the other? If you insist on my view it is that the Roman Church is correct in its customs and the Celtic Church – yours my Lord – is wrong. But that is merely an opinion which up to now I have never expressed, and would not have done so now had you not put me on the spot. In truth, however, I am not a theologian and am not qualified to put forward a reasoned argument in support of my belief. It may be people like you, my Lord, who must put forward arguments in favour of your view against others expressing the Roman position. It is my sincere hope that such a meeting will be arranged soon so that there will be no division between us. I cannot believe that the existence of separate Churches is pleasing to Almighty God. We have gone wrong somewhere. There my Lord. You asked me and I have answered.'

James fully expected Bishop Colman to respond with vigour but he merely grunted, saying nothing for some time, before delivering, what James was pleased to find, was the last word on the subject.

'You think we should soon decide who is right, do you? Well, that may be so; may be so. I am confidant enough in our beliefs to defend them at any time. Perhaps that is what we should do.'

James left Bishop Colman's presence with mixed feelings of relief and distress. Iona had represented the Celtic Church to both Edith and him, and had been a haven offering shelter to two Christian refugees fleeing from barbarism. The island had been a sanctuary where they could worship Almighty God together in perfect safety. To be asked to consider that Church in conflict with another, to find two sides opposing each other yet professing belief in the same God, he found deeply upsetting.

Did it matter when the holy feast of Easter was celebrated? Were the minute details of a calculation based on a cycle of eighty years, or whatever, so very important? Surely, as Father Melchior had said to them so many years ago in the shepherd's hut on the night before he had returned to face almost certain death, it was the *fact* that you celebrated the feast that mattered, not when. If he had stayed on Iona with Edith they would probably have lived out their lives on the edge of the world without any whisper of an Easter controversy reaching them and the tonsure the monks wore would never have excited comment. Of course he and Edith had known that the Roman Church did things a little differently, but they had quickly fallen into the Celtic way of things and, for years now, the Celtic Church had seemed to him to the *the* Church.

But it wasn't *the* Church. There was another with a different pattern of observances which, when he thought more carefully about it, might seem trivial in themselves but were important because they *were* differences. Christ had founded one Church not many. What was true was true and had to be adhered to. People had always tried to challenge Christian teaching. Here, on this very island, he recalled, Segenus reading the Pope's letter about the heresy of Pelagianism. There had been many heresies, James knew, since the foundation of the Christian Church and the errors they contained had had to be refuted and those who practiced them condemned. Holy Mother Church could not condone fundamental differences in doctrine. If she did there would soon have been numerous churches holding different beliefs.

What it all came down to, James supposed, was authority. If he considered Iona as a remote Christian community it was unimportant whether Easter day was April the fifteenth or twenty-second or whenever. That did not matter in isolation but it *did* matter when that community began to come into contact with others. Unless the different geographical sections of the Church accepted authority there would inevitably be division not uniformity of beliefs and practices.

Looked at from the point of view of Celtic isolation – and they had been isolated for over one hundred years, James acknowledged – the practices they had followed for so long would seem correct and they would be loath to give them up. But the Celtic Church was no longer isolated and unless they and the Roman Church resolved their differences they would drift apart and Rome would eventually . . . James could see no alternative . . . be obliged to declare the Celts heretical.

It was a deeply distressing thought when he looked around at the island which had meant salvation for them so long ago. Pray God there *would* be a conference soon or attitudes would harden and each side would become more entrenched still.

James shrugged his shoulders and, trying to put the matter out of his mind, went off to seek out his old acquaintances, all too few after so many years.

Abbot Segenus had died, to be succeeded by Suibhenus and in turn by the present abbot, Cummene, whom James did not know. Eligius and Plenus, too, were no more and Falla had returned to Ireland. But among the senior brethren James was delighted to find Brother Erasmus, sadly no longer able to see well enough to sew, and Brother Linus who, remembering Edith's cure by Aidan, had to be told about their last few days together and the miracle which followed.

Two others, who were anxious to know all about Edith, were Fara and Briga. Fara, now a widow for many years, welcomed him like a long lost son and plied him with questions first about Edith and then Eadfrith. Fara had immediately sent for Briga, who had befriended Edith during their early weeks on the island, and the whole story had to be repeated. Briga was a proud grandmother. Her daughter, the eldest, had two little girls, whilst Briga's sons, born after James and Edith had left the island, had both been tonsured to their mother's great delight. Altogether it was a pleasant reunion, bringing back vivid memories of his early married life, tinged with sadness though these were.

The delay, whilst waiting for Bishop Colman to be ready to leave, was fortunate in another respect – it gave James the chance to spend three long afternoons in the scriptorium with the new 'scriba' Brother Martin, examining the drafts for the early manuscripts of which Brother Eligius had been so fond. It was a curious sensation, reviewing his own work made twenty-eight years ago. In some respects he thought his present work was better but he was reminded of techniques he had used then which he had neglected and which might, with benefit, be employed again, although modified to conform to his present style. He had evidently been using lilac shades then to a far greater extent than now and these too he thought he might reintroduce.

Brother Martin was all praise for the St John gospel destined for Brother Boisil and both men spent a considerable time comparing styles.

They were due to depart for the mainland the following day when James had his last, and most pleasant, surprise. Fursa – a much older and leaner Fursa, now completely bald – returned from a voyage to the island of Tiree.

The old boatman had lost none of his joviality and clasped James to him, slapping him on the back time and again in his old enthusiastic way. Their conversation was punctuated by the old peals of laughter as Fursa described many hilarious things that had happened to him since their last meeting. He had much to tell too. Calen had died only last year, he informed James. The little cook had seemed indestructable as he grew older and older and more and more bent and gnarled. He had been eighty-three or so he claimed – Fursa said, with a twinkle in his eye, and he had gone on preparing meals for the monks until the end.

Then after a long session of "do you remember" Fursa produced not only the parchment James had made for him but Calen's as well which the old man had left to him.

'Pity you are going tomorrow,' Fursa said, as James commented on their dilapidated state, 'or you could make me another.' And he roared with laughter again, before finally saying, 'I hope you remembered all I taught you about boats because, tomorrow, I take you in mine again and that bishop – he is no sailor. You have to work your passage.'

Bishop Colman, it transpired was indeed no sailor. James quickly regained his sealegs and enjoyed a glorious trip with his old friend, whilst the bishop endured the passage in complete misery. James looked at him with as much sympathy as he could muster but, remembering their interview, felt somehow that this restored the balance.

Enfleda had been wrong to suspect Oswy of seeing another woman. The person he was seeing was a child.

There *had* been another woman, of course. During Oswy's return journey from Iona he had passed through the annexed territory of Strathclyde. By then he had been away from Enfleda for nearly three months and one of the petty chieftains had a nubile daughter . . . for how long was a man expected to remain celibate?

Fina was nineteen with bold eyes and a voluptuous figure and no inhibitions. Perhaps she had been put up to it by her father, hoping for some preferment or other, Oswy wondered . . . but that had not been until later, after she had brought him almost to boiling point by her pouting bosom, more exposed it seemed every time he saw her, the suggestive hidden meanings she could impart to the most innocent sounding phrases and the soft contacts with her body that always managed to occur whenever they met.

Well, he hadn't seduced an innocent girl, Oswy realised the first time they were together. She'd been no virgin then and must have known quite well what she was getting into.

The baby was a surprise alright, there was no denying that, thought Oswy, when he went back over the events in his mind as he often did when Enfleda had been particularly loving and his conscience troubled him. At first his inclinations were to leave the boy at Strathclyde but, on reflection, he decided that it was better to have him under his own wing – safely tucked away of course so that Enfleda wouldn't find out. So Ricbert had gone off to bring the child back and deposit him in the nunnery at Coldingham where the Abbess was Oswy's sister, Ebba, who could be relied upon to keep his secret – in return for lavish endowments needless to say. There had to be largesse provided for Fina's family too and a suitable husband provided for her so, all in all, it had been an expensive liaison.

Oswy had found that he quickly became attached to the boy whom Fina had christened Alfrid before the king knew anything about him. He hadn't seen his other illegitimate son at all as a child, since he had remained in Ireland until he was seventeen when Oswy had brought him back to Northumbria after Enfleda's fourth daughter had been born. Ecfrith, his legitimate son, had been brought up entirely by nurses and Oswy had been so involved with affairs of state that he had barely seen his son as an infant.

This third son was a beautiful child who charmed Oswy each time he visited him at Coldingham, which was now becoming so often that Enfleda was getting suspicious. Oswy decided that he must be very careful. If Enfleda found out about Alfrid Oswy's life wouldn't be worth living. Fortunately, at present, she was fully occupied with the arrangements for Ecfrith's wedding to Audrey, King Anna's daughter, in the spring. He was sure he could risk one more visit to Alfrid.

Chapter 15

In the monastery at Melrose the prior was dying. No one was in any doubt of this since he had told them so plainly and he had been renowned for years for his ability to foretell events in the future. In preparation for death he sent for James and Brother Cuthbert.

'I would spend my last days on earth in the study of the mysteries of our faith with you, Brother Cuthbert. I still have much to teach you and, since we have such a short time available to us, we must use it to the full to our advantage. In a week from now I will be no more.'

Brother Cuthbert and James looked at each other, uncertain how to respond to this dramatic announcement. It was the monk who broke the silence.

'Then we must waste no more time, Brother Prior. Will you tell me which is the best book to study that can be completed in a week?'

'Without any doubt, St John's gospel,' replied the prior. 'Here I have a commentary in seven parts. With the help of God we can get through one part each day. If we read this wonderful gospel, which my friend James here made for me,' Boisil smiled warmly at James as he spoke and placed his hand on the book resting beside his pallet, 'in association with the commentary we will benefit immeasureably.

'My reason for asking you to join us here, James,' he went on, 'is to ask your permission to leave your wonderful book in the possession of Brother Cuthbert after I am gone. When I contemplate what is in the future for him I believe he will be in need of the wisdom it contains. May he have it when I die?'

James was embarrassed by the warmth of the prior's praise, and touched to be asked for his agreement.

'He may have the gospel willingly prior. It is yours to give and I can think of no one more fitting to receive it. Brother Cuthbert has been a great influence for good on my son Eadfrith. It will be a small return I can make.'

Soon afterwards James left the two monks alone to begin their study of the gospel and it's commentary. After lying quietly with his eyes closed for a little while, the abbot began their discussion.

'You will find Brother Cuthbert, that the gospel we are about to read has a character which is quite different from the synoptic gospels of Matthew, Mark and Luke. It is specially evident to me as an old man that it is the reminiscence of another old man. There are recollections in it everywhere that have little to do with the story the saint is telling. There are inconsequential matters which remind me of myself talking about days gone by. Sometimes, for example, the evangelist gives us fastidious detail – the netting of one hundred and fifty-three fishes for example – and at other times seems to think we know the story already; when we come to chapter eleven for instance you will find that John tells us that Lazarus naturally comes from the same town as Martha and Mary – naturally because he expects us to know that he was their brother. The saint often recalls conversations which are unconnected but which come one after another into his mind so he puts them down together. He changes the scene quickly in similar fashion when we have no reason to expect such a change. The gospel's unique in character because of these detached reflections and because it gives us too the actual words of our Blessed Lord far more often than the others do.

'So let us make a start,' said Boisil, shifting slightly on his pallet to find a more comfortable position. 'I will lie back and close my eyes. Read the text first, then we will look at the commentary.'

Brother Cuthbert adjusted his chair, took up James' copy of St John and began to read.

'In the beginning was the word . . . '

It was the second day and they had made a good beginning.

'Does anything strange strike you about chapters five, six and seven, which we have just read, Brother Cuthbert?'

Cuthbert turned backwards over the pages to look at what he might have missed and to see if anything caught his eye now. After a time he answered, somewhat diffidently, 'There are some curious references to places our Lord visited in these chapters, Brother Prior.' Cuthbert turned two pages forward and traced the part he was looking for with his forefinger. 'I see here, in Chapter seven, that He intends to centre His activities on Galilee instead of Judea.' The monk paused for a minute, arranging his thoughts and then turned backwards three pages. 'But here, in Chapter 6, He *is* in Galilee, whereas,' moving backwards in the text further still, 'in Chapter 5 He is in

Judea. It seems somehow as if the order is wrong.'

The prior gave a little chuckle and said, 'Well done. I have long thought it possible that Chapters 5 and 6 might have been transposed by one of the early scribes or copyists perhaps. Had that been so we would have had, in the present 6 – which should really, in my view, be 5 – our Lord in Galilee; in 5 – which should correctly be 6 – He has gone to Judea, whilst in 7 He decides to leave Judea and return to Galilee. Furthermore,' the prior continued, pointing to the text in Cuthbert's hand and indicating that he should turn the pages, 'you will find, in Chapter 5 verse 1, mention that the time had arrived for the Jewish festival; this seems likely to have been the Pasch although Chapter 6 says that it is "near at hand". If it was "near at hand" in Chapter 6 it could hardly have arrived in Chapter 5, so it looks again as if the two have been transposed.

'But,' the prior concluded, 'this may simply be St John remembering what happened 60 years earlier. We cannot be sure. What it shows you, Brother Cuthbert, – what it really shows you – is the importance of reading the scriptures very carefully and asking yourself searching questions.'

'Yes, Brother Prior.'

'May it please Your Majesty. Abbot Wilfrid has arrived and will attend upon you at your pleasure.'

Alchfrith, as always, had been scheming. The pinpricks of irritation he was inflicting on his father were a cause for satisfaction but it was time for a bolder stroke. If Oswy were to be overcome at some time Alchfrith must weaken the old man's position and strengthen his own. For that he needed the Roman Church on his side and for *that* he needed Wilfrid.

'Give the abbot my compliments and say I would be happy to see him at once.'

Wilfrid looked wonderfully well as if organising a monastery was agreeing with him. He was thinner, which suited him – the austerities of the Rule no doubt thought Alchfrith – and his eyes sparkled and his step was sprightly. He greeted the sub-king warmly.

'Your servant, Your Majesty. It is with great pleasure that I attend upon you. I am anxious to report upon the affairs of the monastery which you so generously gave into my charge at Ripon. May I tell you of our progress sire?'

'That would be my pleasure, Abbot. There is a matter I have in mind to discuss with you, which is the reason for my summons, but it can wait until I hear about everything you have been doing. But first refreshments. Servant!'

Wilfrid broke in before the order could be given.

'Your Majesty, pray excuse me. The rules we have in our monastery are strict and must be obeyed by all, from the highest – ' Wilfrid gave a tiny smile to emphasise the reference to himself ' – to the lowest, whether we are in our own house or elsewhere as I am now. If the abbot flouts the laws, Your Majesty, who can be expected to obey them?'

'*I* will not tell, Wilfrid. No one will know if we take a little refreshment together.'

Wilfrid shook his head emphatically nevertheless. 'I will know, sire, and more important than that – much more important than that – Almighty God will know. No one can cheat him.'

No one can cheat Him! Alchfrith felt a little stab of anxiety at the Abbot's words. Could seeking an ally of the Roman Church for his own purposes be described as cheating? Not if it brought an end to the near schismatic Celtic Church surely thought the sub-king hopefully. Nonetheless he immediately changed the subject.

'Very well, Abbot Wilfrid. I will take nothing either. As you have, I see, grown thinner I have become stouter and it will do me no harm to follow your example. Now,' he said settling himself comfortably in his chair, 'sit by me here and tell me your news.'

Wilfrid did as he was told and carefully assembled his thoughts before speaking.

'My first act, sire, was to introduce the Rule of St Benedict. It is a rule of masterly simplicity combining, as it does, the three disciplines of prayer, study and physical work. The holy St Benedict devised it first when he set up twelve small priories at the town of Subiaco in Italy, so called,' Wilfrid added, knowing that Alchfrith loved extra details of this kind, 'because, in the days of the Emperor Claudius, an artificial lake was formed by damming up the waters of the River Arno – hence Sublacum, which has become in the course of time Subiaco. Each house had it's prior with Benedict himself in overall charge. Later, Your Majesty, aspects of it were changed, when jealousy of his fame and achievements caused him to move to Monte Cassino, where he constructed a single house for all his monks. Before he began work there he fasted for forty days, as our Lord did, to fortify him for the task ahead. The monastery he raised, sire, is already the most famous in all christendom and will, I do not doubt, remain so for centuries to come.

'His rule, which I have introduced, sire, is fair – firm without undue austerity. Indeed Benedict discouraged self-imposed discipline of great severity. There is a story told of him, Your Majesty, concerning a hermit who had chained himself to a rock near Monte Cassino. Benedict sent him a message to say, "If you are truly a servant of God do not chain yourself with iron but with the chain of Christ". There is much more I could tell you about him if Your Majesty is interested to hear.'

Was he? Not really, although he loved listening to Wilfrid talking – just for the words to flow over him was all he needed, whether about Benedict or not. Still, this was obviously something dear to Wilfrid's heart and he wanted Wilfrid on his side.

'I would hear it all Abbot. Pray continue.'

'Obedience to the rule and to the abbot must be complete, Your Majesty; that was the saint's teaching. In his own words, addressing those who renounced their own will, he called them "the strong and bright army of obedience to fight under Jesus Christ our true king". The rule was tripartite – liturgical prayer, sacred reading and work, all enjoyed together in a community under one superior.

'The responsibilities of that superior were manifold, sire – as indeed they are now,' Wilfrid thought it prudent to add. 'For example one problem of Herculean proportions,' he continued, employing a nonchristian metaphor for emphasis, 'presented to the saint during a famine in Carpania. He gave to the starving everything there was to eat in the monastery with the exception of five loaves. His monks were in despair but Benedict was more than equal to the task. "You do not have enough for today, I know", he told them, "but I assure you by tomorrow you will have too much". On the following morning two hundred loaves had miraculously appeared at the front gate of the monastery. That problem has not yet presented to me,' laughed Wilfrid, managing to convey the impression that he would no doubt find some similar means of dealing with it were it to do so.

'St Benedict stressed that the provision of food and clothing and other necessities was a very important aspect of the activities of a monastery, Your Majesty,' Wilfrid went on quickly, thinking that Alchfrith was going to butt in and wanting to become more practical before he did so. 'It is something I have tried hard to establish at Ripon and much has been given away to God's less fortunate creatures. We have been able to do this, sire, because more than half of the additional twenty hides of land you so generously gave me on my accession have been cultivated and the produce – some of the produce,' Wilfrid corrected hastily, 'given to the poor. But it is costly work, Your Majesty, and I am concerned too to embellish the chapel with objects of sacred art worthy of Almighty God. Not really worthy, of course – nothing could be worthy of Almighty God – but we must strive to obtain the best we can.'

Alchfrith recognised an appeal for money when he heard it even graciously hinted at, as this was. For a moment he contemplated blandly ignoring it but then decided that to have Wilfrid in his debt would pay dividends in the long run. The abbot was essential to his plans.

'I am impressed with the strides you have made, Abbot. More land – shall we say twenty more hides – will be provided and you may commission suitable items for your chapel although,' he added prudently, 'you may care to put your requests to me first for approval.'

Wilfrid was about to thank the sub-king for his generosity but Alchfrith continued speaking. He was beginning to regret declining refreshments, to keep the abbot company, but preferred to show no weakness by getting his servant to bring them now. Better get the rest of this meeting done with first he thought.

'The reason for my com . . . request that you should come to see me Abbot, is to make you aware of plans which are forming in my mind for bringing to a head the dispute with the Celtic Church over Easter.'

Wilfrid nodded but said nothing, realising very well the importance of what was coming and happy to await it now that his monastery was to be further enriched.

'Ecfrith, my half brother,' Alchfrith as always had to force himself to speak of the distasteful relationship 'is to marry soon. His bride,' Alchfrith smiled to himself at the inappropriateness of the term as applied to her 'is to be Audrey, King Anna's daughter. I suppose you were out of the country, Wilfrid, when she first married some Earldorman or other. Well, he died and now my father and King Anna have cooked up this political match between them. She is not quite old enough to be his mother but it is a close thing.' Alchfrith chuckled to himself at the indifferent bargain his half-brother was getting before coming back to his main point.

'What is important for us, Wilfrid – you and me – is that her own people, the East Angles, were converted by the Roman Church – Bishop Felix I believe.' Alchfrith knew this very well; his enquiries had been meticulous. 'So she will be used to keeping the Roman date of Easter – the true date of course,' he added quickly before Wilfrid could make the point. 'She will almost certainly wish to keep the Ro . . . proper date, still, even here, in Northumbria. Well the chance that arises is this,' stressed the sub-king, leaning forward in his keenness to impress Wilfrid; 'I have already suggested to the queen that perhaps she should be keeping this date too. Now, if Audrey does insist on doing that – and from what I have heard she is certain to do so – Enfleda might – just might – be persuaded to join her. In six sixty-three they tell me the dates will differ by a week so when the king is wanting to celebrate the end of Lent with a banquet, the queen will still be keeping Palm Sunday. That wouldn't be important if just Audrey did it but if the queen did too it would be very awkward. Obviously the king couldn't let this go on year after year especially since the year after the difference between the dates is greater still. This ought to be enough to make him agree to a conference to discuss the whole question – there will be a debate which we know we will win. What is your reaction to that?'

Wilfrid's reaction to that was one of wholehearted approval. 'Splendid, Your Majesty,' he answered at once smiling broadly to match the sub-king's obvious pleasure. 'If such a conference could be launched with senior churchmen on each side I am confident our arguments would prevail. I have no misgivings about the correctness of our position, sire – we have ample authority behind us from earlier Church pronouncements – but we might find ourselves outnumbered. It would not be difficult for the Celtic Church to bring together several abbots to support Bishop Colman who, one supposes, would be the leader of the Celtic party. If they thought their position threatened they might even try to obtain reinforcements from, say, Iona or even Ireland. We have no bishop – indeed we have no priest in Northumbria as yet. Princess Audrey may bring one as her chaplain but he would be only one. Hm . . . '

Wilfrid began to ponder on the minimal support of the Roman Church. How could his side – as he was already thinking of it – be strengthened? He looked at Alchfrith who seemed to be considering the same problem. Another thought struck Wilfrid. The sub-king was being very determined in this matter. What was his real reason? As he studied Alchfrith more closely, now that the idea had come to him, he began to ask himself what was behind this move? To be sure the sub-king had been a strong supporter of the Roman Church – or at least of Wilfrid as it's representative – but, as the abbot thought more carefully about it, it seemed doubtful if a burning desire to see Easter kept at the proper time was the motivation for his actions. Was he – Wilfrid – being manipulated? Perhaps, but, even if he was, it had been, so far at least, very much to his advantage. Suppose Alchfrith had some scheme in mind that Wilfrid knew nothing about, were he and the Roman Church going to lose by going along with it? No, he decided – as yet – but better be careful.

Wilfrid coughed to attract the pensive Alchfrith's attention.

'I was about to suggest, Your Majesty, that since we have some time in hand, so to speak – after all, if we are to expect the separate Easter observance to be in six sixty-three, the synod you foresee could not be before the end of that year or more likely in six sixty-four – we should look around for allies. There is Bishop Bertgils of East Anglia for example,'

Wilfrid stopped and drummed his fingers on the arm of his chair for a moment in thought, before going on 'but he might not wish, for political reasons, to have a prominent part were he seen to be against King Oswy. We must try to find episcopal support elsewhere if we can. Canterbury might be brought into it directly, if the queen could be persuaded to use her influence with her Kentish relatives. Or perhaps we will be able to get help from someone else . . . It is something we should think carefully about . . . very carefully.'

It was the fifth day.
'Perhaps you have noticed, Brother Cuthbert, that Matthew and Mark merely state the fact of our Lord's scourging without comment. Luke implies that Pilate intended to release Jesus after the scourging, hoping that the Jews would be appeased by this alone. Pilate would have had his own reasons for this of course other than compassion; it would cause him less trouble as Governor for one thing. It seems clear from St John's account in Chapter nineteen that he *did* scourge Him with this purpose in mind for, having done so, he lets the soldiers mock Him and dress Him up in purple, after which he presents Christ to the Jews as a pitiful spectacle. "Ecco homo", are the words written but "Behold the man" is a poor kind of translation. Pilate would say something like, "Look at this poor wretch. Isn't this enough?" That is what Pilate, for reasons of his own, is asking. Do you agree?'
'Yes, Brother Prior.'

It was the sixth day. Boisil was speaking very slowly and softly and stopping for longer periods to regain his strength.
'You will note, Brother Cuthbert, that St John omits from his account details that would be common knowledge among Christians at the time he was writing because they were included by the other three evangelists. He makes no mention for example of the tearing of the veil of the Temple; no word is said of the bystanders mocking our Lord: he does not tell us of the darkness from the sixth to the ninth hour. If you read his account carefully you will find that he is concerned to tell us *why* things happened not simply what occurred. "These things were done" he says, "so that scripture might be fulfilled".' Boisil paused to get his breath and it was some moments before he could continue.
'You will note too,' he resumed, 'that St John gives us the actual words

which Christ addresses to His mother which the others do not record. "Woman behold thy son", he says. He was writing, as I said at the outset, many years after the event; the others were writing during the Blessed Virgin's lifetime. It is not surprising that for this personal reason they might omit these words.'

'I will rest now, Brother Cuthbert. Tomorrow we will complete the remainder. We are almost finished.'

His Lordship, Bishop Colman, was pondering upon the state of the Celtic Church. On arrival in Lindisfarne he had started gathering information on the subject from a variety of sources and, until recently, what he had learned had been a source of satisfaction. Now he was becoming disturbed.

His Church was of course strong throughout Bernicia, and Colman intended that it should remain so. It was powerful too in the annexed territory of Strathclyde and even further north in parts of Pictland, although he himself had little influence there. In Mercia, although King Oswy's influence had waned, when Penda's son Wulfhere had been proclaimed king, the Celtic Church had apparently flourished under Bishop Trumhere. Colman had yet to meet Trumhere who, although trained by the Scots, was an Englishman and regarded by Colman with some mistrust; regarding people with mistrust was second nature with the bishop. A question mark must remain over Trumhere therefore. If Colman needed help, which seemed likely, it might be wise to look elsewhere.

Cedd, now, the bishop of the East Saxons – he was a different proposition. Bishop Colman had gone to a great deal of trouble to learn about Cedd when casting around for future allies and everything he had heard was good.

Cedd was one of four brothers, all priests and, by all accounts, men of God. Cedd himself had been sent to the East Saxons when Oswy had persuaded King Sigbert to accept the Faith. Colman still had doubts about Oswy but, at least, in that respect he had done well.

Of course the East Saxons had accepted the Faith once before, Colman had discovered, and then apostacised. Mellitus, their bishop, along with Augustine, Archbishop of Canterbury no less, had fled to Gaul the moment it had happened. It just showed the poor calibre of Roman clerics if, at the first sign of trouble, they ran away instead of facing it. This Mellitus had been Archbishop of Canterbury too sometime later. Colman gave a metaphorical sniff and continued his consideration of Cedd.

According to reports Cedd, then a mere priest, had evangelised the whole province of the East Saxons and had so impressed Finan, Colman's predecessor at Lindisfarne, that Cedd had been called northward and consecrated bishop. There was something else he had done too, thought Colman, trying to bring it to mind. What was it? Yes that was it – he had founded a monastery at a place called Lastingham which was actually in Colman's diocese, just south of Whitby where that tiresome Abbess Hilda came from. There was more than that though, Colman felt . . . Something about . . .

Got it! This Lastingham had once been a lawless place in the hills, notorious for the fact that bandits had made it their stronghold. Because of it's Godless associations Cedd was determined to purify it before consecrating his monastery. He had prayed for twelve hours a day and fasted until evening throughout the whole of Lent and, even then, he had eaten only a little bread and some watered milk. There was austerity for you. This man Cedd sounded someone to rely on . . . and it was beginning to look as if reliable people might be required.

It was Alchfrith, sub-king of Deira, whom Colman was worried about. He had only just learned about the fiasco at Ripon when the monks from Melrose, who had been given the monastery by Alchfrith, allowed themselves to be ejected. They were quite right to resist irregular Roman practices, of course, but they should never have given up the monastery without a fight. Colman had been incensed when he had heard about it. He would have barricaded himself in, sub-king or no sub-king, if he had been there. But those cowardly Melrose monks had put up no resistance; none at all. They had just taken all their things and gone back to Melrose leaving the monastery in the hands of that upstart Wilfrid.

That one would have to be watched, thought the bishop. A dyed-in-the-wool Roman if ever there was one. What were they up to – those two, Wilfrid and Alchfrith? Nothing that would benefit the Celtic Church that was for sure. It was all very worrying. Until Wilfrid came the Roman Church had had no foothold at all in his territory and now they had a monastery with, so he had been told, lavish endowments and were, no doubt, increasing their influence as fast as they could. A showdown, that's what it would have to come to – and before the Roman Church became too powerful.

Colman needed a strong supporter. It was no use looking to Melrose, they had no fight in them. Cedd was the man. Colman would invite him to Lindisfarne.

It was the last day.

'The suggestion sometimes made, Brother Cuthbert, that the appearance of Jesus by the side of the lake, which we have just read in John, Chapter twenty-one, is the same incident as that related by St Luke in Chapter five, cannot be substantiated. Both evangelists are telling a story of a fruitless nights fishing, followed by a large catch when they followed our Lord's instructions; that is certainly true. But St Luke is clearly relating a story which led to the apostles leaving everything and following Jesus. John is telling one in which it is the Lord who is leaving and St Peter who will be left as the leader.'

Cuthbert listened intently and nodded his head in agreement. Boisil, scarcely able to raise his voice above a whisper, chose to ask the monk a question.

'Do you think there is any significance in the fact of Christ questioning St Peter three times?'

'I have wondered Brother Prior if our Lord was reminding St Peter of the three occasions on which he denied Him, and so demanding a threefold affirmation of service from him in return.'

'It may be so,' replied the prior 'it may be so . . . ' Cuthbert thought he had fallen asleep and remained very quiet so as not to wake him. But presently there was a second question which Cuthbert had to lean close to hear.

'And when our Lord says to Peter in verse eighteen, "When thou shalt be old thou shalt stretch forth thy hand and another shall gird thee", what do you think He has in mind then?'

The old man's eyes closed and Cuthbert had to wait until he was sure Boisil was awake before answering.

'Then, Brother Prior, our Blessed Lord may have been referring to St Peter's later crucifixion with outstretched arms or possibly, to his profound weakness after a prolonged period in prison so that all he was able to do was to stand like a very old man does, with arms held out, for someone else – his gaoler perhaps – to tie his robe in place before being led out to execution.'

After an even longer silence the prior finally whispered, with barely moving lips, 'And the last question, Cuthbert, for we are at the end of the book. When Jesus replies to Peter, in verse twenty-two, in answer to his question about St John himself, "So he will have to wait till I come", what did he mean then, "wait till I come".'

Cuthbert took longer to reply this time but kept his eyes firmly on the dying man whilst composing the response.

'There have been many suggestions, Brother Prior. It has been postulated that our Lord meant that St John would never die; that is plainly false since he did die. Some said that the second coming was to be before the disciple's death, but that too was false since the disciple is dead and that day has not yet arrived. I think, Brother Prior, it may mean that St John would not be martyred as the other apostles were but would have to await death by natural causes in very old age. That would seem to me to be the meaning, Brother Prior.'

A tiny smile crossed the prior's lips and, fleetingly, he opened his eyes.

'You have learned well, Brother Cuthbert. We are at the end of the gospel, the end of the week and the end of my life. There are some things, now, I must say to you although not all will be to your liking for I know you to be a humble man.'

Cuthbert waited patiently watching the prior with great affection as the still figure tried to gather the strength to continue.

'By common consent of the brethren you will take my place as prior for a while after my death. Then you must prepare yourself for even higher office as abbot, but not at this monastery. That dismays you, I see, but I would remind you of your duty to accept whatever you are asked to undertake.'

Cuthbert considered what the prior had said in silence while the old man closed his eyes again and seemed to drift off into unconsciousness once more.

'Brother Cuthbert?'

'Yes, Brother Prior?'

The old man's eyes were open again but what he said was barely audible.

'One last thing. When you are asked to accept consecration as a bishop will you accept?'

The two men were looking directly into each other's eyes as the prior waited for an answer.

'It will be my duty, Brother Prior. I will accept, but with reluctance.'

The prior closed his eyes again and Cuthbert began to pray for the still figure beside him and for strength in his own life ahead. He did not speak for a long time.

'Brother Prior?'

There was no reply.

Chapter 16

The king and queen of Northumbria were in bed, luxuriating in a post coital glow of exceptional pleasure, in the wake of the departure of the last wedding guest.

There had been times when Enfleda had thought they would never get through it all. Audrey had been impossible, precipitating an ecclesiastical crisis at the outset. In her customary dogmatic fashion she had announced that, of course, she would have to be married at a Nuptial Mass in the Roman rite. Very carefully they had explained to her that Bishop Colman wouldn't agree to that and in any case it was an unnecessary demand since the essential part of the sacrifice was virtually identical in both rites, and why was she making all the fuss? Her retort had been that if the bishop wouldn't say the mass for her in the Roman rite she would be married by her chaplain instead. That would enrage his Lordship even more, Enfleda had pointed out. After all he was the bishop and ought to officiate at the marriage of the king's son, and if someone else was asked to do it it would be an insult and he would take offence – and no one took offence more easily than he. It had taken hours of argument to try to get her to see reason and they had just about reached deadlock when King Anna and his retinue arrived. He had settled Audrey's hash in no time.

'Great heavens, child' (child! Enfleda raised her eyes in astonishment), 'you know there is no difference. You have been to Holy Mass often enough – often enough – in both rites, said by Bishop Felix or Brother Fursey, and never said one word; not one word. They are the same I tell you, the same. You're making too much fuss. I won't have it, d'ye hear, won't have it. So that's settled,' and he had turned to Enfleda, 'the Celtic rite will be fine. I shall enjoy it, enjoy it. Nothing like a good Nuptial Mass.'

Enfleda found that she was just as fascinated by King Anna as she had been years ago. He hardly seemed to have changed at all. Jovial and bubbling as ever, he was like a breath of fresh air after his daughter. There couldn't be much to say for heredity, she thought, if Anna could sire Audrey or, for that matter, she and Oswy produce Ecfrith. At any rate it would be fun having King Anna around again just so long as he didn't disorganise her arrangements. Better tell him his job was looking after his daughter.

Sadly it hadn't needed Anna to disorganise the arrangements; everyone seemed to do that.

In one coterie there had been Paeda of the Middle Angles with his frightful sister Cyniburg, who was married to Alchfrith. Enfleda had tried to be as fair as she could with Alchfrith but, try as she might, she couldn't like him, and it had been a source of great satisfaction to her when she began to think that Oswy didn't like him either. Devious, that was the word for Alchfrith; devious, always making snide comments to irritate his father, never missing a chance to probe some chink in Oswy's armour, making derogatory remarks in, just, audible asides, then being smarmy, with nauseating mock humility which annoyed Enfleda more than his deliberate nastiness. With her he was ostentatiously charming – buttering her up was the expression that always came to her mind. But buttering her up for what? There must be some scheme in his mind but she hadn't so far been able to work out what it was. King Anna's arrival had been providential since Alchfrith had been on the point of supporting Audrey in her demand for Roman ceremony. Come to think of it, Enfleda had said to herself, he was always on about Easter. He was going to adopt the Roman practice, why didn't she? Well, good luck to him, she had thought. She had fallen in with Celtic practices, just to be helpful, when she came to Northumbria and if she changed now it would upset Oswy no end. Alchfrith was plotting something, she was certain, and she intended to deal with him with considerable circumspection until she found out what it was.

The problem of the guests paled into insignificance compared with those with the bishop. Bishop Aidan had been a sweety, Finan, hot tempered and unpredictable but this Colman was sour and self-righteous.

Had there been a way of getting someone else to conduct the ceremony Enfleda would have accepted it gladly, but he was the bishop and had to do it . . . in Saxon. Well, not all in Saxon, of course, since the Mass itself would be in Latin, but the actual marriage part, where he was obliged to ask, 'do you take this woman etc', had to be in a language they could understand. The bishop would have to learn that part – there seemed to be no other way.

'Why should *he* learn', had been his retort . . . through an interpreter. *They* had only to say, 'I will', in gaelic and they could manage that more easily than he could learn his part.

'Perhaps they could, but they wouldn't understand what was being asked in a foreign language which might make the ceremony invalid and in any case the congregation wouldn't understand either. Surely the bishop wasn't suggesting they conduct the only part which would not be in Latin in a language no one else could understand'.

He had been suggesting exactly that, it appeared, and was extraordinarily stubborn about it when everyone – but everyone – was clearly against him. They hadn't had an argument exactly . . . well, with an interpreter in the middle translating everything twice you couldn't really have an argument. . . but they had had an interminable discussion.

There had been a curious end to it though, Enfleda remembered. She had suggested that her kinswoman, the Abbess Hilda, might come over and discuss it with the bishop. This had provoked a violent response in a torrent of gaelic and, somehow, she had got the impression that the interpreter was paraphrasing what sounded vitriolic into quite moderate language. At any rate Colman had surprisingly capitulated and had gone off to learn his part.

Unsuccessfully, it later transpired. By all accounts he had tried but it was too much for him. In the end the Saxon bits were clearly written out for him and he was intensively coached in pronunciation.

He had barely struggled through them nevertheless.

Enfleda pondered for a moment while Oswy watched her affectionately. He had been little help he knew but weddings just weren't his scene – this one most of all. Enfleda had borne the brunt of it and he felt rather guilty that he hadn't made more effort. Besides one thing was worrying him a bit.

'Oswy?'

'Yes love.'

'What's Alchfrith up to? He's as nice as can be to me but keeps getting sly digs in at you the whole time. And Oswy . . . I'm sorry but I can't like him. I did try to but he's very sly if you ask me. Do you know what he's planning? Nothing that will do you any good I'm sure.'

But Oswy wasn't prepared to take Alchfrith seriously.

'He's flexing his muscles, that's all. A lot of sons try it on with their fathers seeing how far they can go I suppose. Don't let it worry you. I can manage Alchfrith alright. I'm not a bit surprised you don't like him. Neither do I but I'm more than a match for him – even if he is planning something.'

'Oswy, what are you doing?'

What Oswy was doing should have been obvious as his fingers fumbled with the button on the back of her gown.

'Enfleda, let's go to bed?'

'Oh, Oswy. What a good idea. Let's.'

And it had been wonderful too after all the frustrations and annoyances of the previous week. They had lain for a long time afterwards before Enfleda spoke.

'We produced a couple of odd sons between us, didn't we? I'm glad you have no more illegitimate ones. I couldn't stand another like Alchfrith.'

Oswy made no reply.

Far to the south, in the country of the West Saxons, events were soon to provide a powerful ally for King Alchfrith.

A man of learning, named Agilbert, had come from Gaul and prevailed upon the West Saxon King, Coehwahl, to allow the evangelisation of his kingdom. Agilbert had made many converts, including the king himself who, in gratitude, persuaded Agilbert to remain among his people as their bishop. Soon the entire region was firmly Christian.

Then, as time went by, Coenwahl began to dislike the notion of a foreign bishop with sole responsibility for his kingdom and, in peremptory fashion, without any prior consultation, he informed Agilbert that a second bishop was to be appointed who would share the see with him on an equal footing. The chosen priest was Wini, a native of the country whom Agilbert considered to be of little sanctity and no learning. In high dudgeon he resigned his see leaving the West Saxons to Wini and the king to his own devices.

But when Agilbert became calmer he realised that he had perhaps been rash. His indignation at the loss of half his see had so inflamed him that he had decided to leave before considering the important question of where he should go. He had been in West Saxon country for many years and his influence elsewhere had waned. He knew few in Gaul and fewer still in Ireland. He would have to remain in England, he decided, travel north and see what might transpire.

Little transpired at several courts he visited until he arrived in Deira where Alchfrith welcomed him with open arms.

A Roman bishop, even one without a see, could be invaluable to Alchfrith's plans. Agilbert was entertained lavishly, given elegant quarters in the palace, allowed to say Mass in the king's private chapel and above all, introduced to Wilfrid.

Wilfrid's exceptional ability had of course been stressed on several occasions before the meeting took place.

'He has most excellent qualities, my Lord, which you will readily appreciate – humanity, peacefulness, devotion to prayer and fasting, kindness, compassion, discretion, modesty, prudence, learning, to name but some. You will also be deeply impressed by his eloquence, my Lord, of that I have no doubt,' Alchfrith had continued, 'and it would be my hope that, should you consider him suitable, you would agree to ordain him priest.'

Agilbert had smiled to himself as he listened to the catalogue of virtues, but he was finding it comfortable in Deira and he had no wish to upset the sub-king.

'From what you say, Your Majesty, he sounds as if he should be a bishop,' had been the tactful reply.

In the event Agilbert *was* impressed with Wilfrid's eloquence and learning, if less so by his humanity, modesty and compassion, but he was in no doubt that he should be ordained priest.

He would be delighted to officiate, at Ripon, on whatever date the king would favour.

Harbouring the king's illegitimate son had brought the nuns of Coldingham luxuries which should have been no part of the life of a religious order. The coarse cloth of their habits was replaced by fine cambric and lawn. Frugal fare gave way to rich plentiful meals. Attendances at canonical hours fell away, prayers became more hurried, penances lighter and self denial a rarity. But the abuse which was to have the most important effect upon the community was their failure to observe the night office of mattins.

When a brand, falling from a fire, unwisely left banked high in the kitchen, sent a shower of sparks into some rags piled carelessly nearby, the nuns were sleeping soundly in their beds and no one was astir to see the early wisps of smoke or to smell the burning. The wind which had risen during the night, blew open the door, left ajar, and, within minutes, fanned the smouldering cloths into flame. The kitchen quickly became an inferno, the fire spread to the refectory, the chapel caught next and then the first of the nuns cells.

Sparks flew in the strong wind. Outbuildings took hold and straw was ignited in the stables. The shrill screams of the horses were added to those of the trapped nuns but were scarcely audible above the roar of the flames and the crash of falling timbers. An ostler was there to release the animals but there was no one to help the women.

The house of the abbess, set a little apart from the main buildings, was the last to be caught by the flames. She awoke with a start, confused by the roar outside and choked by the smoke in her chamber. Fire! Ebba's first thought was for the boy.

'Anne,' she shouted anxiously for her servant. 'Anne. Are you alright? Are you with Alfrid? Anne, where are you?'

Ebba struggled out of her bed in agitation. Was that the boy crying next door? Dear God, she must go to him at once. He was the son Oswy doted on. Nothing must be allowed to happen to him.

Flames were fanned into life the moment she opened her door. Smoke already filled the passage beyond and the fire must be spreading fast. Ebba drew back for an instant but knew that there was no other way to his room. That was Alfrid crying, she was certain now. She would have to go. How long could he survive in this?

'Abbess, wait.'

Anne had appeared by her side and was clutching her arm to restrain her.

'Wait, my Lady. It is too late. You'll be burned to death. NO!'

The last was a shriek of protest as Ebba struggled out of the servant's grasp and, left arm held up before her face to try to protect it from the smoke and heat, plunged forward crying to Anne as she did so, 'Stay there. Don't you come.'

Should Anne go or stay? Could she help her mistress? She could hear noises but could see nothing. No. 'Stay there' the abbess had said and a lifetime of obedience kept her rooted to the spot. How could they both stay alive in there?

There was a cry and a wail, and the figure of the abbess loomed up out of the smoke. Her hair was singed, her face and arms scorched and blistered, her thin night clothes smouldering but she was carrying the child in her arms, bundled up in the covers from his bed to protect him.

'Take him Anne, quickly.'

The abbess thrust the bundle into her servant's arms so strongly that Anne staggered with the force of it but grasped him and managed to hold on.

'Go, Anne. He must get out. Take him to the king. It's too late for secrets now. Go on . . . ' The abbess pushed her servant with both hands in desperation. 'I've risked my life for him. Don't fail me now,' and she shouted at the top of her voice, 'GET OUT, I can follow.'

Anne obediently turned and, bent forward to shield the child from the smoke, hurried back down the passage to the door leading her to safety.

Ebba started after her but the pain in her scorched body brought her to a standstill and she sank to the ground, unable to go further. She knew she should get to her feet and somehow struggle out through the smoke but she could not bring her mind to bear on her own predicament, overwhelmed as she was by the appalling tragedy of it all. How many nuns had survived the inferno? Please God let them not have died without asking forgiveness of their sins – her sins for permitting the abuses to enter all their lives.

'Dear Lord, forgive us,' she prayed, 'in Your infinite mercy. Remember our human frailty and the love we have for you. Forgive us our trespasses as we forg . . . '

The roof beam above burned through and fell with a crash across Ebba's shoulders, pinning her to the ground. Within seconds the flames engulfed her.

The inferno of Coldingham had spared few. Three nuns, whose cells were farthest from where the fire started, had escaped and, although shocked, were otherwise unharmed. Two more had superficial burns and would certainly recover but another three were severely scorched and would surely die. The buildings were razed to the ground and the once elegant nunnery was reduced to a smouldering ruin.

Anne could find no one whom she could trust to escort her south to Bamburgh. If the identity of the boy, Alfrid, became known there was no telling what might happen. If they were captured he might be held to ransom. Worse still both might be murdered if they fell in with the king's enemies who, in these northern parts of his kingdom, were not a few. She had one chance only – to go alone with him to the palace hoping to accomplish the journey safely and to restore the boy to his father. It would take a long time but she dare not consider any other plan. She would collect as much food as she could carry from the one friend she could trust and go south as stealthily as she could.

The king heard the news of the fire one week later and, as he galloped north to search for his son, he passed Anne and the boy who were nearing Bamburgh. They had made painfully slow progress. Anne realised that if she stuck to the coastal strip the going would be easier but how was she to get across the River Tweed by it's wide mouth? She would have to go inland, she had decided, and hope that the wilder hill country she would have to negotiate would not be too much for her. She had to carry the child almost the entire way which meant that she could manage no more than a mile or two at a stretch before stopping to rest. She dared not ask for a ride on the few occasions on which they had been overtaken by a wagon and had chosen to turn off the road to let it pass rather than arouse suspicion.

The river, she had always known, would be difficult and, since she was already feeling the strain of the journey, she knew she would never accomplish the long detour west which would be necessary to reach a narrow crossing place. For almost a whole day she had watched a ferry plying it's trade before, in early evening, when the numbers of passengers had dwindled, they were able to cross alone without exciting any special interest.

The terrain became easier as she got further south and left the rugged country behind her. Nevertheless, her feet were sore and bleeding, Alfrid fractious and hungry and her strength was beginning to fail, but she pressed on determinedly, still fighting shy of any strangers she encountered. So, hearing horses, and not knowing who the riders might be, she had hidden in the bushes until the king's party were out of sight before daring to continue on her way. By the time she reached the castle he, travelling at speed, was surveying the horror of Coldingham.

Enfleda had been astonished at his reaction to the news of the destruction of the nunnery.

'I must go at once,' he shouted. 'Servant! Horses, arrange horses. I will be off within the hour.'

'But what on earth for,' she had demanded, quite unable to understand his excitement. 'It is a tragedy, of course, but *you* don't need to go. Send Ricbert or . . . or anyone. They will report to you. There isn't any need for you to go at all and certainly not in a desperate panic like this. What's got into you?'

But she could get no sense out of him.

'You don't understand,' he kept insisting. 'Don't understand. I must go. I can't explain now. It's important.'

'But why is it important? Just tell me that. Why?'

It had been no use though. She couldn't get a straight answer. He was going and that was that. In fact he was gone. In a trice, it seemed, he had rushed off, shouting orders, behaving like a man deranged and, in no time, was clattering out of the palace with a party of only four men and riding full tilt for the north.

Enfleda was baffled. She hadn't seen him like this before. The fire was desperately worrying him for some reason she didn't know about and she didn't like not knowing about something that was as important to him as this.

She found out the next day when Ricbert asked to see her.

'The king's son. You say a woman has arrived claiming to be bringing the king's son? But why did you let her in? She's an imposter. I don't understand how you ever thought it might be true.'

Ricbert looked unhappy and didn't answer immediately. When he did he spoke quietly and with infinite regret, hoping that the queen would not compel him to reveal the truth outright.

'I too thought she must be liar or a thief or some kind of imposter – up to no good anyway, Your Majesty . . . and I was about to send her away as you suggested, until . . . until she told me where she had come from.'

Enfleda was suddenly alarmed by the certainty in his voice.

'Where?'

'Coldingham, Your Majesty.'

'Oh.'

She saw at once from Ricbert's eyes that his conclusion was precisely the same as hers. Oswy, storming out of the palace as soon as the news of the fire at Coldingham reached him! Oswy . . . in a panic . . . yes a panic . . . there was only one explanation. This *was* the king's son, saved from the fire and brought here while Oswy rode frantically north to find him.

Enfleda was a mass of conflicting emotions. Anger – black anger – at Oswy for his unfaithfulness; horror at the knowledge of another illegitimate son; and yet at the same time, a flash of sadness for him, despite his betrayal, searching up there for the son he would not find and would believe dead. Enfleda brought her thoughts back to the present.

'Will you please bring her here, Ricbert . . . and Ricbert,' as he turned to go, 'we are too late for concealment but the fewer who know of this, yet, the better.'

'Yes, Your Majesty. And, Your Majesty.'

'Yes, Ricbert.'

'Just that I am sorry, Your Majesty.'

Enfleda's thoughts went racing off again as she waited for the woman and child. Coldingham must have been where he had kept sneaking off to when she thought he was seeing another woman. How old would the boy be? How long had Oswy been mysteriously disappearing? She tried to remember but the turmoil in her brain prevented rational thought. Who could the mother be, was the next question to come into her head? There surely hadn't been many opportunities for . . . wait though. Might this be a child sired during that long trip to Iona and wherever? That would make him . . . what? Two perhaps; not much more.

Then her thoughts crystallised into an outburst of fury against her husband.

'You bastard. You bastard. Just you wait,' she cried aloud. 'I'll . . . I'll . . . oh, dear God, I don't know what I'm saying, but I must make him pay for this. I . . . '

The door opened quietly and Ricbert reappeared. He stood respectfully just within the room until she motioned him to come forward.

'Are they here Ricbert?'

'Yes, Your Majesty.'

Enfleda turned away, her instinctive reaction one of rejection of this . . . bastard, she suddenly thought. Two bastards, father and son. God help her, what should she do? It was too late to send him away now.

'Show them in, Ricbert.'

It was the bedraggled state of Anne and the boy that immediately attracted all her attention.

'Have you . . . ? Are you alright? How ever have you come all that way from Coldingham?'

Anne was standing nervously just within the room where Ricbert had stood just a few moments earlier. Now that she had accomplished her task, and the king's son was safe in his father's castle, the enormity of it flooded in on her. This was the queen but not the mother of the boy. She probably – almost certainly – didn't know of his existence. If they had been hiding him at Coldingham his birth was a secret which had been kept from this lady until now when she, Anne, had given the game away. What would the queen do? Worse still, what would the king do to her now that she had let the queen find out his secret? For the first time the isolation of her position overwhelmed her. She sank to the floor, still holding the sleeping child, and began to weep.

Enfleda was not sure what she had expected but it wasn't this. Forgetting everything but this sobbing, crouching figure with the sleeping child, she immediately became compassionate.

'It's alright, alright I tell you. You mustn't cry. There's no need to be afraid. That's right,' as Anne looked up, surprised at the kindness she was receiving when she expected to be upbraided. Inconsequentially she answered the last question she could remember.

'Walked . . . Your Majesty.'

'What?'

'You asked how we got here. We walked, Your Majesty . . . Alfrid and me, from Coldingham. There was no other way . . . no other safe way.' And all of a sudden Anne was telling this lady the whole story, and every anxiety bottled up inside since that dreadful night of the fire poured out.

'If any survived the fire they could only have been a few. There was no other place to keep the boy safe and the abbess had said, "Take him to the king". She was burned, Your Majesty, dreadfully burned by going through the flames to get him out. She gave him to me and said, "Take him to the king". I had to go and leave her for the boy's sake – after all, he had done no harm. I had to leave her and she couldn't get out. She was burned, Your Majesty – burned alive. "Take him", she said. "It's too late for concealment now". She said that too, Your Majesty, "too late for concealment". And here I am.'

Enfleda's anger had been totally dissipated by this pathetic, loyal creature crouching before her, still faithfully holding the boy who slept soundly through it all dead to the world.

'Is that his name, Alfrid?'

'Yes, Your Majesty.'

'How old is he?'

Enfleda was looking at the sleeping child very carefully as she asked her question but she could not see sufficient of him to detect any resemblance.

'About two, Your Majesty. We were not really sure, you see . . . we didn't know when . . . exactly he was born. He was about nine months when he came to us.'

'I don't suppose you know . . . ?' Enfleda broke off her question quickly, thinking better of it, but it was answered just the same.

'No, Your Majesty. None of us knew who she was . . . He was just a baby to us. Alfrid, that's all . . . until the fire,' looking directly at Enfleda for almost the first time, 'then he was the king's son.' And she added nervously just as Ricbert had, 'I'm sorry, Your Majesty.'

Oh dear, thought Enfleda, there's another one sorry for me. I expect they'll all be sorry for me, pitying me behind my back. Blast! Blast! Blast! Sorry – he'll be sorry. I'll give him something to be sorry for.

Enfleda realised that Anne was watching her and immediately became concerned for the boy.

'What are you called?'

'Anne, my Lady.'

'Well, I expect you're hungry and tired and would like to have some clean clothes. I will arrange all this. Perhaps for the time being you will go on looking after him – after Alfrid – until we decide what is best to be done. Will you?'

'Oh, gladly, Your Majesty, gladly. I thought you would be furious with me. You're so kind.'

The beguiling sight of this huddled creature still cradling the sleeping form in her arms almost brought a tear to the queen's eye.

'Oh, did you? Why would I be cross with you. You have done nothing wrong, nothing. You have been a very faithful servant and done your duty. You will be rewarded . . . ' And by Oswy too she ended to herself. He would pay. She would see to that. And that isn't the only thing he'll pay for.

Oswy returned three days later.

Enfleda heard the clatter of hooves and the activity in the courtyard below her chamber and was in time to see him dismount, fling the reins to a groom and enter the palace without a word to anyone. She dismissed the two ladies-in-waiting who were with her immediately, with instructions that, when the king came, they were not to be disturbed. This was to be a private matter between the two of them.

Time and again during her life time Enfleda had regretted her capacity to see both sides of a question. When she wanted to be thoroughly and uncompromisingly mad with Oswy her inate reasonableness always seemed to assert itself and let her weaken. She was determined not to let herself be beguiled now, yet during the long minutes of her waiting for him to appear she felt a stab of sorrow for him believing his son dead . . . a son he must care for very much she realised. She couldn't . . . Her thoughts were interrupted as he suddenly burst into the room.

'Enfleda! Oh dear God, Enfleda what am I to do?'

She had not risen from her chair at his entrance but, in his agitation he failed to notice this departure from her customary courtesy. He flung his cloak aside and fell to his knees before her and wept, deep heart rending sobs, at the pain his imagined loss was causing him. Instinctively she began to smooth his hair and make noises of comfort until she steeled herself to return to her former state of bitterness at the wrong he had done her. Curse him, lying with his head on her lap expecting her to console him. Why the hell should she console him? Why? He was to blame. He was at fault. He had . . . yes, been unfaithful to her and had tried to hide the consequences of it from her. And yet . . . No, she would not weaken but she could not leave him in ignorance any longer.

His sobbing had eased somewhat and she felt him stir. She turned her head away so as not to catch his eye and give in to his mute appeal. She heard him mutter 'Forgive me, forgive me', but closed her mind to the words. Instead, pushing him away, she rose to her feet and stood with her back to him.

'He's alive.'

'What?'

Enfleda could feel his puzzlement and sense his movement towards her. She took two steps further away and repeated her words.

'He's alive.'

'Enfleda what do you mean. The boy? Is it the boy? Don't play with me. D'you mean the boy?'

'Yes the boy, Alfrid. He's alive and here.'

At first there was silence behind her then the renewed sound of weeping and the muttering of prayers. Reluctantly turning to look at him she saw Oswy crouching on the floor, his head bowed down until it almost touched the ground, his hands joined together and a low mumble of prayers just audible. Her hand seemed to move out towards him for a moment until she snatched it back and stamped her foot in irritation at her weakness.

Presently the sound of his prayer came to an end and she heard him get up. He coughed hesitantly before asking very softly:

'Tell me please, is he alright and then you can say what you like . . . what I deserve. Just tell me that first.'

Still keeping her back to him she waited only a moment before replying.

'Yes, he's fine. He hardly suffered at all except perhaps a little from the journey here. No! Just stay there,' as she heard him begin to move towards her. 'I don't want . . . can't look at you yet but you deserve to know about him. The servant brought him. Ebba's servant. The abbess saved his life for your sake and lost her own in the process, so that's something else on your conscience. When there was no one left alive – or scarcely any one – this woman, Anne, brought Alfrid here as Ebba had said she must and when they arrived you had gone and . . . they brought him to me.'

'And you took him in?'

'Of course I took him in.' In her anger Enfleda spun around and began to glare at her husband, venting her fury totally upon him now that he knew his son to be safe. 'What did you expect me to do? Send away a helpless child and a faithful old woman who had kept him safe just because you had wronged me? It's you I should send away – or go myself. You with your promises that you loved me and would never look at another woman again and all the time you've been laughing behind my back and producing a second bastard to match your precious Alchfrith.'

Enfleda was at last able to let herself go. All pity for Oswy's supposed loss of his son had disappeared and her only concern now was to abuse him.

'How many more bastards have you got hidden away, I'd like to know? I expect the monasteries round here are full of them. You're beneath contempt. You're . . . you're . . . ' Enfleda was weeping now in rage and frustration.

'I thought you loved me and all the time you were having it off with any little bit you fancied. Love! You don't know the meaning of the word. But I'll make you sorry for this in every way I can – just you wait. Your life won't be worth living when I've finished with you. I'll . . . I'll . . . '

Unable in her frustration to think of ways she would pay him back, Enfleda sank to the floor beating her fists on it in a furious tattoo.

It took a long while for her to become calmer and her husband remained silent the entire time. At last, as she began to get to her feet, he spoke, full of remorse.

'There isn't anything you can say that I don't deserve. I was unfaithful and I've rued it every day since. Time and again I wanted to tell you but always shied away from it. At first I wanted to leave the boy in Strathclyde – yes,' seeing the look in Enfleda's eyes, 'that's where it happened, on my journey back from Iona. I wanted to leave him, as I said, and now I wish by everything holy that I had. But I thought it better to have him away from there and under my eye. Ebba took him of course when I asked her. I went once to make sure he was alright and . . . and I realised that I loved him.

'Not like I love you, of course . . . Oh yes I do,' seeing the look of scorn in her eyes at his statement. 'I have loved you since soon after we were married. I've been a poor husband perhaps but not because I didn't love you. I do and . . . whatever you do or say . . . I always will.'

Oswy sank wearily into a chair but all the time kept his eyes on his wife who had turned away from him again and was desperately trying to sustain her anger.

'There was something about the boy that I hadn't felt for Ecfrith. I'm sorry but it is true. In some way I can't explain I felt for him and knew I had to see him as often as I could. I even wondered if you might be beginning to suspect something,' he admitted, 'with the number of journeys I was making and I tried to make fewer . . . because I knew that if you found out . . . it would hurt you grievously.'

Enfleda had begun to weep silently again but, sensing that any attempt at personal contact would be rejected, Oswy remained where he was and made no attempt to approach her.

'I knew it would wound you,' he repeated, 'as it has. Terribly, I know. I can think of no way to try to make it up. I can only hope that sooner or later – and pray God it will be sooner – you will forgive me.'

'There is only one more thing I can say now,' he continued after a pause hoping for some sign of forgiveness that he did not get. 'He cannot stay here. He would be a constant reminder to you of my unfaithfulness. If you will just give me a few days I will make some arrangements for him to go away . . . well away from here . . . too far for me . . . ever . . . to see him again.'

Again he paused but again there was no response from the silent queen. Oswy walked to the door and stood by it in bewilderment as if wondering how to take his leave.

'I told you I loved the boy,' he said finally, 'and so I do. But I love you more, far more. Now that you know of his existence I must put him out of my life altogether if that is the only way I can keep . . . regain . . . your love.'

The door closed softly behind him. Enfleda felt numb with shock at the memory of that terrible meeting and was unable to focus her mind on what she should do. Ought she to offer to keep the child. Yes. No. NO! Oswy was right. The only chance of them regaining their relationship was for him to go. Enfleda remembered what he had said. He loved that boy but was giving him up for her . . . prepared never to see him again. He must love her if he was willing to make such a sacrifice. Oh, dear God what was she to do? Go to him now and make up? No, she would not . . . could not, do that yet. But she would be unable to keep this vendetta up for long. Sooner or later, he had said and please God make it sooner. It would have to be sooner for her own sake as well. She couldn't be vindictive. They would have to make up soon.

But until they did, she told herself, she would make sure he felt her displeasure. But how? She wasn't very good at being nasty but she couldn't let him off the hook completely. She would go to see her daughter, Elfleda, more often – that was one thing. He couldn't try to stop her now. If he could go several times a year to one monastery to see his bastard she could surely go to see their legitimate daughter. She was resolved on that at any rate. What else?

Separate rooms, needless to say. She would just refuse to have him with her until . . . until when? Until she could suppress her need for him no longer. She'd make him give her up for Lent. She laughed out loud at the notion and realised that the worst of her anger had passed. Lent. That was another idea. The Celtic Easter was a week earlier than the Roman one next year – or so Audrey said – so Enfleda would revert to the Roman practice and insist . . . absolutely insist . . . that Oswy's fast, which would begin a week earlier than hers, would not be broken until *her* Easter Day, not his. He could keep his own Easter Day if he liked but no feasting until she was ready. After all it would be unseemly for him to be eating heartily – and drinking too – while she was keeping Holy Week. An extra week of Lent would do him good. Audrey would be delighted to have Enfleda join her.

What else? She might have some fun being as difficult as possible and making his life as uncomfortable as she could.

It was a dying man who eventually brought the king and queen back together.

Brother Uffa had been ailing for months. His breathing had become difficult, a harsh cough racked his body and, several times, phlegm, which came up after his bouts of coughing, was bloodstained. His habit began to hang loosely on his thin frame and, on some days, it was as much as he could do to walk as far as the chapel and even then he needed two monks to help him.

When the day came that he was unable to get up at all they sent a message to the queen.

Brother Uffa had not, in fact, acted as Enfleda's personal chaplain for three years. His failing eyesight first caused problems and his hands became so twisted and gnarled by rheumatism that he could no longer celebrate Holy Mass. The queen, reluctant to part with so faithful a servant, had nevertheless been obliged to do so and the sorrowful Uffa had left the palace to spend the remaining days of his life at Lindisfarne.

Oswy accidentally came into his wife's presence soon after the news of Uffa's critical state was brought to her.

Enfleda was finding it increasingly hard to remain distant from Oswy and, time and again, she wished she could find a convenient excuse to make peace. But none of the circumstances she hoped would give her the chance to do so gracefully actually provided the opportunity and she was at her wits end to know how to do it. Oswy offered no olive branch, being content it seemed to go on suffering his penance until such time as the queen forgave him. In the end no contrived pardon was called for.

She was weeping from hearing the news when he came into the room.

She welcomed him, literally, with open arms, her anguish driving everything else from her mind but the knowledge of the comfort he would give her.

'Oh, Oswy. It's Brother Uffa. They say he's dying – can't last very long. Can I go to him?'

At first Oswy could only hold her tightly to him, hoping fervently that, at last, he had been forgiven. When she did not release herself from his arms he let out a grateful sigh and said gently:

'You must go to him, my love, and at once or you may be too late. You can't delay. You would be so upset if you did not see him just once more. Would you like me to go with you?'

At first the old monk did not realise who they were but when Enfleda spoke to him and gently touched his twisted hand he strained his hand towards her and muttered:

'Your Majesty, you shouldn't have come – not for an old monk like me.'

He made an effort to shrug himself up in the bed but she restrained him.

'Now, lie still, Brother Uffa, lie still. There is no need for ceremony. We have just come to say how sorry we are that you are ill.'

The effort of talking seemed to tire him out and he lay back panting for some minutes.

'We will pray for your soul Brother Uffa,' answered Enfleda presently. 'After all, you saved my life here on earth during that terrible storm so I will pray for your happiness in the next world.'

Mention of the storm brought a little smile to Uffa's face and, after a moment, he began speaking to the king as though he had never heard the story.

'I forgot the oil, Your Majesty. All I needed to do was to pour it but, instead, I tried to save the ship and the princess all by myself. Forgot it! Fancy forgetting the oil that Bishop Felix had given me.'

He lapsed into silence again until Enfleda said gently:

'Bishop Aidan.'

'What?' Uffa opened his eyes and peered doubtfully in her direction. 'What was that, Your Majesty?'

'I think it was Bishop Aidan who gave you the oil. Bishop Felix was at the disinterrment, don't you remember? When we were with the East Angles.'

'To be present at that Roman Mass which was held before the exhumation was one of the wonderful experiences of my life, sire. I felt for the first time that I was part of the Universal Church and I had a feeling of . . . belonging to God's Church in this world . . . not just a bit of it as we are here, but all of it everywhere. Many's the time, Your Majesty, that I wanted to ask you if you couldn't do something to bring our Easter differences to an end. But . . . ' He fell silent again for a moment, then rolled onto his back and continued, 'I never did. That shows you what a poor man of God I am.

I should have asked whatever you might have said. Braved the consequences if you'd been cross, sire, But . . . ' he paused again, 'I never did.'

Uffa heaved a great sigh as if deeply regretting his silence. Then he held out his hands towards them as he had done before and said:

'Am I too late to ask now, Your Majesty? Isn't there something you could do?'

And when the king made no reply Uffa seemed to become more agitated and rumbled on,'We're the odd ones out, you know, sire. We're out of step. We're out of . . . communion with the whole world. . . and that upsets me. I should have asked long ago. Am I too late now?'

'Is he too late, my Lord?'

Enfleda was the questioner this time, gently laying her hand on Oswy's arm as she spoke.

'Is there not something you could do for this monk who once saved my life . . . and for me? In return for forgiveness?'

Oswy, watching Enfleda with infinite tenderness, took both her hands in his and raised them to his lips.

'No, it isn't too late. I will do something. . . for you both and you can rest easily, Brother Uffa. Your request will be granted although . . . ' Oswy hesitated for a moment as if uncertain how to frame his words 'had you, in fact, asked me long ago, I don't think I would have agreed. So you see, Brother Uffa, you chose the right time in the end.'

The look on the old man's face was beatific as the king gave his promise. He closed his eyes and his lips moved in a prayer of thankfulness. When he opened them he stretched his hands towards them a third time.

'Thank you, Your Majesty, my Queen. You have made an old man happy. Now I can die in peace. It was preying on my mind that I never asked and then you, in your goodness, came to see me and gave me a last chance.'

He moved his head as though trying to bring them both into his clouded focus then shook it from side to side.

'It's no use. I can't see you. "In the end", you said, sire, "in the end", I picked the right time. That's what this is, Your Majesties . . . the end. I thank you for coming from the bottom of my heart. Now I have much to say to our Lord. I shall be seeing him very soon.'

The guest house in the Monastery of Lindisfarne possessed none of the comforts the king and queen normally enjoyed but their enjoyment of each other, despite their austere surroundings, was ecstatic.

The monastery naturally possessed nothing so conjugal as a double bed but a small dormitory, which normally slept up to four visitors, had been emptied of their rough pallets and two substantial beds brought in instead and pushed together.

The royal couple needed nothing more. Their physical need for each other was overwhelming and they came together the instant they were alone. Afterwards Enfleda propped herself up on one elbow and with a little giggle observed,

'Well, this is the strangest place we've ever done it, Oswy.'

He made no reply so she shook him.

'Owsy, wake up. That was lovely but now I want to talk. Wake up,' giving him a dig with her elbow.

'I am awake. What do you want to talk about?'

Whatever it was Enfleda did not immediately broach it. Instead she ran her fingers through his hair and remarked, 'Your getting thin on top you know which is supposed to ensure virility. How old are you anyway?'

'Is that all you wanted to talk about, how old I am? I am forty-two as you well know and if you'r worried about declining potency put it out of your mind.'

'Declining potency – what a splendid phrase.' Enfleda went off into paroxysms of laughter before, suddenly sitting up and asking, 'Oh dear, Oswy. You don't suppose anyone could have heard us do you?'

'I'm sure they didn't. The guest master was quite reassuring on that point. No one would have known about your abandoned coupling.'

'Abandoned coupling indeed.' Enfleda was immediately back to her former high spirits. 'First declining potency and now abandoned coupling; what a conversation to be having in a monastery. I say, Oswy, you don't think it was sacrilege or anything to do it here do you? Do you suppose anyone ever did it here before?' And she collapsed in hysterics one more.

'No I don't,' replied Oswy with mock solemnity. 'It is reserved for kings and queens. Now, stop all this nonsense and tell me what it was you wanted to talk about.'

Enfleda was beginning to find her nudity cold so she snuggled down beneath the covers before answering.

'Well,' she said presently, 'it was about what Brother Uffa was asking really. I have talked to him about it, on and off, over the years – since before we were married in fact. Do you remember the story I told you about our interlude with the East Angles – we actually mentioned it this evening? Something happened then to make him conscious of Church unity – he told you that too this evening and said what an effect the Roman Mass had had on him. He would have asked you about it long ago I think but, rightly or wrongly, I dissuaded him. I thought it was better that I should conform rather than that we should try to keep two Easters – well you know how awful it was this year when I was being awkward and made you do an extra weeks fasting.'

'Awful! It was devastating,' said Oswy with feeling. He had wrapped his cloak round him and was crouching, with his knees drawn up, at the head of the bed looking down at her.

'That last extra week of Lent was horrible. Still no meat or fish or eggs and only one meal a day – I was hard pressed to last out the other seven weeks but to do an extra one was purgatory – hell in fact – especially with all the others in the lesser hall eating and drinking to their hearts content. Yes,' he admitted with a great sigh, 'if we had had two Easters every year it would have been impossible.'

'So what can we do for poor Brother Uffa?'

Enfleda had got so far down under the clothes that he could see nothing but her eyes.

'Ah, that's the question.'

Oswy, still keeping on his robe, slid down beneath the bedclothes too and they lay side by side facing each other, their heads only inches apart.

'Do you remember asking me about Alchfrith some time ago,' he enquired presently.

'Alchfrith? What about him?'

'You thought he was up to something and I rather poured cold water on it.'

'Yes I do remember now. *Is* he up to something?'

'Oh, yes,' Oswy answered very slowly, 'he's up to something alright. He keeps needling me as you mentioned and getting little digs in here and there. He's been doing that for a while. Then I found he was making up – or trying to make up to my supporters. He tried Ricbert, for example, and several more. Nothing specific said, of course. All very cleverly done but clearly trying to sound them out about siding with him.'

Oswy stopped speaking for a moment, then reached out a hand and tucked in Enfleda's covers more tightly.

'I realised what it all meant,' he resumed. 'He wants Deira for himself without any control from me – Bernicia too if he can get it, certainly when I've gone and perhaps before if he can make himself strong enough.'

Oswy rolled over onto his back but went on with his analysis of Alchfrith's strategy.

'I don't think he's had a definite plan – nothing like outright rebellion. Not yet at any rate. But he's looking for any weakness on my part and trying to strengthen his own position whenever he can. That's why he's been cultivating the Roman Church. He thinks he can get their religious strength behind him and that will be just another way he can bring pressure on me.'

'And? Go on, don't stop there.' Oswy had lapsed into silence again and Enfleda was keen to hear the rest of the story.

'So, the time has come, I think for a little reaction from me to all this and I might start by tackling our religious differences. I'm happy to take him on there and see what he's made of. I've had it in mind – along with other unpleasant matters,' he grinned at her 'for a little while, and I supposed it crystallised tonight when that gentle old man made his appeal. It *is* time we did something and that something will be a . . . convention . . . debate . . . a synod, that's the word, to decide the Easter question and we'll see what happens there.'

'Oh, Oswy. I'm thrilled. Thank you. When do you think it will be?'

'It can't be too early, I fear.' Oswy frowned a little as he tried to concentrate on the problem. 'Next year, six sixty-four, in the spring, I suppose. Very early in the year is too bad for travelling: Lent doesn't seem ideal – so after Easter I suppose. Are you pleased?'

'Please? I'm absolutely delighted. In fact I can hardly wait for it. Come here and give me a kiss. Um – lovely, but that's not enough. It's warm in this bed. Come in here. There's room for us both if we get close enough together. That's right.'

Chapter 17

In the monastery at Whitby there was an elegant little chapel which had once served the first foundation of nuns to be established there. It had easily housed the, then, small number of fourteen, was becoming uncomfortably full when numbers reached fifty and would clearly be hopelessly inadequate when, as a result of Abbess Hilda's growing reputation, novices continued to apply for admission.

A larger chapel had been built soon after King Oswy's daughter, Elfelda, was accepted into Hilda's charge. It's decoration was more elaborate, it's acoustics superior but, for the abbess, it never had the appeal of the original. Plans were laid for using the smaller chapel for one of a variety of purposes then under discussion. Formal deconsecration was undertaken by Bishop Aidan on the only occasion of his visit to Whitby, but somehow the abbess had not been able to commit herself to giving it over to some permanent secular use and it stood largely idle often not used at all for months at a time.

It would prove ideal for the synod.

Hilda had been full of misgivings when the notion of the synod was proposed by the king, and frankly alarmed when he asked her to allow it to take place in her monastery. The Easter question was unusually important, he insisted. They had allowed separate customs to continue for far too long. The issue had to be faced. Here was Abbot Wilfrid becoming an increasingly important Roman cleric in Deira and now was the time to thrash out the rights and wrongs of the two methods of calculation.

Oswy was reluctant for it to be done in any of his royal palaces, he said. Such a venue would easily prove too overpowering to those taking part. If they were to reach a sound decision everything had to be brought out into the open, no holds barred, a frank and free discussion and you couldn't easily have that within the confines of a royal castle.

It couldn't be in Lindisfarne either. Such a move would undoubtedly be opposed by the Roman side as bringing an undue influence to bear. To hold the synod in, say, Melrose would again be seen to be giving a geographical advantage to the Celts and to choose Ripon would unduly favour the Romans. Coldingham was burnt down and Lastingham was too small. Would the good abbess be so kind as to permit this vital meeting to be held at Whitby?

She could hardly refuse of course. When the king pressed you on a matter of such importance you agreed. Still, she had her doubts especially when she learned that the presenter of the Celtic case was to be Bishop Colman.

'But he cannot speak our language, Your Majesty,' she expostulated. 'If we choose him the whole discussion will have to be translated.'

'Even if we don't choose him to lead the Celtic case,' reasoned the king, 'he is the bishop and will have to be made to understand what is being said, so we are sure to need an interpreter anyway.'

This turned Hilda aside from the main issue.

'Whom do you envisage as interpreter?

'Well, I have no preference but Colman seems dead set on Bishop Cedd who would certainly do the job well.'

Would the other side accept him, Your Majesty?' persisted the abbess. 'He is a supporter of the Celtic Church after all. He might be seen as giving them an advantage.'

'I don't mind if they have one of their own, if they wish, to confirm that the translations are accurate and to share the burden – except that they almost certainly won't find one who speaks gaelic.'

Hilda broke the silence after a moment.

'James.'

'What?'

'There is one, James, the "scriba". He is a splendid interpreter.' And Hilda went on to describe a distressing discussion she had had with Colman and James admirable translation of it all. 'He has practiced Celtic Christianity for years, Your Majesty, I realise, but originally he came here with Bishop Paulinus and was brought up within the Roman Church. I think perhaps,' Hilda added hesitantly, 'that he rather favours the Roman method of calculation but keeps ours out of a desire for peace.'

'Splendid. Cedd and James. Excellent. I will arrange it.'

And off he had gone to do so, presumed Hilda, while she gave her mind to hosting the synod.

How many would there be? Surely there was no need for large numbers especially as the Roman side would be sparsely represented. If there were too many Celts it would look like another manoeuvre to exert too much influence. She began to count.

Bishop Agilbert, was he called, would be one; Wilfrid two; the sub-king Alchfrith she knew had promoted the whole affair, three – and his wife perhaps, four; some representatives from Ripon, say, half a dozen or so, ten. Oh, there was another priest with the bishop, Ag . . . Ago . . . Agatho, that was it, eleven. There might be one or two more she didn't know about so perhaps fifteen in all. The Celtic side could field a lot more very easily but the numbers would have to more or less equal – say twenty of them. And of course there would be the king and queen and herself and the two interpreters – forty to forty-five would be around the final number she decided. The old chapel would do nicely and be quite cosy. Hilda began mentally arranging the seating.

The synod was planned for between Easter and Pentecost 664. Once the Easter ceremonies were over – and mercifully that year they coincided – those who were selected to attend would set out for Whitby. It was after all a reasonably central place. The monks from Melrose would have to travel farthest but, at that time of the year, the journey should present no problems. The second Sunday after Easter was chosen.

Abbot Eata had decided that he did not feel up to the journey and he certainly did not relish the thought of a further encounter with the sub-king Alchfrith, nor, for that matter, with the new abbot of Ripon although he knew him only by reputation. As told to Eata Wilfrid was a scheming churchman, out for his own advantage and, in the case of Ripon, getting it. Eata decided to stay at home and send Cuthbert.

Prior Cuthbert had been curiously silent about the proposed synod and, when told of the abbot's intention, had looked troubled. For some minutes he had made no reply but seemed to be puzzling over the affair. Presently he asked:

'What is our position to be, my Lord Abbot? I realise that if a debate is to be held upon the respective merits of our calculations of the date of Easter there is a possibility, at least, that the Roman case might be judged stronger. Thinking the matter over as I have since we were given notice of the gathering, it seems to me that we have practiced our custom because they are our customs. I have never seriously considered any other view – nor, in truth, the fundamental reason for our own. If I am faced with an irrefutable case for the correctness of the Roman case, and this is the decision of the synod, what is our attitude to be?'

Abbot Eata was silent, too, for a long time and when he replied it was in a regretful tone.

'I cannot tell you what *you* must do, Prior Cuthbert, for, on a matter of this nature, I would not wish to insist on obedience. I can say only that were I faced with, to use your words, an irrefutable case for the correctness of the Roman calculation – I cannot envisage such a circumstance, but if I were – I would feel obliged to accept it. Were I shown that what they were doing was right and we had indeed been wrong I have to accept that. To do otherwise would be to refuse to obey the authority of the Universal Church and that I could not do.'

He was silent again for a short time before ending:

'So, if you find this to be the verdict facing you, you must decide for yourself. I, on your return, will accept your account of the events and will advise – not order but advise – my monks here to practice the Roman Easter customs with me. Those who will not must leave.'

'I will stay, my Lord Abbot, if that is the judgement.'

At Lindisfarne it was a very different story.

Bishop Colman had reacted so violently to the king's announcement of the synod that, for a time, his monks thought he would refuse to take part. He was indignant that the convocation was to be held at all and incensed by the choice of Whitby as its venue. The Celtic practice, handed down through generations of monks of exemplary holiness, including the miracle worker Columcille himself, required no justification. It was beyond the bishop's comprehension that such men could be wrong and he saw it as an insult to men of the utmost sanctity that their practices should be questioned. And questioned by whom? A bishop without even a see, who came from some foreign country or other and a novice priest ordained only yesterday. As for Whitby, memories of the Abbess Hilda angered Colman, who never liked losing an argument. The thought of defending his blessed Columcille there of all places was anathema to him.

It had taken a long time to calm him down and, when he seemed to have let off all his steam and to be accepting the inevitability of the synod, Cedd's brother, Chad, started him off again with one innocent question.

'Just suppose, Bishop Colman, that despite the overwhelming strength of our position the judgement goes to the Romans. What will you and your monks do here?'

'Do? Why nothing. How can you even think such a thing. It's abominable.' And Colman's face began to return to it's former shade of purple.

Chad was astonished by the vehemence of the response to his question and, since he was a gentle kindly person by nature, he was diffident about making any comment that might inflame the bishop further. His brother, however was not so easily subdued.

'Chad has a point, Bishop Colman. If we agree to take part we might be faced with an adverse verdict. You cannot even visualise the possibility, I can clearly see, of St Columcille and our forefathers being wrong. But have you not always believed they were right without even considering the other side? Do you know the strength of their case? Are you aware of what you have to contend against?'

Colman's expression was ferocious as he looked from one man to the other.

'You astonish me Cedd,' he said presently after a visible effort to control himself. 'And you also, Chad. There is no chance of the Roman practice being preferred, I tell you. Our historical traditions stemming from St John are unassailable. You are defeatist, both of you. Abject defeatist. I had thought to hear nothing so weak as you suggest ever to pass your lips. You are beneath contempt to consider such a thing.'

Chad was clearly upset by the bishop's rudeness and began to finger his beads to restore his equilibrium. But Cedd came back with a firm rejoinder.

'It matters little to me if you abuse me, my Lord, although I see no cause for you insulting my brother who merely asked you a necessary question – a necessary question which I repeat. What will you and your monks do if the verdict goes to the other side? Abide by it? Reject it? What? And may I add,' went on Cedd quietly before Colman had the chance to answer, 'that a wise protagonist learns the strengths and weaknesses of his opponents. Do you know the strength of the Roman case? . . . or anything about it at all?'

'No, I do not, nor do I require to.' Colman was in a seething rage again, staring with malevolent eyes at Cedd. 'Whatever their case is it cannot stand against the provenance of ours as you should know. I will not . . . will not, do you hear . . . demean myself by enquiring into this flawed Roman practice nor will I allow anyone else from this monastery to do so. Our position is impregnable and if the enquiry is fair we shall win.

'And,' he ground out in harsh insistent tones, 'if the enquiry is so flagrantly biased as to give the judgement to them, my monks and I will refuse to accept it . . . ever.'

Audrey and Ecfrith were discussing the synod in quite different terms.

'By now, my dear Ecfrith, you will be utterly convinced I am sure, of the correctness of the Roman case for the calculation of Easter. The explanations I have given you will have shown you the gaps in the Celtic case and I know . . . '

Audrey, although apparently deeply immersed in complicated

needlework, was keeping up a never ending commentary at the same time. Ecfrith was barely listening. She had expounded the Easter problem to him several times before but her explanation had been anything but lucid. He had tried to follow her reasoning but it seemed to be a little different each time she advanced it.

'You are far from unintelligent, Ecfrith,' she had told him more than once, 'and I am confident of making one convert to the Roman practice in Northumbria, however stubborn the others might be. It will require a little clarification from me, that is all and then we will both sit with the Roman side at the synod.'

Audrey's clarification had been too confusing for Ecfrith but he was learning not to argue and to let her think he was persuaded. It was all too puzzling for him. Someone else – his father, he supposed – would pronounce the judgement after the enquiry and he would not need to cast a vote or anything. And even if it did come to that he would just vote the same way as Audrey did. There was no more to be said. The more he agreed with her the easier life was and the more time he had for his music.

'Yes, dear,' he answered. He was uncertain even what the question had been but 'yes dear' was always the safe answer.

To James the announcement of the synod was splendid news.

His contact with Wilfrid and Bishop Agilbert at Ripon had made him more aware than ever of the two different practices of Easter. It was the uncomfortable meeting with Colman on Iona which had started him thinking about it again after years of being so immersed in Celtic customs that he had almost forgotten that different ones existed. In the early days, after Enfleda had come to Northumbria to marry Oswy, he had half hoped she would continue the Roman practice but she had not wanted to upset her new husband and, after a number of discussions with her chaplain, Brother Uffa, she had agreed to observe the Celtic Easter like everybody else . . . until last year of course when she, with Audrey's help, had upset the entire court by insisting that Easter should be kept twice.

Suppose she had been adamant at the beginning that she was going to follow the Roman practice in which she had been brought up, would James have joined her? To have done so might have caused problems in his family just as it would have done in hers, unless Edith had changed too. Edith had been less concerned about the whole question than he and she would, he supposed, have done what he decided. But Enfleda's agreement to do what Oswy did had avoided any difficulties there might otherwise have been. The queen was a good woman whom James admired and, on reflection, he had been pleased that she had not precipitated a crisis which might have caused difficulties for them all but especially for Bishop Aidan. No one ever wanted to upset the saintly bishop. Perhaps that had been one of the points Brother Uffa had brought up when he had advised her.

They had somehow avoided confrontation until now but James could not help but feel pleased by the king's decision to call the synod. It didn't seem to matter when one Church was carrying on it's practices in isolation but when they came together a solution had to be found. Yes, he was glad the convocation was to be held but a little alarmed perhaps that he was to be a participant, if only to the extent of translating the words of others.

He had been frankly astonished when the abbess, at the king's request, had asked him to act in this capacity. Had anyone else asked him – except the queen of course – he might have refused but you couldn't refuse someone like Abbess Hilda. He had got to know her well over the winter of 633-4. Arriving at Whitby in late October he had stayed on until the spring when of course the synod was to be held. James had developed a greater admiration for her as the weeks passed. He knew she was of royal blood but no one would ever have realised it from her demeanour. Humble and devout at all times, that was the abbess. Never too busy to give up her time for anyone who wished to see her. Always seeming to have nothing else to do but to listen patiently to whatever problem was being brought to her notice. No, he couldn't refuse her.

He had been surprised though.

'Share with a bishop, my Lady? That would be presumptuous surely. And such a one as Bishop Cedd too. A very holy man, so I've been told and strong and determined too.'

'That is why it was thought wise to have another interpreter to help him, James,' Hilda had explained. 'He is strong and determined, even rebuking kings if he thinks it right. Perhaps you know the story of his famous encounter with King Sigbert of the East Saxons?'

James had shaken his head

'Well, it is an interesting and enlightening story from several points of view,' Hilda had continued, 'and since you will be joining forces with the bishop I think perhaps you should know it.

'Brother Cedd, as he was then, converted King Sigbert and the majority of the East Saxons who had apostacised from the faith. But not all the people, even the noble ones, practiced the faith devoutly. There was one, an earldorman, who, despite Cedd's preaching against such practices, contracted an illicit marriage with a woman whose first husband was still alive. The man was excommunicated and Cedd forebade anyone to visit his house or eat at his table.

'The king was a good man,' said the abbess, smoothing the folds of her coarse gown as she told the tale, 'but perhaps weak. He accepted the earldorman's invitation and *did* eat at his table. Immediately on leaving the house whom should he meet but Cedd, now a bishop. Remember this man was the king, James, but seeing the bishop and feeling his displeasure, Sigbert got down from his horse and fell on his knees before Cedd begging forgiveness. The bishop, angry at the events, brought his staff down none too lightly on the prostrate king in exercise of his episcopal authority. As Sigbert glanced up Cedd announced, 'This very house, which you have refused to shun despite my command will be the place of your death.'

The abbess stopped speaking for so long that James felt obliged to ask, 'And was it my Lady?'

'Oh yes, it was. The earldorman and his brother murdered the king soon afterwards when he visited the house again. It was a punishment for disobeying the episcopal decree. So this is the bishop James, with whom you are to share the translation of the synod – and of the words, among others, of Bishop Colman, in which,' she smiled gently, 'you have had no little practice. Perhaps now you see James how we cannot just have a determined translator, one who might project his own views into the discussion. A translator must be exact and impersonal, and to be sure that Cedd acts in this way, James, we need you. Will you help us?'

'Of course, my Lady Abbess.'

And so he would but, if truth be told, he was anxious about his part in the affair. Not so far as his ability to translate was concerned – even to translate vituperation like Colman was likely to indulge in – but concerning his ability to stand up to the demands of such a trying occasion.

He had been experiencing a lethargy for several months now which he could not account for. Tasks which he had previously accomplished without difficulty were now tiring him in a way they had never done before. A year or two ago he would have finished his work at Whitby well before advent and returned to Melrose, or to one of his other schools, to continue his supervision. But by Christmas his task was bearely half finished and even if it had been, he was obliged to admit that the winter journey across Northumbria was more than he could face. He had worked on at Whitby, instead, and had decided to await the coming of spring before setting out on his travels again. Then this plan too was overtaken by the synod.

Would he find it too trying? Was he ill, he wondered? This inertia was so unlike him. Where had all his old enthusiasm gone? He felt like ... yes, like he had done two winters ago at Durrow when he had the jaundice. He had risen at the thought and gone to examine the whites of his eyes in the looking glass. Was there any sign of yellowness? No, he couldn't truthfully say there was. Perhaps he was imagining his symptoms. He would have to pull himself together for the synod.

The participants began arriving in good time.

All the resources of Whitby had been harnessed to avoid the possibility of violent arguments before the synod opened. Hilda had planned well and by rearranging the quarters of her own monks she was able to give those arriving from the Roman side a sufficient degree of privacy.

In fact the days before the synod, so far from giving rise to disputes between opposing delegates were filled with extraordinary happenings.

Then they had a mysterious visitor. A youth, who looked no more than nineteen or twenty, suddenly appeared from nowhere and was found sitting in one of the guest chambers. The guest master, and several others with him, welcomed the young man asking him where he had come from and where he was going. The youth replied that he was stopping only briefly before continuing on his way and did not wish to trouble them. He was, nonetheless, given water to wash his hands and feet and asked to wait until after Terce when a meal would be ready. But after Terce he was nowhere to be found and none could tell how he had left, since a light fall of snow that morning showed not a single footprint leaving the monastery. And in the guest room where he had been sitting they found three loaves, snow white and wonderfully fragrant, and apparently inexhaustable since the whole monastery ate of them before they were used up.

Then two of the party of monks from Ripon, who had been delayed on their journey and were very short of food, told of being fed miraculously by an eagle which plucked a fish from the river before their eyes and dropped it at their feet to sustain them.

Three monks from Lindisfarne, making their journey by boat, were caught in a sudden gale and their boat was dismasted and shipped a great deal of water. They told of seeing the figure of a man dressed in white moving over the waves towards their boat and continuing on until he went out of sight in the distance. And behind him as he walked the sea became calm and the wind fell and they were able to bale enough water to bring them to safety.

There was one strange event at dead of night which only Abbess Hilda and one other monk learned about. Cuthbert was seen by this monk to leave the monastery about midnight on several nights in succession. One night the monk followed Cuthbert and watched him make his way down to the shore and walk straight into the water until only his head was still visible. There he stayed singing psalms and praying in a loud voice to Almighty God for two hours and when he returned to the shore, two otters appeared from nowhere, warmed his cold feet with their breath and rolled on them to dry them with their fur. The terrified monk had confessed what he had seen to Abbess Hilda who had sworn him to secrecy. She had said not a word to Cuthbert and was astonished when he said to her one day, 'Thank you for your silence, my Lady Abbess. I would not have wished the story to be widely known.'

Altogether there was a tremendous feeling of cameraderie and so much mixing between the parties that Hilda began to wonder why she had ever thought it would be otherwise and had gone to such lengths to keep the sides apart.

The great day came at last and everywhere a feeling of excitement prevailed. Hilda and Oswy had spent hours trying to decide the best arrangement for the seating so that everyone would be able to see and hear what happened. The little old chapel had a raised platform at one end where the sanctuary had previously been. To one side of this a rostrum had been placed and, beside it, two chairs for the interpreters. On the other side were thrones for the king and queen. The seats in what had been the tiny nave were now arranged in curved rows for eight people in each row. Colman was at one end of the first row, Wilfrid and Agilbert at the other end, with Alchfrith, Cyniburg, Audrey, Ecfrith and Hilda in the middle. No attempt had been made to separate the remining monks into their constituent parties and James was interested to note that no segregation was attempted by the men themselves.

The king opened the proceedings. Everyone stood as he rose to his feet but he motioned them to be seated again and waited until all were settled. James of course was facing the audience and had a perfect view of them all. Colman scowled and looked thoroughly put out by the entire business. Wilfrid, James saw, was holding a rolled parchment which seemed to indicate that what James had heard was true and it was Wilfrid, not Agilbert, who was to present the Roman case. The abbot looked calm and gazed benignly round at the assembled company in contrast to the dour withdrawal of his opponent Colman.

'My Lords Bishop, my Lady Abbess, Reverend Fathers and monks, members of the Royal Households of Bernicia and Deira, I thank you all for attending this historic gathering. Some of you have travelled a long way and I offer special thanks to you. I offer them also to the Abbess for her wonderful hospitality in this holy monastery. We could not possibly have better facilities for our deliberations.

'We are here, my friends,' Oswy continued, speaking in measured phrases and giving Cedd ample time to translate each phrase, 'to decide on a matter of the upmost import. Two parts of the Church of God celebrate that Church's principal feast on different dates. Is that so important, I have heard it asked, and to that there is only one answer. Yes, immensely important. The Church of God must be one Church and if that one Church cannot agree on the date of it's principle feast what can it agree on? We are not given a choice – I have looked into this very carefully. None of the Fathers of the Church say do it this way or that way – please yourself, we don't mind. No. There is only one time and instructions for calculating it.

'It is these instructions which seem to be the problem,' went on the king after giving Cedd a moment to catch up. 'Should they be interpreted one way or the other? Both,' stressed Oswy holding up his finger to stress his words, 'cannot be right. One is right and one wrong, but which is which?'

He paused for a moment again and surveyed the listeners who, it seemed to James were hanging on his every word.

'That,' he repeated, 'is why we are here; to decide this momentous question. Now, the points will be argued by two people – Bishop Colman of the See of Lindisfarne, putting the Celtic case and Abbot Wilfrid from Ripon, putting the Roman one. Bisiph Agilbert has specially requested that Abbot Wilfrid should speak in his stead since the good bishop would not be speaking in his own language, were he to argue the case, which might result in parts of his presentation being misunderstood. I am sure you will accept that we must find the truth and avoid misunderstanding and so I have agreed. Wilfrid will present the Roman case.

'And now, my friends we are ready to begin. Bishop Colman, as Lord Bishop in the Kingdom of Northumbria should by right speak first to present the case for the calculation of the date of Easter by the Celtic method. Bishop Colman, the floor is yours.'

Colman remained in his chair for some moments after Oswy finished speaking. He gave no flicker of response to the royal invitation to come forward although he could not have failed to recognise his own name nor to understand the meaning of the king's gesture towards the rostrum. He sat motionless awaiting the completion of the translation. Only when Cedd had finished the rendering of Oswy's words into gaelic did the bishop stir.

He rose to his feet in silence and marched out before the whole gathering, ignoring the rostrum and stationing himself in the centre of the floor in full view of all. His head turned first towards the king, then towards the royal party in the front row and back again to Oswy. He stood with feet apart, his left hand clenching and unclenching into a fist in a steady rhythm.

'This is an unnecessary gathering which will achieve nothing,' he began in forthright terms, 'since there is nothing to achieve. The king has said it is important. I disagree. It is unimportant and pointless.'

In his abrupt opening he had acknowledged neither the king nor any of the royal party nor his opponent.

'I protest at this meeting at which I am instructed to defend the age-old customs of my Church which have been handed down to me by men of extreme holiness, men beloved by Almighty God whose computation of the date of Easter could not possibly err.'

Colman made his stance before his audience seem more aggressive still as he squared his shoulders and shook a finger vigorously at them all.

'Those who sent me here as bishop taught me the Easter customs which were handed down to them by our forefathers, men of unsurpassed sanctity. And from whom did they learn them? Why from none other that St John the Blessed Evangelist himself, the man beloved of our Lord Jesus Christ, the disciple who rested his head on our Lord's breast at the Last Supper. Can such a man not know the correct date of Easter? Of course he knew.'

Colman was shouting now and scarcely waiting for the translation in his frustration, 'And so did every Church he founded. What other justification do we need for keeping Easter when we do than to follow the evangelist himself. Why should I be obliged to defend such a practice that was good enough for the beloved disciple. It is scandalous – scandalous – to attack it as these here – ' making a disparaging gesture towards Agilbert and Wilfrid ' – have attacked it. We practice what St John the Evangelist practiced. That is enough.'

Colman flounced back to his chair indignation apparant in his every movement. Cedd struggled through the last part of the translation and glanced towards James who nodded his agreement. No emotion showed on the king's face to let them guess his reaction to Colman's tirade. James and Hilda, who had expected nothing less, caught each other's eye and the abbess seemed to give a little shrug as if to say 'what else could you expect from him'. It was not a convincing explanation of the correctness of Celtic Easter customs, James had to admit. Wilfrid, he felt, would give a far better account of himself.

Abbot Wilfrid was already on his feet in response to a signal from the king. He carried his parchment over to the rostrum and placed it carefully down in front of him, for easy reference, James felt sure, as he unfolded his argument. Wilfrid bowed graciously towards Oswy and Enfleda and then to Alchfrith and finally to Hilda as hostess of the gathering.

'Your Majesties,' he began, 'my Lords Bishop, Holy Fathers and all attending this important meeting.'

Wilfrid was at his most suave and, it seemed to James, was seeking to give an impression of sweet reason after Colman's vituperations.

'The Lord Bishop has told us that his authority for the Celtic Easter customs was handed on to him by his superiors who, through a long line of holy men, received them from St John the Evangelist. Now if – and I stress the if – ' emphasised Wilfrid, holding up a finger to make his point, 'they do indeed practice what St John practiced there would seem to be little room for argument. If,' he raised the finger again, 'they do as the evangelist did, you might be forgiven for wondering why, in the Roman Church, things are done differently. Why,' once more the arresting finger, 'did St Peter decide that a different Easter calculation was necessary. For St Peter did decide this, make no mistake about that. Bishop Colman takes his authority back through a long line of holy men to St John; I take mine back through a long line of holy men to St Peter. It would be difficult on that basis alone, would it not, to decide who was correct. Comparisons are odious as we know. Far be it from me to say that Peter was holier than John or John than Peter. One, as we heard, rested his head on our Lord's breast at the Last Supper but the other was given the keys of the Kingdom of Heaven. Whom are we to believe? We must look much more carefully into this if we are to find the truth.

'The Celtic Church – this tiny organisation on the remotest edge of the world – has opted to believe St John whereas all the rest of the world – mark that,' stressed Wilfrid raising his voice and speaking for the first time with vigour and determination, 'all the rest of the world follows Peter. If Asians and Africans and Egyptians and Greeks and Syrians and Gauls and everyone follows Peter, you may wonder why, in their obstinacy, this tiny nest of the Celtic Church stupidly contends against them.'

'Stupidly! Stupidly!'

Colman was on his feet shouting before the translation of Wilfrid's words was quite finished. Wilfrid had a look of surprised innocence on his face but James could not help wondering whether his choice of the word 'stupidly' had been a deliberate one to provoke his volatile opponent.

Colman had marched out onto the floor in front of the dais and was gesticulating angrily at Wilfrid.

'Stupidly? Can the great Evangelist, St John, be called stupid. If we are stupid so is he and how can anyone, least of all an upstart such as you, call the great St John stupid.'

Wilfrid having obtained, James felt sure, the reaction he wished to provoke was gently persuasive in his reply. He waited patiently until Colman, still glowering, returned to his seat and settled down with a good deal of tugging at his habit and forceful crossing of his legs.

'I had hoped, Your Majesty,' Wilfrid said quietly bowing to the king, 'that we would discuss these important issues seriously as they deserve to be discussed not by calling each other names. Upstart I may be but I know the scriptures and it would seem the Lord Bishop does not. He will find, if he pays attention to my words, that I levelled no accusation of stupidity against St John, but only against those who wrongly claim him as authority for their error.'

Turning away from the king and speaking now directly to Colman Wilfrid began his frontal attack.

'You, Bishop Colman, say that the Celtic Church follows St John in your celebration of Easter on the Lord's Day between the fourteenth and twentieth day of the moon in the first month of the year. Very well. Let us see what the great Evangelist actually did.'

Wilfrid began to tick off the points on his fingers.

'Point one. He began to celebrate Easter on the evening of the fourteenth day of the moon in the first month of the year whether that day was the Sabbath or not. Do you do that, Bishop Colman? No, of course you don't. You do not wait for evening in your enumeration of days and you do not celebrate Easter if that day is not the Lord's Day. So already, in two important matters you do not follow St John.

'You may well enquire,' went on Wilfrid, 'why the Evangelist celebrated Easter at that time. The answer is a simple one – because he was faithfully following the Law of Moses regarding the Passover which, you will read in Leviticus, Chapter twenty-two verse five, was to be, "the first month, the fourteenth day of the month, *at evening*". Note that my Lord, at evening, not before. It was at that time that the great Evangelist began to celebrate this great Christian festival. Why did he make this choice?

'The early Church, you must realise, Colman,' went on Wilfrid in derisory tones as though lecturing a novice, 'followed many Jewish practices for fear of giving offence to their Jewish converts. Was not Timothy circumcised at St Paul's insistence? Did Paul, himself, not offer sacrifice in the Temple and shave his head at Corinth? These things were done so that the many Jewish believers would not be scandalised by what might seem a too flagrant breach of the Law. Are the faithful circumcised now?' enquired Wilfrid, gazing round the assembled company who shifted a little uneasily in their seats. 'No of course not. Such a thing is no longer necessary, but for a while circumcision *was* necessary. Now, my Lord Bishop we come to point number two.'

Wilfrid paused, unrolled a little more of his parchment, glanced around to ensure that he held their attention, and continued.

'Point number two is that Peter, whilst in Rome, realised that our Lord had risen from the dead, and given the hope of resurrection to the world, on the morning *after* the Sabbath. Thus he and his followers celebrated Easter on the next Lord's Day after moonrise on the fourteenth day of the month. If the Lord's Day fell on the day which began on the evening of the fourteenth day he, like John, celebrated Easter then. But if that day were not the Lord's Day Peter waited until the next Lord's Day between then and the evening of the twenty-first day. Peter therefore was celebrating Easter between the evening of the fourteenth day and the evening of the twenty-first day.

'Do you do that?'

Wilfrid had leaned forward and was directing a piercing gaze straight at Bishop Colman.

'Of course you don't. If the fourteenth day of the moon is the Lord's Day you celebrate Easter then, quite disregarding the Law which speaks only of *the evening* of the fourteenth day and *the evening* of the twenty-first. So Colman, do you follow Peter? No you do not. You follow neither John nor Peter but flagrantly disregard what scripture tells you.'

James thought Colman would respond but he remained silent, slumped down in his chair but still fixing his piercing eyes directly on his adversary. Wilfrid unrolled a little more of his parchment.

'Let us just have a look at what the Law says, shall we?' Wilfrid resumed smiling benignly at the scowling Bishop. 'Shall we continue our scrutiny of Leviticus?

'After telling us of the commencement of the Passover at evening on the fourteenth day of the month, we read in verse six, "and the fifteenth day of the month is the solemnity of the unleavened bread of the Lord. Seven days shalt thou eat unleavened bread". So,' went on Wilfrid brightly, 'seven days from the evening of the fourteenth day – or the beginning of the fifteenth, if you prefer – to the evening of the twenty-first is the feast of the unleavened bread. You may wish to quibble about the dates perhaps but they are quite clearly stated, are they not? Still, shall we seek further authority by looking at what is written in Exodus?'

Cedd's commentary was beginning to falter and he had made one or two mistakes which James was obliged to correct. After a short consultation between them it was James who took up the translation.

'Exodus then,' when he could see they were ready for him to continue, 'chapter twelve, you may recall, and – ' he unrolled a little more of the parchment ' – verse eighteen. "The first month, the fourteenth day of the month, in the evening, you shall eat unleavened bread until the first and twentieth day of the same month, in the evening".'

Wilfrid rolled up his parchment rapidly and gazed solemnly at Colman. Then, turning half to his right, he spoke directly to the king and queen.

'What, Your Majesties, could possibly be clearer than that. There you have the evening of the fourteenth day to the evening of the twenty-first – the feast of the unleavened bread which Peter celebrated as a Christian feast on the Lord's Day. John, not to give offence, did not choose the Lord's Day but *he did not begin the celebration of Easter until the evening of the fourteenth day*. I beg you mark that, Your Majesties. Nothing is anywhere said about the fourteenth day before evening although the Celtic Church begins it's calculations then. Moreover, Your Majesties, the twenty-first day, *up to evening*, is explicitly stated although the Celtic Church refuses to count this day.

'Thus, sire, you will realise, I am sure, that the Celtic Church keeps neither the Law of Moses nor Christian practice. It begins the week, during which Easter must be celebrated, on the fourteenth day before evening, for which it has no authority, and it flagrantly disregards specific reference to the evening of the twenty-first day. All this was debated long ago, Your Majesties, at the Council of Nicea in the Year of our Lord, three twenty-five when three hundred and eighteen bishops reaffirmed the correct calculation of Easter as I have stated it. What more need be said?'

First round to Wilfrid, thought James, as the abbot gathered up his parchment and returned to his chair. There was a general stir in the room as the assembled monks turned to each other with comments upon the debate so far. Sensing the need among the older members present, at least, for a short break the king announced that the proceedings would recommence in a quarter of an hour when Bishop Colman would have the opportunity to speak again and Wilfrid after him.

Immediately there was much standing and stretching, and several monks left to answer calls of nature. The queen spoke briefly to the king then rose and moved over to the other ladies on the front row and all went out together. Alchfrith and Agilbert and Wilfrid had their heads together in earnest consultation. Only the king, sitting placidly awaiting the queen's return, and Colman, hunched up in glum silence, were alone. Bishop Cedd, after hovering close by for some moments without receiving any recognition from Colman, eventually shrugged his shoulders and went out also after indicating to James that he should continue with the translation of the next session.

What would happen now, James wondered? If one were supporting neither side, but judging solely from the arguments each speaker had advanced the case for the Roman Easter would win hands down. Colman had been no better than James expected. He had blustered but had produced little justification for the Celtic practice, and the authority of St John, which he claimed, had been shown to be no authority for the customs his Church followed. Unless he could come up with something when he spoke next the advantage would still lie heavily with Wilfrid. Even if Colman did bring up other points, James had a shrewd suspicion that the abbot would be more than equal to demolishing them. They would soon be starting again, he realised. The ladies had returned and most of the men also. Cedd was, as yet, nowhere to be seen and James began to wonder if he had been dismayed by the poor account Colman had presented of the Celtic Church's case.

The king, James saw, was rising to his feet. Various private conversations broke up and priests hurriedly returned to their chairs. Oswy, with a calm untroubled expression on his face, waited patiently as if they were all having a pleasant discussion instead of trying to decide a fundamental issue of such importance.

'My Lady,' began Oswy, inclining his head gracefully towards his wife, 'my Lady Abbess, bishops priests, monks and others,' (no word about Alchfrith noticed James), 'we must continue. Each side has presented it's case; now it is time for the ripostes. Bishop Colman shall have the floor first as is his right.'

This time Colman walked to the rostrum where he stood in silence for a moment. He closed his eyes – perhaps in prayer, thought James, perhaps marshalling his facts. Facts were what he required; what would he produce that he hadn't mentioned already?

'It appears to me,' began the bishop, with notably less bluster than formerly, 'that he,' pointing disparagingly at Wilfrid, 'the abbot, the newly fledged priest, the world traveller, has, despite all his so-called learning and his quotations, forgotten something. Perhaps not forgotten – not known about something which proves our case. I have told him that our most revered Columcille followed our customs. His holiness and that of many before him is attested by miracles. Can such men be wrong? No, no.' This seemed like the same arguments again, thought James, and Colman was certainly getting worked up. 'No they cannot. Did they not base their calculation on the writings of the saintly Anatolius who you,' scowling fiercely at Wilfrid, 'never mentioned – if you knew about him at all. If you read his treatise you will see quite clearly that he wrote that Easter should be kept between the fourteenth and twentieth days of the moon – note that the fourteenth and twentieth days of the moon and answer it if you can.'

Colman stalked back to his chair and sat down brusquely with fists clenched as if seeking a physical not a verbal battle.

Wilfrid, meanwhile, watched the king calmly and waited for the royal assent before taking the rostrum again. When he did so he said nothing for a moment and the thought entered James mind that perhaps, after all, Colman had scored a point. He was quickly disillusioned.

'Anatolius of Laodicea,' Wilfrid began, speaking quietly, 'I was sure he would come up soon.' He paused again briefly and then turning towards the king and queen he started his exposition.

'His Lordship Bishop Colman is referring, Your Majesty, to the sainted Anatolius, Bishop of Laodicea who died around the year two eighty-three. There was another of the same name, sire, who was Patriarch of Alexandria almost two hundred years later with whom our – or should I say, Bishop Colman's, Antolius is sometimes confused. Bishop Colman's Anatolius was an eminent mathematician, Your Majesty, who wrote some – ten treatises on arithmetic and a book, as the learned bishop says, on Easter. But –' Wilfrid was shaking his head in sadness, 'I fear the good bishop cannot claim his authority since he does not follow his instructions.

'Anatolius spoke of the fourteenth to twentieth days but you should know, Your Majesty, that he followed the method of the ancient Egyptians in this matter, regarding the fourteenth day, in the evening – not once more Bishop Colman – *in the evening*, as the fifteenth day. His Easter began at evening and so was the commencement of the fifteenth day and in doing this he followed a cycle of nineteen years. Now Bishop Colman,' continued Wilfrid, relentlessly and in a more incisive manner than formerly, 'either you do not know of this, you being the ignorant one, or you choose to disregard it as you disregard Leviticus, Exodus, St Peter and the Council of Nicea.'

Now it was Wilfrid's turn to leave the rostrum but he had not finished speaking. He walked out into the middle of the floor in front of the gathering as Colman had done but nearer to the bishop so that he was speaking directly to him.

'Let us look Colman, at this Columba of yours, your miracle worker, who with his predecessors handed down his teaching to you. It is clear to me that Columba was a true servant of God, a good and holy man. He and his forefathers were devout, sincere men, if living in primitive simplicity. Such rustics can be pardoned for believing and practicing what had been taught to them since they knew no better. In their extreme isolation few with a knowledge of the truth were able to reach them to show them the error of their ways. And even in their error,' Wilfrid continued, with a gesture of magnanimity, 'what harm did they do while they were not in touch with others practicing correctly. But Colman, but – had they been able, as you have been able, to hear the truth expounded I have no shadow of doubt in my mind that your Columba, genuine and sincere as he was, would have accepted it and abandoned his old ways. He and his forebears may have been mistaken – were mistaken – but were not in serious error since they knew no better. But you, Colman, and others like you commit sin if you continue to ignore the truth when it is explained to you and if you reject the decrees of the Apostolic See and of the Universal Church which Holy Writ confirms.'

Wilfrid spun round on his heel to face the king and queen and stood tensly for a few moments without speaking. Then he began his final denunciation.

'Can Bishop Colman seriously contend that, holy though his Columba and others were, they can take precedence, on their tiny island clinging to the edge of the world, before the entire Universal Church of God everywhere else in the world. And can he,' gesturing to the bishop, 'really be saying that his Columba – and not only his but ours since he was a man of God – full of holiness and miracles as he was should precede the Apostle Peter to whom Christ Himself said, "Thou art Peter and upon this rock I will build My Church, and the gates of hell shall not prevail against it and I will give unto thee the keys of the Kingdom of Heaven".'

Wilfrid returned to his chair in dead silence. Colman had not moved throughout the peroration. Hilda looked perturbed. Cedd was gnawing his lip and a muscle at the corner of his eyes was twitching. Alchfrith looked complaisant as if his side had produced an unassailable case. As a few murmurings were heard in the room Oswy stood up and walked to the spot Wilfrid had vacated. His questions were direct ones.

'Colman, is it true, as the abbot has alleged, that the words quoted were spoken by our Lord to the Apostle Peter?'

'Yes, Your Majesty, it is true.'

'And what authority did Jesus Christ give to Columba?'

Colman shook his head and after a moment said, 'None sire.'

'We must be absolutely clear on this,' persisted Oswy, looking from the bishop to the abbot. 'Do you both accept that our Lord said these words to the holy Apostle Peter and gave him the keys of heaven?'

'We do.'

'Yes.' A pause. 'We do.'

Then Oswy did a strange thing. His expression whilst questioning the two men had been serious but now he looked directly at Alchfrith and gave a slow mocking smile before giving his attention back to the gathering.

'I declare,' he said solemnly, 'that St Peter is the holder of the keys of Heaven and I will do as he commands me in everything as far as my ability permits. If I do not will there be anyone with the keys by the heavenly gate when I stand before them? I further declare that the Roman method of the calculation of Easter is the correct one and henceforth will be followed in my kingdom. Do all here agree?'

Only six people failed to raise their hands in agreement – Bishop Colman, four of his monks from Lindisfarne, and Alchfrith who seemed stunned by the way things had turned out. What he had envisaged as a resounding defeat for the king and the Celtic Church, leaving him champion of the victorious Roman party, had become a triumph for Oswy who had abandoned his former allegiance and, in a stroke, usurped the temporal leadership of the Church of Rome in Northumbria. The Celtic Christians were the losers alright but the king, who had left them to their fate and gone over to the enemy, was the victor. Alchfrith, remembering Oswy's mocking smile before delivering his verdict, realised that not only had this politically expedient change of sides left the advantage firmly with the king but that Oswy was well aware of it and of Alchfrith's own schemes. Agilbert and Wilfrid, whom he had seen as powerful weapons in his own armoury, were now virtually certain to throw in their lot with the king. Without his backing they could hope for little preferrment; with it one of them might step neatly into the See of Northumbria if Colman refused to accept the verdict.

Alchfrith, so wrapped up in his own thoughts and alarmed at finding himself so isolated, took a moment to realise that he was being addressed.

'Are you not going to indicate your agreement,' repeated Oswy. 'After all, it is your own side that has been given the judgement. I had thought to see your hand go up first of all.'

The twitch at the corner of the king's mouth was more openly sneering than before as he waited for some response from his son.

Alchfrith tried to hold the king's eye as he slowly raised his hand but could not sustain Oswy's steady gaze. It was the younger man whose eyes dropped first.

'Good, excellent. Now, Bishop Colman, we have only you and some of your supporters. Will you give your consent.'

'Never.'

Colman was on his feet, his face red, his expression angry, his stance aggressive.

'Never. I will never abandon what my saintly forebears have passed down to me. You others may be bemused by his smooth words but I know the truth and that we have practiced it for hundreds of years – and will go on practicing it for hundreds more. My custom and that of my monks remains the same.'

Oswy waited until James did the best he could with Colman's indignant response, then simply said:

'But not in Northumbria.'

'What?'

'Not in Northumbria. If you wish to continue Celtic practices it will have to be elsewhere. There is no room for them here any longer. I shall require your resignation – immediately.'

For a moment James thought Colman was about to refuse. Few of king Oswy's subjects could have stared at their sovereign with such ferocity. Out of the corner of his eye James saw Brother Cuthbert take a step forward with outstretched hand as if intending to calm the bishop's anger but, before he reached the bishop, Colman rapped out his reply.

'You will have it. As of this instant I resign. My monks and I will leave Lindisfarne for ever.'

And then, as if at last recalling his own position as a priest addressing a king, he added, 'God be with you and with your subjects.'

Turning on his heel Colman marched defiantly from the room followed by the four monks who had voted with him. No one else moved, awaiting the king's lead. Oswy extended his hand to Enfleda who gave him a beaming smile and rose to join him. They made a graceful circle of the room, expressing their thanks to everyone involved – Abbess Hilda first of all for allowing her monastery to be used for such an important synod, James and Cedd for their faithful translation, Bishop Agilbert for allowing so able an advocate as Wilfrid to conduct the case and Wilfrid himself for his brilliant exposition. Nothing, James noticed, was said to Alchfrith.

It had been a tiring day but one of great accomplishment. Despite Bishop Colman's adamant refusal to accept the judgement it seemed as if most if not all of the rest of Northumbria would do so. Abbess Hilda was coming towards him and he stood up politely to meet her.

'That was another splendid task of translation you achieved, James,' she said smilingly.

'Thank you abbess. It was a little difficult to translate the bishop – former bishop perhaps I should say – when he got carried away. Are you perturbed about the outcome, my Lady?'

Hilda did not answer at once and appeared to be considering his question seriously.

'Oddly enough, no,' she replied eventually. 'I suppose the truth is I had never seriously considered the rightness or wrongness of our own Celtic practice as carefully as I should. When I heard the Roman case so lucidly put by Abbot Wilfrid it seemed hard to gainsay – too hard for our former adversary Colman. I have to admit, James,' she went on after a moment, 'that I think we were wrong and that is why I am disturbed now but not by the verdict.'

'Then disturbed by what, my Lady?'

'About our former bishop, James. Stubborn and unbending he certainly is and he will go on sticking to Celtic customs. It is what Abbot Wilfrid said at the end of his speech that struck me so forcibly. When Columba and his friends passed on their practices to others they knew no better way and we went on doing what we were taught. But once the correct way is shown to us as clearly as it was today our duty is to accept it. To practice in ignorance of error is one thing; but to refuse to admit error when the teaching of the Universal Church displays it so clearly is another. I fear that those who will not accept the truth are not far from . . . I scarcely dare say the word . . . heretics.'

Chapter 18

In the aftermath of the synod the year 664 would see many changes. No one doubted that although it was not yet clear what these might be. It soon became apparant, however, that not all would be religious.

Oswy had given permission for Colman and his monks to set out at once, but Alchfrith and his party were not allowed to leave. No explanation had been given. The sub-king must await the king's pleasure before departing. When approval had not been given forty-eight hours later Alchfrith, in high dudgeon, sought an audience with his father.

'Why am I being kept here? If you have something in mind for me may I know what it is? If not may my retainers and I return home?'

Alchfrith was plainly irritated by the delay imposed and was restraining himself only with difficulty. Oswy, on the other hand, was calm and relaxed and seemed to be in full command of the situation. He smiled at Alchfrith but, like that during the synod, it was not a pleasant smile and it caused the younger man some concern.

'Oh, I have something in mind for you alright, Alchfrith, you may rest assured about that.' Oswy never took his eyes off his son as he spoke. 'As to going home there is a difficulty there I fear.'

Alchfrith, who was becoming increasingly annoyed by being kept standing without the curtesy of the offer of any refreshment, was curt in his response.

'Difficulty? I don't understand. What difficulty? Why can't we go?'

'You cannot go home, Alchfrith, because, quite simply you have no home to go to. Deira is no longer your home and certainly not your kingdom. As a king you have always been "sub" – subordinate, that is, to me, and when you decided, as you clearly did decide some time ago, that you found such subordination irksome, and that you wished to rule not only Deira but Bernicia also, that was where you committed your error.

'Don't insult me by attempting to deny it,' Oswy shouted as Alchfrith made an attempt to butt in.

The king was on his feet now and had marched over to stand directly in front of his son but there was nothing paternal nor relenting in his gaze.

'I have known for a long time what you were up to. My trusted servants *are* trusted, Alchfrith, and are not to be enticed away from me by the likes of you. Oh, I know you hadn't got to the stage of open rebellion yet and now you won't because when you return to York – not home because that is no longer home to you – you will find my soldiers there not yours. The moment you left to come here my men moved in. Everyone in your household has been relieved of his position and is under restraint. Your soldiers are disarmed and your captains and lieutenants under guard – including those messengers who set off after you while you were travelling here to try to warn you. I anticipated this move and they were taken before they were a quarter of their way along the journey.

'I've been at this game a lot longer than you have Alchfrith. You should have remembered that when you made your plans. When the day comes that I can be surprised by you and others like you I shall deserve to be deposed – but that won't be yet awhile.'

Oswy was stalking up and down now before the motionless figure of Alchfrith who followed his father with his eyes but made no other move. Oswy suddenly stopped pacing and faced his son again.

'You asked if you could have my permission to go. You may, but you will return to York for the last time – and for long enough only for you to gather together your personal possessions – which I have no doubt, knowing you, will be of considerable value – and your family and retainers – if there are any who wish to accompany you when you leave for Ireland – where you came from. I'm sure they will be delighted there to have you back.'

Alchfrith still stood motionless without speaking.

'Well, have you nothing to say? No last message for your father?'

'Father!' Alchfrith spat out the word. 'What kind of father banishes his son? What have I done to deserve that? You . . . you hypocrit. You say you have evidence of subversion – produce it. When did I rebel? Whom did I kill? When were you threatened? I'm the one who has been attacked – and without provocation. You're supposed to be a Christian – what about all those pious sentiments we heard of during the synod? Put those into practice – be a proper Christian not a vindictive barbarian.'

'Oh ho.' Oswy was smiling with delight at the outburst. 'What kind of father banishes his son, you ask? Well. I'll tell you – the kind that has a son like you – that's who. And if it's evidence of subversion you ask for let's see if we can provide it.'

Oswy looked round the room gleefully letting his eye fall on each of his retainers in turn until he seemed to be looking straight behind Alchfrith who, seeing the direction of his gaze, turned his head.

'That's right, my son, you have found the one as I knew you would.'

Unnoticed by Alchfrith, Ricbert had come quietly into the room during the earlier exchange and remained out of sight behind the sub-king's back.

'Well, Ricbert, can you give us any evidence of subversion?'

Without giving Ricbert an opportunity to reply Alchfrith changed his line immediately.

'Of course I approached Ricbert, thinking that he may, one day, come into my service. Even you won't live forever! One day when you die this realm will need a strong king like me to rule it, not a namby pamby like my virgin half-brother and his platonic wife. I wasn't trying to usurp you but I wasn't going to remain a sub-king under him.'

'Enough!'

Oswy, having earlier resumed his seat was on his feet again glaring steadily at his son.

'Enough, Alchfrith. You protest too much. You have had your chance – a far better one than you deserve and you have betrayed my trust. You wanted Ricbert in your service. Well, he's in your service now – while you go back to York for your goods and chattels and then to see you on your way into banishment. Be sure he will serve you well. You need have no fears about reaching Ireland, need he Ricbert?'

'None, Your Majesty. He will get there. You know you can rely on me.'

'I have never doubted it Ricbert.'

There were two startling events in the year 664 which were not the result of the synod.

The first was a total eclipse of the sun, visible over a wide area, which occurred on the third day of May between the hours of Terce and Sect. The second was an outbreak of the plague which all but eclipsed the Christian Church in Britain and was to bring about a surprising change in James' life style which he could never have envisaged.

He had been back in Lindisfarne for almost three months. He was in excellent health apart from an annoying stiffness in his hands. This seemed scarcely to matter with Eadfrith's work so superior to anything James had done even at his best. The father had endless pleasure examining the son's completed gospels of Matthew, Mark and Luke although Eadfrith was strangely reticent about that of St John which, he assured his father, was almost finished – but not to be put on view until then.

James was in the scriptorium supervising the work of some of the copyists when he was surprised to receive a request from Prior Cuthbert that he should wait on him.

Cuthbert welcomed James graciously and was full of thanks that he had agreed to come. The prior invited James to sit beside him at the table.

'I have a lot to say to you Master James,' Cuthbert began, 'and it will not all be concerned with the future and the request I have to make to you. There are few people whose work has served Almighty God so well as yours and when I think of the many books you have made during your lifetime, I feel sure you must have a great sense of achievement – ought to have a great sense of achievement, at any rate, although I realise that those who achieve most are often the most humble about their attainments. Talking to Brother Eadfrith – and I must ask you to forgive us discussing you in your absence in this way, but I felt I had to know more about you first before broaching the subject that I have in mind – I have gained the impression from him that you feel that you are not perhaps the incomparable artist you once were.'

James smiled broadly at the prior and scratched his head before replying.

'Whether or not I was ever "incomparable", Brother Prior, I cannot say but I am surely surpassed now by my son who is better than I ever was, while my own dexterity is not what it used to be.'

Cuthbert smiled in return at the answer.

'About your son's skill I have no doubt, Master James. He is, I understand, engaged on a major task that he is anxious I should not see incomplete so I am happy to wait until it is finished. But touching on your own lack of "dexterity", to use your own word, this seems to me to mean that you are less likely, now, to be engaged on a major artistic undertaking. Would I be right in that assumption?'

James did not answer immediately but Cuthbert waited patiently.

'Unlikely ever again, Brother Prior,' he answered at last looking rather sorrowful as he spoke, 'at least in the sense of designing and completing the work myself. Oh, I can still design and I still retain, I trust, originality and individuality but someone else would have to put it down on parchment.

Not only that, prior, but I suppose I have done my work too well in one sense. Melrose has a fine artist in Brother Lawrence, Whitby in Barnabas, whilst Brother Clement, who took over the new scriptorium at Ripon, has surpassed all my expectations. There is Lastingham, of course, but I suppose Brother Paul is doing well enough, whilst here Eadfrith is, to use your word this time, "incomparable".' James gave a little laugh and ended, 'If the reward of a teacher is a successful pupil I have been amply rewarded.'

'And deservedly rewarded,' added Cuthbert, 'but since we each seem to be taking each others words, I will take some of yours. "Not needed as I once was", I think you said?'

James nodded.

'In that case I am getting a little nearer my point,' said Cuthbert smiling, 'but now I have to tell you something else before I reach it.'

He rose from his chair and walked to the window and seemed disturbed for the first time during the interview. Then, resuming his seat, and looking very solemn, he began speaking again.

'Almost the whole country, James – not perhaps the north yet but Kent, the Saxon territories, East Anglia, Mercia and further afield, including parts of Ireland – has been visited by a terrible plague. it is not I understand like the one with the buboes which caused the deaths of Bishop Aidan and your dear wife, but is even more devastating. Word has reached us that the loss of life has been very great and, in particular, many churchmen have died. Deusdedit, the Archbishop of Canterbury, died and on the following day King Earconbert or Kent, whilst many more Kentish priests and monks have perished – God rest their souls. Tuda, a worthy Scot who had been nominated as next Bishop of Lindisfarne, became a victim whilst visiting Canterbury before coming here. The East Saxon clergy have been badly smitten and it is rumoured that King Sighere has ordered pagan temples to be rebuilt in the vain hope that the pagan gods will save him and the rest of his people. Further north the virulence of the plague has eased a little but some holy monks and priests have still died – more than thirty I hear have been lost at Lastingham, including the venerable Bishop Cedd with whom you shared the translation at Whitby. So far as I know Whitby, itself, has not been affected, nor anywhere further north but that could still happen.'

'We must pray for their souls, James,' Cuthbert continued, 'and tomorrow a special Mass of intercession will be celebrated for the souls of all who have died and to ask for protection of areas such as ours which are still free of pestilence.

'You are wondering how this relates to you, are you not?' Cuthbert said.

'Well, in this way. I intend to allow some of my monks to go south to the most stricken areas. If we do not help, apostacy, such as occurred among the East Saxons, for example, may be repeated elsewhere. We must not let that happen by keeping all our people here. The monastic life is praiseworthy and an admirable way of serving God but, when the souls of the faithful are at risk, exceptional measures are called for.

'Now – finally – James, we come to you,' went on Cuthbert patiently. 'I know that throughout your life you have been an exemplary Christian serving Almighty God in your own special way. I also know – and I need not tell you how I learned – that, as a younger man, you often taught God's word in this kingdom and even in this province of it, when it was first evangelised by Bishop Paulinus. That is what I hope you will do again – preach the word of God, to help those of us who remain at Lindisfarne to sustain the faith of the people hereabouts when they learn of the threat of plague and may even be – pray God this will never happen – infected by it. You would not need to move far away from this monastery and Bamburgh itself – others can go further afield. I feel you would be of the greatest help, not only now, in the time of such danger, but later when, with God's help, it passes. You said earlier James, that you were not needed now as you once were. I think you are needed in another way – in the way Bishop Paulinus needed you to preach the word and sustain the faith. Would you consider doing that?'

James was so surprised by what Cuthbert had said that he took some time to reply. Eventually he nodded his head and gave a little smile at the prior before speaking.

'How terrible to have such devastation from the plague; simply terrible. The plague – even though you say this is of a different kind from that which killed my wife – has had a particular horror for me since that time.'

Memories of Edith came momentarily into his mind, distracting him from completing his answer.

'Yes,' he said presently, 'yes, Brother Prior, I would willingly do that; would welcome it in fact. When I helped Bishop Paulinus so long ago, explaining the scriptures was a task I greatly enjoyed and it cannot be denied,' he added with a grin, 'that I have read the gospels many times in the course of my work – in fact I am almost word perfect. Yes, Brother Cuthbert, of course I will help.'

'I was sure you would,' responded Cuthbert immediately, 'but there is one more thing I must ask you. The faithful to whom you will preach, and whose faith you must help to strengthen, will accept you more readily if you are ordained deacon. Do you think you could agree to that?'

Deacon! Deacon. James was taken so totally by surprise that for some time he could only repeat the word to himself. The priesthood he had declined long ago but . . . now that the notion of becoming a deacon had been suggested there was something about it that appealed to him. He had no wish to marry again so that was no barrier . . . deacon.

Cuthbert, thinking that James must be finding it difficult to make up his mind, broke in on his thoughts.

'The office of deacon is an ancient and honourable one, James, without all the dignity of a priest, perhaps, but is a holy order the origin of which goes back to the time soon after our Lord's death. Seven Greek-speaking deacons were appointed, you may recall, in Jerusalem, to look after the needs of the Hellenic Christians. St Stephen, the first martyr, was one. St Lawrence, St Cyriacus and St Vincent of Zaragoza. The duties are those I have explained to you in addition to which you would be able to assist at the distribution of Holy Communion although not to consecrate the Host. I know you will fulfill all these admirably and I hope you will consent.'

The prior did not interrupt James thoughts again, being anxious not to press him too strongly. He closed his eyes and murmured a prayer that our Lord would lead James to acceptance if that was His Holy Will. 'Dear God', he prayed, 'help this man who has so much to offer, to . . . '

'I will.'

The prior opened his eyes and saw that James was nodding his head and smiling.

'Yes, Brother Prior,' James repeated, 'I shall be honoured to accept ordination as deacon and to do everything I can to help the people of Bernicia. Do you know, Brother Cuthbert, many years ago Bishop Paulinus first enquired if I felt drawn to the priesthood. I had to say no then and I'm sure I was right to do so. Several times since I have wondered – when I attended Bishop Wilfrid's ordination for example – but I have always been confident that I was serving Almighty God better as a scribe than as a priest. Now,' with a gentle smile at the prior, 'the situation is different. I feel now that, rather than continue to do indifferent work in the scriptorium, I would prefer to accept a new challenge in the office you have suggested. But I shall need a lot of help from our Lord,' he ended. 'Would you come with me now to the chapel, Brother Prior, and together we can ask Him for it?'

Easter in the Year of our Lord 665, the first Roman Easter to be celebrated throughout Northumbria, was almost as late as it could possibly be and, with spring so far advanced, was a happy occasion.

The winter had been mild too and James had been able to make many more pastoral visits than he had ever thought likely and was finding his work immensely rewarding. Dealing once more with peasant people had reminded him of his younger days and of the missionary journeys he had made with the two bishops Paulinus and Aidan. He was revelling in this newly-found human contact, he realised. Not, he said to himself, that he had missed it in the years he had spent in the scriptoria of the kingdom; they had given him a different kind of personal contact, and the monks who had patiently followed his instructions, and reproduced the word of God on parchment, had now been replaced by these simple rustics who listened to those same words given to them by him for which they seemed grateful.

They were grateful too for having escaped the pestilence. Only parts of Deira and the southern fringes of Bernicia had been affected and many of those who had contracted the disease had survived it. There would have to be a period of rebuilding in the Church, of course, since the heirarchy had been decimated. There were of necessity changes everywhere, some of which gave James cause for great satisfaction. Abbot Eata was to be consecrated Bishop of Lindisfarne with – and James could hardly contain his delight – Cuthbert as abbot. The kingdom of Deira was to have a seperate bishop – Wilfrid of course – but James was not sure whether he approved of this or not. King Oswy of Northumbria and King Egbert of Kent had conferred and agreed to send a priest, Wighard, to Rome to be consecrated successor to Archbishop Deusdedit who had been one of the first victims of the plague.

James was hoping soon to make his journey to Whitby. But best of all Eadfrith had completed the Gospel of St John and today James was to see it for the first time.

'I need hardly ask if I will like it Eadfrith?'

'I hope you do, Father, but . . . ' Eadfrith was grinning broadly as if he was amused by some private joke 'there is one tiny part which I hope – very much hope – you will approve.'

'What's that?'

But Eadfrith refused to be drawn.

'Wait and see, Father. Wait and see.'

And here he was at last seeing the initial page for the first time and assimilating all the beauty that he knew would be there.

Since the letters INP of the first words of St John -- In principio erat verbum; in the beginning was the word – resembled the IN at the commencement of St Mark James expected that there would be some similarity between the two huge monograms. And so there was but they were very far from the same. Whereas Eadfrith had left the Mark monogram open and the 'N' filled only with a simple knotwork design in alternating colours, the entire background of the 'N' in John was a seething maelstrom of birds and beasts, bodies and tails, legs and feet, coiling and recoiling in and out of each other. James noticed two beaks entering one corner, two snouts another, toes a third. It was splended!

His eye moved lower and he began to examine the 'erat verbum'. Here was a marvellous curling neck to a bird on the 'e' and another, even more striking, on the 't'. And, there, in the middle of the bottom line was a bird so small that James almost missed it – a cheeky head peering up out of a flurry of wings in the centre of the 'D' of Deum. Was there something he had missed? Eadfrith had hinted at one unusual . . .

'Oh!'

He was so taken by surprise that he hardly knew whether he was pleased or not but the more he looked the more he approved of what he saw. He turned to his son, grinning broadly, and found the boy, once aware of his father's pleasure, grinning back. James returned to his examination of the caricature of his face perched neatly on the end of the tail of the letter 'C' of 'Principio'. The tail tapered in a long curved fashion almost to his chin before broadening slightly to meet it, making him look for all the world as if he had an immensely long pointed beard. As he gazed he felt Eadfrith move behind him and place a hand on his shoulder.

'You put Mother in St Matthew, Father. I thought you should be in a gospel too. Who knows, you may go down in posterity.'

Authors Note

The man on the initial page of the Gospel of St John did go down to posterity as the only human portrayed in Eadfrith's masterpiece, The Lindisfarne Gospels. That he is a portrait of the deacon James is no more than a figment of my imagination and represents merely one of the liberties which I have taken with another masterpiece, the Venerable Bede's History of the English Church and People.

My story is based loosely on St Bede's history. Those who are familiar with this marvellous work will realise that many of my characters are taken from his pages although they are not always as he describes them. The biggest liberty I have taken concerns my hero James. In Bede's account James was left behind in Northumbria when Bishop Paulinus and Queen Ethelberga fled to Kent and he remained there as a tower of strength in the Roman Church. He became a deacon at a much earlier stage in his life than I have described, but he helped Paulinus to spread the Faith and, in Bede's words, 'snatched much prey from the clutches of our old enemy the devil'. James special skill was not sacred illumination but a knowledge of religious music and he taught 'many people to sing the music of the Church'.

Bede's account suggests that James spent all his life in Northumbria until, 'at last, old and 'full of days', as the scripture says, he went to his fathers'. He would not therefore have gone to Iona and certainly not with Edith of whom, since I invented her, you will find no mention in Bede's pages. Other inventions include Father Melchior, the boatman Fursa and the cook Calan, all the people on Iona (except for Prince Oswald and Segenus who was abbot during the time covered here), Brother Uffa and his 2 companion monks, a host of minor characters and, with the exception of Eadfrith, all the scribes taught by James in my story.

There seems little doubt that Eadfrith was the author of the Lindisfarne Gospels which were written in honour of St Cuthbert but perhaps some 20 years later than I have suggested. Scarcely anything is known about Eadfrith's early life until he became Bishop of Lindisfarne in 698. Since the duties of a bishop would seem to preclude the devotion of so much of his time to art it seems likely that the Gospels were written somewhat earlier. The Book of Durrow, the earliest of the illuminated Insular Gospel Books, was probably written at some time during the second half of the 7th century. It's author is unknown and could have been someone like the James in my story.

Bishop Aidan brought Celtic Christianity to Northumbria much in the way I have described. King Oswald had originally asked the Scots to send 'a bishop to teach the Faith of Christians to himself and his people' and 'they sent him another man of more austere disposition' but 'meeting with no success in his preaching to the English, who refused to listen to him, he returned home'. We have no reason to suppose that he was called Gobban. Bishop Aidan died in AD 651, 11 days after the murder of Oswin by his cousin Oswy, but there is nothing in Bede's account to suggest that the bishop's death was the result of plague in the manner described here. Bede's Life of Cuthbert tells how the young shepherd witnessed Aidan's soul being born to heaven, after which 'he decided to enter a monastery'; no earlier meeting between the 2 saints is recorded.

Queen Enfleda in the Venerable Bede's history rigidly maintained the observance of the Roman Easter, along with her court, 'a Kentish priest named Romanus' and James. She may have done so but that aspect of St Bede's account has always seemed to me to have an element of unreality attached to it and I have represented it otherwise, returning Romanus to Kent with a broken leg after the storm at sea and introducing Brother Uffa as the queen's chaplain.

Bede does not go into any detail concerning the precise origin of the Synod of Whitby. He tells us that During Aidan's lifetime 'these differences of Easter observance were patiently tolerated'. He later mentions that during the episcopacy of Finan, 'there arose a great and recurring controversy on the observance of Easter'. This, whenever it was, preceded Whitby about which Bede merely states that under Colman 'an even more serious controversy arose'. The view expressed by the Oxford historian, Henry Mayr-Harting, in his book The Coming of Christianity to Anglo-Saxon England', that the 'chief cause of the trouble which led to the Synod of Whitby was the person of King Alfrith' (which is his spelling of Alchfrith) seems to me to carry conviction and has been adopted in my story. Certainly, after the Synod, Alchfrith disappears from view but whether killed or banished is unknown. My account of the actual debate during the Synod closely follows Bede's.

The episode concerning the exhumation and reburiel of King Redwald of the East Angles is supposition. When the Sutton Hoo ship was discovered in 1939, subsequent detailed examination failed to disclose a body although many of the objects described here, both sacred and profane, were excavated. There may never have been a body although it seems more likely that one was buried and later removed as I have described. If so he was clearly a royal personage and the most favoured candidate at the present time is Redwald. Perhaps it might have taken place as told here. King Anna was certainly a good man who would, I feel, have wished a proper Christian buriel for his ancestor.

King Anna reappears in my story at the wedding of his daughter, whom I have called Audrey, by which name she is sometimes known, although she is more often referred to as Etheldreda. After her first unconsummated marriage to Tondberht, Ecfrith, then about 15 years old, agreed to marry her but allow her to remain a virgin as my story relates. Years later he wished to exercise his conjugal rites but she refused and retired as a nun to Coldingham under Abbess Ebbe. Coldingham itself **was** destroyed by fire 'because of the wickedness of it's members', as Bede puts it, but not until long after the fire described here and after the death of Ebbe; moral laxity did however creep in during her rule.

Miracles are a spectacular aspect of the Venerable Bede's story and some of these have been faithfully represented in mine. I have invented 3 however – the cure of Edwin's toothache, the making of rain and the odour of sanctity which perfused the chapel after the deaths of Aidan, Oda and Edith. Although this last event, as described here, is mythical the emergence of wonderful fragrance from the bodies of some saints (including that of St Erkengota, daughter of King Erconbert of Kent, who died around the year 660) is well documented in Christian writing.

St Cuthbert and St Wilfrid were contemporaneous although Wilfrid lived for more than 20 years after the death of Cuthbert. Not all saints appeal to the same extent and although I am immensely attracted by the sanctity of Cuthbert, there are aspects to Wilfrid's character which I find less worthy. I trust I have not treated Wilfrid less kindly than he deserves.

I have left until last Enfleda who occupies far more of my story than of the Venerable Bede's. The events of her early life are accurately reported here – her birth, escape to Kent and subsequent return to marry Oswy. There is no evidence that her voyage (if indeed she travelled by sea at all) was as dramatic as that I have invented. The miracle of the oil as described by Bede takes place 10 years or so after I have introduced it. When Oswy died in 670 Enfleda became a nun at Whitby. She later became abbess and was followed in that office by her daughter Elfleda. King Oswy was buried at Whitby and during Enfleda's rule the relics of her Father, King Edwin, were translated there.

The reader may like to know how many of the characters portrayed here appear in the Calendar of Saints. Among the men are: Agilbert (who became Bishop of Paris after Whitby), Aidan, Augustine, Boisil, Caedmon, Cedd, Cahd, Colman, Columba, Cuthbert, Eadfrith, Eata, Edwin, Felix of Dunwich, Fursey, Justus, Mellitus, Oswald, Oswin, Paulinus of York and Wilfrid. The canonised women are: Audry (Etheldreda), Ebbe, Enfleda, Elfleda, Ethelberga (later Abbess of Lyming) and Hilda.